FIASCO

D1711006

James P. O'Mealia

ISBN: 1502559455
ISBN 13: 9781502559456
Library of Congress Control Number: 2014917578
CreateSpace Independent Publishing Platform
North Charleston, South Carolina

CHAPTER ONE

"I make vacations."

The sixteen eighth-graders weren't expecting to hear about vacations, and a few smiles could be detected and a couple of authentic involuntary chuckles could be heard. It was an introduction that got their attention and provided the right segue to explain just exactly how we in the financial business made the money that enabled their parents to buy the extras in life, such as vacations. My goal was to try to teach some of the principals of portfolio management through a simple, easy to understand, intriguing dialogue. With a little luck, heck, I might even make them realize how much I loved it and how intellectually stimulating and fascinating it was to manage OPM, or "Other People's Money."

"Yes boys and girls, as most of you know, I am Kathleen's dad, Tom Morris. I have been asked to explain to all of you what it is I do for a living. Some of you may have heard that I am a money manager, an investment advisor, or that I invest in stocks and bonds. Sounds pretty boring, doesn't it? But the truth is I make vacations."

I smiled and explained in simple terms how people, just like their moms and dads, entrusted me with their hard-earned money. When I did a good job, the investments that I made for my clients grew in value and created enough money for my clients to take vacations, buy stereos, CD players and other necessary presents that all children desire. I added that I knew of some clients who had used their growing investment portfolios to pay beach club dues, country club fees, college tuitions, and even a daughter's wedding party. My daughter's classmates immediately started to look at me in a different light and began to ask a lot of questions about how I did my job and how I helped their parents make enough money to buy those vacations and what other exotic purchases did my clients afford; cars, yachts, European homes?

"Have any of your clients gone to Florida?" came from my daughter's best friend Alice, a blond-haired precocious tomboy who was the star of her field hockey, basketball and lacrosse teams.

"How about Europe?" shouted a freckle faced red-haired boy in the third row.

"France?" was the feeble request of an obviously shy girl in the second row, uncomfortable with her presence, glasses and braces, and clueless that she would probably be the most beautiful girl in the class by the time she reached her high school graduation.

"France is part of Europe, duh," came from the class jerk in the back row, lazily slouching in his chair with his legs dangling in the aisle, trying his best to be cool and quick to put down anyone to make himself feel superior.

The kids got into the spirit of the discussion and enjoyed learning about stocks and bonds, why they went up and down and just what it was that their dads pored over in the morning paper before they settled in to the sports pages. They also offered telling insights into the homes they grew up in.

"My dad says technology is where you make the best money!"

"My dad says mutual funds are where you put your money."

"My dad says stocks are only for rich people."

"My mom says stocks are risky."

"I own IBM for the dividends and Microsoft for its growth."

The class got me thinking back to my youth, when I tried to understand just what all those numbers meant in the back of the newspaper. How my own dad had informed me that we didn't have any stocks or bonds other than what Grandpa had given us for our birthdays and that they cost a lot of money. How simple those times had been, when my goal in life was to learn what those numbers meant, wondering how many years of allowance and caddying money it would take to own some stocks of my own. If I could own stocks of my own, I would be on my way to being rich and successful. Little did I know, as a pimply-faced teenager, that the act of owning stocks was not a guarantee of wealth, success, or financial freedom. Even less was my awareness of the stresses and troubles that could befall a portfolio manager responsible for managing hundreds of millions of dollars.

The call from the Securities and Exchange Commission examiner had come just this past Friday, and I could tell from his questions and tone that it was not a routine call. He was quick and direct and all business. "What can you tell me about First American Insurance Corp. of Los Angeles, and CEO Roger Maydock? The chill and cold sweat that immediately formed on the back of my neck had a choking effect and I tried to remain calm and composed as the examiner asked me about my "relationship" with Roger, my roommate for two of my four years at The Hill School, an all boys boarding school 25 years earlier. It was a well-known and respected preparatory school situated in the confines of an old industrial town about 30 minutes outside of Philadelphia, but as far from the Main Line as one could get on the socio-economic scale. In those days, Pottstown was best known as a home for Bethlehem Steel and Firestone Rubber plants, but when you were downtown you would most likely smell not the dust of industrial activity, but the mouth-watering aromas emanating from the Mrs. Smith's Pies' bakeries located just two blocks off High

Street, the main thoroughfare and home to most of the businesses in town.

"Mr. Morris, can girls be money managers too?"

The question brought me back in to the moment and I wondered uneasily if my flash-back had disrupted the flow of the lesson. I reminded myself to follow the script I had in my head on how to explain what Price/Earnings ratios were to a group of kids who had very limited financial knowledge.

"Absolutely" I replied. "In fact, one of my best friends in the business is a woman managing a half a billion dollars for an investment firm in Chicago." The "ahs" from the class confirmed my suspicion that a half a billion probably sounded a lot more impressive than $500 million. Heck, many of these kids' mothers or fathers probably made a million or more last year. The girls in the class all seemed to sit up a little straighter and leered smugly at the boys, their expressions saying quite clearly, "nah, nah, nah, we're better than you are." It's a look that seems mastered by teenagers, but lost when they become adults.

"But the best money managers are men, right? Like chefs?" That came from Charlie on my right in the second row, the athletic star of the class and quarterback of the school football team.

"Not at all," I answered quickly, absolutely sure that I didn't want to get into a boys versus girls abilities debate. Without looking directly at her, I caught a glimpse of a smile from my daughter and could tell that she was starting to feel a little better about the classroom visit by dad. It was her idea months ago, but she had begun having second thoughts in recent weeks and as of this mornings breakfast, was so stressed about how dad was going to perform that she couldn't eat.

The tension and nervousness that existed at the beginning of the class dissipated gradually, but noticeably as the class and I fell into a discussion about what makes stocks go up, what you should look for in a company, 'Is Cisco a buy?' The forty-five minutes passed quickly and there was even a noticeable groan or two when the bell sounded signaling that class was over. I wanted to believe that the reaction was due to my astute observations about the markets and the world, but reassured myself that more likely it was because the bell meant in five minutes they had to be in another class with real teachers and real schoolwork to attack.

My daughter waited for the other students to file out ahead of her and, taking up the rear of the procession, with a semi-embarrassed look came up to me and said, "Thanks Dad. That was good."

"Just good?!!" I feigned hurt, but felt the twinge anyway. "I thought I was great!" It is only with your kids that you can espouse Herculean traits and Einsteinian intellect and get away with it. You know that at some point in those teenage years, your God-like qualities are going to fade from their memory, so you relish it while you can.

"Well, you were pretty good, but, ah, you talked too much about those PE's and other things that I still don't quite understand and you let the boys ask too many questions about stocks they've heard about or own. But overall, it was good." She gave me a peck on the check and said, "Gotta go now. Late for math. Bye." She quickly slung her overstuffed, overweight green and black Jansen backpack over her shoulder and strode out the door. I stared amazed at how tall she had become and how much she was transforming into the near carbon copy of the woman I started dating twenty years earlier. Even her walk was starting to have the same sway…

"Well that seemed to have gone well," said my daughter's thirty-ish, mousy brown haired diminutive teacher, Angie Murphy, as she came to the front of the classroom. Breaking my train of thought, I acknowledged that the kids seemed to have gotten into the discussion, but I hoped I hadn't been too technical. I was still hurting from my daughter's brutally honest appraisal of my presentation. "I'm sure you weren't," she said with a tone of confident assurance, "I overheard some of the boys in the hall saying they wanted to check out charts and graphs on some companies." I felt good again. Independent third party confirmation of a successful discussion was offered and I

remembered fondly explaining how technicians look at only information about how a stock has traded and what its volume characteristics
or money flows were. They didn't care a lick what a company did. I,
on the other hand, looked at a company's fundamentals, met with
management, interviewed competitors, customers and suppliers all
to reach a decision on whether a company's shares were priced at-
tractively given their fundamental outlook. The boys obviously preferred the seemingly simpler way to make money by looking at stock
charts and I chuckled to myself about how many times I wished I
hadn't become so obsessed with fundamentals and longed for the
crisp unemotional ways of market technicians. But then again, it
was technical analysis gone wrong that had sunk Long Term Capital
Management in 1998 when a dozen or so PhD's with great minds and
math formulas figured they had learned how to beat the street. They
had come up with foolproof scenarios to leverage their knowledge
and investment portfolios to make billions for their investors and
themselves. Lo and behold, their outsized bets and arrogance nearly
caused a meltdown of the financial markets.

I said a quick and embarrassed "thank you" to Miss Murphy, not
sure how long I had paused to reflect on Long Term Capital's meltdown and headed out into the linoleum-floored hallway. I thought
about the day ahead. Should I peek in on my youngest son's classroom, stay for lunch, schmooze with the headmaster or head back
home to check out how the markets were faring today?

Yes, it was an obsession and even though I was officially on vacation for the whole week, I could never let it go. So I clicked on my
Blackberry to check my e-mail and get a glance at the markets and
headed to my car, knowing that if I didn't spend some quiet time
catching up on the day's activity in the markets and responding to
the e-mail that are the bane of all of today's businessmen, I would be
swamped for days when I returned from my vacation.

Seeing a message from Roger Maydock, I stopped in my tracks
and someone walking behind me bumped into me, books first.

"I'm so sorry," I said earnestly as I turned around, startled and embarrassed.

"Its okay Mr. Morris," said my oldest daughter's friend, Kristin. "I am late for class and shouldn't have been so close. No problem. Got to go and by the way, I really liked your class." Off she went, without missing a beat and darted quickly into the classroom just ahead of us to the left as the bell sounded.

The halls had emptied and I looked back down at my Blackberry to read Roger's message. "J. Thomas – Need to talk, call me. Your office says you're out and your cell phone's off. What gives? Need you to come to Calif. ASAP to discuss a business opportunity that requires your handiwork. Big bucks!! Call me. Work or home – CALL!"

I knew Roger was doing incredibly well running an insurance company in California. Not one to worry about picking stocks or investments, Roger had built a huge firm gathering assets, annuity products and mutual fund companies, and had a stable full of investment firms managing the money. A marketing genius and graduate of the Thunderbird School, he had built an empire in La La land, our colloquial term for Los Angeles. He seemed on top of the world without a worry the last few times we had spoken. I quickly typed a reply.

"Tied up now, will call in an hour or two... everything OK? All the best—J. Thomas."

Not many people called me J. Thomas, only my old prep school buddies, and then as a term of endearment. It certainly was a nicer nickname than some of the others I'd had over the years. It had started innocently enough. We had snuck off campus to smoke some contraband in a secluded wooded area near the school's intra-mural soccer fields. Hidden from sight in the overgrown brush and trees which had escaped the pruner's shears for years, we were sitting on logs we had pulled together to form a campfire-like sitting area, without the fire. Roger pulled out a joint and asked "J, Thomas?" As I took the rolled cigarette, Roger chuckled and remarked, "Hey,

that's a good one. J. Thomas instead of Thomas J. Sounds important, like J. Paul Getty. I like it! Besides, we can use it as a code when
we want to sneak off for a doobie."

I didn't think much of it at the time, but as Roger started using the nickname and calling card freely and we increased the fre-
quency of our dereliction, our friends caught on and soon it was my
preferred name throughout the school. We got the biggest chuckle
though, when some of the younger teachers, trying to be accepted
and close to the student body, also adopted my new nickname! For
Roger and me, it was another one of the secrets we kept to ourselves,
part of our code and slang which no one else could decipher.

I focused on the Blackberry again and Roger's message and saw
that it came in at 8:30 AM, which meant Roger had sent it at 5:30 AM
from California. I knew he was always an early riser, but this bordered
on lunacy. How long had he been up when he sent me this message?
I remembered that since the investment world in the U.S. worked on
New York time, the downside of working on the West Coast was that
brokers and portfolio managers usually had to be at their desks by 5:00
AM to get pre-market research calls and updates from the big brokerage firms in New York. Roger had probably been at his office at 4:00
AM so that he would know everything going on in the world of finance
when his own investment people arrived at work. He had probably
taken a break an hour before the US equity markets had opened to
send me a note.

My morning had started as usual at 7 with my daily dose of the
Wall Street Journal, Bloomberg News and a pair of Diet Cokes. I
hadn't heard of any unusual activity in the markets before I headed
off to school this morning, so I couldn't fathom what was going on
at Roger's company which was so important. I figured I would check
out the major news stories and stock and bond market color before
calling Roger and headed off to my car once again. Then again, maybe it was related to the call from the SEC. A quick glance at my market minder indicated that stocks were slightly higher, bonds off a bit,

crude oil slightly higher and gold continuing its recent move higher on continued Mid East tensions.

Keeping an eye out to make sure I didn't bump into anyone else, I enjoyed seeing the handwritten stories in big uncertain block letters adorning the cream-painted cinder block walls and the pictures drawn by the students of their favorite subjects -- mostly cats, dogs, horses and hockey players. I couldn't help but notice the drawing of a hockey player with the New York Rangers logo across his chest taking a slap shot and knew that it had to be the handiwork of my ten year old, Michael, who had graced his room with no less than a dozen similar efforts in the past two months. Michael's love of life and having fun were truly endearing, and while he was a mathematical whiz, he had no real interest in schoolwork. His greatest passions, hockey and getting detentions kept my wife Missy and me on our toes and made us wonder how uniquely wonderful and different each of our three children were.

Leaving the hallway of the future leaders of arts and letters and walking through the brick lined foyer, I stepped out into the cool, crisp fall air and wondered what was up with Roger and how warm was it now in Southern California.

CHAPTER TWO

The ride home from school was quick, as we lived only three-quarters of a mile away. The leaves on the trees were beginning to turn colors in their irregular autumnal ritual, with flashes of red, orange, brown and flaming yellow mixed within the greens that hadn't gotten the memo yet that fall was here. I marveled at how peaceful the roads were on these weekday mornings when most of the world was at work or school and the housewives were off at the health club, country club or doing those chores that husbands heard at night made their days so stressful. As I turned up our hill, I passed the teams of landscape crews milling about their trucks and vans ready to assault the fallen leaves to create the park-like atmosphere that greeted the bread winners when they arrived home from their busy days. I counted five workers in front of my house and thought to myself that maybe $100.00 a week wasn't such a bad deal. A quick calculation of the hourly rate for two or three hours a week made me feel that it was well worth the money as it would take me a whole weekend to achieve what they did. Like most men, I felt a twinge of guilt that this was another one of those house duties that I had abandoned over the years, but it did give me more time to see the kids' games and have a little bit of a life on those precious breaks from work when the markets were actually closed. On weekends, I slowed down and limited myself to Barron's, the New York Times, and a couple of hours of research on Sunday night.

I pulled into the circular driveway, noticed that our sixty-year-old white colonial digs were in need of another paint job, pushed the thought of paying for a fresh coat out of mind, hit the garage remote and headed into the house to get to my office and the markets.

The dogs poked their heads up, somewhat confused by my presence in the middle of the day as I passed through the kitchen, threw my keys on the black granite counter and thought with a wry smile, "Gee, that will go over well." Missy hated it when I cluttered up her pristinely clean bare counter space. I passed through the kitchen and breakfast area and walked into the War Room.

At various times we referred to it as my office, sanctuary, my kingdom and a host of other names, but most importantly it was my home away from the office. Outfitted with computers with lightening fast cable connections, Bloomberg, fax, copier, satellite TV and no less than three phone lines and a remote, I had all requisite toys and capabilities my other office provided, save for the fact that I had no Tina, my trusted and efficient secretary and assistant, no typing skills and no technological support. My father's handed down antique mahogany desk took up the rear one-third of the room, while the sitting and reading area in front of the wall unit, stereo and TV gave me a place to read research and watch baseball or hockey games in the corner of my eye till the wee hours of the morning. Of course the concept was that it would be my space and my space alone, but with the best TV in the house and most comfortable seating arrangement, the kids and Missy had adopted it as their favorite place to hang out in on weeknights and weekends. Nevertheless, during the day and when they were asleep, it was truly my castle with a private bathroom to boot. If I had convinced Missy that I needed a refrigerator, I could have locked the door and disappeared for days or weeks at a time.

I settled into my desk chair, enjoyed the whoosh of the seat cushion of the blue leather chair as I sat down, and logged on to my computer to check the day's activities.

Not much change from my update of ten minutes earlier at school, but gold had crept eerily higher and was on the verge of breaking into new high ground. I congratulated myself for putting 5% of my clients' assets into some gold producers, but wondered if I should sell some covered calls to collect a little extra income. "There's plenty of time to figure out if this move is real," I told myself, remembering the rule that investment decisions need to be well thought out. I moved on to find out what was going on with the rest of the world.

Industrials look OK; glad I bought that Allied Industrial, up another 3% today. Utilities still can't get out of their own way. Someday, they've got to turn. Oils and service stocks generally higher, now how about that oil exploration company Roger told me to keep an eye on. I flipped to my next screen and saw it up another point. 'How much has that run in the past month?' I asked myself. Had to be at least 30%. I pulled up the chart. From 9 to 13.60 in a month – wow 45%. He did have a knack. But now what was he up to?

As I dialed Roger's private line in California, I leaned back to watch the ticker cross the bottom of the TV screen, saw the big hair on the too-young- to-know-anything announcer and wondered how many people really thought he knew what he was talking about. In the investment business gray hair is earned, and this guy wouldn't be worth listening to for years. The mute button never had a better use than to suffocate the dribble that came out of the mouth of this "stock analyst" and "market commentator."

"Yello!" came the familiar voice.

"Rog."

"J. Thomas?"

"Yup – what's up? Got your message."

"Hey, I can't talk right now. I'm in a meeting. Tell me you can be out here by the end of the week."

"What?" I wasn't ready for this.

"You've got to come. We've got to talk. Can you do it?"

I stammered a feeble "I'll have to look into it and talk to Missy."

"Let me take care of all the arrangements, my company will pay for everything. Airfare too." He was pushing hard, but at least he was trying to make it painless on my wallet.

"I've already got my girl looking into it. She's checking out flights as we speak."

"Whatever you do, make sure you have her coordinate your trip with Paula, my assistant. Paula will take care of everything. She's a pistol. Tell you what; I'll have Paula call Tina right now to start working on it." He liked being in control, but at times it was annoying to get pushed around.

"I haven't even agreed to come out yet," I protested.

He answered impatiently; "OK, call me back and let me know, or at least have Tina keep Paula up to speed on what plans you do make. Promise?"

"Alright already, I'll have Tina work with Paula, but I am not promising to be there this week. I have some juggling to do at home and you have to realize, you can't just order me around. I do have a family to think of and a business to run." I didn't like raining on his parade and reminding him that he didn't control my destiny, but he took it in stride.

"Yeah, I know. But I really need you out here, and I was kind of hoping you could come out Thursday night."

"We'll see," I said, then trying to change the subject, mentioned nonchalantly "You know I got a call from the SEC last week asking about you."

"Yeah, that's part of it, but not a big deal. Gotta go, OK?"

"OK" I said, and heard the click of the phone on the other end.

Leaning forward to put the headset back in the receiver, I turned away from the ticker and thought "What could be going on that is so urgent Roger needs me in California?" Then in a flash I remembered I was supposed to be on vacation, and if I even thought about leaving to see Roger, there would be hell to pay at home. Missy would freak. Things had been pretty rough around the house lately, and this week was supposed to be time for us to spend 'quality time' together. But Roger was my closest friend and we were supposed to be... no... we had to be there for each other in times of need.

My watch said it was 11:12 AM, so Missy wouldn't be home from the health club for another 45 minutes. My mind started to race. Better have the office start checking into flights. How would this go over with Missy? I knew I had promised we'd go to see Tommy's squash match Wednesday afternoon. Nothing else major was on the calendar. Kathleen had a basketball game Tuesday, but the rest of the week looked clear. If I got out Thursday morning, I could meet with Roger and take the red-eye back Thursday night – no, Friday night, and still be back in time for Michael's soccer game Saturday morning. "Can't miss the weekend," I said to myself, recalling the oath. "No business on weekends. Family first. That's our pact." Missy and I had a deal.

Speed dialing my secretary got me the pleasant professional voice of my most trusted employee, Christine, a proficient and organized saint of a woman, who at age 28 had somehow thus far avoided the trappings of marriage, was devoted to her work from 8 till 6, then disappeared every day.

"Mr. Morris' office, can I help you?"

"Tina, it's me. Anything going on?"

"No, a couple of calls in your voice mail from people selling things you don't want, that new client in St. Louis wants to know if the contracts were received, signed and sent back. Told him they were Fed Ex'd to his lawyer Friday and a call from your friend, Roger, but he said he would track you down."

Everything I needed to know in a flash.

"Yup, got him a minute ago – I need you to check out flights to L.A. Leaving this Thursday morning and returning on the Friday night red eye. See if there's room up front. Can't bear to think of squeezing into the cattle car in back for six hours at a time and Roger said his firm would pick up all the expenses. Said you should coordinate all travel with his secretary, Paula, who if I know Roger will be calling you in a minute or two."

"Got it. Should I book it or hold it?"

"Try and save a seat, I'll know later today."

"Some vacation you must be having – Monday morning and you're already looking to go cross country. Don't you have to see your son play something?"

"Yup, but, like a memory, you've got some elephant. That's Wednesday." It was a banter we fell into naturally and off she went to book my latest trip, a feat she performed better than any travel agent or secretary I had ever relied upon.

"I'm at home if you need me for anything," I added.

"We'll survive without you somehow; we've already made it for four hours without a crisis. You're on vacation. Relax."

"OK, but you know where I am if you need me. I'll check in later."

"Yes, boss."

"Thanks, Tina."

That done, I turned to the Bloomberg screen and started reviewing the day's news stories, earnings reports and checked the rest of my e-mail.

CHAPTER THREE

The barking in the kitchen gave me a start and I realized that Missy must have returned from the morning's activities and be in the kitchen. My watch showed ten minutes after twelve and I realized that I had fallen into that delirium known as focus where time, minutes and hours disappear. I had learned from my stint at the Bloomberg terminal that the world of stocks and bonds was copasetic for the time being and one of my holdings had announced they were going to beat Wall Street's high-paid analysts' earnings estimates causing its stock to move 5% higher. Three corporate insiders revealed that they had bought stock in Mid West Railroad Transport, another stock which I owned, causing a surge in activity, mostly buying as the stock was about 4% higher. Some days the world of equities made sense and today appeared to be one of them.

"Honey?" came the standard beckoning.

"Coming" came the standard response as I headed into the kitchen, pulling my body out of my favorite chair to the sound of clicking knees that had experienced too many years of too many sports with too little padding and too little stretching.

Missy was standing at the sink putting the dog's lunchtime feast together and looked like a sports bunny with her tight black warm-ups and white sleeveless vest. I sidled up to her, poked a kiss on her cheek and said, "So how's the star paddle player today? Good practice?"

"It was fun, but we're not sure who's going to be able to play back-hand with Julie in #1. She's too strong willed to play with Hannah or Bonnie, who can't take being told what to do. It'll probably have to be Nancy or me, who aren't as good, but can follow Julie's orders. She is an unbelievable player. What's up with you today? How did the class go?"

"I think it went well. The kids seemed to have fun and I didn't embarrass Kathleen too badly. All in all, I'd give myself a B+/A-."

"Sounds positive, you going to the gym or spending the afternoon on the phone watching the stock market channel?"

She knew me too well and while we talked about how I needed to spend more time exercising and trying to get into better shape, I just couldn't seem to do it while the U. S. equity markets were open. Sure, when we went away on trips or I was with clients playing golf, I could justify leaving it alone for a few hours at a time, but when I had these off days around the house, I couldn't seem to break away.

"I've got some calls to make, and oh, by the way, Roger called."

"Oh really! What's up with Rog?"

There wasn't an easy way to slip the news in, especially since Tina was already working her magic with flights. "He said he needs me to come out to L.A."

"Yeah – when?" she asked innocently, still pleasant and unassuming.

"This week," I answered meekly. The bomb dropped with a silent thud that I could feel reverberate through the walls and floor.

"You can't, you couldn't. You didn't say yes."

All wars started with a single shot.

"I know, I know. But actually, I could fly out Thursday and be back in time for the soccer game Saturday morning."

"But you promised," she protested, with more than a hint of anger in her voice.

"I know, I know, but this will work. We'll still make it to the squash match Wednesday and I'll be back for Michael's soccer game on Saturday. And it's for Roger. You know I have to go."

She didn't know and didn't understand the bond. I had told her countless times through the years how much Roger's friendship meant to me. How he was the brother I always wanted, to stick with through thick and thin, who'd take a bullet or give a limb, organ or any body part that I might need. In the end, it was my future that he had saved when he said that it was his stash of pot in the footlocker of our room at prep school nearly 25 years ago. Truth was, it was both of ours, as we pooled everything we had, from allowances to smokes to pot. Well, almost everything. Girls were the one thing that we didn't share. It was funny that his girlfriends came and went on a regular basis, but in the end, I was the one who stayed friends with them as he moved on to other pursuits and conquests. But Roger said we needed a plan and whoever got called into the dean first was going to claim ownership of the contraband. He got the short straw as he got called first, said it was his, wouldn't give up the name of the dealer and thus ended his prep school career. Missy would never truly know or feel the hell that we went through, the torture of that night as we waited for the call, the pain I felt as we packed his bags and belongings and the guilt that I had lived with for the past twenty-five years.

"So you're saying I have no choice, you're going."

"No, we can talk about it," I offered meekly.

"There's nothing to talk about, go make your calls."

"But I'll be here for the squash match and back for soccer."

"I'm not in the mood…Go make your calls…. Has Tina booked the flights yet?"

"No," I said firmly, with a renewed sense of conviction.

"Is she working on it?"

"Just checking flights to make sure it will work with our schedules."

"You mean your schedule."

The tone was clear, the frost filled the kitchen and grew as we had our tete a tete, and I felt a perceptible shiver as we ended our conversation. I put my tail between my legs as the dogs looked on and I slinked out of the room, back to my sanctuary, which in times like this felt more like an isolation chamber. I knew that I would have to make the next move. She would leave me alone until I surfaced again, giving her a chance to stew with the impending alteration of plans. I would have to let enough time pass to make our next encounter manageable. Move too soon and be doomed to failure. Wait too long and Missy's disdain for my insensitivity would grow in hyperbolic proportions, the ice thickening with the Arctic air.

A quick call back to Tina confirmed my suspicions that the Thursday morning flight to L.A. was available. I could have dinner with Roger Thursday night, stop by his office in the morning, and have lunch with the CFO of a heavy oil company that I had invested in a few years earlier. I had invested in his oil company as a tax shelter and way to start building up some income producing assets, but as I had gotten to know him over the years, found him to be a font of knowledge about the oil industry and a valuable resource when I had questions about the energy industry.

"But is this passing muster at home?" Tina asked. She knew that my vacations were supposed to be 'family only'. But she also knew that I always seemed to mess them up, straining marital and family relations. As a result, I was usually in a bad mood for at least a week or two when I returned from these vacations that were supposed to recharge my batteries and mend the fences at home. I always passed off the foul moods to the piles of work awaiting my return. Tina knew better. Mountains of paper didn't faze me, an unhappy partner at home did.

"It'll be fine, but yes, I do have some serious groveling and repair work to do."

"Thought so. This plan has trouble written all over it."

"Yeah, yeah, move on…where do we stand?"

"I have a courtesy hold from Southern Airways for the 9:00AM from Newark Thursday, returning on the Friday night redeye getting in at 5:30 AM Saturday. The fare's $368.00 if you book today, but it jumps to $772.00 tomorrow due to the fact it's within the 3 day window and yes, if you want to pay for up front, there are some seats available. Only two seats are left in first class going out and only one left on the redeye coming home…What should I do? Want to think about it"?

I had already weighed the pros and cons and Missy knew I was going anyway. I was going to be playing damage control, but the damage had already been done.

"No, book it." It hurt to say it. It was going to hurt for awhile, but we had made our way through these potholes on the marriage highway before. I added, "And go ahead with First Class. Remember, Roger said First American would pick up the tab."

"Yeah, I've already spoken to Paula twice in the past half hour. She's the one who found the seats up front. I'll have the tickets dropped off tomorrow."

"Thanks, anything else new?"

"No, usual stuff…We're handling it and you did let everyone know you were going to be out this week!"

"I know, just checking."

"Relax. Enjoy your time off. Sounds like you're winding down already."

"Ha ha—talk to you later today, or first thing in the AM."

"I'm sure you will."

CHAPTER FOUR

The First Class section of the Boeing 757 outfitted by Southern Airways was roomy and as comfortable as one could hope for as I settled in to the soft tan leather seat for the flight west. Armed with extendable footrest, pillow, blanket and personal video terminal to watch movies, it was an opportunity to escape reality for 5 1/2 hours. Armed with a briefcase full of Wall Street research reports, the latest novel from my favorite author, Sam Black, and a file full of notes and calls to organize for my return to the office next week, I looked at the crisp jacket of the novel's hardcover and longed for the time when I could take a break from the grind of keeping up with the world to enjoy a good read. The only time I ever seemed to be able to float away into a story was on plane flights of 3 or more hours, so I only read two or three novels a year and would wait for one of my favorite authors to come out with a new yarn before I dove into a new story.

I put the novel in the pouch of the seat in front of me and promised I'd get to it soon and closed my eyes to reflect on the past few days and the trip ahead.

Missy's attitude had thawed somewhat, partially due to the passage of time and partially due to my over-zealous, perfect-Dad routine. Bringing the kids to school on Tuesday and Wednesday morning and letting Missy enjoy the peace and quiet of an un rushed morning capped off by hand-delivered Mocha Grande coffee from Starbucks certainly helped. Or was it my volunteering to assist coaching my son's winter hockey team? Intimacy was not a possibility, as previous battles had proven, and my quiet acceptance of pre-trip celibacy or penance was a lesson well learned after all those years of marriage. Yes, we still have a healthy sex life, I reminded myself, and nothing could be more satisfying that just waking up together and holding each other in our semi-naked condition, but this was not one of those times. Maybe when I got back on Saturday night.

The squash match was exciting, as my oldest rallied to win after being down two games to one. Missy and I topped it off with a nice dinner together with the victor, marveling on the way home how poised and mature our son had become. It is amazing to watch your progeny grow from infants to children to semi-adults in a flash. Tommie had developed physically and mentally at the prep school where Roger and I had met and it seemed like he was getting more out of it than we or our friends did 25 years earlier. Now he was a man of seventeen with incredible energy, focus and drive and the pages of his future were white as snow.

Roger and I had taken different paths; at times by choice; at times by luck, and the luck wasn't always good. Maybe it was destiny. And look where we were now. Things had worked out pretty well through the years for both of us, but what was up with Roger now? He was the one that always seemed to be caught up in something, but always seemed to come out better off no matter what.

"Would you like a drink before takeoff?" The attractive, thirty-something brunette stewardess was speaking to the passenger on the aisle to my left, but jostled my thoughts nonetheless. I opened my eyes and noticing my awake condition she asked, "And you?"

I thanked the stewardess and declined, for the last thing I wanted was to get my bladder working too hard and to have to repeatedly wake up or disturb my unknown companion in mid flight. Lessons from the road included Never Drink Too Much and absolutely Never Eat Too Much of the processed, tasteless food for fear of actually having to use those toilets in the planes. The things you learn, you never forget!

The plane boarding process was nearly finished by the masses heading west, an odd and seemingly random collection of our melting pot. If anyone ever wanted to get a true cross section of American culture and society, they should look no further than a flight like this one. Students with their back packs bulging, businessmen with their faces gray and eyes hollowing with circles, senior citizens visiting family or going home, couples getting away from it all. I chuckled to myself about the lunacy of the brilliant airline executives who fashioned the industry to its current comical state of financial panic. There were probably no less than a dozen different fares for the travelers on any give flight. Furthermore, they charged the businessmen that flew the most exorbitant rates while they filled up the majority of the plane with cost conscious consumers looking for the cheapest flight. 'Repeat after me', I said to myself. 'I will never buy an airline stock. I will never buy an airline stock.'

"Wonder how the markets are opening?" I thought to myself. If there is one vacuum of isolation for a stock market junkie, it is being 40,000 feet above the world. I knew I could sneak a peek at my Blackberry once we got airborne, but after 5 to 10,000 feet even that electronic marvel's capability was useless. As the plane took off and began its ascent to heaven, I took a quick peek at the e-mail of the morning…Useless chatter from work about clients adding or taking out insignificant sums as their pension plans paid off retirees and collected premiums, or profit sharing plan participants who needed to add or subtract from their various asset pools. Lots of the usual upgrades and downgrades from securities analysts trying to make their mark as their exclusive proprietary research had caused them to change an earnings estimate for a multi billion dollar company by a whopping one or two cents.

It amazed me that so few investors understood that the analysts who crafted the most detailed and accurate financial models were often the worst stock pickers. That is, they knew what a company was going to earn, but had not developed the knack for knowing when to recommend buying or selling a stock. Indeed, some of my best investments over the years had been to buy stocks that the famous high priced analysts had finally given up on and to sell stocks when the locusts of Wall Street have all decided that a company was hitting on all cylinders and had to be a great buy. Like moths to a flame, the 'can't miss' opportunities always seemed to burn out, and the few analysts who realized how to make money usually decided to manage their own money or they went to work for hedge funds where the rewards could be truly huge. The bull market of the late 90's made too many of these analysts believe that they were geniuses, because golly gee, anyone could start a hedge fund and make millions if they were good stock pickers, right? Now, my email in box was sprinkled with resumes from a half dozen geniuses a week trying to get back in the game now that they had vaporized their life's savings, and usually their friends' and families', too.

The satellite connection ended abruptly and I knew that I could officially be called unavailable, a phrase Tina had used for countless other possibilities. She knew that family, close friends and my closest business relationships could always be told if I was available or when I was likely to be able to get back to them, but for the legions of cold calls from people trying to get a piece of my time, I was always unavailable.

Perusing through a stack of research, I noticed a short note on Spindletop Energy, the exploration company Roger had told me about a month earlier and since it was from a regional brokerage firm that didn't have an investment banking relationship

Spindletop; I looked closer than usual at the firm's assessment of the company's valuation and prospects. While the analyst was intrigued with Spindletop's exploration efforts and the potential of its drilling efforts in the Slaughterhouse Trend, he pointed out that the area where the company was focusing its drilling activity was remote, not tied in to existing pipelines or other needed infrastructure and that even if the company found the oil it hoped, he questioned whether the company had the financial wherewithal to "bring home the bacon." At least he had a sense of humor and some wit, I thought. I pulled the report out of my stack and put it in my briefcase to discuss with Roger if we had time. I decided Frank Howell, my friend and partner in the heavy oil business, might be able to give me some insight into the company and its prospects at lunch on Friday as well.

Roger and I hadn't spoken since Monday, but between my right-hand man (Tina) and his right hand man (Paula), we had confirmed reservations for a dinner meeting at 6:00 PM. I was to call when I checked in to my hotel on The Avenue of the Stars, and we were scheduled to get together again Friday at his office at 8:30 AM. Tina's handiwork was obvious since Roger would schedule meetings as early as 5:00 AM and Tina knew no matter what the occasion, she would never schedule a meeting for me before 8:00 AM. My preference was actually 10:00 AM since that would give me time to read the Journal, check overnight market activity and get through a morning batch of e-mail. I always felt lost on days when I was forced to do an early meeting, didn't feel sharp if I hadn't consumed the Journal with and as a part of my breakfast.

"Would you like coffee or juice Mr. Morris?" asked the same brunette stewardess who offered me a pre-flight drink. She said it with what seemed like a sincere smile.

"No thanks, I'll wait until breakfast is served."

"And what would you like with your meal?"

"Just apple juice, thanks."

"Certainly, Mr. Morris. My name is Karen and I'll be your server today. Just let me know if there's anything I can do to make your flight more enjoyable."

Now that was a loaded statement if I ever heard one. I thought about what kind of thoughts and responses that line created for most businessmen on their way cross country for a six-hour flight away from their wives, families and girlfriends and smiled to myself. Men are pigs. Their minds are and will always be in the gutter, and with the slightest encouragement most would suffer instant amnesia and dementia if a woman, any woman, propositioned them. Of course, guilt immediately settled into my mind about how could I possibly risk my marriage and family for a feckless dalliance. Sure, it would probably be fun and exciting, but for how long, and look at the downside. Risk/Reward convincingly terrible. Potential repercussions unfathomable. But hey, she was cute and did smile at me. And I remembered what smiles like that meant way back when -- before jobs and kids and wives.

"Not a coffee drinker?" my seat mate asked.

I looked up and noticed that the early forty-something mustachioed man had his laptop open to Microsoft Outlook and was obviously going through his email in box. Quick guess was a senior salesman for a division of a major Fortune 500 company. Talkers on flights were often salesmen and the mustache was strike two. The cheap cufflinks and the two-toned shirt clinched it for me.

"No, never developed a taste for it."

"Pretty unique in this day and age."

"Yeah, but I do love caffeine and drink enough soda to stay wired and alert through the day." Shut up, I said to myself or this could go on for hours.

"I, myself love the stuff, couldn't give it up. Wouldn't give it up for the world." He was starting to drone.

"Yeah, I know what you mean." I quickly reached for my novel and hoped that burying me in a book would bring quiet and solitude once again.

"What's that? The new Sam Black?" he asked.

Oh, shit, backfire. I really didn't want to get into an involved conversation. I tried to set up a graceful exit, stage left. "Uh huh, really want to finish it by California."

"You could, he's always a fast read."

"Hope so," I said quickly and looked down at what I hoped was my pass to peace and quiet.

"Haven't read that one yet, but it got really good reviews.

"If I finish it by California, I'll let you have it."

"Gee, thanks," he said quickly, his salt and pepper mustache rising as he showed a white-washed set of model-quality teeth.

"No problem," I replied, trying to end the discourse quickly. "And if I happen to close my eyes, just tell the stewardess I'll pass on breakfast."

"Sure. No problem."

Could I have put an end to the suffering small-talk? I refocused on the book and started to read the forward, a standard part of every Sam Black novel that developed the story line. The book's forward was a newspaper story about a random killing that had occurred with sketchy details and, according to the police report, no apparent motive. The question for the reader and the plot would unfold was about how Sam, the intrepid private eye, was going to get involved and how he would solve the crime. Off to the fantasy land fiction escape. I lost myself in the story for thirty pages before I closed my eyes and drifted off to sleep.

Mid-morning cat naps are a good idea only if you don't have a timetable for when you have to be awake and alert. The captain's voice over the speaker above me startled me out of my slumber. I really didn't need to know that we were now cruising at 37,000 feet or that it was sunny and 76 degrees in L.A. The one important piece of information that he relayed was that while we were a little late leaving the gate, due to weak head winds we should be on time for our arrival into L.A. The stewardesses were busy keeping the working passengers caffeinated,

fulfilling the wants and needs of the fussy ones and repelling the flirting advances of the scourge of the air, married businessmen hoping to
develop a relationship meaningful enough to get them in the sack for
their layover. Not so meaningful that they would tell the truth about
their marital status, number of children and town that they lived in,
but what the heck, what was the downside?

Karen stopped by with a steaming towel and a smile and I smiled
back a sincere "Thanks." Sitting by the window didn't give me much
of an opportunity to engage in conversation and I certainly didn't
want to start a conversation I couldn't stop with Mr. Mustache, so I
kept my head in my book for breakfast and figured I'd have a little
chat with Karen when I needed a potty run. Her wholesome looks
started to grow on me and each time she passed by I'd try to get a
glance or smile or just a peek to get a better read on her face, eyes
and body for my fantasies. Looking out the window I was surprised
to have passed the flat farmland of the Midwest and assumed we must
now be near or in the Colorado Rockies. In an amazing stark picture
of black and white, the tops of the mountains were pure and freshly
white. Everything else was a jumble of seemingly lifeless vegetation
and the crevices in the mountains that filled with snow from afar
looked like veins in a spectacular creation.

As we passed over the Rockies and into the waves of mountain
ranges and canyons, I marveled that anyone would have ever attempted to cross parts of the country like this, or were able to survive
on what little sustenance the land below appeared to offer from my
perch of 37,000 feet. The roads that wore their way across the landscape reminded me that not much of our great country had avoided
being explored, conquered and made accessible.

"I wonder where the Slaughterhouse Trend is," I thought, looking across the barren landscape before me. I remembered it being
somewhere remote in the Rockies. If it were near here, I guessed the
name came from being in an area where cattle roamed or were processed. It would be neat to find out, I thought as I excused myself to

Mr. Mustache and exited my seat to find the lavatory. It never ceased to amaze me how some words continued in existence ever after we had a suitable replacement. Why keep the Latin-derived lavatory when bathroom was such an able replacement?

Karen was sitting on the jump seat next to the plane's boarding door across the aisle from the cramped kitchen area and, after satisfying my biological needs, I moved on the emotional and psychological.

"So, heading home or just starting out?" I asked. Looking up at me in green eyes, she said, "Finishing up a round trip, but we've been flying for four days. Get a layover in L.A. for a day and a half and then head home to Cleveland on Saturday."

"Sounds like fun" I said. God, I was bad at small-talk when I was single and reflected that I probably hadn't improved much through the years.

"Actually, it's not bad," Karen offered with a smile. "This crew has been a lot of fun. It is what you make of it and I love seeing new places and being able to visit friends and their families."

"Really, how long have you been a stewardess?"

"Flight attendants, that's what we are called now," she corrected me, feigning hurt. "Funny, you don't look that old." Was that a compliment or a flirtatious opening? "I've been flying for eight years now," she added.

"So, do you have friends in L.A.?" Maybe I wasn't so bad at small talk.

"Yes, my old roommate from college lives there with her two children and I usually stay with her. But she got called out of town on business and her ex has the kids, so not this time."

"Where do they usually put you up?" I added, enjoying the small talk.

"Actually, for security reasons we're not supposed to say." Her smile was gone.

I must have crossed the line and I had thought things were going so well.

"And why are you going to L.A.?" she added. Another opening, I thought.

"Business. Meetings tonight and tomorrow then back on the red eye on Friday night."

"Your schedule sounds busy."

Oh no, don't shut off all the possibilities.

"Actually, it's an early dinner and my meeting's not till 8:30 AM tomorrow. So, I might sneak out to have a look see at some of the sights. Go for a drive."

"You better know where you're going" she said, cautioning me. "Everyone says, and even the airlines tell us there are parts of L.A. to avoid completely."

"I'm definitely going to stay on the main drags. Might go down to Hollywood Boulevard and check out the Walk of the Stars and play tourist." Where was I going with this?

"I hear that part of town stays open late," she offered, adding, "But it sounds like fun. I've been down there once, but only by car."

There it was! My opening. "Well if you want, we could hook up somewhere."

"Oh no, thank you. The airline really frowns on that."

"No problem, no pressure. Just figured it would be more fun with someone else along." What was I doing, I thought to myself. How would Missy react if she caught me trying to drum up some companionship? Of course this conversation was innocent enough; there wasn't really anything to it. Was there?

"Well, have a good time in L.A. Hope your meetings go well," Karen said which make it clear that my dalliance had reached its appropriate end. The smile that she gave me, though, made me think that maybe a connection had been made. Strong eye contact. Had consciously avoided letting my eyes wander to parts of her body while we spoke. If there was one thing I had learned through the years, women like to look good and feel good about how they looked, but very few wanted a man to visually undress them and have his mind fondle their bodies. 'Yes' I thought, 'all men are pigs.' I wondered how I looked, how Karen viewed this forty-three year old man, with slight wisps of gray hair near the temples, obviously carrying a few too many pounds. I knew from my daily weigh in it was thirty-five, but I had learned long ago that by standing up very straight and having a wardrobe of mostly dark clothes made most people think it was less. At least that's what my buddies at the club said when we talked about how much we needed to lose to get back into shape.

Sidling back to my seat, Mr. Mustache got up so that I could get in easier. I said thanks and hoped I'd avoid getting into a long conversation.

"She's cute" he offered unsolicited as I sat down.

"Huh?" I answered, surprised to have another topic to avoid with my seat mate.

"The stewardess you were hitting on. She single?"

Dumbfounded, I wondered if there was a sign flashing around me with a scarlet A. I managed an "I don't know" and a feeble "Just passing time."

"Who can blame you?" he said. "Great body and some rack, huh?"

While I had some of the same passing thoughts, hearing him say it repulsed me and the French word "cochon" came to mind. Pig didn't have enough syllables to do him justice.

"She seemed very sweet," I said matter-of-factly and dove back into my book. But the incident nagged at me. What was I doing? Was it cheating on your wife to talk to another woman? Was I starting conversations with unknown women because I hadn't had sex with my wife for two and a half weeks? Would I be doing the same thing if we had had wild intimate sex last night? The questions of the universe. Was it because of my inadequacies or shortcomings that I had these wandering thoughts? I'd never really cheated on Missy, though I did enjoy a good flirt now and again. What's the difference? 'Enough, enough, it's over', I said to myself. Back to the novel and away from this guilt. Nothing happened. No blood. No foul.

CHAPTER FIVE

The limo driver was waiting at the end of security with a "MORRIS, J.T." sign boldly identifying that he was there to drive me to the hotel.

I had slithered guiltily off the plane, sure that I had made an ass of myself with my conduct and attempts at what, flirting? I couldn't even think to try to speak with or have eye contact with Karen, even as she handed me my navy blue blazer as we prepared to land.

Extending my hand to the driver, I said, "I'm Tom Morris. The J. is an inside joke."

"Hello Mr. Morris. I'm Jeff. Any luggage today, sir?"

"No, thanks. Just this overnight and my briefcase."

"Then if you'll follow me, we can go straight to the car. Let me take that for you."

I offered up my overnight bag, but would never give up my briefcase, a black Tumi traveling office that was almost permanently attached to my shoulder when I traveled. Its sturdy strap was slightly cushioned and enabled me to carry my important research and papers, money, wallet, emergency items and of course, address book.

Once we reached the black stretch limo, I climbed into the back seat, got out the address book to get Roger's phone number; dialing him up on my cell.

He answered on the second ring. "Yo, Thomas."

"Caller ID, huh? Can't get away with a thing. By the way, the stretch is a little over the top. A sedan would have been just fine."

"Don't worry my treat. Company's paying. If I can't spend it on you, who can I? It's yours for your stay. Jeff will take care of anything you need, bring you anywhere you need to go."

"We still on for dinner?"

"Yup, I'm going to the health club at 3:00 for a workout and sauna. Meet you at the restaurant at 6?"

"That's pretty early, but sure."

"I have to sleep some time, you know. Bed by 10, up at 3. We have to fight the New York bias of the world, remember."

"See you then. Casual dress?"

"Come on. California defined casual. Wear a suit and I'll make you regret it."

"OK." It was fun just to be a part of Roger's energy and enthusiasm. It didn't surprise any one who knew him well that he was going to be a huge success in whatever he concentrated his efforts on.

As I clicked on my Blackberry, I noticed that we had made it to the outskirts of the airport, near the rental cars and satellite parking. Now there's a joke for a comedian, I chuckled. Are you supposed to park your satellite there or maybe there could be a joke about you know you've made it when you have your own satellite and can park in satellite parking…..hmmm, have to work on that, I thought. I made a mental note to put the thought in my list of jokes for my stand-up routine when I burned out on the markets.

The Blackberry let me know that the markets and office had somehow survived my absence for the past six hours, and as I scrambled through my messages noticed that Tina had sent me a summary of phone messages, including one from my son at school thanking me for coming to his match and one from the SEC, calling with some more questions.

"What is going on?" I thought. I couldn't figure out what they were after and how Roger was involved, but was sure I would find out at dinner. Tommie, I would call when I got settled in.

We pulled into the horseshoe shaped entrance of the JW Marriott on the Avenue of the Stars, which would never be confused with the Walk of Stars on Hollywood and Vine. Slightly different neighborhood. Being a movie lover, I enjoyed knowing that the office building across the street was used in one of the first "Die Hard" movies. I took a quick peek and smiled as it was just as I remembered it from my last stay and seemed not the worse for wear, even though it was almost completely destroyed in the movie. Only in Hollywood!! Jeff brought my bag to the front desk, gave me his card and promised to be waiting and ready to serve at a moment's notice.

Roger had obviously researched where I was going to stay, for when I arrived at the front desk; I was informed that I had been upgraded to the concierge floor and that all charges were being taken care of by First American Insurance. Special key and all, with complimentary beverage service and snacks 24 hours a day. Nice touch. One hour pressing available and overnight shoeshine as well. What a way to live. If you were going to have to travel for business, this was not a bad way to have to suffer through.

The view of downtown LA from my room was spectacular. The sun was just beginning to set in the distance and the first hints of pink and yellow were starting to work their way into the mosaic of the day's end. I started my Road Warrior routine – the moves I used when in a new hotel room. Unpacked the briefcase, laid out the papers for tomorrow in piles on the white duvet bed spread, plugged the computer and Blackberry chargers in to the wall, the cell phone charger into the plug beneath the light on the small writing desk, then put each of my electronic necessities into their respective chargers. Moving on to the suitcase, I hung up my folded shirts and pants from the overnight bag and got out my toiletries. A shower felt like a great idea. I started dumping the contents of my jacket and pants pockets; money, keys, cell phone, and then something I didn't expect and couldn't place. It was a folded napkin with the logo of Southern Airways imprinted on it.

I didn't remember taking a napkin while in flight, so I picked it up and saw on the back of it written in pen, "Karen Clarkson – Airport Hilton. Sightseeing?"

Startled, excited and suddenly scared to death, I didn't know what to do. Does she know my name? "My God," I thought "of course she does, from the list of passengers." It wasn't making any sense to me. Was this real or a joke? But the note did appear to be written with a flowing feminine hand, textbook perfect script that no man I knew could emulate after age 15 or 16.

CHAPTER SIX

I met Jeff in the lobby at about 5:45 PM, just minutes after I called to let him know I was on my way. He assured me he knew where we were going, a short drive to meet Mr. Maydock at the Hoofs and Spurs, one of the trendiest, but best steak and seafood restaurants in L.A.

"Is your room satisfactory, Mr. Morris?"

"Absolutely. Couldn't be nicer. Do all of Mr. Maydock's guests stay here?"

"No, only CEO's and his most important clients," he said with a suitably deferential impressed air.

Either it was a line that made all of Roger's clients and prospects feel important or I really was being given the red carpet treatment. The air seemed cooler as we left the lobby and headed to the limo parked boldly front and center in the valet parking area, and I was glad that I had grabbed my navy blue blazer at the last minute as I left my room. In reality, I had taken it so I had more pockets to hold my cell phone, Blackberry and cigarettes, hating the look of electronics bulging from my pants pocket. Now, in the cool early evening air I felt justified for reasons other than vanity.

"You may smoke in the car, Mr. Morris. I should have mentioned it on the drive from the airport."

"No problem. Thanks," I answered, as I reached into my shirt pocket and pulled out my pack of Marlboros. I knew that my cigarettes had been in my jacket when I rode from the airport, but Jeff must have noticed them in my shirt pocket when I met him in the lobby. Sharp guy, I thought to myself. As we drove to the restaurant, I looked at the palm trees lining the street and in the distance the haze that permeates the horizon on most afternoons. The pastel colors of the haze were pleasant enough, but the thought of the pollution that they represented was not.

Taking a drag on my cigarette, I saw a billboard advertising the lowest prices on new cars, followed by one displaying a gorgeous woman's face and the promise of the finest live dancers in the L.A. area. I chuckled to myself that those establishments promising dead dancers didn't stand a chance. Sick humor. It's a good thing I didn't speak my random thoughts. Like what was I going to do tonight? Eagerly looking forward to finding out what was up with Roger and his insurance company, and what in the world the SEC was interested in? If he was in trouble, he would have called sooner and I would've been able to tell it in his voice. Wouldn't I?

"Excuse me, but will you be going out this evening, Mr. Morris?"

The question stopped me in my tracks. I fumbled, "You mean after dinner?"

"Yes, sir," came the crisp and professional reply "The Lakers are out of town, but many of Mr. Maydock's clients like to go to nightclubs or jazz bars after dinner when in town for the evening."

"No thanks, I'll probably just go back to the hotel after dinner." I didn't know what I was going to do after dinner, but one thing I had decided was that I was not going to use Roger's limo. If I was going to go for a ride, I would just take a cab. Besides, I still hadn't decided what to do with the napkin in my pocket. Throw it away. Call her. I was torn with the moral consequences of even thinking about calling her. "Put it out of your mind," I said to myself. "You're here to see Roger."

We pulled up to the restaurant, our limo taking up most of the valet parking space and I told Jeff, "Don't worry. I can let myself out."

"I'll be here waiting for you, Mr. Morris. Take you time and enjoy your dinner. I hear the surf and turf is the best in town."

"Thanks, Jeff," I said as I climbed out of the back seat. While limos look impressive, I thought, they are a pain to get in and out of.

As I approached the huge mahogany double doors, a doorman dressed in fox hunting attire, replete with red jacket, polished brass buttons and white pants pulled on the gold bar that ran the length of the door and served as a door handle. I walked into the dark mahogany paneled foyer with brass globes offering a subtle soft light that took me a second to adjust to. I stood in the entrance as my eyes adjusted and heard from my right, Roger's familiar voice.

"J. Thomas. Over here."

I saw Roger sitting at the bar on a swiveling black leather-backed stool. Looking fit and tan, he stood up with a bright engaging smile. Roger said something to the gorgeous blonde in the navy blue satiny dress with a slit up to her thigh seated on his right and she laughed as he put his hand on her arm and rose. As I walked toward them and heard her shooting down his advance, her response said a lot about Roger. Namely, some things never change.

"Thanks for the offer, but I'm quite sure my fiancé would not approve of a little innocent dinner sometime. It was a pleasure meeting you though and thanks for the drink."

I remembered the many times we had met in bars in our youth. Usually by the time I arrived, Roger was talking to the most beautiful woman in the place, already assured of a partner for dancing, drinking and most likely a night that lonely guys like me only dreamed about. He had the looks, the charm and the obvious physical characteristics that drew women like bees to honey, or was it bears? Fortunately or unfortunately, the relationships usually flamed out after the one night. At 6'2" and a fit 180 pounds of muscle, he had it all and I could never figure out if it was his need for conquest or whether he was looking for the unattainable. However, we all wished we had his problems, whatever they were. Now that we had passed into our forties, I had a wife and kids, dogs, house, fence, mortgage and tuition payments. Roger was single, between wives two and three. We hadn't met number three, but knew it was just a matter of time, even if she wasn't in the picture yet.

"How the hell are ya?" he asked as he hopped off the stool and gave me a bear hug. It would have been embarrassing if either of us cared, but we had long ago dropped concerns about what people thought of us when we were together. The bond was that tight. "God I miss you. You gotta move out here one day."

Well, that answered my first question. "So how the hell are you and what the heck is up with the SEC?"

"Let's go to our booth. We've got plenty of time for all that. Hey, you're looking good. Missy got you working out again?"

"On occasion, but not the animal you are. You know me; good health is a passing fad that I fight constantly."

"Still holding onto the freshman 20?" he asked as he put his arm around me and squeezed my love handles. "Yup, still there," he remarked with a playful smile.

"That's enough, Rog. And thanks for noticing, you bum. Let's sit down before you decide to check out any more of me."

We chuckled and Roger led me to the back of the bar area where a booth in the corner appeared to be waiting for us. The maitre d' appeared and with classy poise slid the table out so that first I and then Roger could sit down.

"And how are you this evening, Mr. Maydock?"

"Just fine, Henri. Thanks for asking."

We sat down, were offered a wine list and some suggestions from Henri about the specialties of the evening, as well as what were suggested to be the perfect wines to accompany each entrée. Naturally, no prices were mentioned, but I knew from the look and smell of the place that we were looking at a couple of hundred dollars even without wine.

Roger interrupted. "Henri, no need to go any further. My friend will have the crab meat cocktail, Caesar salad and your finest filet mignon, medium rare, with a little of your special béarnaise on the side. And yes, some of those delicious potato crisps that Francois makes would be perfect on the side. We'll split some creamed spinach. I'll have the escargots and chicken marsala. Sound about right, J.T.?"

He knew me like a book, and even if I had changed my diet as Missy was always suggesting, I would've let it pass just to watch Roger in action.

"Perfect," I said, adding "You of all people know old habits die hard."

"Ain't that the truth? So what can we get you to drink, club soda with a lime?"

"Right again," I answered, suddenly wishing maybe he knew me too well. Roger knew I hardly drank anymore, but tonight maybe I could have tossed back one with my buddy for old time's sake. But then again, I remembered quickly, how would I feel in the morning? If I had one, I'd probably have five and live to regret it. I did want to have all my faculties working when we got down to talking business in the morning.

Roger had no such worries and I was envious. "I'll have your best dry white wine with dinner and a Johnny Walker Black on the rocks to keep me company for now."

"Very good, Mr. Maydock" said Henri, never taking his eyes off Roger and never threatening to write down our order. I couldn't even see evidence of a pen in his crisp white shirt or in his black tuxedo jacket.

Roger broke the ice. "Damn it's good to see you, JT. Been too long. OK I'm ready. Give me your best shot," he offered, challenging me to stump him with some kind of trivia. It was a game we played for hours in our youth and now used as a starting point whenever we got together. Since we were both Yankee fans and I still lived in New Jersey, I always chose a Yankee baseball trivia question. It didn't hurt that I watched at least half of their games each year and therefore, had a constant stream of recondite tidbits from the broadcasts.

"April 16, 1929" I said, laying down the challenge.

"Hmm, April 16, 1929. Babe, Gehrig and crew, probably an opening day, and someone unknown probably hit a home run or Ruth hit two, but I am sure it is more than that." I could see his mind crunching statistics, history, memories, and facts in his head as he spoke and his tanned forehead scrunched into lines as he thought and then, as always, I could see the answer come to him.

"Numbers!" he said. Dammit, how did he know? "The first time numbers were put on baseball uniforms and it was done on Opening Day 1929 by the Yankees. Want to know who batted where?" He was insufferable, as he now became the teacher explaining that the Yankees assigned numbers to players based on where they batted in the order; Ruth 3rd, Gehrig 4th

"But how did you know?" I asked.

"Wild guess," he said smugly. "My turn."

This is where he made me feel like an idiot. Since I was an English major in college, Roger always challenged me with a language related question and, more often than not, the derivation of a word.

"Caddies" he said.

"Huh?" I said, as I tried to milk the moment. "The cars made by General Motors?" I knew better.

"Where does the word caddy come from? You know the guys who carry your golf clubs!" He smiled knowing that more often than not he would stump me.

"Well, it's obviously slang and altered through the years." I tried to act like I wasn't sure and was feverishly trying to develop a thought, but I was playing with him and knew this one cold.

"Hold on," I pleaded and strung him along. "Don't tell me. It's there somewhere. Caddy, caddies. Is it French? No, the English and Scots invented the game and carried their own bags. Remember where the name for the game came from: Gentlemen Only, Ladies Forbidden. But I digress…. We've been there and done that. Anyway, when the rich and aristocracy played golf, they would need caddies. Common folk wouldn't. Then that would mean it could be a military term?" I could tell by Roger's expression that he was surprised and pleased. I went for the big finish: "I believe that when royalty played golf they used young cadets to carry their clubs and the word morphed through the years."

"That's not fair. You knew that one and made me think you didn't." We smiled, laughed and set about feeling like we had dinner together every night. It was like slipping on your most comfortable shirt, soft, easy and no pressure. Damn it was good to be together.

"And you, my friend, are still a cad," I added. It was fun to rib him and show off a little at the same time. "You do realize that cad has the same derivation as caddy, don't you?"

"Enough already, I want to eat," Roger said with mock disapproval.

After drinks arrived and the appetizers were served, we worked the conversation into the meat of the issue.

"So why am I here?" I asked.

"Because you wanted to see me and get away," came the glib response.

"Always," I answered cheerily. "But you know that already! What's up? Why is the SEC calling and why do you need me out here now?"

"I need some help. Pretty simple, really."

"Money?" I asked, but knew it wasn't that simple. Just filling in the conversation to see where we would go.

"Nah. Actually, there are two issues and they are interrelated. You know that oil exploration company I told you about, Spindletop Energy? Well, we've become very involved with it, provided them with a junk private placement where we got equity warrants in addition to a cool 12% coupon. Normal financing deal for our mezzanine finance group except for the fact that one of our subsidiaries participated in the deal and has put it in their mutual fund."

"Sounds not too much out of the ordinary, so far. I was actually just reading some research on it on the flight out here. One analyst questioned whether they could bring home the bacon... was this the Big Cahuna?"

"I saw that, too. Cute, huh?"

"Is it true?" I asked.

"You're getting ahead of the issue," Roger interrupted. "Any way, do you remember that investment management company in Las Vegas we bought two years ago? Remember that deal?"

"Of course, it made the front page of the "B" section of The Wall Street Journal. Remember, I called to congratulate you on having your mug in the paper and how the pen and ink sketch made you look young?"

"Yes, yes." Roger was starting to get frustrated. "Well, the subsidiary put its bonds in Spindletop into one of its mutual funds and apparently has used some pretty aggressive pricing on its bond holdings. The pricing or value assigned to Spindletop's bonds in particular is being investigated by the SEC."

It was starting to become a little clearer. In the world of private placements and bonds that rarely traded, it was sometimes difficult to put an appropriate market price on certain securities. Some firms and pricing services simply used a matrix that attempted to take into account how strong a company's credit profile was with an appropriate spread or margin over other issues to compensate for the issue's risk of default. There were constant rumors that significant pricing discrepancies existed in the bond market and most sophisticated bond managers tried to avoid the pit-falls of illiquid issues. Others relished the opportunity to play in those markets.

"So you took a few liberties with your women, oh I mean pricing," I said, paraphrasing the famous line from Animal House and gave Roger a wink. He wasn't smiling.

"We found out that this guy is more of a slime bag than we thought when we bought his firm." Roger was deeply serious. He whispered, "In fact, we've come to realize that this could be the tip of the iceberg."

"Sounds serious, especially with mutual funds and the public element." It was starting to become clear what was at issue.

"That's right. Since mutual funds are priced every day and investors can get in or out based on unit values that are supposed to represent actual and accurate prices, there is a potential fraud issue." This was all starting to sound like Roger's firm or at least their mutual fund was heading for a front-page expose in the Journal.

"Sounds like you got in bed with the wrong guy," I concluded, trying to soften the seriousness of the conversation.

"It's worse. We've realized that this guy is bad news in more ways than one." I could feel the proverbial other shoe beginning its descent. "He's been totally uncooperative and we're hearing rumors that he lied to us about how the firm is run. He's a control freak and we're hearing rumors he is abusive with his employees, especially the women. Nothing definitive, just rumblings so far. No one seems to want to talk and we don't know the staff out there very well."

"A little sexual harassment to top off your soufflé?" I joked.

"It's not very funny. This is going to come out and it's going to get ugly fast."

"The SEC swooping down?" I asked.

"Yeah, that's part of it," Roger answered.

"What else?" There had to be more, but what was it?

"Well, I've been working on a plan," Roger said and seemed to finally relax a bit, leaning back for the first time in minutes. Henri seemed to sense the opportunity and instantly appeared with two waiters to present us with our entrées and fresh drinks.

"I can't wait to hear it," I said as the plates were presented.

"That's why you're here. You are an important part of it." Roger was smiling again.

"What do you mean?" This was starting to scare me.

"I want you to come help me fix this. Take over managing the company we bought until we can put in a new management team. Short-term project. I figure it will take six weeks to two months for you to straighten things out for us." He smiled and took a quick whiff and then sip of his glass of white wine. "Perfect Henri" he said, looking back at me as Henri departed with bow.

"How?" I protested, after the pause. "I've got a job, a company to run, portfolios to manage. I can't drop everything. There's Missy and the kids." This was snowballing into dangerous territory. Was this still friends having dinner and a chat, or had we crossed the line in our relationship without me realizing it? Roger was obviously enjoying my discomfort.

"Relax," he said calmly. He did have such a smooth, calm way about him, even as he threatened to turn my life upside down. "We can talk about how to work this all out tomorrow morning. Let's enjoy dinner. Don't be so tense. Look at you. I wouldn't ever make you do something you didn't want to do." He smiled broadly, as we both knew that Roger had talked me into doing and trying more things than we would ever admit to and would never share with anyone. The trip to Vegas. The acid weekend.

"So where'd the SEC come into the picture?" I asked trying to complete more of a still fragmented puzzle.

"Actually, we contacted them when we found out about the pricing discrepancies between where we were marking the Spindletop bonds at fiscal year-end and where this slime bag was marking them in his mutual fund. As an insurance company, we only have to mark-to-market problem credits, which we do at quarter end and year-end. The rest of the time we just sit back, clip the coupons and baby sit them. It's part of the beauty of insurance industry accounting. If we plan to hold a bond to maturity, we can assign a market value equal to our cost, which is usually the price the bond was issued at. Pretty neat and simple."

Some of this I knew and a few more pieces of the puzzle had just fallen into place. "So, why did the SEC contact me?" I asked.

"Seems you bought a few shares of Spindletop for your own account." Roger smiled and my heart stopped and my sweat glands got their cue to react.

"Oh shit," I moaned. My appetite suddenly disappeared into what had once been a stomach and had instantaneously been disintegrated by the ball of acid bouncing against the inside lining of what was moments before a useful functioning organ. So that's what tied this all together. Was my career about to go up in flames because of a measly five thousand share position in a little oil company? I bought five thousand shares of every company Roger passed on through the years that he found "interesting, intriguing or worth a look." He had a gift, or so I thought, but was that gift about to come back biting me in the ass?

After letting me stew in my bile for about fifteen seconds, Roger came to the rescue.

"You're clean. Don't worry. We checked it out."

"What do you mean?" I asked, intrigued by the hope in his quick assessment of my predicament.

"You must have bought the stock the first time I mentioned it to you because your purchase occurred before we got down to receiving or reviewing the company's projections and seismic data. Do you buy every stock I tell you about?"

"Naturally," I responded, feeling safer already. I could feel blood beginning to flow through my body again and almost believed that moving a finger could be a possibility again this evening.

"You bought five thousand shares of Spindletop on March 17th, a full three weeks before they came to our offices and went on our company-wide restricted list. We had the company check the holders' record. So, you're clean as a whistle. If anything, the SEC is going to want to know if you had any conversation with Spindletop and why you made the purchase. It's really a non-event." No wonder he could be so smug.

"You son of a bitch. You could have saved me the heart attack," I scolded, feigning my most serious expression, but I know I wasn't very convincing as I was giddy to be free again.

"So what's this about a job?" I asked. "Do you think I'm nuts? I don't need another turnaround situation on my resume. Been there, done that. Too many hours, too little sleep and they are known to ruin marriages. My last one almost ended mine!"

"Yeah, I remember," he said with a wisp of concern. "Missy really put you over the coals on that one. But not to worry, let's enjoy the night and the food. We'll have plenty of time in the morning to go through my plan. No pressure. Oh, and by the way, where do you think the expression catty-corner comes from?"

"Hmm, French again, eh? Un, deux, trois, quatre…" He knew I had him and pouted.

CHAPTER SEVEN

O nce Roger and I had dispensed with the business chatter, we
settled into familiar territory, much like any other dinner we
had in the past ten years. Roger worked his way through the obliga-
tory questions about Missy and the kids and how they were doing:
"How old are they now?," "What are they up to?," "Does Kathleen have
boyfriends yet?"

It was a question that made me uncomfortable. As the years had
passed, I, as a father, had come to think in terms of how to keep my
daughter away from guys like Roger. Now that she was becoming a
woman, the last thing I needed was having Roger, the man's man
with a Baskin Robbins assortment of conquests under his belt, talking in sexual terms about my own daughter. Roger had never been
able to make the adjustment to commit to one woman, one partner,
regardless of his two previous attempts at marriage. In a way it had
put a distance between us. I quickly tried to steer our conversation to
his love life and what supermodel-type woman he was now dating, a
relatively easy process as Roger was always comfortable talking about
himself and his conquests.

"You should have seen this girl I was dating last month. She said she was twenty-seven but I think she added about three or four years to try and seem more eligible. Hawaiian Tropic model for the last two years and man, what a body. What a tan. Total airhead, but god was she fine; great in the sack, too. Really aimed to please. Know what I mean?"

He winked in knowing confidence, but the charm of Roger's exploits seemed hollower as the years passed. Why didn't he just find a nice normal woman closer to his age with a decent head on her shoulders? A partner to talk to, confide in and support him in the tough times. Missy and I had been there enough to realize that marriage did have its benefits.

A sudden chill ran down my back as I thought about Karen and the napkin in my pocket. Who was I to talk? But I reminded myself that I had not acted on the urge, even though the temptation was great. To be thousands of miles away from home with little or no chance of being caught. Tempting yes, but I wouldn't give it all up for an affair, would I? Maybe I should pass her name on to Roger and try to set them up. Nah, she seemed too nice and Roger still didn't seem ready to move up in class. He certainly wouldn't go for a plain, moderately attractive Midwestern girl, who flew around the country for a living and one that seemed to care about kids and families. Roger lived his life to be with his male friends as much as possible and seemed to use women to fill in the gaps. Bad pun, I thought to myself.

"So what's this month's flavor?" I asked somewhat disinterestedly.

"I'm dating this knockout girl," he gushed. "Not going to last, of course, but I already have a couple of prospects waiting in the wings so to speak." Roger winked mischievously. "I met her at the opening of the Impressionists at our local museum. I'm on the board you know." Roger was almost as impressed with his female accomplishments as he was with the Boards he had bought his way on to.

"How many does that make?" I asked, stroking his ego and happy to get off the subject of women and sex.

"Seven" he said proudly. "Four non-profits. Do-good stuff. Makes me a pillar of the community. Three companies, though two are because of some intricate business relationships with First American. Got those because of workouts and restructurings where we need to keep a close eye on our investment"

"Sounds like you're a busy man, as usual. How do you find the time?" I asked. It was fun to let the line go after you had the hook in. Play with the fish for a while, but keep control of the game.

"You know, a rolling stone..."

"Gathers no moss" I finished. It was one of his many mottos that kept his life's purpose simple and understandable. I was waiting for "Live fast, die young and have a good-looking corpse," but he seemed to use that one less now that we had entered our forties. Maybe he was starting to think about his own mortality.

The dessert was now two empty plates before us and it was getting late in Roger's world. He seemed to think we were at an appropriate time to finish up, as he nodded to Henri, who came over to slide out our table. Roger spoke as he stood up, "well now it's time for me to show you a little bit of the L. A. night life. A little trip to Silicone Valley. Get it?" The wry smile told me exactly what he was suggesting, and he had used the expression before to describe the topless bars in town. Gentlemen's Clubs he called them, as if anyone believed that they were for gentlemen. They would have more appropriately been called "Horny Male Hangouts," which is how Missy and any other woman I ever spoke with about the subject viewed them.

"Any plans for the night?" Roger queried. I knew it wasn't an invitation as Roger had long ago come to the painful realization that a few hours of watching girls dance naked had lost its appeal for one of us, and it wasn't him. I really did prefer to watch a good ball game or read a novel when out of town on business. There were so many ways we had drifted apart.

"Not really" I answered, as we started walking to the door. "I was thinking of taking a ride downtown for a little sight seeing to see what the crazy youths of our country are wearing. What they're doing to their hair? Important reconnaissance work on what to expect in my own house in about two years."

Roger chuckled. "Scary stuff, I tell you. There are even some kids starting to wear their hair as long as we did in prep school. Remember that?"

"It's a vague and foggy memory," I responded. "I try not to let the kids see too many pictures of me in that era. Though I don't think I'd react quite like my father did."

Roger lit up. "Yeah. Remember the time your dad picked us up and said 'If you happen to be a child of mine, you will be stopping at Anthony's barbershop on the way home!' Man, did that freak me out. I thought he was going to order buzz cuts for two."

I interjected what Roger had learned through the years. "Nope, he laid down the rules for the Morris'. He always said that he couldn't raise other people's kids for them, much as he'd like to."

"Yeah, good man, your dad." His voice softened and he seemed genuinely reflective and somber, a rare feat for him.

We walked outside in silence to be greeted by two limos. Jeff was standing outside of mine, and a carbon copy of Jeff, though a bit stronger looking and perhaps a little taller, in front of what had to be Roger's chariot.

"Tell you what" Roger said, "Why don't we have an early night cap at The Doll House? It's a half a block away. We can walk there and the cars will wait for us. Come on, what do ya' think?"

"I think it's a bad idea" I answered, but regretted saying it immediately. How could I refuse my best friend an after-dinner drink? It wasn't like we hadn't spent time together in any of those places before. Quite the contrary. We had probably experienced a couple dozen different topless bars together through the years and had probably collectively stuffed over a thousand dollars in the G-strings of semi-naked women..

"Oh, so you don't like women anymore?" he taunted me, obviously disappointed with my response.

I knew that I had hurt his feelings and needed to fix things quickly. "Just foolin', ya' ninny. Of course I can have an after dinner with you. Anywhere you want and yes, I still like women!"

Roger's mood improved instantaneously, "Then follow me, you lecherous old man."

"Hey be nice," I protested weakly. "It was your idea" I said, trying to remind Roger as to how we had started down this road.

"I know," he responded, "but we know what I am. Just wanted to make sure you hadn't changed on me. After all, you know what they say about leopards, don't you?"

"Yeah, they don't change their spots." I wasn't exactly thrilled with how Roger had steered the conversation to an analysis of me, but went along with the jousting. "Okay" I said with a forced smile, "take me to your lair, you pain in the ass. We'll burn in hell together."

We walked the short distance down the block to the Doll House bar, and upon entering had no fewer than three of the first four women we passed say "Hi Roger."

It was a great opportunity to give Roger some grief and I took it. "So this is your secret life, Walter Mitty! Come here often?"

"Hardy har," Roger answered without embarrassment. "Yes, I've been here before, but not that often." It was a feeble protest and one he knew I'd never believe, but it didn't really matter between friends like us.

We settled in to a booth in the back of the room, with a perfect view of the two wooden platform stages ahead, ordered drinks from another of Roger's friends, and sat back to enjoy the view. We didn't talk business, didn't have a care in the world, and shamelessly rated the dancers on their most attractive and appealing body parts. Bonus points were given to those who Roger decided had the best overall "attitude," and I wasn't sure if he was talking from experience or making it up on the fly. It didn't really matter. I was having trouble not thinking about Missy at home and my experience, if you could call it that, with Karen, the stewardess, er flight attendant on the airplane. After about twenty minutes and the promised night cap we got up together and headed outside.

"Well, got to get up early, you know. Cause the early bird….."

"Gets the worm," I answered. The game was not as much fun as it used to be, but it was one I knew we would continue until one of us died. Certain things in a relationship would not change. They were an obligation that couldn't and shouldn't be questioned. It was part of the bond between us.

Night had fallen, but due to the darkness of the Doll House's interior, the initial reaction to the lights outside was as if we had just stepped out into the daylight.

We stood there for a second letting our eyes adjust and I saw that our limo's had in fact followed us to our latest venue and were waiting curbside. I wasn't quite sure what to do or say, when Roger turned toward me and stepped forward to give me a hug. "Damned glad to see you, buddy. And thanks for joining me for an after-dinner. I know you're heart wasn't really in it." He put his arms around me and said. "We'll see you in the morning and I'll show you how much fun we're going to have working together. It'll be great."

Somehow I wasn't any more convinced and I thought to myself, would I be working with Roger or putting out a fire for him. With what I knew so far, it seemed like a project from hell. Going in to play the heavy and take over one of his struggling divisions, one that was being investigated by the SEC, no less. Then again, I did love the thrill of turnarounds. The rush from taking charge and fixing a broken company was as good as it gets. And it was how I had been able to put together enough of a nest egg to put my kids through school and give Missy and me a comfortable life.

"I'll wait and see" was my laconic response.

Roger smiled. "Later," he said as he ducked into his limo, door professionally held open by Jeff's bigger clone. "Parting is...."

"Such sweet sorrow," I finished, but the door was closed and Roger was off in an instant. I looked at Jeff, took out a smoke, lit it and said, "Well, I guess that's a wrap." I smugly complimented myself on how smoothly I would adapt to the Hollywood casual lingo. But then again, I thought, it's probably an expression only used by those of us who secretly dreamed of someday being in show business.

"Back to the hotel, please" I said, feeling guilty for trying to be so Hollywood hip and probably appearing only the more foolish in the effort.

"Very good, Mr. Morris. And please, as I said earlier, feel free to smoke in the car."

It sounded like a good idea, for why should I have to stand out here on the sidewalk just to enjoy the pleasure of an after dinner smoke. The world was getting far too restrictive and politically correct for my taste. And besides, wasn't it my right to indulge myself once in a while. Life, liberty and the pursuit of happiness and all that.

"So will that be it for the evening, Mr. Morris?" Jeff asked as we pulled away.

"I guess so," I said, still struggling with the guilt of wanting companionship and a smile. It probably been procured at the Doll House for a couple of hundred dollars, but that didn't have much appeal any more. Been there, done that and learned a few lessons along the way.

"Well, if you change your mind, I'll be at the hotel until 9:30 PM and will give you my card with my cell phone and pager numbers on it."

I looked at my watch and realized that it was already approaching 9:00 PM. "Thanks," I said, thinking even if I did go out and called Karen, I wouldn't want Jeff and most likely Roger to know. The time had passed where we needed to know everything about each other's lives. This wasn't prep school anymore.

CHAPTER EIGHT

Neither the Sam Black novel nor the Los Angeles Kings hockey game on the TV in the background were able to hold my attention, as my mind raced back and forth between just what was Roger planning to lay out for me tomorrow and the indecision and trepidation I felt about calling Karen at the Airport Hilton. I pulled out my Blackberry to check to see what late e-mail had been sent to me and turned to the all-night business channel to find out what was going on in the markets overseas and how the futures were acting. Nothing like the markets to take your mind off women – or whatever else was bothering you.

The commercial breaks were annoying, yet I was amazed that Cal was still selling cars at what he promised were the lowest prices, just as he had for at least the last 20 years. Now that's impressive, I thought to myself. Must be a heck of a businessman. Not a business that many have succeeded at and he's been doing it for as long as I've been traveling to California. The ads for class action lawyers offering help to anyone who had been hurt, injured, terminated wrongly were the same as I had seen throughout the country, but the personal chat line ads were something I had not yet experienced.

"Are you lonely? Looking for friendship? Someone to talk to?" came the question from what had to be one of Roger's conquests, a curvaceous, tanned blonde bombshell of about 25 in an electric blue bikini that left nothing to the imagination.

I switched channels back to the hockey game and thought to myself; I wonder who actually calls those numbers. Does Roger? How about Karen? Is she stuck in her room wondering if I am going to call?

I decided the honorable thing to do would be to at least call her and set the record straight. I played the conversation in my head. "Karen. Hi. It's Tom Morris from the plane. I'm happily married and won't be able to see you tonight."

Seemed pretty simple and straightforward. I got out the phonebook and realized that in L.A. there were three phonebooks and I had the wrong one, two for the yellow pages and one white. I had the wrong part of the alphabet for "Hotels." Finding the correct book and phone number for the Hilton, I picked up my cell and dialed. I had gotten screwed enough times by hotels with their in-room phone charges and had vowed long ago that I would have to be nuts to ever use their phone for anything other than wake-up calls, calls to the front desk or room service.

"Airport Hilton. How may I direct your call?" came the woman's voice. The accent seemed European; probably German was my best guess.

"Could you connect me with Karen Clarkson's room, please?" I could feel the nerves bundling up inside me as I spoke and realized that maybe this wasn't such a good idea.

"Very well, sir. One moment, please."

Should I disconnect? Did they even have a Karen Clarkson staying there? It was pretty presumptuous of me to even think that she would be there. The second ring was interrupted by a questioning "Hello?" It sounded like Karen.

"Hello" I fumbled.

"Yes, who is this?" came the request and I sensed uncertainty and maybe even fear in her voice.

"Uh, it's Tom Morris. I met you on the plane." I could hardly breathe. As I paused, she said

"Oh hi, I'm glad you called." The tone was much calmer and friendly. "I was wondering if you were going to find my little note." She chuckled; a sweet and gentle sound that I envisioned had to be created with a smile.

"Yes, I did and I wasn't sure if you meant it or if someone was playing a joke on me."

"No, I meant it. You seemed nice and I thought it would be fun to go out and see the sights. The rest of the crew is so much younger and were going clubbing, which had absolutely no appeal." She spoke smoothly and was easy to talk to.

"I can imagine," I said. "Haven't been to a club in I don't know how long." What are you doing, I asked myself.

"So do you want to go out for a bit?" Karen asked. "I haven't been downtown in years. Check out the hand prints on the Walk of Stars?"

I had to stop this. "I'm married," I blurted. I didn't know what else to say.

"Ok, so then why the phone call? Why the invitation on the plane? I guess we both made a mistake then. You just seemed like you could use some company and I thought it would be fun. We seemed to relate." She seemed disappointed and her tone changed.

"Um, I don't know," I stammered, not knowing how to react. This wasn't part of my script. Now I felt guilty for calling, guilty for leading her on and guilty for letting her down. What should I do?

"I wasn't trying to lead you on," I apologized, attempting to save face. "You seemed sweet and I thought it would be more fun than staying in my hotel room alone. I could go out for an hour or two, if you're still interested." Where did that come from?

"You make it seem so appealing," she said sarcastically, but with a hint of a more pleasant tone.

"No, it will be fun. I could come by and pick you up in about a half hour." What was I doing? How did I get into this?

"Sounds great, should I meet you downstairs in the lobby?" she asked perkily.

"Uh, sure. Looking forward to it," I said, dumbfounded, as I clicked off my cell phone. What am I doing? I looked at my watch, 9:05 PM. I started the calculations. If I pick her up at 9:30 PM, take her downtown for an hour or so, bring her back to her place by 11:00 PM, I could be back in my room by 11:30 PM. That's not too bad, I thought, even though I had absolutely no idea if the timing of going from here to there and back made any sense whatsoever. The other side of my brain reminded me that California was three hours behind and it would be 2:30 in the morning. Markets open at 9:30. Want to be up by 6 California time to watch the pre-opening and check out the early earnings reports. Meeting with Roger at 8:30AM. Six hours of sleep. "Not so bad," my devil-directed conscience said. "It's actually about what you usually get at home!"

I called the front desk from the hotel phone next to my bed and asked, "Do you have any cabs available?"

"Yes, Mr. Morris, we always have a few outside. I can see three out there now. Or if you prefer, we could call your driver, Jeff."

"No thanks. That won't be necessary."

CHAPTER NINE

After organizing my papers, briefcase and clothes for the next day, I contemplated just what I should wear for my non-date rendezvous. Realizing that I only had one pair of casual slacks and the folded, dry cleaned white shirt was reserved for tomorrow's meetings made the fashion quandary a joke. I had what I was wearing and that was about it.

I grabbed my wallet and blazer, but left my cell phone and Blackberry behind, as I didn't want to lug around my electronic companions. Who was I going to call anyway? It was past midnight in New Jersey and the only e-mail I might receive at this hour would be span anyway.

I rode the elevator down and decided that I would walk straight out to the cabs, hoping the front desk clerk wouldn't notice me. The lobby was empty, so I couldn't help but notice the clicking of my shoes on the marble floor and assumed that anyone working at the desk would hear me as well. I glanced over to my right and was pleasantly surprised to see that the desk was unmanned at present.

The cabs out front were waiting, as promised, and as I headed to the first one in line, a beaten-up, heavily dented, ten-year-old, white generic cab, I chuckled to myself, "At least she won't think I'm rich." I told the three-hundred-pound and then some driver that I was picking up a friend at the Airport Hilton and we would be heading down to the Mann's Theatre and Walk of Stars. I doubted his seat, tilted halfway into the back seat would survive his size or the trip and wondered if there would be enough room for Karen.

As we headed off to the Hilton, Joe, as he called himself, asked if I would want him to wait for me or to act as a tour guide. I thanked him for his offer, but felt that I could probably do better on my own. I would be willing to take the risk. Speaking of risk, just what was I doing? I had never cheated on Missy and while I had my share of flirtatious encounters with random strangers and even some of our mutual friends, I had never gone so far as I had tonight. Me and another woman alone together! I reassured myself that I hadn't crossed the line yet and I didn't plan to. I would be honest and keep the encounter nonsexual in nature.

We pulled up to the valet area of the Hilton's parking lot and I realized how hard it was going to be, as Karen stood out front looking far different than her stewardess role earlier in the day. She had let her hair down to reveal a long wavy brunette mane. Decked out in fitted jeans, low- heeled boots and a white cotton blouse that was buttoned just low enough to show the presence of a full bust. The green sweater tied around her neck and hanging over her shoulders completed a classy but sensual look that I knew would be hard to keep my eyes off.

"Is that your babe?" Joe asked, adding without waiting for a response, "She's hot."

"She's not my babe," I corrected and decided I really didn't want to have Karen ride in this clunker with this driver slobbering over her. "And actually, I am going to get out here. I forgot that we were going to have a drink here first."

"Okay," said Joe. "Want me to wait?"

"No thanks" I said. "That won't be necessary."

Karen's look of recognition turned to one of surprise and then confusion as I climbed out of the cab.

"I'll tell you later," I said, as I grabbed her arm and led her back inside. "Let's have a drink before we head out."

"Well, if that's what you want. Everything okay?"

"Everything is fine" I assured her, "and by the way, you look great." She smiled and turned to look at me and I noticed just how pretty she was. Her makeup or the light made her hazel green eyes sparkle and I noticed that she had soft eye shadow and wore an inviting wet looking shade of pink lipstick. I looked away as I led her inside, but couldn't help but notice the opening in her shirt and the lack of a brassiere underneath. That bordered on unfair. Did she have any idea how perfectly delectable she looked and how impossible it would be for any male to think about anything but sex with her looking the way she did.

We walked into the hotel lobby and I noticed the bar ahead and to the right. Entering, I thought to myself that the darkness of the bar and lounge area might save me from myself, and I led her to an empty table in the corner. "You really didn't want a ride in the cab that I came over in," I explained.

She laughed. "I was wondering if that was an ad for Rent-a-Wreck or you were just trying to impress me!"

I couldn't help but laugh myself and she said,

"You have a nice smile. You should smile more often."

I wanted to tell her she was gorgeous, but said, "Thanks, want me to get us some drinks?" The activity in the bar seemed confined to five men seated at the bar and the lone bartender had not made an indication that he was planning on leaving his port. No bar attendants appeared to be on duty to serve us, so I rose to play waiter.

"A glass of white wine would be just great," she said.

"Coming right up," I offered with a false bravado as I rose.

I sidled up to the empty end of the bar and waited for the bartender. "What can I get for you this evening?" he asked after what seemed like an inappropriate delay.

"A glass of white and a club soda with a lime," I requested.

"I'll bring it right over," he said genuinely attempting to be helpful. "Could I get you some peanuts or would you like to see a menu? The kitchen is open "till 12 and we have great burgers and sandwiches."

"No thanks," I answered, and then reconsidered, "but actually, you can bring along some peanuts."

I went back to the table to sit down, cognizant that all twelve eyes at the bar were checking out Karen in the corner. They obviously were trying to figure out if we were together, dating or married, in the hope that I was only a date and that if I were to crash and burn, this beautiful woman with "the look" would be fair game. As I looked at her, it pained me that she had made herself into this persona, exuding sex and sexuality. If ever a cat looked on the prowl, she fit the bill to a T. Now what was I going to do about it?

"Nothing," I told myself. "Nothing….Don't even go there" I heard the echo of the old Lost in Space episodes as the robot warned, "Danger, Will Robinson, Danger."

Karen gave me a big smile as I returned and sat down. "Should be just a minute" I said.

"Great and by the way, I'm glad you're back. I was getting a little uncomfortable with the looks I was getting from those men at the bar." She was serious and the smile quickly faded as she spoke.

Trying to calm her, I reassured, "Don't worry. They look pretty harmless. And after all, I'm here to protect you." As soon as I put my hand on her thigh, I knew it was a mistake. It had seemed innocent and more for effect, but when she put her hand on my other hand and let her fingers playfully circle and stroke the little hairs, I drew back as if given an electric shock, the current building quickly as I realized how deep I was in and either fear or remorse kicked in. The delayed but abrupt withdrawal of my hand from her thigh and the other from under hers startled both of us, but it was Karen who remarked.

"What's the matter?" she asked startled. "What happened?"

I didn't know how to respond, but felt so guilty that honesty won out. "I'm sorry," I blurted. "I just realized how inappropriate my touching you was and how I shouldn't even be here. I'm happily married."

"So you said," Karen said somewhat perturbed. "Listen, I'm not going to rape you, try to ruin your marriage, blackmail you or do whatever else you are afraid of. Yes, I find you attractive and yes, if things had gone a little differently, I could've seen us spending some time together. But you've got so much guilt; I doubt you'd be able to get into any trouble." The sarcasm stung like a razor cut and I felt myself flinch. "So give yourself a break and relax."

"I'm sorry," I said again. Foolish and embarrassed, but relieved just the same. She had said all the right things. Maybe a man could talk to a strange, beautiful woman and not have sexual thoughts coursing through his brain. I doubted it, but figured the least I could do was keep her company while we had our drinks. They arrived as I was about to continue.

"Stop saying I'm sorry," Karen said, as the drinks were put before us. The smile returned to her face as she said, "So tell me about your wife. How many kids do you have?"

The bartender shot me a quizzical glance as I gave him a twenty and said, "Thanks, keep the change." I wasn't sure if his glance was a function of my being a big tipper or him overhearing Karen's questions about my wife and family, but I didn't really care. The question put me at ease, lightened the noose that I had felt choking my neck and enabled me to breathe again.

"My wife?" I repeated. "She really is great, but I have to admit this trip did not go over very big at home. I was supposed to be on vacation this week and got called out here on business." It wasn't really business, I thought. "Actually, a friend of mine needed some help, so I had to come."

"Is he hurt or sick?" she asked.

"No," I said. "His business has some problems and he wanted me to come help him out." She still seemed puzzled. "It's hard to explain, but see my best friend growing up wants me to run one of his businesses for him. He said I'm the only one he knew he could trust to do it."

She was intrigued. "What kind of business? Are you one of those turnaround experts?"

I was taken back by the question. "How do you know about turn-around experts?" I asked.

"My ex was an investment banker," she said, seeming embarrassed to admit it. "Seemed like a nice guy when we met in college and got married. He fell in love with his job and out of love with me. Better for both of us that it's over." She spoke pretty matter-of-factly about something that had to have been brutal emotionally. I had the best marriage of any of my friends as far as I could gather, but had my share of moments when I could see taking a vacation from trying to make it work; like the past week, no fun at all.

"How long ago?" I asked.

"Almost ten years ago," she answered. "Actually, in another month it will be ten years." I could see memories were floating in front of her as she spoke.

"So that's when you headed off to the friendly skies of Southern Airways."

"Yup," she said as she raised her glass to take a sip of her drink. "Had to make a change. Had to have a life of my own. Too many hours in a big apartment waiting for my husband to come home. Had to see what was out there. What I had missed while I played servant to my college sweetheart. He was more concerned with whether I remembered to iron his shirts or pick up his dry-cleaning than if I had had a good day. Not a rewarding or satisfying experience." She took a quick and deep swig from her glass, more like taking a shot of whiskey than wine

I could feel the bitterness and resentment build in her voice and quickly did a self-evaluation as to whether I had exhibited those same traits at home. I gave myself a quick B- and thought, "Make a note and step up the concerned questions at home. How was your day etc.? You don't want to mess up a good thing."

"So are you happy?" I asked.

"Yes, very much so" Karen replied, adding; "I'm having the time of my life. I'm visiting friends, family and new places. At first I did it to get away. Now, I'm making the best of it."

"And the downside?" I queried.

"It gets lonely on the road."

"But I'm sure you'd have your pick of guys," I protested. "You must be fighting them off."

"Well, that's the problem," she explained, obviously having analyzed the situation over many long hours. "Think about it, you get on a plane for a short flight of an hour or two or three, sit back in your seat and relax. Next time take a moment to notice the three people serving you and busting their butts for 95% of the time. Not a great time to meet someone. Though, yes, there are plenty of offers. Mostly from jerks looking for a one night stand." She paused and took another sip of her drink. She was becoming very caught up in her story.

"The married businessmen are the worst." She smiled and gave a little chuckle. "Free tonight, babe? Wanna grab a bite? Hey honey, what ya' doin' later? Some really classy propositions," she said with disgust.

"So why'd you say yes to me?" I wondered.

"You weren't really trying too hard, weren't pushy. And you had nice eyes. They looked honest." As she said it, our eyes met. I looked closer into her hazel green orbs, still brilliant in the dim light, but she looked deeper into mine trying to reassure herself that I still had honest eyes. I grinned self-consciously and turned away briefly to scan the bar; having been entranced from the moment I sat down.

The group of men had gotten louder and only one seemed to be staring at Karen as I glanced over, a notable improvement.

Trying to regain my composure and honest look, I turned back to face Karen again.

"You know, I was right. You are honest," she said, and then looked away just as I had seconds earlier to check on the 5 guys at the bar.

When she glanced away, feeling slightly proud of myself but somewhat embarrassed, I didn't know what to do. I looked down for a second, only to be confronted with the subject I had been trying to avoid all night. The gap in Karen's white blouse mesmerized me and I noticed the fullness of her breasts was stretching the weave of the cotton fibers around the buttons ever so slightly. I could feel my cheeks start to warm and could feel their pink color building as my embarrassment worked its biological reaction.

"Well, let's not get carried away," I interjected. "I'm a decent human being, who is basically honest and try to be fair and good to people I know and work with, but I'm no saint."

"Hey, the saints were sinners before they were saints, and you've already proven yourself in fifteen minutes to be more honest than 99% of the men I've dated in the last five years. Don't sell yourself short." She either hadn't noticed or didn't mind my honest eyes' adventure down the front of her shirt.

"That's an interesting expression for a stewardess--" I corrected myself-- "Sorry, flight attendant to use."

"Actually, some expressions are hard to kick. I do understand where it comes from though. Shorting stocks. Selling what you don't own. In this case, don't bet against yourself. Probably, yes, did pick it up from my ex."

I was fascinated and enjoyed the confidence she had in what she was saying, the way she presented herself. "Where did you go to school?" I asked.

"Resume time?" she asked. "Well, alright, I'll play if you will. Penn, as in University of. Coming from the Midwest wanted to be in the East, in a city. Experience the bright lights, big city...all that stuff. Majored in English and figured I'd be a teacher someday. Get tenured at some prestigious university and travel to England to research Shakespeare. Pretty standard stuff." Her eyes lit up as she spoke remembering the excitement of her youth. "Had a great time. We really knew how to have a good time in those days. Frat parties at Saint A's." She paused for a second and looked at me quizzically.

"Do you have any idea what I'm talking about?" she asked. "Or is it all, God, pardon the pun, but Greek to you?"

"No, I get the picture," I said. "Had some close friends who went to Penn and also said it was a blast. Then what, after Penn?"

"Well, I met a Wharton guy. Smart as a whip. Fell in love with his mind. Funny, smart, good-looking, good family. All a girl could want. Well, almost. The sex wasn't great, but I didn't know any better."

"And?" I prodded.

"Like I said before, he fell in love with his job and we lost that connection that was so natural. It's amazing how simple life is when you're young and in school..." She bit her lip before continuing, her top teeth temporarily resting on her lower lip. "And how different things are when you start working and worrying about bills, car payments, rent." She shivered as if the movement would shake the memories of those days away.

"But enough about me. Your turn, I've babbled enough and said far too much. It is amazing what you will admit to a perfect stranger, isn't it?"

"Nah, I'm not that perfect," I countered. "Actually, it's fascinating to look back and see the twists and turns our lives have taken and how we got where we are. The good news is it all worked out and you're happy, right?"

"Yes, very. But no more about me, it's your turn."

"OK, OK" I said. "Where to start...youngest of three boys; two older brothers, who went Ivy League, Harvard and Yale. I had too much fun in prep school to match up to their standards. Learned how to party and somehow got away with it." My mind raced back to The Bust and Roger. "Not all of us did. I went to NYU, where I fell in love with the city life. Scraped my way through the first two years until I took an economics course that fascinated me. Changed majors from English to Business and found my element. Got a job with a small Wall Street research firm and worked my way up to be a portfolio manager, managing other people's money. Became moderately successful and started my own business." Short and sweet, how simple it was to condense years of education and work into a few short sentences. How scary, really.

"And your wife?" Karen asked. "At some point you must have met, dated…all that stuff."

I was embarrassed to have left out Missy and the birth of our children. How insensitive had I become? Did they really mean so little to me that I omitted them? Was my subconscious avoiding bringing them into the discussion?

"Actually, we met in grammar school. She was a grade behind and I really didn't even notice her. I ran into her again during the summer of my junior year in college at a local bar in my old stomping grounds. We started dating and had a long distance relationship until she graduated from Boston College. Spent lots of weekends traveling to Beantown until she got out. We got married the summer after she graduated. Three kids followed in the next five years. Talk about changing your life! But watching them grow up and being a part of it has been more than I could have ever hoped for. Great kids, two boys and a girl, and the two younger ones still think I'm always right." I could feel the smile of pride form on my face uncontrollably.

"How old?" she asked, smiling back at me, obviously enjoying the story or having the focus be off her.

"My oldest son is sixteen, looking at colleges already. My daughter is thirteen and the youngest boy is twelve."

"Must be a lot of work," Karen interjected. "My friends say the teenage years are the toughest. My best friend, Amy, says she feels more like a taxi driver than a parent."

"That's the truth," I answered. "Lots of times my wife and I have to go in different directions to make it all work. I think that there are some people who don't actually believe I have a wife since we're hardly ever able to go to their activities together." It was a line I had used many times before and had grown to like. And now saying it, again, I was without my wife, talking to a beautiful single woman, who had seemed to move closer to me without my noticing. How did that happen? And was I hallucinating or had she planned to lean forward so that every time I looked at her my eyes were drawn to the opening of her blouse and the soft and inviting flesh inside? "Stop it," I told myself as I stared into the abyss. "It's a normal biological reaction," I reassured myself. "What would they feel like?"

"Hello," Karen said, shaking me out of my daydream.

I looked up and she was almost giggling.

"Welcome back," she said, her bright smile showing brilliant white teeth.

"I'm sorry," I said. "Lost my train of thought. Where was I?"

"Down my shirt, I believe," she joked, not embarrassed, enjoying the moment and the effect she was having on me. She leaned back and I couldn't help but take a longing look at how her breasts pressed against her blouse, stretching the buttons and fabric.

Not knowing where to look, I glanced at our empty glasses on the table, looked at my watch and realized it was 11:45 PM. We were now the only people left in the bar, except the bartender, who noticed my glance.

"Another round?" he said over the expanse of three empty tables and a vacant bar.

I looked at Karen and thought that the smart thing to do would be to cut and run, much as I wanted to stay. Talking to Karen was a welcome relief to a lonely hotel room, but I knew I needed the sleep and tomorrow was going to be a big day.

"No thanks, I think we're done," I said and apologized to Karen. "I really should get going. Early morning meetings and all that."

"I understand," she said. "Hey it was nice to have someone to talk to. Better than being cooped up in my room or suffering the lame advances of the drunken crew that was in here before. It's not easy being a single woman on the road."

"I can only imagine," I said and thought about what I would have done if I had been confronted by the presence of a beautiful woman like Karen alone in a bar. "Men are pigs," I blurted, "Only after one thing."

"Well, not all of them," she countered. "You behaved yourself, at least most of the time," she chuckled. What a sweet laugh.

"You sure you don't want to come up for a nightcap?" she asked.

The thought of heading off to her room had been racing through my mind off and on for the past hour but now that it was before me, I felt uncomfortable. I felt like I was on a first date and afraid of going too far, too fast. 'And you're married, you idiot,' I reminded myself.

"We could raid the mini-bar. Southern Airlines covers mini-bar charges!" The offer seemed genuine and all of a sudden less trashy. Maybe it wasn't a sexual invitation and I was just flattering myself.

"I really have to go, but it is an enticing offer to say the least." There, I did it; walk away with honor. I was proud of myself.

"Will I ever see you again?" Karen asked. Now sounding uncertain and a bit less cheery, but still with a positive and pleasing undertone.

"I would like to" I admitted, "but I don't know when. Is the California route your usual fare? Don't you fly all over?"

"Yes and yes. I make the California trip about three times a month and other than that regularly fly to Houston and Las Vegas. Never quite sure what my schedule is until a week or so in advance. But if you give me your email address, I can keep you posted on my buddy list. I have a dozen or so friends that I forward my schedule to when I get it."

It sounded innocent enough, so I reached into the breast pocket of my blazer, took out my wallet and removed a business card. As I handed it to her, she looked at it closely, as if memorizing something on it.

"President, huh? Looks impressive," she offered with a smile.

"It's just a piece of paper," I deadpanned. "For $12.95 anyone can be anything they want to be." I was proud to be president of my own company, but not comfortable actually saying the word in public. It looked better in print. In my mind it sounded unnatural and egotistical when someone identified themselves as President of a company in conversation.

Karen picked up her Dooney and Burke tan purse, similar to one I had purchased for Missy once, opened it and slid my card inside. She pulled out a white card of her own, handed it to me and said: "This is my card. It has a work number where I never am, but the email address is my own."

"Thanks," I said, and started to walk out of the bar with Karen following close to my side.

"Last chance for the mini bar raid," she said lightly.

"I'll have to take a pass," I said, wishing I could live without guilt and fear and take her up on the offer.

"Walk me to the elevator?" she asked, putting her arm in mine.

"Absolutely," I said. "Which way?"

"Follow me," she offered. And off we went into the lobby and through the plush decorated sitting area with overstuffed couches upholstered with flame-stitch patterns to the elevator bank at the back of the room. She reached out to push the UP button, not leaving my arm until the bell rang and the doors opened.

"Till next time?" she asked as she slid her arm free and turned to face me, her eyes sparkling in the too-bright lobby lights and her near auburn hair shining as it swayed across her neck. Karen offered her hand to say goodbye, and when I held it to say goodbye, I felt the warmth of her flesh. I immediately regretted saying no and hated the existence of guilt and my conscience. She pulled my hand rather than shaking it and as I tilted toward her, gave me a kiss on the lips. Not a long kiss, not a tongue-lashing or probing kiss, but more of a kiss than what you would give a sister, mother or close friend. Her lips were moist and soft and the meeting of our mouths was electric, for me at least.

I pulled away, released my hand from hers and said, "I really have to go."

"I know," she replied. "Thanks for the drink and the company. Maybe next time we will see the sights on Hollywood Boulevard."

I had completely forgotten what the original plan was, and as she turned and stepped into the elevator, I looked longingly at the jeans, the heels and the back of the white blouse I had fallen into.

"Yes," I stammered, "next time."

She turned, smiled and winked as the doors closed and I was faced by my own confused reflection in the golden shiny elevator doors. I looked at myself and wondered, "Will there be a next time?"

CHAPTER TEN

Roger rose from his desk, smiling broadly when he saw me walking down the hall to his glass-enclosed spacious corner office. It was decorated with shiny brass tables with transparent glass tops and white leather chairs and sofa. His desk appeared to be simply an eight foot by four foot piece of thick glass resting on two brass semicircles. No drawers, no visible files, just a set of manila folders lining the right side of his desk. A computer terminal and phone occupied the left hand side of the desk and the tall high-backed white leather chair was rocked back and forth as he rose out of it.

"J. Thomas, old buddy, how the hell are you?" he asked as he came from behind the desk and greeted me with a hug. "Sleep well, everything OK at the hotel?"

"Just great," I replied. "They treat you like royalty there. Or is that just for your guests?" I asked.

"Well, I do have some pull there" he admitted sheepishly. "Glad you didn't switch to the Airport Hilton," he added matter of factly, but stopping my heart and making me feel as if I had just be caught shoplifting with my hand still in the cookie jar. Noticing my surprise and unease, he added, "Don't worry, your secret is safe with me."

I stammered a feeble "How did you…" before Roger interrupted.

"The hotel keeps a close eye on my guests. You should have used Jeff, by the way. By using a cab, the hotel got suspicious."

I didn't know what to say, how to respond. I felt like my privacy had been violated, raped. It was not a pleasant feeling. Roger on the other hand was enjoying the moment.

"Not to worry. We'll talk about it later. Right now, we need to get to the conference room and discuss strategy. Follow me." As we walked out of his office, he introduced me to his secretary, Paula, a plain looking but efficient woman in her mid to late forties wearing a classic two-piece tan khaki outfit with buttons all the way up to the neck. I would have expected flash and skin from Roger's secretary. He could read what I was thinking and as we walked down the hall confided,

"Best damn secretary I ever had. First one I haven't been in the sack with either." He smiled. "Honest. She types 95 words per minute, no mistakes, takes shorthand, knows how to write a letter and keeps my life at the office manageable. Strictly a pro. Every time I make an advance, she threatens to quit; I give her a raise and promise to be good and she stays. I've tried to corral my manly needs when I'm around her, but every once in a while I relapse. Costly though, she's probably already the highest paid secretary in L.A. She made close to a hundred grand last year with bonuses!"

"Wow," was all the response I could muster. But I immediately took a liking to her for beating Roger at his game and maintaining her honor.

"Makes twice what her husband makes." He added, "She's on call from 5 AM to 5 PM; I'd be lost without her."

We entered the glassed in conference room, the focal point being the huge rectangular oak table that had ten brown leather chairs on either side with one high-backed leather chair at the far end, probably where Roger sat, I thought. An easel with two-foot by three-foot pages of white paper and a half dozen color markers in its tray. The view of downtown L.A. was spectacular as we were on the 53rd floor, you could see the Pacific Ocean in the distance, the masses of ants and miniature cars below and the orangey haze on the horizon; smog's contribution to the landscape before us. Virgin white legal pads and crisply sharpened pencils were placed on the table in front of each seat. A buffet of coffee, Danish and croissants was set up in the back of the room, behind what appeared to be Roger's seat. Three men in their late thirties to early forties were chatting in cocktail party pose, coffee mugs in hand in a semicircle. Roger went directly to them and said: "Let's get this show on the road. Everybody, this is J. Thomas Morris, my lifelong friend and the man who is going to help us fix Ocular Asset Management."

He pointed to me with a wave of his hand and said, "Why don't we all take our seats. Thomas, why don't you sit on my right and we'll put the brain trust that got us into this mess on my left."

Roger introduced me in order from left to right to Mark Hanes, Chief Financial Officer, and a thin and pale faced man with wire rim glasses that appeared not to have seen much of the Southern California sun. John Reiss, his Chief Investment Officer was next; a muscular sandy blond haired man, who appeared to have spent many days on the golf course, the tanner right hand a giveaway that his left hand spent many hours covered by a glove. It had to be a batting or golf glove. My bet was golf. Finally, Carl Huthwaite, his general counsel, appeared slightly older than the rest, with gray hair evident at the temple areas and sprinkled in his well-trimmed brown hair. His eyes occasionally darted about the room through the introductions, as he appeared to be randomly reviewing important thoughts in his head, and then refocusing on where he was. They seemed an amiable but quiet group, obviously subservient to Roger's whims and his control of the meeting.

After a few pleasantries about the weather back East, Roger got to the heart of the matter at hand.

"So here's the deal. As I explained last night at dinner, we bought a money management firm, Ocular Asset Management, which had great numbers. Unfortunately, now that we have gotten into it, issues have come up about the management. Quite frankly, the founder, Terry Burroughs, is a dirt bag that we never should have gotten in bed with. What we have put together is a consulting agreement for you, Thomas, to work for First American in an advisory role, to get the lay of the land at Ocular and to recommend what we can and should do to fix it. These are my right hand men, who I put on my left because they fucked up so badly on this one. They are available for anything you need to do this job."

I figured I better step in before Roger sent me to a new office for the afternoon.

"Whoa, Rog. I haven't agreed to anything yet. I've got a successful business of my own to run. I can't just drop everything and move to California and leave my family and business behind. I'd love to help, but..."

Before I could continue, Roger interrupted, "We've got that covered. This contract is a $500,000 consulting fee and will not require you to move to L.A. Ocular is located in Las Vegas and the way I figure it, if you spend a couple of days there and make them report to you about everything they do from buying individual stocks and bonds to ordering paper clips, you can oversee this from New Jersey. Just fly to Vegas every other week or so to check in. I'll meet you there and we'll review what's going on. You'll report directly to me, but if you have any questions or run into any roadblocks, my brain trust here will be at your disposal."

This was starting to sound more interesting and after all, Roger knew I enjoyed an occasional trip to the tables. We had spent a lost weekend in Vegas when we were young and foolish and just out of school. But still, the time commitment scared me. Turnarounds always took longer than expected and Roger was making this all seem too easy.

"Pardon me, but what makes you think this is going to be so easy and why me?" This all sounded too pat.

Roger was ready. "A couple of things. First, you and I both know that you have a great record turning around investment firms. Better than anyone else we looked at and we looked at a few. Second, you own your own business so you have the ability to manage your own schedule. Third, you are intensely involved in the markets and your knowledge of junk bonds and private placements will be critical to determining if there are fraudulent practices being used by Ocular. Fourth and foremost, I know you and I trust you." Roger always sounded in control and seemed to know exactly where conversations were going. He also knew how to bait the hook and land the fish. I knew that somewhere Roger had probably scratched out a probable question and answer cheat sheet on a pad of paper to rebut any negatives I might have. The consummate salesman, as always.

"And how does Ocular and, what's his name, Terry, feel about this plan of yours?" I still didn't feel like we had peeled more than the first layer of an onion. Interesting proposition, but so far not enough substance about what I was going to do.

"In the immortal words of Rhett Butler, 'Frankly Scarlett, I don't give a damn.'" Roger loved his quotes and metaphors. "At this point, Terry doesn't know shit about 'our plan', as you say. We have a board meeting with him next Wednesday and I am hoping that we will have you signed, sealed and delivered by then. That's when we lower the boom."

I thought about how this might play at home and the queasiness began to churn in my stomach. "Of course I will have to think about this and will obviously have dozens of questions. Would need access to the firm's trading records, internal research." A real negative popped into my head. "And what about my business? If I have intimate knowledge of what Ocular is buying and selling, I would have to be restricted from owning or trading in those securities in my own business."

Now it was Roger's team's turn to prove that they were up to date with the plan and had been involved in putting it together. John Reiss, the CIO piped in,

"Actually, there is minimal crossover in the securities Ocular invests in and what you own in your client accounts." He sensed my unease and was ready to ease my concern. "We checked the 13-D and 13-F public filings and there is no overlap on the stock holdings in Ocular's mutual fund and what you have listed in your pension client equity holdings. Ocular is a special situation small cap shop while your firm apparently focuses on only mid to large cap stocks. Ocular does own some bonds in companies where you have equity holdings, but there doesn't seem to be much to worry about there. Ocular is not going to have any non-public information on the companies you invest in."

Time to get a little more serious, I thought. Let's see how they react to a blast from left field.

"And what about the SEC investigation into Spindletop?" Roger didn't react, but I detected some serious squirming on the part of the brain trust. John Reiss, the CIO came to bat.

"Obviously, that's a concern and one of the reasons you are here." He suddenly seemed less tan and though he tried to appear calm, his upper body stiffened slightly and the vein in his neck had become more prominent. "First American did purchase some private placement debt of Spindletop and furthermore, we have become the largest owner of their bank loans. Since Spindletop is a public company, we cannot divulge what we know about the company, its oil and gas production forecasts, its earnings or cash flow projections, nor can we comment on their recent drilling activity or the speculation that exists about their Wyoming properties."

This response seemed pretty cold and rehearsed and was more of an 8-K or legalistic disclaimer than I needed. Still, it sent an unpleasant message. "But if I'm to oversee Ocular and they own the debt and equity and saw the private placement projections, won't I need to know what they know?"

Dancing-eyes Huthwaite joined the fray. "Actually, you are right. But legally, until we have employed you as a consultant, we cannot distribute or disseminate internal projections provided to us by Spindletop."

"And what about the shares of stock in Spindletop that I own personally?"

Carl was prepared. "Based upon my reading of securities laws, you have a few options. One, you could sell the stock before you become a consultant or relinquish control of the stock by contributing it to a blind trust that would be managed by someone other than yourself for the time that you are under contract. Either way, you would be able to work out the issues surrounding Spindletop."

"Ahem" came from Roger as an indication that Carl was finished for now.

But Carl had opened up a new issue. "What do you mean the issues surrounding Spindletop?" I inquired. This was a completely new wrinkle.

Roger took charge again. "What Carl so indelicately was referring to is a corporate matter. As John mentioned earlier, we are Spindletop's largest lender and as such, we have effective control over them if they should run into any problems achieving the financial targets they agreed to and specified in our bond indenture. These covenants, as they are commonly referred to, are meant to protect us and serve as a kind of leash we can keep the company on to stop them from doing anything we don't want them to do."

"Sounds pretty straightforward," I added. "Nothing I am too unfamiliar with. Sounds like they're bumping up against some of their covenants, generally not a big deal. Especially when you are the largest lender. So you relax a few covenants, get some extra fees from the company and let them live another day even more under your control. Get them to pledge their assets so that if they really get into trouble, you take control of the company. It's pretty standard stuff."

The nodding of heads around the table indicated I was on the right track. Roger said approvingly to his brain trust, "See, I told you he was our guy."

"So what's the big deal?" I asked. "Why the big secrecy?"

"If we tell you, you won't be able to turn back," Carl said. "It would be inside information under SEC guidelines and if you were to trade on the information, it could open you up to potential insider trading violations."

"OK. So, I won't trade on the information," I assured them. "I'll even sign a confidentiality agreement right now if you want. It's not that big a deal and hell, I only own 5000 shares of the stock."

Roger said to the brain trust, "I told you he'd catch on. Carl, you have a copy of the confidentiality agreement handy; don't you?"

Was this orchestrated and had I been set up? It seemed pretty remote to me that somehow this meeting was going to lead to a conversation about Spindletop and that they were going to have a confidentiality agreement at the ready. I must have let them lead me to exactly where they wanted. Carl rose, walked purposefully around the table behind Roger, went to the door, opened it and picked up a manila folder from the reception desk outside. He placed it in front of me on his return and settled back into his seat across from me.

Upon opening it, I saw a boiler plate confidentiality agreement that forbade me to use, disclose or disseminate any non-public information regarding Spindletop Exploration Co. It was standard stuff that I had signed dozens of times before in private equity and debt financing deals. Taking out my black Uniball micro ballpoint, I signed the agreement next to the space indicated by the 3 M sticky that said "Sign here" and slid the folder across the table to Carl.

"OK," I said. "Now I'm sworn to secrecy. What the hell is going on with Spindletop?"

Mark Hanes' role finally became clear as he said, "you were spot on when you reasoned that Spindletop was getting close to violating their financial covenants. They are right on the cusp now and we anticipate they will be in violation at the end of this quarter. They got so excited about the geology of the Slaughterhouse Trend that they kept a 100% interest in the wells they are drilling out there. Most companies will farm out or sell interests in very high-risk speculative drilling areas, but they hung on to this entire one. They fell in love with the prospect, even though they knew going in that the wells were going to have to be very deep and very expensive. The target depth is below 18,000 feet and the geologic formations above the structure created some of the hardest rock the drillers have ever encountered. It has been eating up drill bits and the delays have eaten up the company's cash flow."

The tag team continued as John Reiss gave his analytical input.

"We've talked to the best geologists in the country and the consensus is that this is one of the most exciting geological structures in the country. The big oil companies have speculated that there is a huge field in this trend and many companies have taken their turns trying to strike black gold there, but the same drilling problems keep coming up. Each time the drillers have to stop and restart, it costs time and money. Drilling an oil well is like opening a telescope backwards – you start with a big hole and it gets smaller and smaller the deeper you go. Each time a well is sidetracked or runs into problems, it gets smaller still as new pipe is laid in the hole. Just imagine how hard it is to push a four mile long string of pipe through incredibly hard rock at the bottom of a hole. Really amazing stuff if you think about it."

I had a general knowledge of oil and gas drilling procedures, but if it got more technical from here, I was about to get lost in the vernacular of the business. John continued his tutorial.

"So companies that have drilled this trend have basically run out of workable pipe or money before they got to target depth. That is why it has been nicknamed the Slaughterhouse Trend."

I had to ask the obvious. "The logical follow-up question is, why did Spindletop think they were going to be more successful than others who had gone after the same play?"

John Reiss had done his homework and answered knowingly: "Quite frankly, the advances in drill bits and drilling technology made them think that they could get there, to target depth, with enough hole left to have a meaningful shot at having a productive well."

I thought for a second about the ramifications of what he was saying. "So you have a company running out of money, creditors on its heels and you still don't know what's down there. If there's oil or gas."

"That's correct," John answered matter of factly.

I wasn't convinced. "Sounds to me like you are taking a bit of a crap shoot on this company."

Roger decided that it was his turn to set the record straight. "Actually, this is a no-lose situation for us because if the company violates its covenants, we can accelerate their debt obligations, force them into bankruptcy and virtually assume ownership of the company in its restructuring. But we know that the company's proven oil and gas reserves outside and apart from the Slaughterhouse Trend are worth more than two times its debt obligations. So we could actually do better in bankruptcy than by throwing them a lifeline."

Finally, he had lost me. "I don't understand your logic," I admitted.

Roger leaned forward, looked me in the eye and gave a wink. "Follow me to its conclusion. Spindletop runs short of cash, we force them into a Chapter 11 bankruptcy whereby they have to restructure their debt. As the largest creditor, we control the restructuring; force all other debt holders to exchange debt for equity and all of a sudden we are the largest stockholder in the company. If the wells come in at the Slaughterhouse Trend, who cares if we don't get paid back on our bonds and bank loans. We would just sell the stock and get what it's really worth. It could be one of the greatest home runs we ever hit. We're looking at a double on proven asset value already and if Slaughterhouse is worth what we think, this could be a ten or twenty bagger."

He leaned back, smiling, put his hands together and concluded. "So whaddya think, J. Thomas? Pretty good plan, eh?"

The plan was brilliant. He had figured out the next ten moves on the chessboard and knew he had checkmate in hand. It was a masterful play and he knew it. But wait a second, I thought. If this was a lay down slam-dunk winner, why was I here and why was I involved? "Sounds impressive to me well thought out. Makes a ton of sense obviously. But where and why do you need me?" Go ahead, hit me over the head. I still didn't get it.

Roger leaned forward again, his face scrunched up into lines I had never seen before, grimacing through his teeth as he said,

"That fucking bastard at Ocular, Terry Burroughs, doesn't want to go along with our plan. He has offered to give them a temporary loan, a subordinate convertible bond that will ultimately increase his equity ownership of the company and lessen our claim on the assets. Furthermore, it will give them the lifeline that they need to stay out of bankruptcy. He can ruin everything."

Ouch, I thought. The proverbial fly in the ointment was one of their own employees in a company in which they were the majority stockholder!

"But can't you control what Ocular does? You are their parent company, after all."

Roger continued to fume and his brain trust members were looking intently down at their blank white pads. "You'd certainly think so, wouldn't you? But when we made this deal to buy 75 % of his company, we put in writing that we would never try to influence or exercise control over the investment decision making process at his firm for as long as he continued to be the President and Chief Investment Officer, which happens to be the entire five fucking years of his employment contract."

The brain trust refused to move or act, and I noticed even Carl Huthwaite's darting eyes could suddenly only focus on the white pad in front of him. Obviously, they knew that they had screwed up this one big time and as General Counsel; Carl had to be the one most at risk because all contracts and legal documents had to be signed off by him.

I looked at Roger, still leaning forward, waiting for an answer, with none of the "old pal" smile that he usually looked at you with. It was a side of him that I had never seen before and I didn't like it or feel very comfortable on the other end of it. The intensity of his hatred for Terry Burroughs was so strong that I half wondered if Roger had started looking in the yellow pages under H for Hit man or M for Murderer for hire. I had visions of Guido, the pimp in Risky Business telling Joel, "Don't ever fuck with a man's livelihood."

"And where do I come in?" I asked, not quite sure I wanted an answer or any response from Roger at this point.

"Your mission, Mr. Phelps," Roger said, quoting the Mission Impossible line, but with a tone which showed no humor, "is to find out what is going on at Ocular, what Terry Burroughs is doing in client accounts and in his personal accounts. Find me something that will give us reason to fire him. Nobody is totally clean and we think there is plenty of dirt for you to dig up. But we've got to do it fast and we can't send in one of our own people. We can, however, as part of our purchase agreement of Ocular, force them to accept our 'consultative help' in the management of their business. That's what you're going to be, our consultative help."

So now I knew what they wanted from me. A little spying and reconnaissance work. All the rest about turnarounds, and how perfect I was for the job, was staged to make me feel good and to put the net out to catch me.

"I see," I said. "Obviously, I will think about it. Roger, you know I will do whatever I can. But I'm not sure that I have the time and of course I'll have to talk to Missy."

"Oh no. You're going to help," Roger responded, a knowing smile forming. "We have to move fast and I want you to start immediately. You know you can't say No to me."

"Sure I can," I protested, trying to force a smile to defuse the tension in the room.

"We'll see about that. By the way, where did you say you were staying, the Airport Hilton? We want to messenger over a cashier's check and engagement letter later this morning."

It may have been meant as a veiled threat, but I suddenly felt awfully naked hearing it. The brain trust looked at me. They must have known that all of Roger's clients stayed at the posh Park Hyatt down the street. Was Roger blackmailing me or threatening to tell all about my rendezvous at the Hilton last night? I didn't do anything, but I had been followed. How did he know about my little trip?

"No, I'm staying at the Park Hyatt," I countered, not at all pleased with the web that Roger was weaving. Was I just another chess piece? My God, had he set everything up, including Karen? My mind began to race as I tried to reconstruct just how I had gotten myself into this predicament. But this was no place to collect my thoughts. I stood up and said, "I will think about it, but right now, I've got to get ready for my next meeting. I have a business lunch to prepare for. If you need me, I'll be in my hotel room or via my cell phone." I looked at Roger and wasn't in the mood for a hug. I said thanks and extended my hand.

Roger shifted gears flawlessly, putting on the 'old pal' smile, grabbed my hand strongly and said, "Great, ole buddy. I'll walk you out."

We said goodbye to the brain trust, collectively sighing their relief that the meeting was wrapping up and looking less concerned now that Roger and I were leaving the room. Carl's eyes rose from the pad before him and were once again darting everywhere but at us. Roger put his arm around my shoulder and tried to apologize. "Sorry I had to play a little rough in there. Just business, you know. No blood, no foul. Right? I really need your help, though. I'm counting on you."

"I don't know, Rog," I said. "I'll have to think about it and talk to Missy." I wasn't sure what to do or what I could do. One thing I was sure of was that Missy would not be a big fan of anything that would take me out of town on business any more frequently than I already was.

We reached the elevator and Roger made one more plea. "Come on J.T. You can make this decision on your own. You don't need Missy's permission. It's your racetrack, your car and you're the driver. You're in control of the race."

I looked at him closely, and he smiled content and impressed with his metaphor. I tried to force a smile of my own and said as the elevator door opened, "Yes, that may be, but Missy controls the pits." I stepped into the elevator and said my customary goodbye, "Later, Rog."

CHAPTER ELEVEN

Jeff and the limo were waiting outside to take me wherever I wanted to go. I still had an hour before my luncheon meeting, so I asked him to take me back to the Park Hyatt. After the meeting with ole pal Rog, I felt like I needed a good shower. I felt like I had been raped and unaware of what was happening until it was too late. More than that, Roger had gone over the line and, no, dammit, it wasn't all right. I knew what I really needed to do was call Missy to check the temperature and gauges and see how the rest of the pit crew was doing. I also needed to talk to Tina and find out how the office was surviving without me. First and foremost, I had to see what the markets were doing and check my e-mail.

The Blackberry found its signal almost as soon as I turned it on and immediately started buzzing as it loaded my e-mail I lit a cigarette and started to check how the market indices had fared in my hour absence and got real time updates on where my top stock holdings were trading. Thankfully, the pluses were beating the minuses and it looked as if my clients were closer to their vacations today, even though the market averages were flat to slightly down. When all the hard work turned in positive results, it was as rewarding an existence as any that I'd heard of. But every day was a battle and you can't win every battle if you plan on winning the war. The trick is to control the depression that follows those bad days and weeks that settle in like a cold or virus. Thankfully, we were getting a clean bill of health today.

I punched in the ticker symbol for Spindletop, SPN, and thought that as far as tickers go, it wasn't very original. While companies don't always have control over what their ticker symbols will be, it was always more fun to have one that implied something about what the company did. Some of the classics or personal favorites included JAM for Smuckers, GAS for NICOR, a natural gas pipeline company, OO for Oakley (the glass manufacturer) and OIL for Triton Energy, a high- flying energy company in the 1990's. And Spindletop got SPE. Oh well, unexciting stock symbol or not, the stock appeared to be under accumulation, Wall Street lingo for moving higher. With all the uncertainty as to whether or not they were going to run out of money drilling in the Slaughterhouse Trend, I couldn't help but be amazed at how well the stock was doing. Had Roger told me everything? Had I learned the whole truth or was Roger putting his own spin, pardon the pun, on Spindletop. But Roger and his team should know more about what was going on than anyone else. Were investors buying the company's stock because they knew about the drilling potential or simply because it's technical chart looked good? Did they know about Ocular's plan to do a private convert with them? All rhetorical questions and quite frankly of no matter, as I had signed away my right to buy or sell shares in the company.

The limo stopped in front of the Park Hyatt and Jeff quickly hopped out of the front seat to come around and open my door before I had time to put my electronic toys back in my briefcase and put out my cigarette.

Opening the door Jeff asked," Would you like me to wait here, Mr. Morris? I understand you have a luncheon meeting and I would be happy to drive you to your next appointment."

Had my itinerary been posted on the web somewhere? This was getting a little spooky, but as there was no secret rendezvous or clandestine meeting, I decided it would be better than risking a ride in a dumpy cab like last night.

"Sure, that would be great" I said as I exited the limo.

"I've got a noon luncheon meeting about 10 minutes from here, or so I'm told. I'll be back down between 11:30 and 11:45. Okay? Got to make a few phone calls."

"That will be fine," he answered. "The valet will let me park just off to the side here and I'll be waiting."

"Thanks. I'll be down shortly."

I entered the lobby, crossed the marble floor and took a glance to see if I could identify where and who the spies were that ratted out my adventure last night. Naturally, not one of the three attractive women behind the registration desk paid me any attention as I walked loudly to the elevator, my loafers making sharp clicking sounds, with me feeling foolish for my suspicions.

Arriving back at my suite, I took off my jacket, turned on my cell phone and put CNBC on the television as I called the office. Tina answered on the second ring.

"Mr. Morris' office, this is Christine. May I help you?" What a sweet voice; clear, business-like and professional.

"Hi Tina, it's me. What's up? Anything going on?"

"Oh, thank God, it's you," she said with a concerned, nervous tone in her voice.

"What's up?" I asked again. "Is something wrong?" I could tell by her tone that something definitely wasn't right.

"I don't know" came the response from someone who always knew what was good news and what was bad news. New or happy client:

Good news. Losing a client or having an unhappy client: Bad news. Stocks up: Good. Stocks down: Bad. Not many other possibilities in the investment business.

"You had a call this morning, about a half hour ago, from a Mr. Stanford T. Sowers." She paused for a second trying to control her emotions and keep her delivery calm. "He said he was from the SEC and that it was, what did he say, critical was the term he used, critical that he meet with you as soon as possible."

My heart constricted. My ability to breathe disappeared for a second and then I reminded myself that I had done nothing wrong and had nothing to worry about. Sounded like a good rationalization, but my mind and sensory organs weren't convinced. It was like the feeling I would get as a teenager driving down the road when I saw a policeman, creating a shiver and fear even when I hadn't done anything wrong, wasn't under the influence and hadn't broken any laws.

Tina continued, "He asked if he could come here on Monday morning at 9:00 AM to meet with you. I know you don't like early morning meetings, so I lied and said you were busy until 10:30. Is that all right? I wasn't sure what to do. Is everything OK?" She was perceptibly flustered so I decided if I couldn't control my own fears, at least I could allay hers.

"Fine. Fine," I said. "Relax, I was expecting him to call and there's nothing to worry about." A little lie but it was important to calm Tina down. "Besides, when they ask for an appointment, it means you're not in any trouble. It's when they show up without an appointment, that you better start worrying."

"I hope you're right," Tina said, seeming partially relieved. I too, hoped that I was right.

The "critical" nature of the meeting did concern me though. Time to change subjects and get Tina out of the Fear Zone and back to the efficient office zone. "Next?" I asked

"Well, other than that, not much of importance. Your friend John called asking about golf tomorrow. I told him I thought you were already committed with family obligations."

"Correct. Next?"

"Some reporter for the Wall Street Journal called and said he wanted to talk to you. He was different from the usual ones that want a comment on a company. I asked him which company he was calling about and he said he wanted to talk to you about other matters. Very secretive."

"Save the number. I'll call him on Monday, or better yet, e-mail it to me on my Blackberry and if I have time before my flight I'll call him back today. Next?"

"Two client calls, nothing to worry about, can wait till next week and they both said they were glad you were taking a vacation."

Some vacation, I thought to myself. What was a vacation anyway? My eyes drifted to the ticker scrolling on the bottom of the TV screen.

"I told them you were relaxing and spending time with your family and friends."

She was right in a way.

"Anything else?" I asked. "Not much time before my luncheon."

"Everything else is fine. We are surviving and I've cleared off most of the junk that had started to pile up on your desk and put what looked important in an envelope. Want me to drop it off at your house tonight?"

She was the best you could ask for. "That would be great. Thanks for everything. I'll probably check in later."

"I know you will, but you don't have to" she argued. "It is 2:30 PM on a Friday afternoon. Not much can happen that can't wait until Monday."

"I know, I know, but if I have time, I'll check in."

"If you must" she said with a mock exasperated tone, but I knew that she liked it when I called even if it was just an opportunity for her to give me grief about my obsessive work habits.

"Okay, later" I said and pushed the red END button on the cell phone. Checking my watch, I figured I still had time for a quick call home. They probably weren't there, but it was worth a shot. After five rings, the answering machine picked up and after hearing my daughter's cute greeting and the beep, I left my standard out of town message.

"Hi, honey, hi guys. Sorry I missed you. Hope all is well. Can't wait to see you. Will try again later if I have the time."

Critical family duties done, it was now time to find out how some of my other investments were doing. After the visit with Roger and crew, I sure hoped it was better than Spindletop. Besides, maybe Frank Howell, my luncheon date and the CFO of Bakersfield Petroleum, a heavy oil company, could answer a few questions for me. While the partnership I was in with Frank focused on old oil reserves in Southern California, slow and steady "stripper" wells as they were known, Frank had been in the "ahl bidness," as he called it, for over forty years and knew more about geology and oil production than any Wall Street analyst I had ever met.

I met Jeff downstairs and set off to the offices of Bakersfield Petroleum, a simple single story stucco building in what appeared to be an industrial wasteland, save for the presence of a half dozen oil pumping units slowly bobbing up and down in the expansive dirt yard. As a partner, it was always satisfying to see that Frank didn't spend all of our money on fancy modern office space and instead put my money and theirs into the ground to develop oil reserves and generate as much cash as possible. As the limo approached the chain link fence surrounding the property and pulled up to the gate marked Private, No Trespassing, we were met by Frank, who stepped out of the building just as Jeff was about to get out of the car. Wearing faded jeans, cowboy boots and a faded denim shirt with snap ivory buttons and a black but dusty Stetson cowboy hat, he hadn't changed in the ten years I had known him.

"Come on in," he yelled to Jeff, as he pulled what appeared to be a garage door opener out of his pocket and the gates slid open. "We've been expecting you. Remember how to find us OK?"

Through my rolled down window I answered, "Of course, how could I forget? Just look for the donkeys." He had once used this term to describe the pumping units around the property.

"Well, come on in and lets get some eats, put the old feed bag on, eh?" It was an expression I didn't like, but seemed natural and unobtrusive coming from him.

I followed him into the building, past the gray-haired receptionist answering what had to be the company phone, a touch tone slim line model that was probably obsolete when they purchased it. I knew that Bakersfield Petroleum had more than one phone line out of necessity, but Frank and Ida, the receptionist, would probably have felt more comfortable with rotary phones. The carpet was dusty brown and threadbare in the pathways to the three offices surrounding the reception area and to the conference room. There was a pair of brown metal folding chairs in the waiting room, on either side of a simple square fake oak veneer end table bedecked with oil magazines and a lamp made out of a miniature drilling rig. Frank showed me into the conference room, where he pushed a pile of rolled up maps to the side of the four by eight oak table and pointed to the seats. "Take a load off. I wasn't sure what you wanted so I ordered a turkey and a roast beef. Your choice," he said as he pointed to the two sandwiches still in their white deli paper wrapping. "Got sodas, too, both kinds. Coke and Diet Coke," he added.

I sat down, chose the sandwich closest to me and said, "Coke will be fine for me."

Sitting down and joining me for our modest meal, Frank told me how the higher oil prices of the past few months were making this Bakerfield's best year and proudly offered that the company's cash distribution would probably end up being a record, up about 30%

over last year. Heartening news, to say the least. Since we had time on our hands, instead of having Frank explain the nuances of oil recovery and water floods and fracturing, a well stimulation strategy, I decided to pick his brain.

"Frank, you've been in the drilling business for what, 30 to 35 years? Drilled just about every major basin in the country, right?"

"Forty-two years," he corrected. "I'm older than I look."

It was high time I got the skinny on what people in the know knew about the potential of the Slaughterhouse Trend. "Well, what can you tell me about the Slaughterhouse Trend? I hear there's some speculation that it could be a biggie. Major league potential."

Frank didn't hesitate. "Boy, that there play has busted more 'ahl' company budgets than OPEC." He got fired up as he spoke, taking time for a drag of his trusted Lucky Strike. Not often did I see Luckies anymore, but Frank had been smoking them for as long as I knew him. "I remember one time when I was with San Juan Pete, we had some of the best damn seismic, saw the bright spots and just knew we had a major prospect. But that ole well just chewed up bits like a rank thoroughbred and spit them back at us like there was no tomorrow. Hardest damn cap rock I ever encountered."

Sounded like he knew it well, but I wasn't feeling like I was completely following the lingo. In my business, a portfolio manager gets to know a little bit about everything, but becomes an expert in nothing. His slang was on the verge of losing me completely.

"Frank," I pleaded gently, "keep it in simple terms for me."

"Right, right," he apologized. "Sometimes I get carried away. OK. So when you want to drill in an area that has some real geologic potential, you usually start off by shooting some seismic. That means sending sound waves down into the earth and measuring how long it takes for those sounds to return. You do it lots of times over an area and let the sound waves give you a map of what the geology looks like thousands of feet below the surface. It's a way of trying to find a structure that can trap the oil and gas. With me so far?"

"Yup, you're doing great," I answered. So far I seemed to be keeping up. I had heard bits and pieces through the years of how seismic worked, and it all made sense so far.

He gave me a wink and said, "Here's the fun part. When the sound waves bounce just right off the hard cap rocks and the softer more porous rocks where the oil and gas is trapped, the sound echoes a bit stronger and faster and you get what we call a 'bright' spot on the seismic map of the area. The Slaughterhouse Trend has at least a half dozen bright spots, real potential, but the prospects are all very deep and no one ever could get a decent size hole down there. Just imagine you're a straw trying to get through the bottom of an aluminum can. It is pretty easy to get to the bottom of the can, but getting through it's a bitch. We tried three times and every time, the same thing. Drill bits wear out as they chew their way down a hole and the drill bits just couldn't seem to get through that damn cap rock. Helluva challenge. Someday, someone's gonna get through. The new diamond drill bits just might do the trick, but I'm too old to go wildcattin'. Heart can't take it. Bank account can't take it. I'd just as soon milk some of these boring old stripper wells and earn a decent wage."

Fascinating stuff, I thought. Frank took a break, lit another Lucky off the one he was nearly finished and snubbed out the old one in the crowded ashtray on the middle of the table. I wanted more, so I prodded.

"How big did you guys think it was, or could be?"

"Shit," he said, thoughtfully. "You never know till the well comes in, if it comes in, whether you get oil or gas, or strike out with a dry hole or a wet one."

"What's a wet one?" I asked.

"A well is wet when you get water and nothing else. See there are three things you can get flowing out of a well; water, oil or gas. Did'ya ever shake up some oil and vinegar salad dressing then watch it separate? Well, oil and gas and water work the same way, with gas at the top, followed by oil and then water at the bottom and when you are drilling, you don't want water. That usually means that oil and gas have oozed off into other nooks and crannies, other faults underneath. Get the picture?"

It was making a little more sense to me now. "So how big could it be? What would a big well be in this area, the proverbial company maker, home run?"

"Well, hell, with as expensive as it is to get to, probably at least $25 to 35 million a well these days, probably even more with some problems along the way. It would have to be at least a hundred million barrel field to get people excited. Real company makers would probably be five times that or more. But hell yes, it is possible. Why all the interest?" he asked. "Have you been sold some penny stock hoping to make a killing? Doesn't sound like your style?"

"No, no," I reassured him. "Just hearing about this company Spindletop making the play. Own a little stock personally, but not too much."

"They're a good group of guys. Good geologist founded the company. Came out of Amoco. Cashed in all his company stock and decided to try to grow something out of the leftovers from the majors."

Before I had a chance to ask, he followed. "Those are the exploration prospects the big boys think are too risky or don't have enough return potential. They have a word for it that makes it seem like it all makes sense—non-core assets. Well hell, they've got a 100-year history of leaving some of the great finds on the table for the little guys and once the little guy finds it, proves it and begins to develop it, they buy the whole damn company or step in to help fund the development to get a share of the production."

"Sounds like a decent business?" I added, trying to imply that I had kept up with him.

"Yeah, can be, but just remember the number of oil companies that have made it are a small fraction of all the ones that have tried and disappeared."

"Caveat emptor" I said, meaning that someone should know the risks before jumping in, translating to buyer beware.

"Nope, never heard of those guys," Frank said as he searched the rolodex of his mind, "Foreign outfit?"

CHAPTER TWELVE

T he view out the window of the plane as we left the bright lights
  of L.A. was exciting, as the many dots of light below twinkled
like a Christmas scene. I thought to myself, I wonder what Roger is
doing now. He can't be happy that I didn't sign the consulting agreement before I left, and now, thinking again about the opportunity I
took out the manila folder with the contract and cashiers check for
$500,000 made out to Morris Asset. I had to discuss it with Missy
and really wasn't sure I wanted to play the role of spy to bring down
Ocular's Terry Burroughs and ultimately to force Spindletop into
bankruptcy.

Who was the bad guy? Was it Terry Burroughs or Roger? Roger,
my buddy, my friend, my pal. He had saved my butt in prep school
and now he was cashing in the chip. Or trying.

As the plane rose into a pillow of clouds, the mild turbulence
caused me to change my focus, from the white outside my window to
the choices ahead of me.

The offer was an attractive one bordering on the obscene. A
three-month consulting fee of $500,000 would make my family

blush, my friends gasp and acquaintances sick with envy. Little did they know that taking on the consulting project had the possibility of threatening my marriage, ruining my reputation and damaging my relationship with my best friend. But was he still my best friend? After our meeting in L.A. and the threat to expose my night at the Airport Hilton, I wasn't exactly sure where we stood.

The young, tanned and jet black haired male flight attendant interrupted my train of thought and offered me a drink. He asked what my dinner entrée preference would be: chicken Kiev or steak au poivre, and as I mumbled the choice of chicken, I wondered where Karen was flying off to. Back to Cleveland? Or off to find more excitement with fools like me who fill the airways. I was half glad that I was being served by a male flight attendant as I had some serious decisions to make and didn't need the distraction or guilt of conversing with another young stewardess, er... flight attendant.

I opened up the manila folder to review the documents inside for the third time in three hours; a signed original of the confidentiality agreement relating to Spindletop, a copy of the proposed consulting agreement with First American and the cashiers check. Missy was going to flip and I probably shouldn't even think of taking on this project, but did I have a choice? The actual consulting agreement was as open-ended as any contract I had ever seen, no promises or guarantees. I simply provided consulting and advisory services to First American and any of its subsidiaries for a period of three months. Timing was critical, according to Roger, as they were playing a game of Beat The Clock. The Spindletop well was due to reach target depth within the next few weeks and he and First American needed to have Terry Burroughs and Ocular towing the corporate line and soon.

Roger had backed down a bit and on his first call on Friday afternoon suggested that I take the weekend to think it over with Missy. He stressed, however, that whatever I decided, at a minimum he needed to know by Tuesday morning so that he could prepare documents for Wednesday's board meeting. He also thought that we could meet in Las Vegas a week from Friday, so that I could get acquainted with Terry and Ocular, maybe do a little work over the weekend and have some fun at the tables on Saturday night.

"I really need your help on this one, J. Thomas," he had pleaded. "And besides, we can have a little fun in the process. You could even bring Missy out for a little romantic getaway."

"With you in tow, I doubt she'd see the romance," I countered. "Besides, she'd never leave the kids for a weekend. Too many games, parties and other craziness on the calendar to deal with. Which is one of the reasons I just don't see how I'm going to be able to swing this, Rog."

"Well," he finished, "You'll do what you gotta do. You know what they say. Women. Can't live with them,"

"Can't live without them," I answered. How true it was.

The chicken kiev arrived and I closed my folder of conflict. Luckily, the flight wasn't full in first class and I had an empty seat next to me, so I pulled my indestructible Tumi briefcase off the floor from its safely stowed hiding place underneath the seat in front of me and put it on the vacant seat to my right. I put the manila folder away and decided that the Sam Black novel was going to be my escape. Take my mind off things. Sam's private eye was in the midst of bringing down a money-laundering operation and had just found out that his wife's uncle might be involved. Things were heating up and I needed to get away from Roger, First American, Terry Burroughs, Ocular and Spindletop. My head was spinning with all the twists and turns of the past forty-eight hours.. I was tired of trying to solve the puzzle before me.

I decided to take a quick look at my Blackberry to see if it had a signal and if there were any late important emails that I could deal with before my return. The signal was gone, but I could still read what had been sent to me. Any responses I made would be stored until we dropped back below 10,000 feet or so tomorrow morning.

Luckily, there wasn't much of importance other than Tina's end of the day note.

"Thomas, I will drop off your research folder on my way home. Enjoy the weekend. Some vacation!! I sent Missy a dozen red roses in your name and said, 'Can't wait to see you.' I'm sure she needed it. Just looking out for you. Monday looks pretty calm except for 10:30 AM with the SEC. He called to confirm late today. Take care. Tina."

The SEC called to confirm. I thought to myself, either this guy is obsessive or they have too much damned time to waste if they confirm every appointment they make. What were they fishing for anyway? Obviously, Roger was a part of it because in the first call, he had asked about my "relationship" with Roger and First American. Was it because of my little purchase of 5000 shares of Spindletop as Roger suggested? Or was there more?

I wracked my brain and couldn't think of any other reasons why they would find it "critical" that we meet so soon. I wasn't one to risk my career playing some of the games other portfolio managers did. Marking up stocks at the quarter end to boost performance. Touting the virtues of stocks in the press that I wanted to sell, trying to get the stocks to move up so I could get out at a better price. I still looked at the violations of securities laws listed in the Wall Street Journal every month to remind myself of what not to do and to see what the regulators were focusing on. Nobody's perfect, but I prided myself on being an honest person who tried to play it straight and above all to be fair. Most often, it was retail brokers that got fined for trying to screw investors out of their money by trading excessively, deceiving them by issuing false statements with bloated valuations on illiquid stocks. That was just one of the many reasons I stuck with liquid, well-known blue chip stocks. I slept better and the clients slept better, knowing that we were invested in real companies with real assets. We were invested in companies that provided valuable-necessary products and services. Furthermore, I focused on companies that had generally been doing it better than anyone else for a long time.

I remembered some of the firms that I had worked at during my career and how unethical they were in their trading activity. How at quarter end and year end, they just had to buy more of this company or that, running up the stock prices in the last few hours, knowing full well that they were just trying to game the system and improve their portfolios' performance, regardless of whether the stocks in question were cheap. If the SEC really wanted to get the crooks, they should take a look at which firms were buying stocks in the last hour of the last trading day of a quarter or year. I found the practice so distasteful that for the ten plus years I had my own firm, the only orders I executed on those days were sell orders. Let them play their games and give me a chance to sell stocks at stupid inflated prices.

Before I mailed my name off to the Vatican to nominate myself for sainthood, I reminded myself that I had plenty of faults and my little adventure with Karen should be confirmation of just how human I was. Should I or would I mention her to Missy? How I had been tempted to eat the apple in the proverbial garden? What the hell was I doing in the garden in the first place? Some things are better left unsaid, I decided, and chuckled to myself, that Roger would say, "Let sleeping dogs...." Lie, I thought.

I picked up my Sam Black novel, eager to change focus and dove into the story. As exciting as it was, the stress of the past two days and the late hours conspired to send me into dreamland a short time later.

The steward shook my arm to wake me as we made our final descent into Newark, and I quickly put Sam and Company back into my briefcase and tried to wake myself up for the landing. It was going to be a long day, but we were on time and yes, I was going to make it to the soccer game on time.

The approach to Newark in the early morning light as I looked out the window was cold and gray. I couldn't feel the cold, but some things can be sensed with the eyes. The leaves on the trees were brown and many were barren of any life. It appeared as if Newark was asleep and that the only signs of life were the cars moving along the New Jersey Turnpike and the airport's access roads. Had the weather turned that quickly from the bright warm days and colors of a week ago? Was it still red and yellow and brilliant at home when the sun shone bright? Or had we lapsed into the cold and damp and dreary of another New Jersey winter already? What a difference from the warm, sunny, dry climate of Southern California just a few short hours ago.

Looking at my watch, I realized if the car service was on time and had its driver at the ready, I would be home in an hour or so. Just in time for breakfast with the family and the soccer game. The smart thing to do would be to climb into bed and catch a power nap for a couple of hours, but I needed to stay alert and stay sharp if I ever thought I was going to be out of town on a Friday again, coming home on a red eye. No, I reminded myself, it's not a short leash. Missy and I agreed that it had to be this way.

Missy. What could I say? What should I say about the events of the past 36 hours? What a trip. How much had changed in that short period of time.

The drivers at the bottom of the escalator looked ashen gray, a condition that seemed a permanent affliction of drivers that picked me up at any of the New York area airports, regardless of the time of day or the season. What a life they must have, I thought. I picked out MORRIS from the group of men holding their car services' mini-signs and noted that once again I had a new driver. Joe, as he introduced himself appeared to be in his late fifties or early sixties, of slight build with well-groomed gray hair, horn rimmed glasses and a somewhat worn, but high quality suit. I hoped he wasn't one of Wall Street's latest batches of cost reductions and prayed that he wouldn't want to chat about the markets. Luckily, he seemed less interested in talking than I, and after the compulsory "any luggage" discourse, we headed off to the car and to home.

I half dozed the ride home, having make the simple request for a classic rock station, and closed my eyes to the sounds of CCR,

Chicago and Bruce. Relaxing rock for an old middle-aged fart like myself. I thought about how in the early days of our marriage, Missy would meet me at any hour at any New York airport. Was it marriage, the kids or both that had changed all that? Stop analyzing and get some rest, I told myself and dozed off somewhere in the strains of an Allman Brothers jam.

"We're here, Mr. Morris" the wake-up call from Joe in the driver's seat. Rousting myself, I grabbed my briefcase, patted down my navy blue blazer for a general content check and slung my overnight bag over one shoulder and briefcase strap over the other. The house appeared quiet, almost too quiet. There were usually more lights on at this hour on Saturday mornings, for while my youngest son might have trouble getting out of bed before 8:00 AM on Monday through Friday due to a lack of interest in what school offered fifth graders on a daily basis in the way of learning, Saturdays were a different story. Playtime, cartoons and a variety of sports activities were what he lived for and we could sometimes hear him on Saturdays at 5:30 AM, logging on to his computer to check the late sports scores, and playing video games that he knew were off limits and too violent. But heck, what's a kid to do? And how many parents would leave the pleasure, comfort and warmth of a king-sized bed to yell at a child. I, for one, dreamed of sleeping in past ten o'clock and was happy to get anything past eight on any given weekend.

I saw the vase of roses Tina had sent at the side of the double dutch white front door and figured Missy must have missed seeing them as she usually went in and out of the house through the garage.

I quietly put my key in the front door, undid the lock and gently slipped inside to find out where my family was. Who was awake and who was asleep. I could hear the dogs rustling in their cage/crate/ house in the kitchen and decided that heading straight upstairs to our bedroom was the safer, quieter play. Maybe I could slip in a few hours of nap time.

The door to our bedroom made its customary 'I need WD40' squeak as I opened it, cringing and hoping I wouldn't wake Missy. As I peered in and started to put down my briefcase and overnighter, I noticed the bed was made, apparently not slept in, with an envelope on the pillow on my side of the bed.

Feeling instantly alert and no longer caring about the volume of noise, I dropped the briefcase and bag and half ran to the envelope. I instantly recognized Missy's handwriting on the envelope, with "Thomas" written in her polished handwriting on the middle of the envelope. Well that should rule out kidnapping, I thought to myself. Opening the envelope my eyes raced through the words and my heart sank as I read:

"Gone to Mom's. Couldn't take being alone another night. I've got the kids. Feed the dogs. Hope it was worth it."

This was not good.

CHAPTER THIRTEEN

S tunned, I sat down on the bed and tried to figure out the situation. Was this just one of the many random getaways to my mother-in laws? Had I done or said something to set this off? I knew things weren't completely warm and fuzzy when I left, but they didn't seem too bad. I had called in as usual and though we hadn't had a chance to talk, I had only left two days ago. So one night alone had set this off?

I looked at my watch and the hands seemed uncertain. I then noticed my left hand was visibly shaking and I tried to focus. 7:10 am. She would probably be up, but I couldn't fathom trying to sort this out over the phone and dreaded the prospect of talking to my mother-in-law, who had never really liked me and who felt that I wasn't a good enough father for her grandchildren and husband to her daughter. She never said as much to me directly, but her tone spoke volumes when we talked. She preferred to let Missy know how she felt about my shortcomings and deficiencies when I was out of town on business and Missy was at her most vulnerable emotional state. As a result, our reunions when I arrived home were usually stilted and difficult until the web of my mother-in-law faded from memory. Usually a two day process at the most. I hoped that this was all this represented.

But Missy had never left me a note on the pillow. No message on my cell phone, nothing to forewarn me.

I started to focus on the issues at hand and set up a battle plan. First, feed the dogs and let them out. Second, boy did I need a shower and a shave. Third, the soccer game was at 9:00 AM and she would have to be there with Michael, our twelve year old. Fourth, I had to get up from the bed and get moving or I would lie down and sleep for hours. It was 4:10 am California time and I only had about three hours of sleep in me. Not enough, but it would have to do.

Feeding the dogs made them happy and took my mind off my problems temporarily. I stood in the shower until the hot water was gone. From history, I knew that when I took showers until the cold water settled in, I had disappeared into the pleasure of the running jets of water for a good fifteen to twenty minutes. It was worth every minute of pleasure, and as the cool and then cold water fought its way into the mix, I started to come to life again.

I dressed in nicer clothes than I preferred khaki's and a striped button down dress shirt, knowing that my favorite jeans were on Missy's wish list to burn on an annual basis. I shaved because it was just something old guys had to do in today's society if you didn't want to be scorned and because the stubble came in almost uniformly gray now, making me look and feel older.

Back downstairs to let the dogs in, I decided to check the voice mail to see if any more clues could be found. Maybe Missy left a message on the phone. When the machine told me I had seventeen unheard messages, I knew it was bad. When Missy got angry, she shut out the world and friends and retreated into a shell, not wanting to interact with anyone. She shunned contact with the outside world and didn't appreciate me trying to talk things through either.

Three of the messages were from me, unheard and ignored. The rest were either my friends calling about possible golf games (two), friends of Missy's trying to put together paddle tennis games (five) and the rest of the calls were for Kathleen or Michael trying to get together to play or go to the movies.

I saved all of the messages, except for the two from my buddies and checked the calendar on the bulletin board next to the kitchen phone to find out where the soccer game was.

Armed with the knowledge that Missy was going to be in one of her moods, I set off to try and begin the Herculean task of working my way up the food chain from slime to some other higher form of Darwinian evolution. I would take what I could.

Not focusing on driving, I did arrive at the soccer field as warm-ups were occurring, and was relieved to see that Michael was out in the middle of the field practicing passing with two of his teammates. Looking around the perimeter of the field, I found no trace of Missy or her car in either the stands or the parking areas.

I called out to Michael to let him know I was there, and when he heard my call he turned toward me and frowned.

"Hi Mickey" I said again and added cheerfully, "Promised I'd make it."

"Yeah" he grunted as he turned toward me on the sidelines. "But Mom is mad at you." As he walked closer he said," Mom said you really did it this time."

"Did what?" I asked, now even more concerned as my greatest fears were becoming reality.

He shrugged his shoulders and said, "Something about making the wrong choice for the last time. Something about Uncle Roger, I think."

"What else did she say?" I asked. Hoping for more details on just how low I had fallen in the evolutionary chain.

"I dunno." He looked down at his muddy cleats groping for recollection of the phrases and words that she had used. A brilliant memory, he could recall conversations with incredible accuracy. "Something like, 'This time you've really done it. Gone too far. I'm not going through this ever again.'" He looked up at me with beseeching sad eyes and asked, "What does she mean Dad? Are you and Mom okay? She seems really upset. She had Grandma drop me off this morning and said Grandma was picking me up, too."

It meant trouble and I knew it. "It's nothing, Mickey," I reassured him. "Nothing to worry about. Get back to practice and let's see you score a goal today, okay?" I tried my best to be upbeat and supportive and get Mickey to focus on the soccer game ahead instead of the storms that were obviously brewing in Missy's head.

"Okay, Dad. But you know these guys are supposed to be pretty tough. They're in first and have only lost one game." He was back where he ought to be.

"Yeah, but you guys have only lost two games and those were early in the season. Play your best and you'll beat them, you'll see. Don't be intimidated. You're as good as any team in this league." His eyes looked up at me approvingly. Whatever else was going on, he still looked up to me physically and literally for support and advice. He jogged off to practice some more with his teammates, giving a smiling, "Thanks, Dad" as he left. All was well with part of my life at least.

I tried to focus on the game, and watched proudly as my son played his heart out, not scoring, but setting up the game's only goal with a crisp crossing pass that was booted past a sprawling goalie by his best friend, Timmy. A hard fought game, but at least this time the good guys came out on top. I gave God a quick "thanks, he needed that" and actually kept my fingers crossed in my pockets for the tense closing moments of the game. But my thoughts continually wandered back to the state of affairs with Missy and the status of my marriage.

Missy's mom didn't make life any easier when she sat in her car in the parking lot glaring at me for the last ten or so minutes of the game, refusing to get out and watch Mickey from the sidelines. From her vantage point, she couldn't see the soccer game, but she could see me, and that appeared to suit her just fine.

At the end of the game, after the players shook hands and the coach gave his customary post game wrap-up pep talk, I walked Mickey over to his Grandma's seven year old black Saturn, which looked like it hadn't been washed or waxed in as many years. Now I don't care if a car is dirty, but if you plan on never washing it, you would think you could choose a better color than black, which shows dirt more than any other color. It was a pet peeve that I could joke with Missy about when life was calm at home and our relationship was in one of those stretches where you felt that your mate was in fact your best friend that you could say anything to without a care. No airs, no pressure to be anything other than yourself. Honestly letting any thought or feeling roll off the tip of your tongue without worrying about how it would be received. That's what marriage is supposed to be and seemed to be most of the time. Now, obviously, we were on the dark side.

"Hello Jane" I said as politely and as humanely as I felt capable of as I approached Grandma's brown dusty black car. "I hear you're bringing Mickey home from the game. I could take him home with me, if it's any help."

"We don't need any of your help," she curtly replied, and the scent of venom laced the words as she spoke. "You've done enough. Mickey is coming home with me and you can do whatever it is you feel you need to do." I noticed her eyes narrow as she spoke and scrunched up in disgust. She might have been attractive once, when the gray hair was blonde and before the lines from years of frowning and distaste for how people lived their lives settled in. Now, years later, there was nothing attractive about this frail body driven by disdain and contempt.

"I just thought maybe I could help." Then I tried to work her for some info that could put this situation in perspective. I didn't care much about her or how she would react, but what I could find out about Missy was important. "Is Missy planning on coming home today? We were supposed to go out together for a friend's fortieth birthday party."

"Well, I'm quite sure that she has no plans on joining you for some fortieth birthday party. She is absolutely livid and rightly so. How could you?" She hissed the words as she spoke.

"What have I done that's so bad?" I asked incredulously. "A friend of mine needed some help. No, my best friend needed help and I had to be there for him. She knows that."

"So your friendship with an old prep school buddy is more important than your relationship with your wife and family." The venom shot out with the intent to maim. "I told her you were no good." She looked away from me to my son, who was trying to act uninterested but was riveted to the dialogue in front of him. He looked up at me when Grandma uttered her assessment of me being no good and was obviously trying to resolve in his mind what to do with this information. I tried not to flinch, not react in a bad or embarrassing way and as I thought through what to say in response, I could not find the words to respond.

Grandma settled that by saying to Mickey, "Come on Mickey, we're going home. Your mom needs you."

Mickey looked up at me for direction and I decided that this was not the time to do battle with Grandma. I gave him a hug, which he appeared to genuinely appreciate, hugging back, which he usually didn't do and said, "Don't worry, Mickey. It'll all be all right. Go with Grandma and I'll talk to you later today or tomorrow. Tell mom I said hi and I love you."

Grandma had had enough and said, "Get in the car, Mickey."

I let go and said to Grandma, "I'll call Missy later today."

She wasn't in the mood for any more conversation, let alone any effort toward reconciliation. "She doesn't need to talk to you or see you for a long, long time. Stay out of our lives and we'll all be better off."

With that, she and Mickey pulled out of the parking lot, leaving me alone and confused. What was I supposed to do now? When could I talk to Missy and patch things back up? Where should I go? Home seemed like the only logical alternative and I self consciously looked around the parking lot to see who might have noticed the row with Grandma, and importantly, who would notice that I was now one of those fathers without a family. I had seen divorced men show up for games alone and slink off into their cars after the games as their wives took their children home with them. I never thought I could or would be in that situation. Right now, I felt like going home to my empty house and hiding from the world for a while. Sounded like the best plan I could come up with and, with the other players' parents milling about, the sooner the better.

When I got home, I tried calling Missy at her parents' house, hoping to catch someone other than Missy's mom answering the phone. Alas, the answering machine spoiled my advances and not knowing what to say, I hung up before the beep offering me the chance to leave a message. It was a folly I would repeat a half-dozen times again over the course of the weekend, but concerned I left messages the other times I called -- sadly with the same result.

CHAPTER FOURTEEN

Monday morning took forever to arrive. I looked forward to getting back to my routine in the office and the challenge of trying to beat the markets. My calls to Missy at Grandma's on Saturday afternoon and Sunday became simple grovelings. "Please return my call. Would like to talk things out and see you and the kids. Hope all is well." What else can you say to an answering machine that you knew would be erased before Missy ever got a chance to hear the message?

Exhausted and stressed, I slept for eleven hours Saturday night, missed church Sunday and felt more tired when I woke up than when I went to sleep. Sunday dragged on as well, but at least I had a New York Giants game to put on in the background and the stack of research from Tina to pore over.

When I walked into the office on Monday morning at 8:00 AM, Tina was the first to mention it.

"You look like hell. What happened to you this weekend? Did you stay over and take the Sunday night red-eye instead?"

"No, just had trouble getting back on East Coast time. You know it's always been easier for me going there than coming back." She, of course, looked bright and chipper in her fall outfit of khaki skirt, brown sweater with golden and red leaves embroidered into it. She wore her casual and what she called her most comfortable Doc Martens and had her shoulder length red hair pony-tailed with what I had come to learn was a scrunchy. All in all, it was a very professional and classy look. She served as a model for the other female employees, who generally took their cue from not only how she dressed, but how she acted toward me and current or prospective clients.

"Are you ready to go over your calendar, yet?" she asked, a visibly concerned look on her face which, I assumed, was from the dark circles around my baggy eyes. I looked like hell and I knew it, but there wasn't anything I could do. Besides, I did not and do not believe in missing work because "I'm not feeling well."

"Go ahead, shoot," I said, mentally trying to get up for the day.

Without looking at her notepad, Tina said, "You wanted to go over the markets and the outstanding buy and sell orders with the traders at 9, Mr. Sowers from the SEC will be here at 10:30. You have lunch scheduled with your friend Sam, the lawyer, and the rest of your afternoon looks pretty clear. Anything else you want me to do?"

My heart skipped a beat when she mentioned the SEC. I hadn't forgotten about it, but was trying to focus on what the markets had in store for the day and week ahead. It was in baseball terms a changeup which had me off balance from the moment it left Tina's lips.

"Right" I said. "We'll probably want to have Mr. Sowers meet me in my office. Make sure we have some coffee available and let me get caught up now on the paper and e-mails. Anything important or out of the ordinary?" I was trying to make everything seem normal.

"Well," Tina hesitated. "You did have two calls this morning. One from your friend Roger wanting to know if you've made your mind up and one from Missy saying she'll be out of town for a week. She is going to your summer place on Long Beach Island, but do not disturb her. She wanted you to know in case the alarm went off." Waiting for my reaction or response and not getting one, she added,

"Is everything okay at home? She sounded upset and usually never calls here before eight."

To be honest, I wasn't sure how things stood at home, or what was left of my home life. The lack of communication from Missy made it pretty clear though how Missy viewed things and I wasn't very excited about the prospects. I had never before been faced with the scenario being played out before me and I felt like a detached observer watching it happen to me, not knowing how to react.

"I'm sure things will be fine. Missy just needed a break."

"So the trip out west didn't win you any brownie points at home," she said trying to sound lighthearted.

"No" I said trying to force a smile. "Rolled a gutter ball on that one I'd say, nothing that can't be fixed. I'll pick up the spare." I still amazed myself at the stupid analogies that just came into my head at the most awkward and sometimes inappropriate moments. A shrink would have to say it was a kind of defense mechanism. Whatever it was, it game me a chuckle and I patted myself on the back for my wit and decided that I had said enough for now.

"Okay, back to the salt mines you go" I facetiously ordered, and set about getting ready for the day, reviewing news stories on the Bloomberg and checking e-mails.

"And what about Roger?" Tina asked as she began to walk away. "He said something about needing an answer."

"He'll get it," I barked at her, not in the mood to face that issue now. "I'm sorry," I quickly added. "Didn't mean to snap at you, Tina. Yes, I will answer him, I promised him by tomorrow. Not to worry. Now, off you go." I rarely snapped at Tina and she knew it, so she had the decency to leave it alone and said,

"I'll try to keep the brokers at bay and let you get some work done," closing my door behind her as she left.

Some days you can consume and digest reams of information quickly and efficiently, but this day wasn't one of them, so when Tina knocked on my door at nine to tell me it was time for the meeting, I didn't feel very prepared. As a result, I let my trusted lieutenants; two traders and my protégé analyst do most of the talking. Thankfully, the markets were quiet, none of the companies we owned had made any significant market-moving announcements and the meeting was over in about fifteen minutes.

Now all I had to do was get ready for the SEC examiner's meeting at 10:30. As I left the conference room, I asked Tina to put together a compilation of all trading activity in my personal account in the past two years and copies of my last two monthly statements.

"No problem. Will get right on it," Tina said and buried her head back into her computer, her fingers working their magic on the keyboard as she answered.

I went back into my office, surveyed the setup and tried to decide how and where to face Mr. Sowers. The love seat couch and sitting area seemed too informal to me and I decided that one of the leather chairs across from my desk would be most appropriate. It would also keep me close to my financial world of quote machines, Bloomberg terminal and phones enabling me to quickly summon anyone or anything that might be needed in an instant.

But this was going to be a simple visit, after all, wasn't it? Roger had said that the one issue the SEC was sniffing around was my purchase of Spindletop, and now in my briefcase I had a signed confidentiality agreement that I would show him if needed.

Piece of cake, I reassured myself. Much ado about nothing.

CHAPTER FIFTEEN

M r. Sowers arrived at 10:23 AM and declined Tina's offer for coffee, use of restrooms or phones and sat waiting in the reception area for the three minutes it took me to get off the phone with an analyst who was writing bad things about one of our larger holdings.

He was still sitting with his tan trench coat on, hands resting on the handle of his worn leather brief case when I came out to introduce myself and bring him into my office.

Mr. Sowers didn't give a first name, but presented me with his business card instead of a welcoming handshake as he rose. A quick glance at the card indicated that I was in the presence of Stanford T. Sowers, Senior Examiner of the Securities and Exchange Commission. I offered to have his coat hung up in the closet by Tina, which he politely and curtly accepted. Finally releasing his briefcase and placing it on the floor, he took off his London Fog which Tina hung in the nearby closet.

"Why don't you follow me to my office, Mr. Sowers," I suggested.

He nodded his assent and followed me down the hall to my office. I indicated that he would probably be most comfortable in one of the two leather chairs facing my desk and offered fresh coffee or soda.

"A glass of water would be fine, thank you," came the reply. I buzzed Tina for a glass of ice water and asked him to sit down.

"So what do I owe the pleasure of your visit, Mr. Sowers?" I asked, trying to be cheerful and amiable, without the slightest hint of worry or concern. "It's not time for our regular SEC visit again already is it? We just had one about a year and a half or two years ago, I believe."

"No, this visit does not concern your firm, Mr. Morris. We are investigating the First American Insurance Corporation in California and your own personal trading transactions." He paused, either waiting for effect or to see how I'd react. I wasn't wild about his choice of the word transactions, as Roger had only mentioned my Spindletop stock purchases as being under scrutiny. Mr. Sowers continued, "You are, I believe, friendly with Roger Mason Maydock, the CEO of First American?"

Honesty had to be the best policy. So I decided to let him know I would do anything I could. "Very well, actually we went to prep school together, were roommates, have remained close and I just saw him last week."

"Yes, we are aware of that," Mr. Sowers said flatly.

This was not a good sign, I thought. How did they know and why did they care if I had seen Roger last week. I assumed I was supposed to fill in a few more blanks to prove my undying devotion to the sanctity of the SEC. I continued:

"He wanted some advice and actually offered me a position as a consultant to his firm. He feels that I would be helpful in reviewing the policies and procedures at one of his firm's subsidiaries." It sure sounded like I was the above board perfect consultant to me as I said it and hoped it would sound as good to Mr. Sowers as it did to me

"Did Mr. Maydock mention that we were investigating numerous areas of his firm, its pricing policies and internal controls as they relate to the securities transactions of its employees and subsidiaries?"

"No, not exactly" was the truthful response and the one that I offered.

"Did he also mention that we are reviewing whether or not he violated securities laws by providing material non-public information to his friends, employees and people that may work for or at some of his firm's subsidiaries?"

"Not exactly" I answered again and wished that I had (1) a better vocabulary and (2) a sense of where this interrogation was heading.

"Well, honestly, we have been investigating First American for over a year and some of the most questionable activities include the pricing policies used by First American and its subsidiaries as well as potential violations of insider trading statutes. We also wanted to discuss why it is that you have purchased the shares of a half dozen companies in your personal account in the past two years. We are especially interested in the trading activity of Spindletop Energy and noticed that you had purchased 5,000 shares of the company's stock about three months ago."

"Yes, I did" I said, letting out a hopefully silent sigh.

"And why did you purchase those shares?" Mr. Sowers asked.

"Actually, Roger Maydock suggested to me in a casual conversation that I should take a look at it, and after doing some research, thought it might be a worthwhile investment opportunity. It's too small for any of the client funds that we manage here, as we are a large and mid-cap shop. So, I bought the shares for myself." It was the truth and I relayed my explanation with confidence.

"Did he tell you that First American was the largest lender to Spindletop and that he or his firm may be in possession of material non-public information?" The tone was not as pleasant as I would have liked and boarded on the accusatory.

"Absolutely not. I have, however, subsequently learned of First American's significant financial role with Spindletop." I wondered if I should go further and decided quickly that I could either work with Mr. Sowers or suggest that any further questioning be done in the presence of my lawyer. I decided to hope for the good cop and offered, "Actually, this past week I signed a confidentiality agreement regarding Spindletop as a result of my meeting with senior officers of First American."

Mr. Sowers leaned forward and took his pen away from his pad of paper, genuinely interested in this latest revelation. "And why did you do that?"

"Because the officers at First American have asked me to serve as a consultant to their firm and as part of those discussions felt that I needed to be aware of their role as a lender to Spindletop and the status of certain negotiations that have transpired recently with the company." Take a bite out of that one, Mr. Sowers, I said to myself.

"Very interesting" Mr. Sowers remarked, leaning back and thinking to himself probably about his next move.

Mr. Sowers reached into his briefcase and pulled out a stapled set of papers. He looked at it for a second and then leaned forward to hand it to me.

"Now tell me, Mr. Morris, why did you purchase the shares of the four companies highlighted in yellow on the pages before you?"

The pages in question were a computer printout of all trades done in my personal account, my wife's account and children's trust accounts for the past two years. Highlighted in yellow were four other companies that Roger had "suggested" I take a look at. Roger hadn't mentioned anything about these companies being involved with First American and I didn't quite know what to say. While I considered my response, Mr. Sowers tightened the noose a bit around my now perspiring neck. "Did Mr. Maydock ever recommend that you purchase any of these companies?"

"No, he just suggested that they might be worth looking into."

"Have you ever paid Mr. Maydock a fee or compensation for investment recommendations?"

"No, I haven't," I answered quickly.

"Has Mr. Maydock ever suggested that he would like to be compensated for his investment ideas?"

"No, he hasn't."

"Has Mr. Maydock ever disclosed that he may have been in possession of material non-public information regarding any of these companies?"

"Alright, I think I've had about enough of this." I was getting fed up with the Spanish Inquisition routine and wanted to let him he had gone too far. "Is the SEC trying to stop college buddies from swapping stock tips!?! Because that's gonna put a few thousand guys out of work in New York City." I said it facetiously, but as I heard myself put the situation in those terms, it did seem to border on the ridiculous.

Mr. Sowers however did not see the humor in my response. He looked at me sternly and said, "No, not all college buddies. Just the ones where we can be certain that one of these so-called 'college buds' does have inside information. That's the case we have here."

All of a sudden I didn't see the humor in the situation anymore. This was getting unpleasant and I felt like maybe I shouldn't have jousted with Mr. Sowers. "Before we go any further, I am getting the feeling that I may want to have a lawyer present before I answer any more questions."

"I don't think that will be necessary," Mr. Sowers said with a little less of a nasty tone, one that was almost conciliatory.

"We're almost done," he said.

I breathed a deep fresh gulp of air for what seemed like the first time in our meeting.

"Tell me about the consulting opportunity that First American offered you." he asked.

Now that was a change of pace, I thought. It took me a second to refocus. "First American has offered me a consulting job to advise them and review the operations of one of their subsidiaries, Ocular Asset Management." I didn't know if the SEC had looked into Ocular and just how deeply they were investigating First American, but I was happy the conversation had for now drifted away from my personal securities transactions.

"And has Mr. Maydock tried to pressure you into accepting the consulting arrangement?"

"Well, yes, but I believe it is because of my experience in turn-around situations, knowledge of financing alternatives and because as the owner of my own company, I have more scheduling flexibility than other people or firms that he may have considered." That explanation seemed plausible in LA a few short days ago. I suddenly remembered the money that was being offered and thought it worth noting.

"First American has offered a very lucrative fee for this consulting engagement, so it's not like I'm being forced into it." But then again, money is a form of blackmail and remembers the comment about staying at the Airport Hilton versus the Park Hyatt. I looked back at Mr. Sowers to see where we were heading now.

"Here's the deal," he said, closing the cap on his pen. "We believe that there have been a number of Securities Act violations and that Mr. Maydock induced you to purchase securities in companies where he and his firm had material non-public information. You may or may not have been aware of First American's involvement with the companies in question, and as we have noted, your purchases of these companies is not inconsistent with your other personal transactions. Nevertheless, while you say that he has not asked for compensation and we could find no record of cash or checks written by you to Mr. Maydock, we believe that he will try to seek compensation from you in another form. Quite simply, we believe that he will attempt to induce you into acting in a manner that could subject you to securities law violations. We believe that by doing so, Mr. Maydock will attempt to insulate himself and First American from wrongdoing, but will use you as a puppet or a pawn, call it what you will, for a grander scheme."

I was flabbergasted and didn't know what to say.

"It is a unique situation and one that has been troubling us for some time. We at the SEC have been trying to figure out what First American's next move was going to be and how we were going to be able to find out whether they were violating securities laws. We know they are playing hardball with Spindletop Energy, which has contacted us to get our view of whether First American's tactics could be violations of securities laws."

"So, what do I have to do with all this?" I asked, somewhat lost in what had become a pretty scary look at the world through the SEC's eyes. Even worse, I had the sinking feeling that they were probably spot on in their analysis of Roger and First American. I didn't like the idea of being a pawn for Roger's play on Spindletop and decided that no amount of money was going to talk me into agreeing to accept the consulting job.

"Actually, you present us with a rather fortuitous situation," Mr. Sowers said, a slight wry smile forming in the corners of his mouth.

"I don't follow" I said, meaning it.

"We want you to take the consulting job. You can be our eyes and ears inside First American and Ocular."

Talk about feeling a body blow to the stomach that you didn't see coming. The oxygen I thought I had stored in my body vanished and I could feel my face and body lose touch with blood cells and all other necessary sources of life or energy.. I didn't have any interest in being Roger's pawn, as he put it. I had even less interest in being the rat who helped the SEC take down my best friend and his company.

"And if I say no, I'm not interested," I said faintly, still reeling from the blow.

"We would still have the matter of your potential violations of securities laws and insider trading statutes to discuss."

CHAPTER SIXTEEN

Roger was ecstatic when I called him later that afternoon to tell him that I was going to take on the consulting arrangement and would do what I could to find out what was going on at Ocular. I don't know what my decision ultimately would have been without my visit from Mr. Sowers, or if I hadn't had lunch with my best friend and lawyer Sam, who told me Missy had contacted an attorney about a trial separation, and who in turn had contacted him this morning. Missy wanted her lawyer to discuss with Sam, our children and visitation guidelines, on a lawyer to lawyer basis. "All very pleasant" Sam said, "Seems like a reasonable guy. So you didn't tell me the marriage was on the rocks. What happened?"

What a good question. What had happened and how had my life been turned so upside down in the span of what, 48 or 72 hours? It was all a blur. Sam told me that first and foremost, Missy was angling for the kids and the house. She wanted me out and soon so that this "situation" would be handled in a way that didn't disrupt the children's routines.

"Not a chance," was my quick response. "I am their father and intimately involved in their 'routine' as she put it. I'll fight that to the end."

"I figured you'd say that and said as much to her lawyer. You're more involved in your kid's lives than just about anyone I know." It was good to hear an impartial outsider's view of my parenting matched my own view.

I told Sam about my little visit from the SEC earlier in the day and how I was probably going to have to be in Las Vegas the following weekend. He said it probably wouldn't hurt my legal situation with Missy and the children if I had to go to Las Vegas, especially if the SEC was almost forcing me to go.

I wasn't inviting him to come along for the ride, but he offered a quick, "I'd love to go to Vegas with you, but we're having the Austin's over for dinner Saturday night and we have two football games Sunday morning. Have fun though, really."

Fun! The SEC was trying to pressure me to rat out my friend in case his firm was doing anything wrong. Roger was pressuring me to do some sleuthing of a firm he bought that wasn't following orders from the top and to top it all off, my wife wanted a trial separation and had taken my kids from me. What a blast!

After lunch I told Tina to get me a flight to Vegas on Thursday night returning Sunday. The last thing I wanted to do was hang out alone in a five bedroom, three and a half bath center hall colonial for a weekend. The dogs would be better off in a kennel anyway. It was no life for them to have a ten minute stint outside in the morning, put in a cage for the day until I got home and then a late dinner and poop before bed. They needed the kids and Missy to be around. Hell, I needed the kids and Missy around.

Tina did as she was told, didn't ask any questions, and could tell my situation wasn't very good and that I wasn't up for a discussion about my personal life. She did look at me sadly and told me that she wasn't very busy this week, so if there was anything I needed, she could put in some extra time if I wanted. Being pitied wasn't a good feeling, but at least she showed some concern for my mental health, unlike Sam, my friend the lawyer. From his tone you'd have thought I had lost a money clip, not a wife.

Sam had been more interested in the consulting agreement: "Pretty loose contract" was his instant analysis. Of my meeting with Mr. Sowers, "Sounds serious; better do what they want." Sam was one of the few lawyers I had ever met who was able to make a quick decision and that was one of the reasons I respected and liked him.

I buried myself in my Bloomberg and various research reports, trying not to think about my current state of affairs. There is nothing like hard work to clear your head. Without fail every time I checked the prices of my investments on the Bloomberg clarity returned, at least in that world. Spindletop was inching its way higher again. Didn't these people know the company was on the verge of bankruptcy? Then again, I thought, if it weren't for my little trip to LA last week I wouldn't have known either. Its scary how little investors really know about the companies they own and how much companies are able to withhold from an unsuspecting public.

Tina popped in on a regular basis to offer help and to make sure I was 'Okay' and effectively warded off unwanted calls from brokers with great ideas. After all, they had these great ideas no less than ten times a day. She did let calls through from my buddies, who were trying to set up in no particular order, golf games, dinners and a card game. We had a monthly card game that actually occurred three times a year. It was a running joke with us because we had a blast when we played and wanted to do it more frequently. However with kids, wives and social duties, we had trouble getting the three or four nights a year that we did. But it was fun to think about and plan and it looked like we had a chance of pulling one off in about three weeks. As for golf, I used my standard line: see you at the course in late fall.

"Come on Joe, you know I have a sixty degree rule. If it's not gonna be sixty and I can't wear shorts, I'm not playing golf I'm getting ready to lace up the old skates." I tried to sound jovial and upbeat, but I could hear in my voice that my heart just wasn't there. I only hoped my friends couldn't tell just how depressing my situation had become. Not one of them mentioned or even asked about Missy, which was odd. Did that mean that they already knew? We lived in a small town, but even I didn't know where things stood until lunchtime today!

I went back to checking my e-mails and when I saw one from FlyKarnFly my heart raced. I'd forgotten that this was the e-mail address I had given her, but as I thought about it, I realized I must have decided that I didn't want her conversing with me from home. Like it mattered now. Opening it up, I saw that it was her upcoming schedule of flights for the next three weeks and that I had been added to her list of friends. There was no personalized note, just a global: "Here are my upcoming trips and layovers. If anyone will be in any of these areas, give me a buzz." Scanning the itinerary, I couldn't believe my eyes. After trips from Cleveland to Houston and Newark she was flying to Las Vegas on Friday night and had a layover until Sunday night. I was going to be there Thursday night and through the weekend.

I started typing a response and then stopped myself. "What the hell do you think you're doing?" asked my guilt ridden self-conscious. "But you are a free agent now" came the rejoinder from the other side of my brain. I reminded myself that I was going out to Vegas for Roger, for the SEC and who knows who else by Thursday. First things first, I told myself. After all, Roger was going to be out there and wanted to hit the tables together. Hell, we had all weekend.

"I am going to be in Vegas this weekend. Sightseeing or dinner interest you?" I sent it before I could stop myself and wondered how soon Karen would see it. How would she react? I'm sure I didn't impress her too much as I stumbled out of the gate like a two year-old thoroughbred, green and not knowing just what to do or say. "Heck" I said to myself, "nothing ventured, nothing gained." I immediately thought about Roger, as it was a line he would have used. But more importantly, why did he have me followed or tailed or spied on when I was in LA?

I got rid of the rest of my emails, saved the one from Karen and went back to the world of trying to make money. Tina interrupted me about a half hour later and said, "Your friend Roger is on the phone, want to talk or should I deflect this one?" As I pondered whether or not to talk, I felt sudden pangs of guilt for not picking him up immediately. After all we'd been through, I still owed him that.

"No, I'll take it" I told her. I tried to smile and said, "Thanks" as she closed the door behind her. Line two was the only one flashing, so I knew where Roger was parked.

"What's up, Rog?" I said, false cheer in my voice but the best I could manage.

"Just trying to get logistics taken care of." Roger had his list ready and ran through it quickly. "At the Ocular board meeting tomorrow, I'll lay the consulting agreement on them. They'll squawk, but can't stop it. My PR guys will have to do a Press Release, will fax you a draft tonight. I hear from Tina and Paula that you get into Vegas on Thursday night in time for a late dinner. I've got us staying at the Belfair because someone I can't mention owes me one and they know how to treat you right. On Friday morning, the car picks you up at eight to head to Ocular; I'm letting you sleep in, so no questions. I'll be up at five not knowing what to do with myself for three hours, so I'll already be there. I'll introduce you around and let you get started. I can't stand being in the same room with Terry Burroughs, so I'm going to get back to LA for the day and come back on Saturday afternoon. We can have dinner and hit the tables Saturday night. Maybe go down the road for old time's sake. My treat. Whaddya think? Sound like a plan?"

It amazed me that he was able to breathe as he rushed through his plans and itinerary. Still living and talking at a pace that proved you can't take the city out of the boy. Everything about the plan seemed workable. The wrinkle about his leaving town Friday gave me pause and I thought, hey, maybe I could hook up with Karen. The comment about heading down the road was a reference to a trip we had taken to the fabled Mustang Ranch an hour outside of Vegas on our cross-country trip the summer after we graduated from college. It was a great plan until we found out that while you could get just about anything you wanted from a woman sexually, between the two of us we only had enough money to have one of us taught the ways of the world. We pooled our money and sent Roger in on the reconnaissance mission while I drank the complimentary beers at the bar, playing the role of a drunken eunuch to a T.

Roger, impatient as always, interrupted my memory. I didn't know how long I had paused, and he asked again "Well, whaddya think? Sound like a plan?"

Flashback over, I mumbled, "Yeah, sounds good, except for the trip down memory lane. Been there, done that."

"No" Roger corrected and joked. "We've been there, but it was only I that done that."

"Nevertheless," I said, "No interest." Time to change the subject. "My flight gets in at 7:35 PM. Will want to check in and freshen up. Dinner around 8:30 sounds good, if all goes well with the friendly skies" I chuckled to myself about how friendly the skies had been or could be.

"Sounds great, J. Thomas. I'll be waiting in my room for your call and will reserve us a table in their best restaurant. Can't tell you how great it's going to be to be working together. Missy okay with the deal?" The question was innocent enough but found an unintended mark and hurt. I lied, "Yeah, no problem there. She thinks I could use the break." Well, a half-truth was better than a lie, wasn't it?

"I'll fax you a copy of the Press Release. The guys say it's almost done. Can't wait to see you, buddy. And don't forget, 'While the cat's away......'"

"The mice will play." It didn't sound very nice from my end and I was tiring of this game. "See you Thursday night then."

We said our good byes and I buzzed Tina that I'd had enough for the day. Told her to hold all my calls and let me concentrate on work for a bit. No, I wouldn't need her to stay late and thanks again for the offer. The trading day was winding down, my wife had left me and the SEC was on my tail. Sounded like a bad country music tune in the making and it felt like months had passed in the past week. With the way things were going, I was sure Tuesday was going to be a blast.

I started packing up some research to read for the evening, as I sure wasn't accomplishing much at the office. Took a last look at my Bloomberg messages and e-mail and saw a response from FlyKarnFly.

"Are you following me? Can't believe we're going to be in Vegas at the same time. Are you on my flight? Would love to get together. I get in at 7:35 PM on Friday. I'm up for dinner and the sights!! Can't wait. Fondly, Karen."

Talk about coincidence, same flight just a day later. "Fondly" I thought, good choice. Respectful, not a trite "love" when we couldn't be there. Too overused by far too many. I didn't believe in using it except for oldest and dearest friends and family. All in all, it was a mature and encouraging response. I clicked save on the e-mail and thought; maybe Tuesday won't be so bad.

CHAPTER SEVENTEEN

It wasn't Tuesday that all hell broke loose in the markets, but Wednesday. Why did it always happen when I was trying to get out of town for a business trip or vacation? For the Crash of '87 I was at a utility conference at The Breakers in Florida and that seemed to set the stage for my investment career. Always trying to assert damage control from afar.

The event that spooked the market on this Wednesday was a terrorist attack on the Linden Cogeneration facility off the New Jersey Turnpike. It was the first terrorist event in the U.S. in months and complacency had returned to the markets. People had felt safe again in their homes. Even the U.S. Government had lowered the ongoing terror alert status a notch to yellow just a week earlier.

The attack was amazing in its simplicity. In broad daylight in front of hundreds of witnesses, seven rocket propelled grenades were fired from a van parked innocently enough on the shoulder of the New Jersey Turnpike. The van drove off into a confused traffic jam and onto the streets of Elizabeth before anyone could figure out what was going on. The NJ Turnpike was shut down for precautionary measures as the fire at the facility was contained, due to the fear that the blaze could spread to the surrounding refinery operations.

The missiles were fired at 9:17 AM, at the tail end of normal commuter traffic, but at a time when the markets were getting ready to open. The New York Stock Exchange governors met briefly to decide whether or not to open the markets on time and after meeting with the specialist community decided that a half hour delay was appropriate. The specialists opined that stocks could open down seven to nine percent in the absence of better or at least more information.

Over the counter stocks looked even worse, and the NASDAQ officers went along with the New York Stock Exchange decision to delay the opening as well. All eyes turned to CNN and CNBC to get live shots of the fire in New Jersey and to wait for official word from somebody about what happened, why and what was going to be done about it.

I pulled my investment team together to put together a list of what stocks to buy and at what price, reminding them that these crazy markets were what we were paid to react to. The junior people were scared, wanted to be on the phones with loved ones, but most circuits were busy anyway. So we set up a battle plan for the markets. Sell our defense issues if they spiked up more than 20 % as they were nearing full valuations. Hold the golds and energy stocks at least initially. And when they creamed the consumer stocks, the Disney's, hotels and retailers, buy 'em for at least a trade. Keep an eye on the banks, I said, and if we have any money left, we might want to buy some Citibank.

I was drenched in sweat as I dismissed the troops, leaned back in my leather chair and broke one of my unwritten rules. I lit up a cigarette in the office, thought maybe I shouldn't, but decided what the heck and opened a window to let some of the cool fresh air in. I wondered which way the wind was blowing and if we would soon smell the smoke from the Linden fire, thirty miles to our north.

The smoke from the World Trade Center attack had enveloped the area in about an hour's time, and I couldn't forget how many friends had been crushed and burned in that horrific event. The world would never be the same and today was just another reminder.

Focusing back to CNN and CNBC on the two televisions in my office, spot power outages were occurring in the Northern New Jersey/Newark area. Newark airport had been closed temporarily as a safety precaution and the tunnels and bridges to New York were closed. Scenes of dozens of fire trucks rushing to the area were on CNN, while CNBC had aerial footage of the fire from its NBC affiliate helicopter, propitiously hovering in the area because of its regular morning traffic report.

Initial reports put the number of dead or missing at between five and fifteen people and I wondered why they even guessed at such an early stage. Imagine having friends or relatives working at the facility and hearing the unemotional estimate of 5 to 15. To top it off, the reporter emphasized that the bigger problem was if the pipelines and refinery cat crackers were damaged, which provided gasoline and heating oil for much of the New York metropolitan area.

Game plan in place, I got on the phone and started to do what everyone else was doing, trying to touch base with my kids. I knew Missy didn't want to hear from me, but I wanted my children to know I was all right, not traveling into the city today and that I loved them. Unfortunately, the phones were jammed, my e-mail appeared to have jammed or frozen, I never knew what the appropriate technical term was and I switched tactics to cell phone and Blackberry. My cell phone had the same reaction, not a chance. "Your call could not be completed as dialed, please check the number and dial again." Alas, my trusty Blackberry at least let me send out e-mails and I sent notes to my sons, Tommy and Michael and daughter Kathleen. I promised Michael that I'd come see his soccer practice tonight, told Tommy away at prep school that I loved him and would try to call tonight, and to Kathleen that I had fun at her class and that I missed her dearly. I signed all "Love, Dad," and thought to myself, now that's when it means something. I wished they were all with me right now.

The markets did open at 10:00 AM, as it appeared for now to be a random act of terrorism. It was however, an ugly opening, as the sea of red flashing on my screen meant millions of people were all of a sudden farther away from those vacations I tried to make. It hurts to see so much wealth disappear, and while I had about fifteen percent cash in most clients' portfolios, it wasn't going to help much with the other eighty-five percent down my trusty up to the minute computer was able to calculate the 4.6%.

It took about a half-hour after the official opening for all major New York Stock Exchange listed stocks to have their first trade, as the specialists were swamped with sell orders and chose to post order imbalances instead of opening individual stocks on very little volume. There just weren't enough buyers yet so they indicated their stocks down by a wide margin to entice investors like me to put together bids where we would buy a block of stock.

We spent 10% or two-thirds of our clients' cash by 11:00 and while some stocks drifted slightly lower from their first trades, the opening prices were mostly the lows of the day and by noon the markets were rallying big off their lows. Now down 3%, some semblance of normalcy was returning to the world and it appeared that no further ramifications of the terrorist grenade attack were unfolding. There were even rumors circulating that the attack was carried out by a group of disgruntled former employees, the subject of workforce reductions a month earlier. Newark Airport remained closed for the time being, stretches of the NJ Turnpike remained cordoned off to all but emergency traffic, while the bridges and tunnels were being reopened with heightened security and LaGuardia and Kennedy Airports were open and operating at one to three hour delays.

As the news services updated the airport situation, I wondered for the first time about my trip to Vegas and whether it was still going to happen. It would be a perfect excuse not to spy on Ocular, but it would be nice to get away from the problems at home and stay out of the social spotlight for a change. I couldn't recall what charitable dinners or cocktail parties we were supposed to attend this weekend, but I was sure there had to be some. It seemed every weekend there were at least two or three great causes that we absolutely had to be a part of. "After all, so and so is on the Board or Dinner Committee and they invited us to such-and-such so we really owe them." It was one part of my life I was happy to be without for a weekend. Of course, the fact that Missy and I were not going to be there would only lend credence to whatever rumors were already spreading about our marriage situation, but so what. Let them gossip. If there was going to be a new chapter in my life, it was going to be my chapter and I was going to write it the way I wanted to.

The day wore on and the markets continued to work their way higher, though still down 1.5% for the day. I took a glance at my personal holdings and saw that they were down about 3% on the day. Pretty standard stuff so I tried to take it in stride. The companies I owned in my personal account were riskier than the ones I owned in client accounts, generally had more debt and had more market volatility. If you could stand the short term swings and pain it usually meant better returns in the long run. As I scrolled through the companies one by one, I noticed that Roger's stocks, which I affectionately called Roger's Ramjets because they often flew higher, all seemed to be down more than the rest. I couldn't calculate exactly how much his picks from the past were down, but most seemed to be down 5% or more with a few down in excess of 10%. Spindletop had not escaped the carnage and was down 9%. I wondered if news was leaking out. Boy, Roger must be having fun today, I thought. I perversely felt like calling Roger and saying, "Live by the sword" and see if he would finish the saying, but decided that would be too cruel a joke to play. Maybe I'd use it in Vegas this weekend.

Tina came in at 3:00 PM, plopped herself down in the leather chair in front of my desk and asked seriously, "How do you do it?"

I didn't have a clue what she was talking about. She hardly ever sat down and talked. It was usually just business banter between us and though extremely close in a business sort of way, we had totally separate lives. She never plopped herself in one of the chairs in front of my desk. "What do you mean?" I asked, clueless as to what she was talking about.

"Well the world's gone crazy, terrorists attack less than 30 miles from here and you take it all so calmly. Everyone else in the office is frantically trying to make sure their families are OK; they're worried about their friends and family and to you today was what you called it, just another buying opportunity. Don't get me wrong, everyone appreciates how you took charge and they are amazed that you pulled off another great move for clients, but people are starting to wonder if you have ice water running through your veins."

I still wasn't sure where she was heading. "Is that a compliment or a criticism?"

"Well, both I guess. Do you realize that most businesses have decided to shut down early today so that people can be with their families? Schools have almost all closed early, and most...no...all of us are wondering what we should do."

It hit me hard. "I'm so sorry. I totally spaced and it didn't even occur to me. Absolutely! Tell everyone to go home and get their kids or do whatever they have to do. We don't need to do any more trades today and we can reconcile trade tickets tomorrow morning. Send everyone home. I'm so sorry." I meant it. I tried to be a compassionate boss and make sure people enjoyed working for me, but sometimes I got so wrapped up in the investing side that the personal side went lacking. I felt lower than I had in years, not only had I let my wife down, but now my loyal employees as well. What a schmuck. I thought.

"Please apologize to everyone for me. I'll have a meeting tomorrow to thank everyone for today and to say I'm sorry if I offended anyone. I've had a lot on my mind." It wasn't much of an excuse, but it was true.

"I know. Sam told me about Missy. I'm so sorry." Tina looked as if Missy had broken up with her as well and I thought I could see her eyes welling up. And thanks Sam, I thought for keeping a secret.

"Don't worry" I reassured her. "It'll all work out for the best. Things always do. You just need to have a little faith some times." I sounded more like Missy than me when I said it and hoped it was true.

"But you two seem so right for each other," she lamented.

"Don't worry. Everything will be fine. She'll be gone for a week or two and then realize what a fool she was for leaving this hunk of good looks." I was out of character, but trying to defuse the situation and keep it from getting all too maudlin. If I let Tina keep it up, I'd be crying too.

She chuckled, sniffled and smiled all in the course of a few seconds and got up to go.

"I'll go tell the troops to go home. I'm sure they'll appreciate it. You're not such a bad guy after all." She smiled more broadly. "I can still stay if you need me to" she offered as she opened the door.

"No thanks. I'll be fine. I need you the most when I'm out of town and you're the one running this place. You know that, don't you?" It was the truth and she knew it, but I felt she needed to hear it.

"You're the best," she said as she closed the door. No, I thought, you're the best.

I went back to my world of Bloomberg news and responding to emails, which had now returned to normal. I had 78 emails thus far and more than a dozen from friends making sure I was all right. Usually in a day I would get one or two from friends at the most. As I scrolled through and responded, I noticed one from my son, Tommie, away at school. He wrote:

"Dad, Hope all is well. Heard about the terrorist strike. Everyone is talking about it at school. Glad to hear you're OK. What's up with Mom? She sounded weird on the phone Sunday night and even more detached last night. Everything OK between you two?"

Maturing faster than his years, he could sense something was up and probably noticed it before I did. I answered back.

"Tommy, Thanks for the note. Mom's going through a tough time and needs some space. It will all work out. Don't worry. Love, Dad."

I moved on to the others on the list, said thanks for your concern. There was one from Kathleen already.

"Dad, Home from school early. Thanks for the update. Thought you were still in town. Grandma, the witch, won't let us call. I'm fine, but Tommie's pretty sad. He really appreciated you being at the game. P.S. He doesn't have practice tonight. Can't wait to see you. Rescue me!! Love and kisses, Your Kitty Kat Kathleen."

Well, it was good to know my children hadn't been poisoned against me. At least not yet. I decided that when I got back from Vegas, I was going to pick them up from school and have them live with me. What gave Missy the right to take the kids, leave them with Grandma the Witch--Good name Kathleen!—and then head out of town. I made a note to call Sam and discuss my plan before I got thrown in jail. I had no idea what my rights were.

Toward the end of the stream of messages I saw FlyKarenFly had sent me another email. Opening it, she wrote, "If all goes well in the next day or so, I should still make Vegas. So far it looks like some delays in Newark, but the airline is hoping for flights to be back on schedule soon. They aren't changing any crew schedules as of yet. Keep you posted. Karen."

I wasn't sure how to respond and decided at this point there wasn't anything to say. We'd just have to wait and see what happened with the world first.

I waited for the markets to close, called Sam, but found he had gone for the day as his office voice mail gave the night time greeting. I punched in his extension and left him a message to give me a call when he got a chance. I figured I was done for the day; no calls had come in for over an hour, so I decided maybe I should stop by the health club for my biweekly visit. Had to make that monthly fee get some use. Besides, what else could I do at 4:45 PM on a Wednesday? It was too early for dinner and I suddenly felt very alone.

Before I left, I looked at Karen's latest email again. I didn't know where she was staying, had no interest in Roger's spies keeping too close an eye on me, so I decided to set a time and place out of the way. Binion's, I thought, in old downtown Vegas was a great gambling hall. I'll go gamble for a bit and meet Karen for dinner, then go for a walk under the light show on Fremont.

I sent off a response to Karen: "Friday night dinner plan: Binion's Steak House at the Casino in downtown Vegas. I'll be waiting at the restaurant bar at 9:00 PM. Hope you can make it. If not, leave a message at the restaurant or email me before tomorrow afternoon if your plans change." I sent it off before I could change my mind. We would just have to see what Lady Luck had in store.

CHAPTER EIGHTEEN

L as Vegas has an aura and pulse to it like no other city in the world. I could feel it from the time the pilot said we were making our final descent. I wondered, "Should I hit the tables before dinner, get in the mood with a few hands of $10.00 blackjack just to get my feet wet?" I didn't have a lot of time before dinner with Roger, so I scolded myself to control the fever. There would be plenty of time for playing and I'd have to be sharp the following morning.

With all the excitement of Wednesday, the Press Release about First American's Ocular Investment Management subsidiary hiring "noted turnaround expert J. Thomas Morris" as a consultant caused barely a ripple. I chuckled to myself that Roger still had a sense of humor. The news wires didn't pick it up until 5:48 PM and most of the business world, including me, had gone home for the day. The skeleton crew at the news desks must have been on duty for nowhere had I ever been mentioned in print as J. Thomas Morris. A fact checker would have corrected the press release to Thomas J. or simply used Thomas Morris in this story. The release indicated that I would continue to manage the private investment company that I founded seven years ago with the wealth I had amassed turning around troubled companies. I wouldn't have put it that way, but Roger said it had the feel he needed, so I left it alone.

Roger promised he'd give me the play-by-play about the Board meeting with Ocular at dinner Thursday night and I could only imagine how happy Terry Burroughs was going to be to see me bright and early tomorrow.

As was becoming custom, Roger had a limo driver waiting for me at McCarran Airport with J.T. Morris on the placard. He was a clone of Jeff in Los Angeles. The driver was all business, no small talk:

"Any bags, Mr. Morris?" After we retrieved my black fold-over wardrobe case from the baggage claim, "The car's this way, Mr. Morris." A white limo awaited us outside in an area that appeared to be restricted and Jeff's clone put my bags in the trunk before saying, "Your driver Mark will take you straight to the Belfair. You are already checked in and Mark has your room keys."

Service to another level, I thought. Was this Roger playing "Can you top this" or was this the Belfair's doing? It didn't matter to me. It was fun being treated like a high roller or royalty. If they only knew that when I really got going the most I played for was $50.00 a hand, they'd call me a cab and say 'good luck, maybe you want to try next door'.

I marveled at the yellowish orange neon glow in the sky as we left McCarran Airport and headed to the Belfair and remembered the first time Roger and I drove to Vegas at night on our cross-country trip. The orange hue in the distant horizon started glowing more than thirty miles outside of town and got brighter as we approached until we entered the outskirts of the city and could barely tell that it was night. It was one of the most powerful memories I have of that trip or any trip. Even more so than the stint at the bar at the Mustang Ranch. I changed focus and checked end of the day stock quotes and e-mails, noting nothing of importance and nothing more from Karen.

As we pulled into the Belfair valet parking area, my bags were re-moved from the trunk and whisked away before I even had a chance to extricate myself from the limo. Mark, the no-talk driver, handed me an envelope with "J. Thomas Morris – Room P2501" typed across the front. Mark finally spoke with a hint of a German accent, "Your key will activate the private elevator just inside to your right. You are on the penthouse floor and your bags will be waiting for you."

As I exited the car, I noticed the valet parking area was missing the normal throng of casino patrons and realized this must be a sepa-rate entrance for the "I don't want to be seen or noticed" set.

I followed instructions, walked inside the golden brass door be-ing held open by a doorman doing his impression of a soldier outside an ambassador's residence. Not a look, a movement of the head or any sign of acknowledgement, the stone-faced doorman waited until I walked inside and then let go of the door and in one step stood astride the doorway as a military officer might, denying entrance to a post with his presence. I didn't see a gun at his side, but everything else about him said Black Belt, Special Forces and 'you don't want to fuck with me'

As promised, the empty lobby had a small private elevator door on the right. There was no one behind the polished mahogany re-ception desk on the left and no one at the expensive antique English ball and claw desk and chair. It was eerie how empty and silent the entrance area was.

I stepped into the elevator, noticed that there were three doors inside, inserted my key into the slot as directed and saw P2501 light up on the display. No floor keys to press, it knew where I was going. A silent, but lightning fast trip to the top and the door to my right opened into my room. No hallway, no fumbling with where to go. It was my room, or should I say palace in the sky. As I looked into my new digs, I could see the bright lights of Vegas straight ahead as my room gave a panoramic view of the strip. I noticed a black-carpeted stairway in the left corner, a full bar set up on the right mirrored wall, a bottle of Dom Perignon chilling in the glass ice bucket on the counter and plush leather chairs and sofas set up to view both downtown and the huge stone fireplace on my left. Naturally, the fireplace was on, though the room was a comfortable seventy degrees or thereabouts. A huge white bear rug served as the accent in front of the fireplace.

Wondering where I was to sleep, and not seeing any doors to the right on the wall with the bar I moved through the room to the left and saw a wooden mahogany door on the same wall as the fireplace.. Opening the door, I realized that the king sized bed before me was where I was to sleep, and entering the room noticed that the room shared the fireplace with the living room. The tone of the room was burgundy and very male. Dark red wallpaper lined the walls and burnt umber leather couch and chairs were situated in front of the fireplace. The room had the same full glass view of the strip and I thought that this had to be as nice a suite as I had ever seen. Had to cost thousands a night. I wondered what dirt Roger had on the owner to rate this kind of treatment. If First American was paying for this, I'd sell the stock immediately on principle alone.

The bathroom was an exercise in decadence, with white marble walls and floor, solid brass faucet and trimmings, a clear glass enclosed shower in the corner and a Jacuzzi situated in the center of the rear wall that would fit two to four of your best friends comfortably. I couldn't see the toilet, but noticed a door to the right and upon opening it found a walk in closet sized room with his and hers toilet and bidet. Brand new cellophane wrapped toiletries were lined up on the double faucet counter including a toothbrush, toothpaste, a futuristic aluminum shaver and a hot shaving cream dispenser. It was, without a doubt, what dreams are made of.

I went back into the bedroom, found the closet hidden in the mirrored wall and as I should have anticipated, found my wardrobe hung in the closet. Opening it, I got fresh clothes for dinner, khakis, white polo shirt and a navy blue blazer. I put my cell phone and Blackberry in my jacket, went back to the bathroom to freshen up and was interrupted by the phone. I noticed it was ringing not only in the bathroom on the wall, but in the water closet and bedroom as well. Good to know you would never miss a call. "J. Thomas!" Roger blurted when I answered. "It's me. Whaddya think? Pretty cool, huh?"

"Rog, I don't know what you've done or what you've promised, but this place has to cost a mint. You know I'm not a big gambler."

"Cool your jets. It's not a big deal. Someone owes me a few favors. I've steered some very big clients his way – Guys that know how to play and how to lose big. We're paying the casino rate of $89.00 per night. Hot shit, huh?"

He never ceased to amaze me. "Unbelievable" was the only response I could muster.

"So you ready to grab a bite. I've got a reservation for us in the five star restaurant downstairs reserved for the high rollers. Got that comped, too." He was bubbling with excitement, like a kid in the proverbial candy store that had just found a prize in his Cracker Jacks.

"Sure, but how do I get there?" I asked. I had gone one way to my room with not a lot of choices. As I looked around at my surroundings, I realized that the shower idea wasn't happening.

"Not to worry" he said. "Just push the elevator button and when you get to the bottom someone will be there to meet you and escort you to the restaurant. Piece of cake."

"Want to just meet downstairs?" I suggested.

"No can do, old buddy. The setup here is one party in the lobby at a time. Since we're in different rooms, we're different parties. Limo drivers can't even enter the drop off area if someone is in the lobby. Very, very secretive and private. There is a clientele that requires that level of privacy."

"You've got to be kidding. So is your room the same as mine, bear rug, double sided fireplace and a pool for a Jacuzzi?"

"Actually, you got the junior suite. I'm in the full suite and there's a Presidential penthouse that's twice the size of mine. I had a client stay there once and he invited me up for drinks. You ain't seen nothing."

"Why would anyone need all this?" I asked dumbfounded.

"You know what they say. The bigger they come…"

"The harder they fall."

"See you in about 15, okay?" Roger offered.

"I'll be there. Should I bring anything?"

"No, just your pen and your wits. I've got some notes and papers that ought to help you out at Ocular tomorrow."

"So I guess it's a working dinner then?"

"Nah, all work and no play…"

"Makes J. Thomas a dull boy?"

CHAPTER NINETEEN

Freshened up by a splash of water, I took a long look at the lights of Vegas from the living room window and thought about how many people came to this town of neon and promise with a dream of winning it big, only to leave town with less than they brought and most often, having lost far more than they ever planned to lose.

That's the way it was twenty something years ago when Roger and I hit town and lost almost all our money at the blackjack and craps tables. Just enough left for a trip to the Mustang and Roger's adventure. Of course, after our little trip to sin, we headed back to town with no money, desperately in need of a plan on how to get some cash so that we could gamble some more. Roger naturally came up with a plan. He knew I had one of my father's credit cards "for emergencies only" and since we both new my dad's idea of an emergency did not include running out of gambling money, we had to "improvise" were his exact words. How he came up with the idea I'll never know, but when we got back into town, he approached a young cab driver not much older than us and asked him if he wanted to make a little extra money and get a new set of tires for his cab at the same time. The cab driver, Mark, we learned, was very willing to play Roger's game. We went off to the local Chief's Auto Parts store, charged four brand new tires to my "emergency" credit card, top of the line Michelins, and in return got $150 in cold hard cash as a stake for one last shot at greatness at the tables. Of course we lost it all, but we had a blast joking about how we were "burning rubber," "double clutching" and "power sliding" through the night. To this day, it was as the most fun I ever had gambling.

Back in the present with a smile, I headed off to my private elevator and pushed the button. As promised, I was whisked down to the lobby, where I was greeted by Henri, who bowed graciously and said in a soft French accent, "Follow me Mr. Morris. Mr. Maydock is waiting for you at our finest restaurant just down this hallway."

We passed through a door in the lobby, down a carpeted hallway about eight feet wide with silver sconces hanging on the wall every ten feet or so. At the end of the hall, there was a tufted leather swinging door and pushing it open, Henri said, "Et Voila. Bon appetit," bowed and disappeared behind the swinging door.

A six-foot tall, slender maitre d' greeted me and said "This way, Mr. Morris" with what I thought was a Spanish accent. A different nationality at each stage of my journey through the restaurant. That was going overboard, but maybe it was just a coincidence. I was escorted to an almost completely private booth with frosted class barriers, so that no one could see in as they walked by until they were passing in front of the booth. Roger was in the last booth down the aisle on the right. As I stepped up and into the booth, the maitre'd pulled the red velvet curtains hanging from each pole defining the booth together to close us off from the world.

"J. Thomas, ole buddy, come on in, the water's warm." Roger was up to his old jovial self. The stock market damage to his stocks obviously hadn't dented his happy-go-lucky attitude. The only time he lost his cool was when he talked about Ocular and Terry Burroughs and that's what we were here to discuss. I wondered how long he would be in such good humor.

We exchanged pleasantries about our flights, the growth of Vegas, "remember when we came cross-country." We had lots of smiles and memories about the trip. Roger ribbed me "Remember that waitress at Denny's in Southern California. Had more tattoos than teeth and you were hitting on her!"

"Was not," I protested, but he was probably right. She did have a great figure. Back and forth we went, a preamble for the business neither of us seemed interested in discussing.

Roger started it, "So, about tomorrow."

"Ugh, and we were having so much fun." It had been more like our old get-togethers than the difficult one in L.A. just a week ago.

"Your limo will pick you up at 7:45 AM tomorrow morning and bring you to Ocular. I will already be there. We'll meet with Terry Burroughs at 8:00 AM in the conference room. They have an empty office set up and ready for you. Pretty small and cramped, but should do as a starter. A personal assistant has been assigned to you who knows all about Ocular's operations and has complete access to their database and can pull any files you need. And that includes personal transactions of all employees, if you know what I mean."

"But I'm not going to spend my time just going over personal stock trades. You could have anyone do that."

"I know. I know," Roger smiled. "But I swear there's something fishy going on there and I can't let him screw up the deal with Spindletop."

"I saw that the stock took it on the chin the last couple of days."

"Yeah, took a direct hit on the chin and the rest of our holdings got dinged a bit, but I'm not worried. Spindletop, however, is going to fall some more," Roger stated confidently, but with a hushed tone as if he knew something others didn't. "I think the shorts have gotten wind of the financial pressures facing Spindletop, and there's a chance Alan Abelson of Barron's just might do one of his hatchet jobs in this weekend's edition."

"Roger, you are gonna get yourself in trouble," I said and meant it. He was playing a dangerous game. "And I'm not going to be in the middle of it."

"You worry too much" Roger said casually. "Besides, I got you to protect yourself by signing that confidentiality agreement. If you don't trade on the inside skinny, they can't touch you."

Everything Roger did was on the edge and I hoped desperately that Roger was clean and that I would be able to keep the SEC happy, Roger happy and me out of jail.

"I'll bring my sharpest pencils," I said. "Oh, by the way," I said, "You told me I'd get the dirt on Terry Burroughs's reaction to me joining his firm as a consultant. How'd it go?"

"Perfect, just as I planned it. We're hiring this guy as a consultant to see if there are ways that Ocular could be run more efficiently and he said, 'You can't do that' and I said, 'Yes I can'.. Our lawyers said, 'Yes he can' and Terry's lawyer said, 'Yes he can.' He turned a shade of red more like your New Jersey tomatoes than any face I've ever seen. He called me a bastard, threatened to quit and sue me. I said I'd love nothing more, go for it, Terry, and he backed down. Pretty funny actually. He might have protection from interference on the investment side, but I still own his firm, or at least a lot more of it than he does."

"I understand why you two might not be best of friends at this point" I said, stating the obvious. "So, after the intro tomorrow, I won't see you again until Saturday night. Where do you want to meet?"

"Some place that's got great food and maybe a show. Don't worry, I'll take care of it and I might even bring us some dates."

"Don't you dare," I objected and meant it. Roger had rented us dates for dinner before and it was not something I cared to experience again. "I'm very serious Roger, and I mean this. Do not bring me a date. If you want to bring a date, go ahead. Do not bring one for me. Is that clear?"

"Yes, it's clear."

"Are we clear?"

"Yes, we're clear."

"How clear?"

"Crystal clear." We were stealing lines from Tom Cruise and Jack Nicholson in the movie "A Few Good Men," and enjoyed playing our parts.

"Besides," I added, "You never know. Maybe this old fart could get himself a date by Saturday night."

"Is Missy flying out?"

"No," I said.

"We could make a bet on this, but if you buy a date, that's cheating. Okay?" He loved to challenge me.

"No. No bets. And by the way, Missy left me last week. My little trip out west didn't go over too well. She'd split when I came back and wants to talk trial separation. She's out of the house."

"Wow, sorry to hear that." He seemed genuinely concerned and paused, and then changed his expression as he changed focus. "Heck, you know what they say. Women...can't live with 'em..."

"Can't live without 'em..."

CHAPTER TWENTY

I t was difficult to leave my luxurious surroundings Friday morning at 7:45, but at least I was able to enjoy a "room service" extravaganza of steak and scrambled eggs as the sun rose over the mountains surrounding Las Vegas. It was a spectacular reddish orange tint at first, growing in strength to a shade of reddish yellow then a bright yellow cacophony of light. I had forgotten how beautiful a desert sunrise could be and how fast it turned to full splendor.

Mr. Don't Fuck with Me's replacement was a shorter more muscular version of the night before, and the elevator must have sent a signal as he stood at the ready to open the door. My white stretch limo was waiting outside. Armed with my Tumi briefcase over my shoulder, Blackberry, cell phone, HP12c, a half dozen of my favorite Uniball micros and two packs of Marlboros, I figured I had all I needed. The limo driver looked like he moonlighted as a bouncer at the city's toughest nightclub, for while his black chauffeur uniform was perfectly tailored to his hulking body, his size made it appear to be completely out of place for his body, the way a child looks in a suit that he is beginning to outgrow. The black ensemble fit his frame, but just didn't look right or comfortable.

I said thanks to Mr. Don't FWM as he opened the car door as if it were made with balsam, climbed in, pulled out my Blackberry to keep an eye on the market, still in its opening moments and lit up a smoke. I wondered what training regimen these drivers were given and if they had to pass a strongman's test to get the job.

The markets were opening badly, as rumors were circulating that another terrorist act was in the offing and traders were taking their profits of the past few days. Mutual fund managers were said to be building up some cash reserves, just in case the rumors came true and their fickle investors decided to cash out before the weekend. Tensions were high, gold was up and other than oils, the markets felt like they were on the bad side of a hangover. I called the office and Tina answered short of breath.

"Tina, it's me. Everything OK?"

"Yes, Yes. But the phones have been busy all morning. Five clients want you to call them because they saw the news about your consulting agreement with Roger's firm. It was in this morning's Journal. I've been telling them you are still running the show and that you'll be in Monday, and that you'd be calling in shortly. But they didn't all seem convinced. I'm sorry" she said trying to catch her breath. "Hold on, there's another call for you."

She parked me on hold and after about thirty seconds came back on the line. "That was the head of First Firefighters Union #3. Someone told him you had changed jobs and he was worried about who would be handling their money. Tom, this doesn't sound good. People are nervous about the article." She paused for a second and then asked, "What do I do?"

"First of all, calm down." I needed to calm Tina down and give her a plan of action. "Then, make a copy of the Wall St. Journal article and fax it to my attention at Ocular. I'll be there in 5 or 10 minutes. Make a list of who has called and needs hand holding and fax that along as well. Call each one of them, and tell them I will return their call within the hour. And most importantly, don't worry. My business is more important than this consulting agreement and I'm not going to jeopardize what I've been able to build over the past seven years. Have you read the article?" Tina was right, something seemed wrong and the news release shouldn't have created this much of a stir.

"No, I've been too busy." It was a stupid question. Tina had no need to read the Wall Street Journal and I had never requested or expected her to. "But I did notice your picture on the front page, actually, a sketch of you. And I think the headline was something like, 'Trouble Brewing at Ocular – New Prescription Needed' with a question mark after Needed. Your sketch is near the top of the story. The article wasn't in your paper?" She was confused and concerned and it seemed she had every right to be.

"No, my edition didn't have anything about me or Ocular, which is weird because Ocular is based out here." I thought for a second and remembered that sometimes articles in the Eastern edition of the *Wall Street Journal* weren't picked up in the western edition until the following day.

The car stopped and the limo driver popped out, so I knew I must be at Ocular. "I'll call you back in the next half hour at the latest. I promise. Just send the fax now." I had to see the article before I could respond.

"OK. On it's way. I'll try to hold down the fort." Tina wasn't very convincing, but I couldn't do much to change that now.

"Don't worry. It will all be fine. I'll talk to you soon."

"Oh, and another thing before you go,"

"What?" I said, not happy that she hadn't taken my cue to let me go.

"That guy called again from the SEC. The one that was here earlier this week, Mr. Sowers."

"And what did he want? Quick, Tina, I have to go." My tone wasn't pleasant and it was only partly because I was about to be late. I needed to see the Wall Street Journal article and my meeting was supposed to start in five minutes.

"He wants to see you again next week. He said Monday would be best. He said it's important that he see you." She was nervous and I could hear it in her voice. What hell she must be going through without me there. Nevertheless, I was not in the mood for any more from Mr. Sowers.

"Call him back and tell him I will call him when I get back, but that I can't see him until later in the week."

"But..." she started and I cut her off.

"Tina, I have to go. Send the fax and I'll call you back. Stop worrying. It will be okay."

I hoped I was right.

CHAPTER TWENTY ONE

The square six story blue gray glass building that housed Ocular and other companies had a rectangular grass lawn in the front of it, with a circular fountain in the middle spouting alternating bursts of twenty to thirty foot streams of water into the air.. If you were placed in front of the building, you would have guessed you were in Palm Beach, not in the middle of the Nevada desert.

I walked up the white marble path and into the tinted glass double doors and went to the directory straight ahead of me in the otherwise empty lobby. Most of the offices seemed to be financial or asset management companies, with Morgan Stanley and Merrill Lynch occupying alternate sides of the first floor. You could see the neon ticker running across the top of the reception area in Merrill's office on the right, while Morgan Stanley's identical ticker was situated along the back wall of that office. They did, after all, have to prove that they were different.

The directory indicated that Ocular was located on the sixth floor in Suite 601, and the only name listed on the directory was Terence J. Burroughs, President and CEO. The two brokerage firms listed about two dozen managers, Senior VPs, and Vice Presidents each, while most of the other financial and consulting firms had between a handful and a dozen names listed on the directory.

I went to the elevator bank for the building, three elevators at the back of the lobby, pushed the up arrow and looked at my reflection in the polished aluminum doors.

I looked beat and tired and it was only 7:55 AM.

Shuttled quickly to the top, I followed the signs on the tan wall-papered walls to Suite 601, down the hall to the left and then back toward the front of the building on the right. I found the dark brown stained, teak doors with Ocular Asset, LLC's name in shiny brass bold capital letters and tried to open the matching brass door handle only to find it locked. There was an intercom on the right, so I buzzed to announce myself, getting a buzz in return instead of a voice. I tried the door again and the lock had been disengaged. I walked into a spanking new office with a six-foot wide dark walnut reception desk about four feet high three steps in front of me. A silver-haired woman sat in the chair on the left with reading glasses draped around her neck on a silver chain, introduced herself.

"Mr. Morris, I'm Jane. Welcome to Ocular. I believe everyone is here and waiting for you in the conference room. It's just behind this partition."

I nodded my thanks and declined her offer of coffee, tea or soda, but did have other more important business to attend to.

"I am expecting a fax and will need to see it as soon as it arrives."

"It just arrived, Mr. Morris," she answered, handing over a white legal sized envelope.

I stopped for a second to review the contents before I met Roger and Terence J. Burroughs, and saw the list of people I had to call from Tina. I was always impressed with her polished handwriting, which must have gotten her an A in penmanship. Every letter and number was textbook crisp in style and clarity. There were seven names and numbers to call with a note from Tina saying, "Here are the people that need a call back, and the article." I took a glance at the names of the clients who needed call backs and recognized the usual suspects; my nervous Nellie's, as I called them, who called whenever the market tumbled.

"Talk to you soon. Tina"

I turned to the second page and saw the clipped out article and a not so flattering sketch of my visage and started to read quickly.

Tina had gotten the title of the article right, which didn't concern me. It was the start of the article which took my breath away.

"In the dark of night, Roger Maydock of First American Insurance pulled a fast one on recently acquired Ocular Asset, hiring noted turnaround expert and close personal friend Thomas Morris as a "consultant." Sources indicate that Mr. Morris is the leading candidate to replace Mr. Burroughs as head of Ocular Asset Management."

"Holy shit!" I said in a scene reminiscent of "Animal House." The only words that my mouth could form or brain could create were "Holy Shit." So that's why the phones were ringing off the hook back at the office. That's why Tina was getting deluged with calls from concerned clients who all of a sudden needed to speak with me.

This was bad and it was going to take time to manage the fallout from this story, however it got planted. Standing there, in front of the reception desk, I reviewed the possibilities. Did Roger do this as a way of increasing the pressure on Terry Burroughs? Did Terry do this to try to upset my clients and force me to go back home and walk away for the consulting deal? Did Terry's employees or Roger's employees have something to gain by planting this false characterization of my job as a consultant?

It was time for me to take charge of the situation. I could hear John Wayne egging me on, deep in my messed up mind, "Saddle up pilgrim, we're gonna take that hill!" Well no one was going to fuck with my livelihood, my business or my hill! I'd had enough.

I stormed into the glassed-in conference room with its twelve-foot long oval mahogany conference table, saw Roger and his General

Counsel, Carl Huthwaite, talking in the far corner and three men speaking in the rear corner to my left. I assumed the man in his mid fifties to be Terence Burroughs and had no idea who the two thirty five-ish men talking to him were and didn't care. It was my turn.

"I assume everyone is here. Listen up." All eyes turned to me. Roger's smile faded as he looked at me and confusion plastered itself over the faces of the remaining four. Carl's eyes took a quick glance at me before bouncing back to the coffee cup in his hand and then toward Roger.

"I just got a copy of this morning's article in the eastern edition of the Wall Street Journal and quite frankly I am not amused. I don't know who did it or why, but when I find out there will be hell to pay. I'm here to do a job and then get the hell out and back to my life. But right now I am going to kick you all out of here, call some of my most important clients and tell them that this article is a piece of shit. It's not true and I am not going to lose my company while I try and fix some problems the two of you have with each other. So that's it. I was promised an assistant and I want him or her in here with pencil and pad in two minutes or sooner. Right now somebody should be running to get me that person. The rest of you may walk, but get the fuck out of here and now. Terence, I will see you at lunchtime. Feel free to bring a sandwich. No, on second thought, eat on your own time. Just be here at 12:30. Roger, I will see you tomorrow night for dinner. I hope you all enjoy your morning, because when I get to the bottom of this someone's going to wish they had never fucked with me." I took a breath and looked at the stunned faces. No one was moving and they stood motionless looking at me for the next part of my tirade. "That's it. Get the fuck out of my office and get my assistant now."

That got them moving. They looked around for papers, briefcases and personal belongings and half ran out of my new office without a word. I walked over to the window and looked at the sleeping strip of Las Vegas in the distance. The casinos, hotels and buildings had flashing lights still blinking on their facades, but in the bright morning light looked more like a black and white photo, a shadow and understatement of its spectacular nighttime look.

I turned around, put my briefcase on the dark stained conference table and sat down near the middle of the table in one of the leather reclining chairs. I leaned back, took out a cigarette and looked at the list of names and phone numbers Tina had sent, pulled the conference room phone from the middle of the table toward me, laid out my cell phone, Blackberry and pulled a fresh pad of paper out of my briefcase and my complete contact list of client phone numbers..

"Umm, there's no smoking in this building," came from a frightened female voice. I looked up to see a tall attractive brunette woman in her late twenties or early thirties standing in the doorway. She was outfitted in a brown two-piece suit, with a white blouse and appeared uncertain as to whether or not she should enter.

"At this point in time, I don't really care," I said sarcastically "And who might you be?" I asked in a more pleasant voice.

"I'm Susan Emery, your assistant while you are here. I have been assigned to help you in whatever manner you deem necessary." She seemed scared but not resentful. Not sure what straw she had drawn.

"And what did you do at Ocular before I descended upon this fine little institution?" I said, trying to force a smile and defuse an uncomfortable scene. If she was going to be my assistant, I was going to need her on my side, have her trust my every move.

"I work as a receptionist most of the time, assist operations at the end of the month with reconciliation of client accounts and type letters and internal research reports for the analysts when they need them." Her confidence rose as she spoke. "I'm a Katherine Gibbs graduate, type 85 words per minute, take dictation in shorthand and can help organize projects and meetings as well."

"Very good" I said. "Then we'll be fine together. This is how it's going to work. I'm going to give you lists of things to do and things that I need. First and foremost, I want a Bloomberg machine moved into this office and put in front of me. Right here! Do whatever it takes, but make sure it happens within the hour." She was writing as I spoke, a good sign.

"Second, I want two copies of this client contact sheet. One is for me to mark up and send back to my office to Tina, my assistant and one is for you. Third, I want you to go to your computer or the operations department and put together a consolidated report showing every stock and every bond owned by Ocular and the price they were bought at, by date and lot. I would like to see it in a traditional Advent/AXYS report segregated by industry. Do you understand what I mean?"

She nodded her assent and looked up from her pad for more.

Next, I want a copy of the most recent SEC examination letter and any correspondence between the SEC and Ocular relating to the latest SEC exam.

"Then I want to have all the Compliance Officer's files of personal securities transactions for employees for the past year brought into my office and placed on the table over there," I said pointing to my left. "Which reminds me, I want you to call a locksmith and have him here within the next hour. He is to report to me directly and no one else. I will also need keys and security codes to have full access to this building and these offices." I took a breath.

"Back to the AXYS database information; I want a run of all securities transactions executed by Ocular since December 31st of last year, meaning the past ten, well almost eleven months, in chronological order. You can put it on that side of the table" I said, pointing to my right. "I want a copy of all trade tickets and trade blotters for the past month put right there, on the table across from me, also in chronological order. And finally, I want to see the performance by quarter of each account in a spreadsheet by asset class, equity, balanced, fixed, whatever. Any questions?" I asked, thinking that this would be a great start.

"Priorities," she answered, "between Bloomberg machine, copies of client list and locksmith?"

She was good; those were the things that I said had to happen first. "Good question and by the way, I will never complain or curse if you ask for clarification or are unsure what has priority over what. I will get upset if you don't ask and make a wrong decision. So, copy the client lists, return them to me, call the locksmith and then find someone who can move the Bloomberg in here. I don't care if it happens while I'm on the phone, as long as I can hear the other end of the line and there's no hammering or drilling involved. Oh, and in your free time, order lunch for yourself and get me a roast beef on rye with mayo, nothing else. And yes, a diet Coke with caffeine, if you could rustle one up now, that would be great."

She half-smiled and said, "Piece of cake. I'll get right on it," and walked out. My eyes were drawn to her as she walked out the door and I noticed her light brown hair was long, pulled back and held together by a simple yellow bow. The brown suit was cut to hide the shape of her figure; her calf muscles were well defined and tightened as she walked away in her tan high-healed pumps. She walked confidently and I tried to guess what she would look like in a bikini. As I thought about her beachwear, I marveled once again that men were pigs and I was a card-carrying member of the species. I also realized that I had to focus on the job at hand and get back to Tina and my client calls.

CHAPTER TWENTY TWO

I spent the morning on the phone with clients, letting them know that the article had it all wrong. I was not going to give up running my firm and leave to manage Ocular Asset. In the meantime, stocks continued their slide. A Bloomberg terminal was set up in my new office in about fifteen minutes, for someone had had the foresight to wire the conference room for a terminal when the office was set up. At about 9:30, the locksmith came and at my direction installed matching locks on both doors to the conference room and gave me what he promised were the only two keys. I slipped him a fifty and told him that he was not to accept any other work at Ocular for the next three months, unless it came from me. I gave him my card and cell phone number, and asked him to call me if anyone tried to contact him to get a copy of the keys to my office for any reason.

"I'm cool" and "interesting office" were his only comments as he left.

Susan was working her magic making copies and delivering reports through the morning, efficiently and exactly as I had ordered. She was a keeper, I thought to myself. I had empowered another super capable assistant who could move mountains if I needed her to, and she loved it.

At 10:30 AM, I gave her a new set of instructions. "Find a bunch of different colored highlighters and report back here and I'm going to have you work on some of these documents. Does cigarette smoke offend you?' I realized that by now my office probably would be reeking of cigarette smell, even though I had the air conditioning system pumping out fresh cool air to keep my office at 67 degrees. Too cold for some, but I seemed to feel more alert at a mid-sixty level.

"No, I worked my way through college as a waitress and it never seemed to bother me too much." Susan seemed to be enjoying the challenge of keeping up with my projects and seemed genuinely happier as the morning wore on and she knocked things off her checklist.

"Are you having fun?" I asked trying to take a mental break from the phones and the markets.

"Absolutely" she answered quickly. "I've been stuck out at the receptionist desk for fourteen months. I was hired to be an assistant and found out that most of the assisting was answering phones. I can do a lot more. Heck, I put myself through Katie Gibbs to do more than answer phones and sit in a chair all day. I hate sitting still."

From the shape of her calves and trim figure I guessed she was a daily workout animal at some health club.

"Well, I'm glad to hear it. Now, your next job is going to require sitting, though you can stand if you prefer, but you will be able to use your mind. I want you to take those colored highlighters and go through the firm's master list. Highlight a stock like Spindletop and set up a cross-reference between when it was purchased in the firm's accounts and when it was purchased in employee accounts. "How many people trade their own accounts here, anyway?" I asked.

"I think about seven of the eighteen employees have a trading compliance file. Most of the secretaries and support staff apparently don't trade or own mutual funds. That includes me," she added.

"Which?" I asked, then regretted asking a personal question. "Never mind, it's none of my business."

"It's not a big deal," she said unemotionally and without offense. "I don't make enough to really buy much and I'd rather save my money for a house. I've been a renter for too long."

"Okay," I said trying to regain focus. "So I want to do a check on who bought what and when. Make sure that no one has been front running the firm's trades, a little compliance check." I tried to gauge her response, but she waited expressionless, either not understanding or not caring. "Any questions?" I probed. "Thoughts?"

"So project number one is to find out if anyone here has been trying to profit from knowing what the firm is going to do. Buy or sell before the firm does."

"Exactly" I said complimenting her. "And well put. What do you think?"

"When people here find out what you're doing, you are going to have fewer friends than when you walked in."

"Did I have any?" I asked jokingly.

"Actually, most of the support staff was looking forward to you coming here. They whisper amongst themselves that there are things that go on here that they don't think are kosher and are scared to death that they are doing something that might be illegal, but no one dares ask any questions. They just do what they are told and keep their mouths shut." Her attitude and forthright manner were refreshing and she was obviously resentful of how she had been treated since she was hired.

"So why do they stay? Why have you stayed?" I was getting more curious by the minute.

"They need the money. This is one of the best paying firms for support and operations people in the Las Vegas suburbs. They can't afford to leave."

It made sense, but there was more I needed to know.

"So what do they think they might be doing that could be illegal or get them in trouble?"

"I'm not sure. But it seems to have something to do with the trading area. The traders are in a separate room and Mr. Burroughs doesn't let the traders get instruction from anyone else but him. Something fishy is going on, but no one wants to jeopardize their jobs or careers."

"Will anyone talk openly to me?" I asked.

"Not a chance. They have decided that as long as Mr. Burroughs signs their checks, they are going to keep their mouths shut."

"Alright" I said. "At 11:45 AM we're going to take a break and you are going to introduce me to the traders and support staff, especially the back office or operations people, whatever you call them."

"That would be the operations and performance group."

"Okay. Now start organizing the personal trading records and make notes of anything that you think looks suspicious. You probably won't find anything because as a firm, the employees must know that the SEC will come in at least every five to seven years to look at this stuff. But before you start, get a copy of the firm's compliance manual and find out what it says the do's and don'ts are for personal transactions. Next, get two copies of the last SEC review, one for you and one for me and we'll see what the SEC said the last time they were here and we'll put you in charge of doing the dirty work."

"I have that right here" she answered confidently, "It was on your first hit." She was proud to have a chance to show her efficiency and capability.

"That's great" I remembered. I'll want to take a look at that before I see Mr. Burroughs. "By the way," I added, "how's the mood out there among the employees?"

"Scared to death. They have no idea what you are doing or what you are going to look at. Your little tirade this morning shook 'em up a bit." She smiled.

"Tell them I'm not so bad. No, actually keep them guessing, at least for now. How about Terry Burroughs and his research staff or portfolio managers?"

Her smile quickly disappeared. "You don't want to know" she said with a tone that indicated just how much love I had instilled in Terry.

"No, go ahead, I can take it. Lay it on me."

"Well, after you kicked him out of his conference room, he cursed out Mr. Maydock and Mr. Huthwaite in front of a bunch of the employees. Then he stormed into his office, slammed the door and could be heard yelling snippets, "No one talks to me like that. How dare he? In my company."

"That's not so bad" I said feeling Terry deserved it and could probably use being put in his place, especially if he was behind the article in the Wall Street Journal.

"There's more," Susan said, pausing for a second, obviously unsure if she should continue, but too far along to stop now. "He also could be heard yelling, 'I'll kill the bastard. I'll kill the fucking bastard.'"

CHAPTER TWENTY THREE

Damage control on the phones for the article was tedious but progressing. Susan faxed Tina the client list with the names of who she should call to let them know I would be calling them today or Monday. Tina would fax back notes on who she had reached every half-hour to forty-five minutes with comments as to who would be at their office available for a call. I was making steady progress calming down my nervous Nellies and no one I talked to seemed too concerned after I had a chance to set the record straight.

Stocks stayed deep in the red as the rumors continued about possible terrorist activities occurring "imminently." I took a break every fifteen to twenty minutes to check the e-mails flooding my Blackberry. There was one from Roger at 11:18 saying, "I'm back in L.A. Some show you put on this morning. It wasn't me, and thanks for the vote of support. I'll see you tomorrow night and tell you what I can find out about the article. Have my contacts working on it. Your friend, Rog, you big idiot" I felt bad, but was not totally at ease with what Roger had gotten me into. This was not the job I was expecting.

Flykarnfly checked in at 11:21 with the message: "Flights might be delayed but it looks like Vegas is a go. Will meet you at Binion's. Wait for me!!" In the excitement of the morning, I had totally forgotten about Karen and my dinner date. I wasn't quite in the mood for a date with anyone right now and was going to be exhausted by the time I was done at Ocular for the day. Hell, I thought, I should probably move a cot into the office and spend the weekend trying to sort it all out. I e-mailed back a feeble "Okay" and figured I'd be sleeping at the bar when Karen arrived.

Susan came in at 11:45 as instructed to take me on a tour of Ocular. I had Susan wait for a few minutes while I gave the SEC examination letter a thorough once over and found that Terry had, in fact, been cited for buying and selling within the trading day window that the SEC felt no personal transaction should occur. They recommended and Ocular agreed to adopt a seven-day blackout period before and three days after for personal transactions in companies Ocular was buying or selling. They also recommended that all of Mr. Burroughs's personal trades be placed through the trading desk to further ensure compliance with the proposed personal trading policies. She introduced me to the employees as "Mr. Morris, our new consultant." The operations staff had their bottoms seemingly glued to their chairs, not one rising from their post to greet me. Their eyes were fixated on their computer screens in front of them, as if they would be given an electric shock every time they looked away. They took turns looking up fearfully to say hello as Susan introduced them one by one, but were obviously more comfortable looking at their screens than me.

The trading room was contained in a separate office with three desks merged in the center of the room in the formation of a T. After introductions, I asked where the third trader was and Jerry, the older and more senior of the two with the white hair and one hand permanently attached to the key-pad in front of him informed me "That is Mr. Burroughs' seat."

"And why does Mr. Burroughs need a seat?" I asked innocently enough, but seemed there was something not so innocent about Mr. Burroughs.

Jerry answered again, "Mr. Burroughs likes to listen to what trading desks are telling us and likes to oversee the trading when we are doing trading blocks. He also usually sits there at the end of the day and allocates the trades we have completed.

"And what are you doing today?" I asked trying to get a sense of what they did and with how much direction.

"Not much, we are adding to our positions in a couple of stocks. Mr. Burroughs has given us a list of how many shares we should buy at what prices. He updates it during the day." Jerry showed me a yellow legal pad sheet with the ticker symbols of a half dozen stocks on the left side and the number of shares to buy in a column to the right. The sheet had the number of shares crossed off on three names with bigger amounts written to the right and one stock had the number of shares crossed off three times with a total of 40,000 now being the amount he wanted to be bought.

"And what accounts will these stocks be put in?" I asked.

Jerry took the lead. "Mr. Burroughs makes all allocation decisions. We do not know when we place the orders which accounts will receive the shares that are bought or which accounts will be selling them. We also do not know how many shares we will be buying or selling on any given day, as Mr. Burroughs often updates the amount he wants to buy or sell during the day."

"And why is that?" I asked, thinking this was a suspicious way of executing trades.

"Mr. Burroughs feels that if we don't know the total shares involved, the trading desks we use can't know our intention and can't front run our orders. He doesn't trust many people and especially doesn't trust the trading desks at the major wire houses.

"So which brokers do you use most of the time? How do you protect yourself from front running?"

"Mr. Burroughs decides which brokers and brokerage firms are to be used for each trade. You can see on the column on the far right of the trade blotter the initials or short name we have for which broker has the order." I saw what he was talking about and was amazed at the simplicity and obsolescence of the Ocular trading procedure.

I decided to keep going with the inquisition. "And where is yesterday's blotter?"

"It's on Mr. Burroughs' desk," Jerry answered. Trader #2 continued to look at his screen, refusing to be a part of the Q&A, nervously punching up stock quotes and acting like we weren't there and that he was conducting critical business. He appeared to be in his mid to late twenties. He had the boyish fair looks of a Southern California surfer, with blond hair and tan arms in his white polo shirt. I found the trade blotter and it looked almost identical to the one from today, but with fewer crossing outs, which I surmised meant less activity.

"We generally trade more on down days, like today," Jerry added with a hint of pride in his voice.

"But where does it say what accounts these were allocated to?"

"Mr. Burroughs got tied up yesterday afternoon, getting ready for today's meeting and promised he would come by this morning to give us instructions." The resignation in Jerry's voice told me that he knew that this was definitely not okay. He added, "We just place the orders as we are instructed. Mr. Burroughs takes care of the rest."

"And how often does Mr. Burroughs fail to allocate the day's trades on the same day?"

"Oh, I couldn't say. I really don't know."

"Yes, you can say, if you have any interest in being able to work in the financial industry." I was threatening him, a tact I didn't like using but I wasn't going to pussyfoot around with my consulting deal. I wanted to get to the bottom of any issues that may be worth a second look and take that second look immediately.

Jerry fidgeted, wondering what to do, knowing now that either way he chose to reply, his job was at risk either from Terry or from me.

"I would have to guess that it's a rare event, but I really think Mr. Burroughs would be better suited to answer that question."

Smart answer, I thought. Cover your ass and send the problem packing away from you. Toss the hot potato quickly and far.

"Well, Mr. Burroughs and I will be having a chat at lunch time and I'll make sure to talk to him about it. Susan, you getting all this down?" Susan had been quietly taking notes since I began my query and I wasn't sure if she was making notes to herself or hoping to help me, but I figured it would add some worry and concern to the trading area if they felt they were being deposed.

"And do you have anything to add?" I asked of the silent junior trader.

"No sir. I just do what Jerry and Mr. Burroughs tell me to do." His voice quavered with fear and I could see the drops of "Oh shit" forming on his forehead and around his face.

"Well, thank you both for all your help," I said flatly and with a hint of disappointment. "Please make a note to yourselves that as soon as the allocation decisions are made that a copy is forwarded to me when I am here or hand-delivered to Susan, who will fax it to me wherever I am."

"Yes sir," they both said in almost military fashion. I wondered if that was how they responded to Mr. Burroughs.

"Oh, and one more thing," they both looked at me in dread waiting for the next shoe, "I would like a list of all brokers that you use, how much each has made in commissions, what rate they are being paid, where your soft dollars are going, and what they are paying for."

Jerry answered meekly, "Yes sir." It was not a fun project and he knew where I was going with my line of questioning. Soft dollars were commissions that money managers paid to brokers who provided research products and services to investment firms like Ocular and Morris Asset. The SEC was getting very serious about the soft dollar issue and I figured I might as well get a sense of what services Ocular was not paying its own hard cash (or hard dollars) for. It was an area that was also rife with possible shady deals and from what I could gather so far, Ocular's support and documentation for how it chose brokers and allocated trades was sorely lacking. The week before, the SEC had fined and censured a hedge fund for having a broker pay not only its rent and computer terminals, but a trip for the firm's principals fishing in the Caymans!

"Thanks, it's been a pleasure meeting you both," I said ready to move on. "Susan, why don't we head back to my office, grab a quick bite and go over those Policy and Procedure documents?"

I couldn't wait to ask Mr. Burroughs about his role in the firm's trading of stocks and bonds and discuss how Ocular satisfied the SEC requirement to provide clients with "best execution." In particular, I wanted to review what procedures determined which specific broker-age firms were chosen to execute trades. Finally, I wanted to understand the process and justification for the allocation of those orders to client accounts upon completion. Boy, was Terry gonna love seeing me!

CHAPTER TWENTY FOUR

Terence J. Burroughs came into my office, his conference room, at precisely 12:30 PM, looking as if he had run around the building a few times before he entered. He wasn't perspiring, but his face was red and his breathing heavy.

"Hello Mr. Morris," he said offering his hand. "I don't believe we've been properly introduced. I'm Terry Burroughs."

"Thanks, Terry. Please call me Tom. I wish we could be meeting under more pleasant circumstances. I assure you my role here is strictly as a consultant, hired to see if there would be changes that I could identify to improve the operations and ultimately the value of Ocular for First American."

It was obvious from his expression he did not see it that way and he let out an audible harrumph. He tried his best to respond professionally. "While I appreciate how you may view your role here, I'll have you know that I, like you, built a very successful money management firm from scratch and ran it pretty damn well for the fifteen years before you showed up."

I could see the passion he had for his firm and felt the sincerity in his voice. I also noticed that his eyes were slightly bloodshot; his cheeks scarred from what must have been tough teen-age acne. He also had well-creased lines in his forehead that deepened as he spoke. I knew the press release had put his age at sixty, but the wear and tear of the markets and the events of the past week had caught up with him and he looked five to ten years older than his true age. A full head of almost white hair looked like it might have been blonde in his youth, for his light complexion and white eyebrows seemed to fit the mold. After a pause and no response from me, he added,

"Quite frankly, I resent your being here. I view it as an insult and an unnecessary waste of both your and my time."

"Well, thank you for being so candid," I said. "I like someone who tells it like it is."

He smiled an engaging smile and instantly appeared to be years younger. The creases in his forehead dissipated and his eyes lit up, de-emphasizing the red in his light blue eyes. "In that case, I'd like you to know that I have work to do, a firm to run and if you need anything, Susan or someone should be able to help you find what you need. Enjoy your time in Vegas. I think that about does it." He stood up and said goodbye, as if he expected he would never meet or have to speak with me again.

"Excuse me," I said, interrupting his departure. "I actually do have a couple of questions that I would like to ask before you go."

Terry stood there uncertainly, not knowing whether to sit back down or if he could dispense with me quickly. He looked at his watch and said, "Yes, well okay. You do realize the market's going to close in about twenty-five minutes."

"Yes, I do. And by the way, that brings up an interesting point. How often do you delay allocating trades in client accounts? I stopped by the trading area and some trades from yesterday still hadn't been allocated." I waited for a response and the reddish hue began to return to his face. He was trying to control his anger at having some outsider taking a peek behind the curtains to see what he was doing.

"You realize that we have more than two hundred clients and money flows in and out on a daily basis." He sat back down at the edge of his chair somewhat unsure if he was going to stay for a while.

"So what does that have to do with following industry standards about treating clients fairly?" It was an attack, but I wanted to see his reaction.

"Listen here, Mr. Morris," the creases were back, the face building up to a sunburned look, "we have pension and endowment funds, mutual funds, partnerships and taxable investor clients. As you know, it takes four days for trades to settle, otherwise known as 'T plus three' in the industry and while I appreciate your concern, it's not a big deal. The trades from yesterday have been allocated and I would have done it yesterday afternoon, except that I have been very busy this week due to the Board meeting with First American. I've also had to speak to a lot of my clients to tell them what the hell was going on since the press release came out about your role here. Obviously, today's *Wall Street Journal* article didn't make my life any easier either. So in a way, Mr. Morris, we're in the same leaking boat if you will. You work on bailing out your end and I'll bail out my end. When we plug the leaks, I would just as soon you got off my boat."

It was an interesting analogy, but didn't quite answer my question. "And as far as the clients are concerned, you feel your practice to not immediately allocate trades is fair?"

"Listen here, when we are buying or selling a company's stock we do it across the board. The trades that were done yesterday and today had nothing to do with that and were proper."

"And why haven't I seen a trade blotter? I asked your traders to get me a copy as soon as yesterday's trades were allocated."

"Because, dammit, I told them to give you a copy at the end of the trading day when they distribute today's reports. They are busy enough without having to answer to your every whim. Do you realize that after your little get together, Jerry, the Silver Fox I call him, came into my office and offered to resign? Do you realize he's been with me since I started this firm and in your first four or five hours you have one of my most loyal and trustworthy employees scared that he's about to be fired by you. Thanks a lot! Just what do you plan to do for an encore?"

As I thought how to respond, I was glad that I had ruffled some feathers. Most people dropped their guard when they got emotional and flustered and revealed more about themselves than they intended.

"The day is young yet," I jabbed.

"You son of a bitch" the steam could be seen rising from his head as he rose from the chair. "If you think you can come in here and ruin what I spent 15 years building, you've got another thing coming. You are going to pay for this, bucko. You'll see." Terry Burroughs stormed out of my temporary office, slamming the door behind him with such force that the windows rattled.

I had him right where I wanted him. Now if he would just leave me a trail of what he was doing that I could use against him, all would be well with the world.

CHAPTER TWENTY FIVE

I n between phone calls with clients, I spent the rest of the day looking through the trade blotters and personal transactions of Ocular's employees and tried to review the stacks of information that Susan had put together for me. Susan continued to color code the personal transactions and Ocular's client trades.

Tina and the crew back on the East Coast had put in a long hard day helping keep things together in the midst of turmoil, rumor and a sick stock market fading even lower at the close.

I thanked her for all her help and told her she not only deserved a raise, but was getting one on Monday. "How does an extra ten thousand a year and an extra paid week of vacation sound?"

"Just what the doctor ordered," she beamed. "If you change your mind over the weekend, I'll understand. It will be nice to dream about over the weekend anyway."

"What can I do now?" Susan asked, stirring me out of my daydream.

"Ummm, just label or put notes on each of the piles to let me know what they are." My watch said 3:30 PM, but I could tell the din outside had decreased and realized most of the Ocular employees must be gone for the day. After all, the equity markets had closed one and a half hours earlier and I assumed that most of the employees had been at the office since six or seven in the morning.

"By the way," I asked, "what time did you get here today and when do people usually leave?"

"Oh" she answered surprised, "I got here at five-thirty and I guess most people are usually gone by three or four at the latest. I usually leave at three or four depending on the week. See, I alternate with the other receptionist for the early shift of five-thirty to three or six-thirty to four, so that the phones are answered. This week was my early week."

"Well, you don't have to stay on my account. But, before you go, anything jump out at you or seem worth a second look?"

"Don't worry about me" Susan assured me. "I can work for awhile longer. I don't have anything planned until dinner at seven, though I would like to go home and change first. But honestly, it feels great to do more than answer the phones all day. Today was fun."

"Glad you enjoyed it," I interjected.

"In terms of anything suspicious, obviously the trading area is suspicious, but there's no way for me to figure out how often trades are not allocated until the following day or later."

"That makes sense. Keep going." She was pretty sharp and had great instincts.

"The thing that just doesn't smell right is that there are no compliance glitches with personal transactions. Well, that's not so surprising, per se. In the Policies and Procedures manual for personal transactions, there is a black out period of seven days whereby Ocular employees cannot buy a stock before that company is bought in client accounts. In addition, Ocular employees have to wait for three days after clients buy a stock before they can buy it in their own accounts."

"Yup, I read that in the SEC letter. Sounds good so far," I said. "Pretty standard stuff actually, so what's the rub? What smells like Denmark?"

She looked at me lost, not having a clue what I was referring to.

"As in something's fishy... Never mind, go on." Another random association misses its mark, I thought sadly. Seemed so cute in my mind.

"Well, anyway, in Mr. Burroughs' account, he appears to have bought just about every stock that the firm has bought in his personal account."

"That's not so surprising. Most money managers want to own their best ideas. Go on."

"Well that's about it. Except for the fact that most of the time he purchased the stocks in his personal account before clients bought it, usually between one or two weeks before, though sometimes as long as three weeks before."

"That is interesting. Any similar patterns with the other employees?"

"Quite the contrary. The five other employees that do any real investing have always bought the stocks in their accounts after the blackout period."

"That does seem a little fishy," I concurred. "Any other closing thoughts before I kick you out of here?"

Susan looked at her watch and said, "Gee I can't think of any. But what do I do next week and when are you coming back here?"

"I was just about to get to that. First, if you don't mind I would like your phone numbers, cell, home etc., so I can track you down if I have any questions. For instance, I'll probably come in here tomorrow for a few hours and try to wade through this stuff. I will be heading back to New Jersey on Sunday and will call in at eleven in the morning and three in the afternoon New York time to review what's going on with your projects. Don't worry. I'll keep you plenty busy and you will be my eyes and ears about what's going on at Ocular. Are you up for it?"

"Absolutely," she answered enthusiastically.

"Okay. So, I think you should work out of my office here while I'm away. You realize that you are not going to be the most popular Ocular employee."

"Don't worry. I have a pretty thick skin and haven't really developed any great friendships here. Everyone is so scared of Mr. Burroughs that they keep their noses in their jobs or computers and aren't a lot of fun."

"Well, don't let them scare or threaten you. Your job is safe with me and based on what you've shown today, I wouldn't worry too much about your future. You are going to do just fine."

"Thanks. That's kind of you to say." She was feeling proud of herself and you could hear it in her voice, and see it as she stood a little straighter.

"So take one of these keys and get the hell out of here. You've done everything I could have hoped and I'll have plenty of work I can get done without you. Oh, and if you don't mind before you go, please give me your phone numbers."

"Not at all" she said, "but I only have one phone number, my cell. There really isn't any need to have a separate phone at home."

As she wrote it down for me on a yellow pad from the conference table, I realized I had heard about this new generation that didn't believe in having another phone at home, just hadn't believed it was true. Maybe it was time to sell those old phone companies after all, I told myself, big dividends and all. I smiled and wondered what other changes this new generation was going to have in store for the investors of tomorrow.

"One last thing before you go," I said, remembering one of the supposed hot issues that Roger had bought up. "I want to take a separate look at Ocular's high yield investments. You know their junk bond holdings. I'd like to see a list of activity, positions and where each bond was priced at the end of each of the last three quarters."

"That should be pretty easy," Susan said confidently. She was excited to have more work to do. "I'll get right on it," she said as she turned to leave the office to work her magic on a computer somewhere.

"Just create a new pile somewhere on this desk," I said.

"Gotcha. Back in a flash." She was full of spunk and I could only imagine how she had longed to graduate from the receptionist desk.

I started to pore over the stack of personal trade confirmations for Terry Burroughs and noticed the pattern that Susan had seen. More often than not, if Ocular bought a stock, Terry had purchased it in his personal account anywhere between eight and ten days before Ocular's clients. Furthermore, in almost every case, the shares were bought at higher prices for clients than what Terry paid. Pretty fishy, but technically it didn't appear that he had violated the firm's personal trading guidelines that mandated a black-out period of seven days.

Interestingly, however, not every stock Terry purchased made it into Ocular's client's portfolios and there were stocks that client's purchased that Terry did not. While it looked fishy and smelled worse, on paper there didn't seem to be any obvious violations of SEC rules or Ocular's internal rules regarding personal transactions.

I wondered if the whole effort was a waste of time, but the more I dug in to the stack of Terry's personal transactions, the more suspicious I got. Frustrated by the lack of any obvious smoking guns, I reminded myself that no one wanted to run afoul of the SEC, including me. Terry was well aware of what could cause a nasty reaction from regulators. Hecht, the SEC had been very specific in stating that Ocular's previous policy was too loose and had recommended strong changes to Ocular personal securities policies. But still, to trade in the same stocks as the firm's clients, you would think there would be a mistake or questionable trade somewhere along the line.

A dull headache was beginning to creep into my temples, and I looked at my watch wondering how late in the day it was. It was now 4:20 PM, 7:20 back home. Usually when I worked late, I broke for a snack or dinner around 6:30 PM. Now my stomach was growling and my body was reacting to the east coast time zone and my body's need to refuel.

I needed a shower, a shave and dinner, I thought to myself, and not necessarily in that order. Why in the world did I make a dinner reservation for 9:00? I knew Karen's flight wouldn't get in until later in the day, but maybe I should have just suggested drinks.

"Where do you want this pile?" I hadn't noticed Susan enter the room and was startled by her presence. The table was running out of openings and at this point the piles were beginning to overwhelm the table's capacity for organization in the Thomas Morris piling method.

"Just somewhere near the center I guess," I suggested, as there weren't any other logical options. My stomach quietly grumbled a silent reminder it wanted to be fed.

"I think I'm about done for the day," I announced to Susan, "but I'm probably going to come back and play with the pencils on the Group W bench tomorrow." It was a reference to Arlo Guthrie's classic "Alice's Restaurant" and I realized as I said it that Susan would have no idea what I was talking about. Only about thirty years before her time, you idiot.

"I'm sorry," she said confused. "I don't……"

"Never mind, an old failing of mine, random expressions and associations that my mind comes up with, which make friends and family wonder if I've gone over the deep end. Couldn't make you understand if I tried." I sheepishly wondered where to go from here, how to change the subject? My stomach forced an answer, growling again. "By the way, is there someplace in the building or close by where I could get a quick snack or bite? A Seven-Eleven or convenience store would be fine."

"Sure, just down the hall, there is a kitchen area with sodas and snacks and a microwave. It's on the honor system. Soda and juice are free, provided by Ocular, and snacks are seventy-five cents each; chips, pretzels, candy bars, etc. For anything more substantial, there is a Circle K about a block and a half away. Do you have a car?"

That was an interesting question, did I have a car? I hadn't thought about that when I left the limo in the morning and I hadn't taken a card or phone number or anything. As I pondered my predicament, Susan asked,

"Or is that black stretch that's been parked outside all day yours?"

"Actually, I'm not sure. Maybe I should check it out. I'll just get my stuff together and go down and see. Are you going to stay?"

"No, I'll head out with you. And if the limo's not for you, I'll give you a ride back to your hotel if you need one. I'd be glad to call you a cab on my cell if you'd rather." She winked a friendly wink and I wondered just how she viewed me.

"Thanks," I said, standing up and gathering my electronic toys and briefcase together. I decided to leave the piles where they were and figured I could attack them again tomorrow. I locked my office, gave Susan one of the two keys and followed her out. She demonstrated which keys opened the front door of the office suite and which electronic card gave me access to the building's front entrance. As we exited the building, the limo driver got out of the front seat and opened the door. Since it was the same driver as this morning, I assumed it was in fact for me. As we approached, the driver said,

"Mr. Morris, glad to see you again."

I was nonplussed. "Have you been waiting here all day?" I asked.

"Yes, Mr. Morris. I have been assigned to be available to you from 7:00AM to 7:00PM. I am to take you anywhere you want to go. At 7:00PM, my replacement takes over."

Susan was impressed. "Hot stuff," she remarked. "I guess you don't need my help anymore." She turned and began to walk away.

"Susan," I said, trying to interrupt her departure and faced with a wonderful view of her walking away, calf muscles showing their shape and definition with every step in her pumps. She turned her head, but not her body.

"Yes, Mr. Morris?"

"Thanks for all your help, you were really a huge help in there and made my day very manageable."

She completed the turnaround and faced me from about ten feet. "No. Thank you." She stepped closer, looked at the driver and appeared to be deciding what to say. "I really enjoyed having someone trust me to get things done." She paused and once again seemed uncertain. "I hope you find whatever you're looking for in there. I really do want to help" she offered empathetically.

"Well, OK," I said. "Thanks again. I guess I'll be seeing you in another week or two and talking to you a bunch next week."

"Actually," she said, "if you're working tomorrow, I'd like to come in and help out. This has really primed my interest."

"Gee, that would be great," I answered enthusiastically, "I could really use the help and you seem to know where to find everything I need."

"Great, I'll see you tomorrow then." She turned and began to walk away, once again giving me my favorite view. Men are pigs, I thought, but at least we appreciate beauty in whatever form it presents itself.

"But not before noon," I said loud enough for her to hear. "And dress is casual." I tried to say with emphasis. She turned her head and winked again.

Was she flirting or was this her standard way of communication? And what was I thinking agreeing to let her come work with me tomorrow? I made a quick resolution to stop getting myself in to these situations.

"To the Circle K," I said to the limo driver, who nodded his assent, closing my door behind me after I climbed in. A quick bite, a shower and a shave, I thought. In three and a half hours, I would be meeting Karen, if all worked out with her flights. Memo to self: Add some rest to the itinerary next time or you're going to burn out.

CHAPTER TWENTY SIX

As we approached my cozy little hotel's entrance, I called up to the limo driver, "Excuse me," I started, "I was wondering how it is that I never see anyone else when I come or go into the hotel? Aren't there a lot of people that use these suites?"

"Well, yes, Mr. Morris. But you see, each set of suites, as you call them, has its own driveway and the hotel has eight of these private residence complexes each with nine suites so there are 72 of these special rooms in total. Some of our guests actually stay here on a weekly basis and no one else uses their rooms. As you are in Suite 2501, if any elevator is in service in your set of suites, my car will not be able to enter the private drive. My computer code will not be accepted until the resident or guest has left the lobby and either entered his or her car or the hotel. State of the art privacy, if you will, for our special guests."

I was speechless as I listened to the degree to which people's privacy could be and was being protected. The costs had to be staggering. As if reading my mind, the limo driver added,

"I hear that some of our clients require it and the casino's pit bosses say they get enough play at our special high roller tables to make it all worthwhile."

"So why am I here?" I thought out loud, not realizing I had spoken loud enough for the driver to hear until he answered.

"Well, if you are not planning on betting a couple of hundred grand this weekend, you must have some pretty important friends."

"So it would appear," I replied, leaning back to ponder my status at the hotel. Was Roger really in that deep with the hotel's owners to rate such a fawning? Did he have this status as a lender? Or, had Roger become a high roller and one of the quasi-residents who jetted here on weekends? I took a last bite of the hot dog I had picked up at the Circle K and as I burped and experienced the aftertaste, scolded myself for succumbing to such a random unhealthy food. The good news was, I could brush my teeth when I got upstairs and wouldn't be seeing anyone soon.

We entered the private drive and I headed in solitude up to my room, now understanding the set up and reasons for the lack of human contact. I felt out of place, preferred being in the presence of others and realized the whole experience was making me a bit uncomfortable.

As I got off the elevator, I noticed fresh flowers had been put in vases on most of the tables and I saw an envelope on the table closest to me. "MR. MORRIS" was typed in bold on the outside. Opening it, I saw that there was a personalized message from the Director of Special Client Services, Leezil, offering me complimentary meals at any of the casino's restaurants, promising to be on call twenty-four hours a day at her extension.

I put my briefcase down on the table next to the envelope and sat in the oversized leather chair near the living room's fireplace looking at the fading daylight of the Las Vegas skyline. On the coffee table in front of me was a remote, which I picked up wondering where the TV was. Pushing the TV button caused a forty-inch plasma TV to descend from the ceiling above the fireplace and when in place above the mantle, turned itself on to the casino/hotel's information channel. I followed the instructions to activate the satellite TV and its hundreds of channel choices, settling in on ESPN's coverage of the New York Rangers game versus the Boston Bruins. The Rangers were losing 3 to 1 in the second period, which was no big surprise, but it was comforting to have familiar surroundings. I turned up the volume so that I could hear the action and got up to take the much needed, long overdue shower.

The shower was unlike any shower I had ever been in, for when I turned on the dial to start it, the water waited to come out until it was the temperature I had chosen. After standing under the hot streaming jets of the shower for about thirty seconds, round silver metal ports came out of the wall and began misting my body from top to bottom. I'd never heard of such decadence, but experiencing it, I had to admit I enjoyed it and wanted it in my shower at home.

'Home', I lamented. I resolved to myself to fix my home life as soon as I got back to New Jersey in the following week and wondered why hadn't Sam returned my call?

After soaking and luxuriating under the streams and mists of water for a sinful time, I got out, grabbed an oversized white fluffy towel from the towel warming rack and gave myself an old fashioned shave. The heated shaving cream made the act of shaving feel like a gentle massage of my face and beard. I made a mental note to myself that this was another necessary indulgence that I was going to have to make part of my life.

They say ignorance is bliss and they're probably right, for my little taste of just what it was the folks who already 'had it all' had was depressing and enlightening. I realized that knowledge was expensive, for I knew it was going to cost me big bucks to recreate some of these luxuries at home.

Pulling a pair of black Dockers slacks and a yellow button-down oxford shirt out of the closet, I tried to remember what I wore the last time I met Karen. I was not much of a fashion coordinator and didn't want to show up wearing the same outfit she had already seen. 'My God', I thought, 'you haven't worried what outfit you were wearing for fifteen years. Just relax' I reassured myself, 'it's not like she fell for your snazzy clothes in the first place!'

Looking at my watch, I noticed that it was almost seven thirty and that I still had an hour and a half until Karen was due to meet me at Binion's. I checked my Blackberry for messages, and read through the headlines of my daily Internet spam offering sure-fire ways to increase my penis size, breast size and to let me know I could get cheap Viagra rushed to my door. Scanning through the messages, I was disappointed that there was nothing from *Karen*.

The good news, I decided, was that if she were delayed, she would have had a chance to e-mail me, but since she hadn't, she was probably still in the skies somewhere across the country on her way to our rendezvous.

Not quite sure what to do with myself for the next hour or so, I sat down for a minute in front of the Rangers game again, but when they gave up their fifth goal, putting them down by three, I decided I had better things to do.

As Roger would have said, when in Rome, do as the Romans. When in Vegas, gamble.

Now that was something that would take my mind off things for a bit. The question was, how much of a stake should I give myself for the night? It was always a tricky question, because you didn't want to blow too much in one night and feel sick and remorseful for the weekend. Then again, if you had one of those defining moments when you had to split pairs of eights four times and double down on three of them, you couldn't be short on cash.

I could feel the surge of adrenaline as my mind started to contemplate possibilities and knew at once that I'd have no problem staying alert tonight. The flow of cards and numbers, of dice and possibilities was a rush that could stimulate my body and mind for hours on end and I remembered quickly how many times I had left a casino in the brightness of a morning sun. Vegas, Tahoe, AC, it didn't matter where; the rush was the same at every gambling hall/casino I had ever been in.

I settled on a stake of two thousand and for good measure, put an extra five hundred in the buttoned inside pocket of my black and brown hounds tooth blazer. Just in case. The last resort. I didn't think I'd really need it and didn't want to, but if I really, really needed it, it would be nice to have. After all, I reminded myself, remember that time in AC when I dipped into the emergency stash and make that huge comeback and won 25 grand at the craps table?

I knew it was a rationalization, but I didn't care. After all, anyone that tempts lady luck knowing the odds are stacked in the house's favor needs a good rationalization.

My magical elevator brought me to my empty lobby, my Special Forces doorman and to no surprise, my own personal limo and driver waiting outside. The sun had retreated below the mountains, the neon lights were up doing their duty and the night air had a crisp refreshing feel to it.

"To Binion's, please," I requested matter of factly to my driver of the night before, giving him a nod of recognition as he opened my door.

"Absolutely," he replied, "Home of the World Series of Poker."

CHAPTER TWENTY SEVEN

With all the glitz and glamour of neon lights, most of Las Vegas is as fake as a three dollar bill, but walking into Binion's is real! It's like stepping back in time to the days when a good casino was a comfortable smoky old joint. The place had aged through the years, but to a gambler who only wanted to gamble, it had aged as it should. Not gracefully, per se, but like its players, unevenly. The green felt on its card playing tables was almost obscene in its freshness, yet the leather swivel chairs that surrounded the black jack tables looked on average about fifteen years old. The chairs in the "world famous" poker pit did not swivel, did not have a lot of cushion left and probably wouldn't fetch more than five dollars a piece at a garage sale.

In a word, perfect.

Let the weekend wonders that built this down dump their money in brass, crass casinos up the road. This is where the real gamblers lived and played.

I could smell it and wanted to taste it, too.

Hanging out on the perimeter of the poker pit, I realized it would be a while before I could get a seat to play with the big boys. Looking at my watch and noting that it was now nearing eight o'clock, I decided sitting down to play poker was not a good idea anyway, with my date with Karen only an hour away.

It was Friday night, the California weekenders and overnighters were starting to fill the casino, and I decided to try a little $5 and $10 blackjack to whet my whistle and get me into the flow. I found a seat at a $5 table inhabited by a group of serious-looking players with significant piles of red and green chips in front of them, the universal sign of gamblers' net worth in five and twenty five dollar increments, respectively. I plunked down a hundred dollar bill for starters and waded right in, playing for $10 a hand.

Two twenties, two dealer busts and a black jack in my first five hands and I was on my way to a happier state. 'Life is good,' I thought to myself.

One of the great differences between Vegas and Atlantic City is that in Atlantic City, black jack, or 21 as it is sometimes called, is dealt from a shoe that contains six or eight decks at a time and you are not allowed to ever touch your cards. It's fast-paced and efficient, but impersonal and structured to increase the speed with which you can lose your money. It is also the casino's way to deter professionals and card counters from getting an edge over the casino. Binion's had real dealers dealing cards that you could pick up and hold and they used one deck at a time. The way it used to be and the way it should be!

I settled into a rhythm, playing solidly and by the rules that most good black jack players say you have to follow and slowly scratched my way to a profit of about two hundred dollars from my initial stake.

I had no idea what time it was or even where I was when someone patted me on the arm and asked with a sweet voice, "Is this seat taken?" The voice sounded familiar and recognition began to creep into my head as I turned to answer.

It was Karen.

Oh, was it ever! Bedecked in a spaghetti-strapped loose, velvety green dress that plunged into men's hopes, all eyes at the table turned to her as if a cease fire had just been ordered. Her hair was down around her shoulders and more wavy than I remembered it. Her green eyes sparkled in the bright casino lights and the dress swayed as she moved and breathed, stopping the table's action in its tracks. No one moved, two jaws dropped and I smiled broadly not ready to respond. Someone at the end muttered with a Texas twang,

"Well there's always room for a pretty little filly like you."

I tried to stake my claim quickly. "Ah. She's with me." As if to seal the deal, Karen leaned closer and kissed me on the cheek.

"Sorry I'm late. Miss me?" she offered with a big smile.

I told the dealer to cash me out and glanced at my watch, noticing with regret that it was 9:35 PM and it was I that was late.

"I'm so sorry," I said standing up to leave the table. "I totally lost track of time. Did you go to the restaurant?" I was embarrassed.

"No, I was walking through on my way there and happened to see you. I actually watched you play a few hands. God, you are intense. I don't think I've ever seen someone so focused on a game of black jack playing for ten dollars a hand." She was smiling but serious in her analysis.

"I do get kind of wrapped up in thought sometimes, I guess," I admitted apologetically. Not comfortable talking about myself in front of my fellow gamblers, I tried to change the subject quickly, "So do you want to grab a bite to eat?" As I said it I realized that my stomach was agreeing, not happy with sustenance offered by a stream of diet cokes and the Circle K snack of three hours earlier.

"Famished" she said, putting her arm in mine and waiting for me to lead the way.

"I hope they haven't given away our table. I have to admit, I lost track of time while I was playing and didn't call to say I would be late."

"Are you always so brutally honest?" Karen asked. "I wouldn't worry about it anyway. If there is one thing that these casinos don't mind, it is someone gambling into their dinner reservation. I'm sure we'll be fine."

"How do you know so much about casinos?" I asked.

"I do fly here about once or twice a month, you know," she said as if I should have known. I probably should have, but was trying to focus on getting through the crowded casino to the restaurant as most of the men and some of the women turned to look at the spectacle of sexiness and green on my arm. Even the players' eyes in the Poker pit lifted from their tables and followed us as we walked.

"Silly me," I joked. "Now let's get away from the wolves." I really wanted to get a better look at what everyone was looking at, and while I knew it wasn't me, I figured there would be time for that.

"Do you know where you're going?" Karen asked.

"Sure, the restaurant is just ahead here, downstairs. Very cozy."

"Umm, Actually I don't think so," she offered and when we reached the staircase that I remembered, it was blocked by a red velvet rope. "The only time I ate here, about a year or two ago, the restaurant was upstairs on the top floor. Follow me."

Now I was the confused one holding onto her arm as she led me to the elevator bank, where indeed there was a brass sign advertising the Steak House on the twenty third floor.

"I could have sworn the restaurant was downstairs. Last time I was in town, I had two dinners there," I explained apologetically.

"Sure you did," Karen said mockingly. "Don't worry, I won't tell."

We stepped into the elevator and I wanted to face her, drink it all in, but contented myself with her reflection in the golden brass doors. She was stunning. Looking about 5'8" or 9" because of her green high-heeled pumps. I noticed that her dress was an uneven length, cut diagonally so that it covered her left thigh and below her knee, but was cut to a level that showed all of her right leg and most of her thigh. Karen was on my right, so I could not tell just how high it was cut, but her outfit made you want to know more. If you had a pulse, that is. Mine was strong and I could feel it beat nervously as we rode the elevator to the top floor.

The doors opened and we were confronted with a small lobby area. As we entered the foyer, I noticed dining tables off to the right down a couple of steps from the maitre`d's podium, and a bar area to our left. It had the same brown and burgundy feel of the restaurant I remembered in the basement, but was much brighter. As we approached the podium, I realized why. The restaurant perimeter was completely made of glass so that everyone in the restaurant facing the outside had an unobstructed view of the old part of downtown below and the neon lights of the more modern strip in the distance. It was a gorgeous crisp night and the blinking; flashing signs and marquees of the casinos gave the appearance of a huge fantasy land.

We were directed to one of the tables up the stairs and to the left, past the old oak bar and into the smoking section. I realized we hadn't discussed it and I asked Karen apologetically, "Do you prefer smoking or non? I didn't think to ask."

"Either is fine with me," she answered. "I'll take the one with the better view. I'm not really a smoker, but every once in a while when I have a few drinks, I just have to have one."

"Well I do smoke, but I promise that I don't smoke when someone else is eating at the table. Of course, I mean in those states where you still can smoke. I know it's a bad habit and someday I'm going to quit, but I haven't been quite ready to pull the trigger yet." Why I blathered on, I thought.

"Well at least you are comfortable with who you are and don't have any preconceived notions about being able to put them down in an instant like some of my friends. This one guy I dated said he didn't smoke, thinking it would offend me or hurt his chances at getting me in the sack! But whenever we went out he would sneak off to the bathroom and have a quick one. Came back smelling like an ashtray and thought I wouldn't notice because he sprayed his mouth with a shot of Binaca! Can you believe it?" She laughed and smiled an engaging smile. It was pleasurable letting her tell her story, watch her get animated and use her hands and arms as she told her tales. Talk about feeling comfortable with her! I realized I just enjoyed being with her, as her positive attitude was infectious and downright appealing. It was something rarely seen in the restrictive confines of our social structure at home. People worried more about how they looked and how they acted than what they were saying, guarding their image and status and suppressing emotion. It would be a treat to see Karen in the midst of the country clubbers. Shake 'em up a bit.

"Had to dump the poor bastard. Felt bad for him, but I will not spend time with anyone who is mean or dishonest. He wasn't mean, but wasn't honest."

Tough standards, I thought. "So, I guess you've successfully narrowed down the male population by a fair degree," I said sarcastically. "Anybody left that qualifies?"

"Still looking, but there are possibilities," she answered, batting her eyes playfully and flirting hard. This was fun.

The waiter came and asked if we wanted to order a drink and hear about the specials. We both said yes and Karen went with a mai tai, while I stepped up to a rum and diet coke. I rarely drank any more, but somehow felt that a little libation was is order to help calm my nerves and get me through a situation in which I wasn't totally comfortable with. We sat and joked and talked, fitting in shrimp cocktail appetizers and steaks as we went, the New York strip for me and filet mignon for her.

I couldn't decide which view I enjoyed more, that of the lights in the distance of the strip or that of Karen laughing and smiling on my right at our square little cozy table. Somewhere around dessert, I felt her toes playfully touching and rubbing against my leg and tried to remember when I had had such a good time.

For our after dinner drinks, we had flaming shots of peppermint schnapps because, as Karen said, they were fun. She was right. I felt a gentle buzz and was feeling loose and frisky. It had been a while since I had more than a drink or two and years since I had really let go. I talked openly and freely about my joy of trying to find good investments and she talked about the fun places she had been. After I paid the check, she put her hand in my lap and said, "So, where to now? A little sightseeing or should we see if either of us is lucky tonight?"

"Let's do both," I offered, not wanting to lose the moment, but well aware that if we stayed here much longer, I wouldn't be able to stand up without embarrassment. "We'll go check out the light show on Tremont and then pick a casino to see if Lady Luck is smiling on us tonight."

"I feel lucky tonight," she bubbled, putting her arm in mine as we got up to leave. Miraculously, shoes were on both of her feet and we headed off to the light show downstairs on Fremont. I was giddy as we took the elevator ride down, unabashedly staring at her reflection in the doors and wondering about the slit up the side of her dress. Then I realized if I could feel her toes, she was probably not wearing any pantyhose. When the elevator doors opened, I had progressed to wondering if underwear was part of tonight's wardrobe and if so, what kind. Maybe I shouldn't have had that after dinner drink, I thought. For someone who hardly drank anymore, I may have gone a little too far. Oh shit, I said to myself keep it together, you idiot!

The reaction to Karen's passage through the casino was even more pronounced this time, whether it was because she was positively lit up and bouncing along like a kid or because the clientele had drunk more and become bolder. Or was it my mind's altered state playing tricks on me? No matter what the answer was, I really didn't want the Las Vegas weekenders fawning over my date. We spilled out onto Fremont, watched the light show above for about ten minutes and started to contemplate where we should try our luck.

"The Girls of Glitter Gulch looks like fun," Karen teased, knowing that it was not a casino.

"I think we can do better than that," I deadpanned unsuccessfully, my grin refusing to remove itself from my face. "I think I have a better idea," I offered.

"I'm sure you do," she jousted, holding on a little tighter in the cool night air.

"No seriously, let me find my driver. I think he said he'd be right over here on this side street." We walked to the side entrance of Binion's and as promised, my limo was at the ready and my driver waiting patiently alongside.

"Excuse me," I said to my driver, "but is there anyplace we can gamble that's a little more private and less crowded. This place is getting a bit crowded for my liking. Must be the Friday night regulars taking over."

"Yes Mr. Morris, our casino has special gambling rooms for our special guests."

"That's not exactly what I had in mind. I don't play for those kinds of stakes," I said apologetically.

"Don't worry, Mr. Morris. There are no minimum bets and no maximum bets in our private gambling rooms."

"Sounds like fun," Karen squealed. "Let's go show them how it's done. Do they have dice? I love craps. I have no idea what anything means, except the pass line. I know that one. Let's go!"

I couldn't refuse her and fell into the limo to be driven to my casino hotel. "By the way," I asked, "what hotel are you staying at Karen? Where did the airline put you up this time?"

"Wherever you are," she answered dreamily and laid her head on my chest, her hand falling into my lap.

"Uh, driver," I said, speaking up so that he could hear me, "I'm sorry I don't know your name. But would it be possible to drop me at my hotel room first. I might need to get some more cash and freshen up."

"Absolutely, Mr. Morris."

"Good idea, Mr. Morris," Karen echoed, tilting her head up and kissing me on the lips, firmly and ravenously this time, not at all like our first encounter.

I didn't stop her, didn't refuse and gladly and recklessly plunged into the abyss.

CHAPTER TWENTY EIGHT

My eyelids sensed light and had no interest in opening. I could
feel a bed under me and sheets over me and other than that I
wasn't sure of much. Vague recollections about last night floated into
my head. The embrace with Karen in the limo. The hungry groping. The sweet smell of her neck. The elevator ride that bordered on
indecency. Who says that you can't smoke in an elevator? The tearing
off of clothes as we entered my palace in the sky. The things we did
on the bear rug in front of the fireplace for all the world to see if they
happened to be flying by our wide open view. The shower where we
scrubbed and cleaned each other dirty --- till we had to retire to the
bedroom for Round Two.

More parts of my body awoke as the tape of the previous night
played back in my mind.

I squinted open my eyes and was blinded by sunlight. Was it
morning or afternoon, I asked myself? Rolling away from the bright
light to look at my watch, I was confronted by brown waves of hair,
the naked back and the curves of Karen's partially covered bottom. I

touched her lightly-tanned, soft skin to make sure I wasn't hallucinating, and she stirred. Maybe it had happened the way I dreamed it.

The hands of my watch were trying to tell me something, but I was having trouble finding both of them. I opened my eyes further and realized that the hands were on top of each other and it was 9:40 AM. Wow, I haven't slept past 8 AM in months, I thought. As my head throbbed, I reminded myself I also hadn't had that much to drink in years either!

Rolling back toward the windows on the world of Las Vegas, I got out of bed gently and headed off to the bathroom. Along the way I noticed parts of last night's attire strewn about the floor and smiled as the memory of when and how it came off returned.

The mirrors in the bathroom laughed at the sorry, stiff figure passing by and after using the his of his and hers sinks. After brushing my teeth, I headed back to the bedroom. The thought of climbing into the shower was intriguing, but climbing back into bed won in a landslide.

Climbing back in, Karen rolled over, opened her eyes and said with a smile, "So maybe you're not such an old fart after all."

"Huh" I mumbled confused. "Is that a compliment?"

"You look like you're ready to go for a little morning delight, you stud, you."

"No, all men look like this in the morning," I countered, but realized that the lingering memories of the night before hadn't completely left my body.

"We'll see about that" she said, taking the challenge and my manhood in her hand. I couldn't remember the last time I had been touched by a woman down there. It certainly wasn't while I was married to Missy, but it felt good and I wasn't going to wait another twenty years.

The thought took a few seconds to register, but hit me in a flash when it did. Missy. Oh my God, what have I done?

"What's the matter?" Karen asked aware that my mind and body had changed focus.

"What? Umm. Oh God, what have we done?" I said as the guilt and remorse came over me.

"Nothing you have to be ashamed of," Karen answered somewhat perturbed. "In fact, you should be proud of your performance last night. I almost couldn't keep up with you." Her smile returned as she continued, "And don't forget, she walked out on you. You told me all about it last night. I know it sucks, but you have to accept the fact that she left you. If it's meant to be, she'll be back. But you needed last night more than you know. Trust me. I can tell."

I wasn't quite sure what to do with her analysis of my plight. But as she walked through it, I felt the tension and guilt dissipate from my body. Not completely gone, but at least pushed back into the 'I'll figure this all out later' category of my mind. Not saying anything, I closed my eyes and focused again on the pleasure my body was feeling, the warmth of Karen's body next to mine. The warmth of Karen's mouth kissing parts of my body that needed to be touched, the heat of Karen's body on mine. We didn't speak a word. No signs of the ravenous animalistic frenetic couplings of the night before. But happily, my body experienced and felt the pleasure more.

Afterwards, I waited in bed while Karen went to the bathroom and when I heard the shower start, I decided that I too should get up. But after last night's escapades and this morning's dalliance, a communal shower would be anticlimactic to say the least. So, I sat up on the edge of the bed, looked aimlessly ahead at the bright expanse of casinos and mountains before me and did an inventory of where I was.

Slumming in Las Vegas in a high roller's suite, separated from my wife for a week and having slept with another woman, working for my best friend that I didn't completely trust anymore, and oh yeah, with the SEC on my ass. My kids had been stolen away from me, terrorists on the loose, someone planting stories in the Wall Street Journal that could only be with malice and aiming to make my life miserable. My head began to throb and I couldn't tell if it was due to last night's alcohol consumption or the crap that was filling up my life. Quite frankly, I didn't care what it was. I wanted to freshen up, get some food and get on with the day and my life. After all, I did have to get to Ocular and check out trade blotters, pricing and the rest of the garbage on my desk away from home.

I walked into the bathroom, and thankfully Karen was just turning off the shower. I grabbed a towel for her, put it around her when she opened the glass door and stepped out and got a peck on the cheek in return. "Thanks," she said warmly. "You're so sweet."

"You're most welcome," I said straining to keep an upbeat attitude. "Listen," I continued, "I don't know what you've got planned for today, but I actually have to work today. I have a pile of papers that I have to get through."

"So do you want me to leave now?" came the hurt reply.

"No, not at all," I said apologetically. "I'd really like to clean up and get some brunch first. Are you hungry?"

"Famished," she said with a smile. "You take your shower and freshen up. I'll call room service and try to get this place looking a little more respectable and afterwards I'll go shopping and check out the Strip. The walk will do me good. You go do what you have to do. When will you be back?"

I hadn't thought that far in advance, so I guessed. "Probably somewhere between five or six at the latest."

"Some fun you are," she said, putting on a pout that caused immediate regret from me. Her wet hair dangled loosely in thick strands around her face and without her makeup she looked as wholesome and homespun as when I first met her on the plane. But somehow, she was no less adorable or sexy with her wet dangling locks. "Are we having dinner together or should I make other plans?" she probed nervously.

"No, we're on for dinner. You might just meet the friend I told you about."

"The one you are helping out?"

"That's him," I said, now knowing that I had made a decision that I couldn't undo and feeling uneasy as soon as I said it.

"That sounds like fun," she said in her bubbly, happy way, eyes lighting up again and a spring in her body returning. She unwrapped her towel, letting it drop to the floor and game me another peck. "Enjoy your shower. I'll get room service to whip up something fast and I'll see what I can do about finding something to put on." She walked out of the bathroom naked, a beautiful lilt in her walk and I thought to myself, she doesn't have any clothes here to wear other than last night's dress. But looking at her curves as they walked away from me, I decided I wouldn't mind if she didn't find anything to wear for a while.

CHAPTER TWENTY NINE

We rode down the elevator to my always-waiting limo at around noon, having decided that we should drop Karen off at her hotel on the way to Ocular. My daytime limo driver was waiting and neither he nor Mr. Special Forces doorman commented or looked askance at Karen in bare feet, my black boxer-style bathing suit and a white golf shirt.

We giggled to ourselves as we climbed in and I said, "Don't worry, I'm sure they see it all the time" even though I wasn't quite sure what "it" was.

The limo dropped Karen at Circus Circus, where the airline had put up her flight crew for the weekend. It was sad to see that the once glorious casino had aged so poorly through the years. I remembered how I marveled at it when I stopped there on my first trip cross country and how fresh and clean it looked, just like it had in the James Bond movie, "Diamonds Are Forever." Now, a tired and faded façade greeted us, and the paint on the huge clown out front was chipped and in serious need of a fresh coat. The sign out front of the casino advertised 50 cent craps and ten-to-one odds, which showed just how far, down the pecking order of casinos it had fallen.

As Karen stepped out the open door, I half-followed her out and asked the driver holding the door, "Excuse me, but how can Ms. Clarkson get into my room?"

"Well actually, she can't," he said apologetically. "As you are the only registered guest, I am not permitted to bring anyone else to your suite and am not authorized to permit her or anyone access to our complex unaccompanied by you. I'm sorry, but the rules are quite clear and designed to protect our guests."

It was a wrinkle I hadn't contemplated. "Well, I guess I'll just have to come pick you up on my way back from Ocular," I said to Karen, who no longer appeared to be bouncy and happy, as the driver had just made her feel like a less-than-reputable companion for one of the hotel's special guests.

"Why don't I just pick you up on my way back from Ocular?" I suggested.

"Okay, if Mr. Limo Driver will let you," she said in a nasty tone that I hadn't heard from her before.

Mr. Limo Driver said nothing, but continued to hold the door open as Karen and I tried to get our logistics in order.

"Tell you what, be here at 5:30 with your bag and I'll pick you up on my way back to the hotel. And when we get there, I'll see about getting you registered."

"Okay," she said, happier. "I'll be waiting with bells on." Considering her current attire, it wouldn't be hard to improve upon.

She walked off into the hotel casino in her bare feet looking like she was going to a health club, and Mr. Limo Driver got back into the driver's seat and pulled away.

"I'm sorry, Mr. Morris, but there really isn't anything I can do. We have to protect the guests."

"Not to worry," I said, understanding his position. "I'll take care of it later."

I leaned back, lit up a cigarette and closed my eyes. I was already feeling stressed and my day hadn't even begun. When we pulled up to Ocular's headquarters, I noticed the fountains were turned off, which gave the entrance a barren, deserted feel. I was surprised to see that the parking lot to the right of the building, the one that Susan had walked away to yesterday afternoon, had a handful of cars in it. I wondered if one of them was Susan's and who else would be at work on a Saturday afternoon. Must be some cold-calling brokers from the Merrill Lynch or Morgan Stanley offices, I surmised.

I used my credit-card-like passkey to unlock the main door, rode up the elevator and fumbled for the next pass card to open the main door at Ocular. Still fumbling through my cards as I walked down the hall, I noticed that the main door at Ocular's suite was ajar. Had Susan gotten there early and left it open for me I wondered? As I opened the front door the rest of the way and walked into the reception area, I noticed that one of the doors to my office/conference room was open and I could hear raised voices in the background.

I walked around the receptionist desk and saw through the glass windowed conference room wall that Susan was indeed there, seated in one of the chairs at the end of the conference room table, but she was not alone. Terry Burroughs was standing over her with a stack of papers in his hand and was firing questions at her near the top of his voice.

"And what is this pile supposed to be," he yelled, obviously exasperated and fuming. His face was beet red and beads of sweat were glistening on his forehead. His light blue golf shirt was sweat stained under the arms and on his breast plate, as if he was in the middle of a workout.

I rushed into the room and shouted, "Terry, just what the hell do you think you are doing and how did you get in my office?"

Susan answered for him, "I came in about a half hour ago and he just barged in, started going through the piles and yelling at me. Told me if I didn't tell him what's going on, he'd have me fired." She sniffled. "I'm scared. All I wanted to do was get my work done." She meant it with Terry still standing over her ominously,

"This is my company," he said forcefully and looked directly at me, "and I have every right to know what the hell's going on here. I don't know what you're looking for or what you're trying to do, but I'm not going to sit by and have you ruin my company or snatch it away from me."

"Cool your jets, mister," I told him with disgust. "First of all, I want you to leave this office right now. I'll see you in your office in fifteen minutes. In the meantime, I'm going to talk to Susan right now and try to figure out if I should call the police, have you arrested for assault or harassment or anything else I can dream up. But right now, if you want to have any chance of staying out of jail or keeping your company, you will sit in your goddamned office and wait for me and think of all the reasons I shouldn't have you fired first thing Monday morning."

Terry began to get ready for battle, something he obviously did often. I decided that he probably bullied his way to get what he wanted on a regular basis. Terry tried to take control of the situation. "You have no right to come in here..."

I interrupted his tirade forcefully, "Now stop right there, Mr. Burroughs. I have every right to be here and you know it. Now get out of here before I call the police. I'll see you in fifteen minutes." I turned away from him and focused on Susan, sitting in the chair cowering and sniffling away her tears. I gave her my handkerchief and told her to calm down. I glanced at Terry, who was standing there seeming confused and told him, "This is your last warning. By the count of three, if you are still in this office, I'm having you brought up on charges. One, two...." On two, Terry dropped the stack of papers he was holding onto the table and stormed out of the conference room. For good measure, I shouted, "Three," just as he got to the doorway, which caused him to look back at me, glare, grab the door handle and slam it closed so hard that the window wall shook violently, reverberating to the floor and desk.

I turned to Susan and said, "Don't worry. It's safe now. I'll make sure he never bothers you again. Now what happened?"

Susan tried to gather her wits and I could tell she was trying to focus and piece together what happened. "I came in, like I said, about twelve. I wasn't sure what time you were going to be here so I came in to your office and sat down to sort through some of the piles. I wasn't here for more than ten minutes when Mr. Burroughs came storming in and wanted to know what each pile was. He was relatively calm at first, but then with each pile got worse, yelling things like, 'Insider trading, my ass,' and 'Lots of luck on that one' and had that crazy wildness about him. I think he's lost it. You came in as he was asking me about the pile of high yield portfolios that I got for you late yesterday." She finished relating her story and looked up at me for direction. "I'm sorry," she said, "I didn't know what to do." I'd heard about Terry's out bursts, but had never had one directed at me. They say he has these moods where every thing is fine until, wham, he loses it. I never realized how venomous he could be.

"You did just fine," I said trying to console her. "There was nothing else you could have done. I'm just sorry he put you through that. It's my fault. I never should have let you come in today." While there had been rumors Terry was tough to work for. I hadn't realized just how tough, nor how much he might feel threatened by me rummaging through his and the firm's trading records.

"I just wanted to help I had no idea he was even here," she argued. "I still want to help."

"Don't worry. You will. But right now, we need to straighten out these piles and figure out where we stand before I meet with Mr. Burroughs."

"Okay. I'll do what I can," Susan offered, getting up from her chair and recreating the piles she had organized yesterday that Terry had strewn about in his fit of rage.

After calming Susan down and giving her something to focus on, my task was to try to figure out what to do with Terry Burroughs.

Things were spinning out of control and I had to get to the bottom of what was going on at Ocular, and fast -- before Terry could harass Susan or any other employees, before he could disrupt my project any further. I couldn't spend all of my time fixing Ocular's problems while I still had a life and a company to run twenty five hundred miles eastward. God, I missed my kids. And yes, I missed Missy, too. I had to figure out how I was going to get the kids away from Grandma the Witch, as Kathleen had so aptly dubbed her. I didn't know if I had lost Missy forever or if she was just having one of her moods. Nevertheless, she had never had a mood like this.

"I think I've gotten the piles back in order," Susan said, interrupting my reverie. "What should we do now?" She was back in her element, doing things that took her mind off the hell of fifteen minutes earlier.

"I really want to focus on the trading situation. I want to figure out what Terry is doing in his personal portfolio and when and why stocks are bought in client accounts. Let's focus on that first."

Susan perked up and walked me through our stack of trading records. "Okay," she started. "I've gotten all of Mr. Burroughs' personal trading information in this pile here," she offered pointing to the sheaf of papers in her hand, laying them in front of me. "And in this pile I have the firm-wide purchases of stocks color coded and cross referenced when Mr. Burroughs bought his stocks and when the firm's clients did. I color coded the names as you suggested." She was proud of her work and the thoroughness of her completion of the task. "Unfortunately, for your purposes, I can't find any times when he bought within a week of the firm buying the stock. You can see I have daily totals of activity for the firm, and no conflict or, what did you call it, front-running seems to have occurred."

"Well, let's have a closer look," I said smiling. "You know what they say about crooks, they always slip up somewhere."

Susan forced a smile and sat down in the chair next to me. "Where do we start?" she asked.

"Did you notice any other patterns?" I asked, not expecting any substantial clues.

"Well, just one," she said sheepishly, "but it probably doesn't mean anything. I'm almost embarrassed to mention it because it probably doesn't mean a thing."

"Never mind about that," I said. "I have two mottos. One. There is no such thing as a stupid question and two, you never can tell what is important on the surface. In life, it's the little things that are often the most important. That goes for picking stocks, figuring out who your real friends are, who you fall in love with." Probably the wrong thing to bring up, I thought. Susan was waiting, listening, absorbing and seemed unfazed. "You know wars can start with a single errant shot." Where was I going with this tutorial? "Anyway, back to the issue at hand. "What else did you find?"

"Well, it probably isn't anything, but I found it odd that Mr. Burroughs always seemed to buy 10,000 shares of stock when he bought a new name."

"That's not all that odd," I offered. "When I buy stocks, I usually buy 5,000 shares of each company I buy. Don't worry, it was worth mentioning."

"Well then isn't it odd that when Ocular would start buying a stock, they also usually bought 10,000 shares the first day they started buying a new name." She looked across at me quizzically, not knowing what it meant, if anything.

I closed my eyes, leaned back and thought for a few seconds as to what the trading pattern might mean, and then it dawned on me.

"Do you remember off hand, if when Ocular bought stock in a company, was it bought on successive days and at a higher or lower prices?"

"I don't understand the question," Susan replied, confused.

My mind was racing. "Never mind," I said. "Show me Ocular's trading blotter summary. The list of purchases and sales by date."

Susan handed me the bigger sheaf of papers and said, "Here it is, but I'm still not sure what you're looking for."

I scanned the first few pages and noticed that Susan was right. Ocular usually did start buying a new name with 10,000 shares and often didn't buy more the next day unless the price was a point or more lower than where it bought its first shares. In a vacuum, that would make sense. But there were a number of instances where Ocular didn't buy any shares the day after it started a new position and a few times when it waited three days before it began buying more shares. When it did delay purchasing more shares, the stock price usually had dropped before it began adding to or building its position.

I quickly flashed back to my meeting with the traders and the issue of not allocating trades on the same day. "This is it!! I think we've found the proverbial smoking gun!" I exclaimed. "I think it's time I had my little chat with Terry Burroughs," I said, grinning ear to ear. All of a sudden I felt like I was unknowingly irritating Roger "Don't you worry, that son of a bitch is going to fry." Then remembering how threatening Terry had been in his rage toward Susan, I paused to consider how best to approach the situation at hand. After all, I wouldn't put it past him to have a gun in his desk to threaten people, and then I debated whether or not it would be loaded. Maybe this was not an issue I wanted to bring up in an almost empty building on a Saturday afternoon with a man who had been on the verge of physically attacking Susan a short while ago.

Maybe I needed to figure out Plan B.

"What have you found?" Susan asked. "Have you figured out what you wanted?"

"Yes, but I'd rather not tell you. Nothing personal, but as they say, what you don't know..."

"...can't hurt you?" she asked.

"Tell you what," I said to Susan, reconsidering my strategy. I would like you to make a copy of these two sets of documents and put them in a FedEx envelope and go put it in the FedEx box outside immediately. Send it to my office with a note to Tina that this information is for my meeting with Mr. Sowers on Monday." Then all of a sudden, I realized it was Saturday and the logistics immediately became an issue.

"Is there a Saturday pick up here at the FedEx box?" I asked concerned now that I had the paper trail and how would I protect it or make sure that it got into the right hands.

"I'm not sure," Susan answered. "But I can call FedEx and see if there are any boxes locally that have a Saturday pick up and drop it off for you."

"That would be great," I offered half-heartedly, still not convinced that I could guarantee that the smoking gun would make its way east.

"You know I could also fax it or scan it and e-mail it as an attachment to your office, if you want."

I looked at Susan, got up, gave her a quick thumbs-up as she sat waiting for direction and said, "Do all the above, and thank God for technology."

CHAPTER THIRTY

After watching Susan fax, e-mail and put copies of our notes in the FedEx envelope, I decided I was ready to confront Terry Burroughs. Not about his personal trading or the firm's trading I would save that for later, I would confront him about his threats toward Susan, his dealings with Spindletop and the issues about the high yield pricing discrepancies. I walked out of my glass-walled office, leaving Susan to search out the FedEx location that accepted Saturday deliveries. I told her she had done a great job, had been a huge help and didn't need to come back today. She'd been through enough already.

I took my plain white legal pad with me, innocuous enough except for my three little notes to myself in order in the top right corner: Susan, Spindletop and High Yield pricing. Taking a deep breath as I approached Terry's office, it was as if I were going into a dentist appointment knowing that I was about to have three teeth pulled. I knocked twice on the dark walnut door with the nameplate for none other than "Terence J. Burroughs, President." I heard Terry grunt a disdainful, "Yeah" and walked in.

The darkness of the office struck me immediately, as the dark green vertical blinds were tilted such that very little of the bright Vegas sky could penetrate the inner sanctum of his office. Whatever view the office had of the casinos in the distance was cloaked and hidden from sight. Terry sat hunched behind his desk with his right hand on the computer keypad and appeared to be reviewing news stories on his Bloomberg screens. Pictures of Terry smiling broadly and shaking hands with various political dignitaries dotted the walls and the bookcase/credenza behind Terry's desk was filled with Lucite cubes and other shapes representing deals that Ocular must have participated in.

"Trying to catch up on last week's news stories or playing the futures markets overseas?" I asked light-heartedly in an attempt at a non-threatening opening.

"What do you want?" Terry barked in reply, keeping his finger on the pulse of his computer keypad, but turning his angry face toward mine. The hour or so since our little chat hadn't exactly changed his mood and I could feel the contempt and disgust which lathered over his every syllable. There weren't many of those syllables, which I decided was a hidden benefit.

"Well, I think we have a few items we still have to discuss." Might as well start off with what he was expecting. "You realize I could have you brought up on harassment charges after your little display this morning."

"Listen buster, I founded this firm and I have every right to know just what it is you're doing and what is going on at my firm." He was ready for a fight and wasn't about to try to control his emotions.

"Well, I appreciate your love for your firm and what you created, but let's not forget that you no longer own a majority stake in the firm. "Remember," I lectured, "you sold 75% of Ocular to First American last year."

"…as I am continually reminded by Roger Maydock."

"Well anyway, I believe that for starters on Monday you will announce to your firm that Susan Emery is no longer going to be a receptionist, and that she will be serving as a Senior Administrative Assistant to me, with full unfettered access to any and all parts of the firm. I don't plan on spending any more time in Las Vegas than I have to and Susan will be my eyes and ears for what's going on out here. Contrary to what you may be thinking, I have no interest in running your firm, but remember this, if you so much as raise your voice to her again, I will have you out on your ass in an instant."

"That sounds like a threat," Terry said rhetorically.

"It is, but do you understand? Are we in agreement?"

"Yeah, I guess so," he lamented.

"No guessing about it. Do we have a deal?" I pressed him.

"Yeah. Okay. What else is on your mind? I'm busy. I have work to do."

"Well, I'd like to go over how you price your high yield issues. You know, the junk bonds you hold in some of your mutual funds."

"Yeah, what about them?"

"Well, I know there was a pricing discrepancy on some of your bond holdings versus where they were being priced by First American." I was fishing but he wouldn't take the bait.

"We have state of the art pricing services and our pricing policies are well documented in our offering documents. Maybe you should do some homework before you head off on a wild goose chase. There's nothing there. I don't give a damn how First American values its bonds. The SEC has reviewed what we do and has never had a problem with how we value our stocks or bonds."

"And when was the last time the SEC was here?" I asked, knowing full well that it was two years ago, before the merger.

"You know better than that. I'm not a fool and don't think I don't know the first thing you probably asked for before you got here was our latest SEC review and their recommendations."

"Well that may be all fine and good with the SEC, but give me the Cliff's Notes version. How do you go about pricing illiquid issues?"

"You know how it's done, don't play dumb with me." Beads of sweat were rolling down his forehead, though the dark office didn't feel any hotter than 70 degrees. "We use IDC, Interactive Data, to price our bonds, and when they don't know what the price is or should be, we direct them to the brokers that have been most active in the issues in question."

"And I'm sure they want to keep their clients, like you, happy with the quotes they are making on those bonds." It was a trick that had been around ever since Michael Milliken had redefined the high yield market in the 1980's. But there wasn't much anybody could do about it. Still, it gave me a good segue into the Spindletop issue. So where did you come up with the pricing for Spindletop at year end?"

"Like I said, we got the prices from IDC." He was tiring of the inquisition, and his exasperation showed.

"But how could you value their bonds at a premium to par when you knew the company was running short on cash?"

"It was not our pricing, damn it. It was IDC's price."

"Nevertheless, here's a company that you know is nearly insolvent and you let the pricing services continue to value their bonds at levels that do not reflect their financial troubles. You know you have a responsibility to price their bonds accurately."

"They are going to make it. We are in discussions to provide them with a convertible issue that should tide them over until their well at Spindletop comes in."

"And what if the well doesn't come in?"

"Then we've made a bad investment." He harrumphed. "We've made them before."

"And when will someone tell the public just how dire the company's finances are?"

"That's up to the company, it's not our job."

"Well, maybe the SEC will have a different idea," I said, standing up and walking toward the door.

"Don't fuck with me, mister," Terry threatened. "You'll be sorry."

I turned my head and said, "I already am sorry I met you, but I think it is you that are fucked." I enjoyed closing the door harder than I meant, and hearing the door shake and something on the other side fall and break.

"Goddammit!" Terry shouted to the world.

"Have a nice day," I said to myself, chuckling. "Now I can get some real work done."

CHAPTER THIRTY ONE

The limo was waiting as normal outside when I stepped into the hot Vegas sun at 5:00 PM. Susan called on her cell to let me know she had found her FedEx drop off spot and was going to head to the gym to put in some time on the stair master. I remembered the well-shaped calves and legs and quickly reminded myself that I had enough issues with the opposite sex to keep me busy for a long time.

Mr. No-Name driver dutifully opened my door and handed me an envelope. "In case you want another key to your room, everything has been taken care of. Just say the word and Ms. Clarkson will be registered to be your guest."

"Yes, please. And thank you. Now, I believe she is waiting for us somewhere outside of Circus Circus."

Closing the door he said, "We're on our way. Again, the management would like to apologize for any embarrassment or inconvenience you might have experienced."

I waited until the driver was in the car before I said "it's Ms. Clarkson that is owed the apology."

"Yes sir," was his only reply, which he said to the windshield ahead of him, not looking me in the eye or the mirror.

I checked my cell phone for messages and not finding any, decided to call my voice mail at home to see what was going on with my life 2500 miles away. The usual social inquiries were on the machine, which made me think maybe people at home didn't know that Missy had bolted town. However, I reconsidered and realized that the messages were generally from our gossipy friends, who were probably fishing for dirt and trying to figure out if the rumor mill was true. The last message was from Missy, and hearing her voice, my heart skipped a beat.

"Tommy," she said shakily, "I'm sorry. I didn't know what to do. Call me when you get back, or anytime. I'm still at the beach, but will be coming home at the end of the week. I'm not sure where or what I'll be coming home to, but I hope you enjoy your time away. I know you always liked Vegas. It was a mistake for me to go to Mom's, but I just... Oh never mind, we'll talk when you get back. We need to talk more. Maybe that's it. I don't know. Well, I guess that's it. Have fun. I heard some rumors that your own life hadn't been too much fun lately. Between the terrorist bombing and the article in the Journal, you must be going a little crazy too. Well, I have to go. I'm just rambling anyway. You know how I hate these machines. Call me when you get a chance. I miss you."

My initial reaction was one of elation, but as I thought about where I was and who I was with, a sense of guilt and dread came over me.

'Oh shit' I thought, replaying the message. 'Now what am I going to do?'

"We're here," the limo driver announced and I realized that we were pulling up to the front of Circus Circus and Karen, as promised, was waiting out front looking ready for the night!

Her hair was pulled back except for three or four Bo Derek braids dangling seductively on either side of her face. A red chiffon dress that crossed her breasts in an X showed more than most lingerie, though it fell to her knees. Her red leather pumps completed the "You-got to-want-a-piece-of-this" outfit.

As the limo pulled up, Karen's face lit up almost as much as her outfit. She grabbed her black travel bag on wheels by the extendable handle and came over to the car. I was surprised, but Mr. No Name driver hopped out of his front seat and popped the trunk, grabbed her bag by the handle, opened the door for her and placed her bag in the trunk. I guessed an attitude change had occurred and it worked its magic on Karen as well, who seemed genuinely surprised and appreciative of the newfound courtesy of the driver who had treated her like a whore five hours earlier.

"Hey there," she beamed, climbing quickly into the back seat next to me, giving me a peck on the cheek and slipping her arm through mine and snuggling up close. She smelled fresh and herbal, and looked like a girl you'd dream of meeting some night, but knew was out of your league. "We've got to stop meeting like this," she giggled, then added "or maybe we should keep meeting like this."

Looking at her beautiful smiling face, dangling braids, the plunging fullness of her breasts, I knew I was out of my league. But then again, what league did I belong in? And now that Missy had called and said basically that all was forgiven, what was I going to do?

"Back to the hotel please," I said loud enough for the driver to hear.

"Yes, Mr. Morris," came the professional reply.

"I think I need a shower and a little freshening up," I said nonchalantly to Karen.

"We can get fresh right here if you want," she offered, putting her hand in my lap.

"I don't think that's such a good idea," I answered with a more negative tone than I intended.

She sensed it and withdrew her hand, moving back to her own seat. "You know, I can't figure you out. One minute we have this connection, this feeling. Then all of a sudden, you get as cold as ice.

I'm not ever sure what I'm going to get with you. You know it's kind of, what should I call it, disconcerting, unnerving. I don't know, but it's not a great feeling."

"I'm sorry," I said. "Rough day at the office. I've got a lot on my mind right now, some big decisions to make and all that. I'll be better after a shower."

"I hope so," she said frowning. "I thought this was supposed to be fun for you. Some break. Are all your vacations this much fun?"

"Well no, this is not really a vacation, but I promise, no more talk of work. I'll snap out of it. Dinner with my friend Roger should help liven things up. You'll like him. Quite the character."

"Oh tell, tell. What's he like? This is your friend from growing up?" Her interest was piqued and she had new life.

"Yup," I answered. "That's the one."

"Oh, this will be fun. I'll get him to tell me all about what you were like, before you became so serious. I'll get him to tell me all your deepest, darkest secrets."

Maybe dinner with Roger and Karen wasn't such a good idea after all.

CHAPTER THIRTY TWO

"So, did ya get a date?" Roger asked rhetorically, when he called my room at 6:35.

I could almost see his mouth gape open and jaw drop on the other end of the line when I answered smugly, "Yes, I did, as a matter of fact."

Roger was speechless for about ten seconds, close to a personal best for him I was sure, and then he mumbled, "Well, I, uh, didn't really think that you would, so I didn't want to show you up and I, am, uh, stag. So, uh, what do you want to do?" It was great to hear him unprepared and caught off guard, where he lost his polish and control. I was rather enjoying his discomfort.

"No, we're still on," I said smugly. "Too bad you couldn't roust up a date for yourself. Want me to get you one?"

"Now stop it," Roger protested. "Do you or don't you have a date for tonight?"

"You'll have to wait and see. Where are we meeting for dinner and what time?"

"Seven o'clock in the Samurai Room. It's supposed to be the best Japanese food in town. I've got a private table with our own personal chef. But I've got to know how many we are. Do you honestly have a date?"

Roger was beside himself trying to understand how I could have a date. "Did you hire someone?" he asked.

"That would be cheating and no, I wouldn't do that. You know me better than that." This was fun.

"So there's three of us then?" He asked again.

"Unless you can scrounge up a date, in which case we would be four. See you at seven," I said, and hung up the phone.

"What was that all about?" Karen asked, sitting in one of the plush chairs facing the downtown Vegas skyline and casinos below. She had her red pumps off and was resting her painted toes on a sofa pillow which she had placed on the coffee table in front of her.

"Just having a little fun," I answered smiling. "And yes, I do have fun sometimes."

"So does your friend have a date for tonight? Or am I going to be the only female at this quaint little dinner?"

I couldn't tell if she thought this was a good or bad turn of events. "Just you" I said. "Think you can handle it?"

A smile broke across her face. "Listen, if I can handle a plane full of sex-crazed businessmen, I think I can handle having dinner with two men. Unless, of course, this friend of yours bites, that could be a different story."

"He's been known to," I offered. The tête-à-tête was fun and helped relieve some of the tension that had developed between us since I had spurned her advances on my way to the shower minutes earlier.

"This could be fun," Karen said, smiling mischievously.

"Let's go down to the restaurant and have a drink" I suggested.

"The best idea I've heard today" she giggled, ready for the game ahead. Yes, that was it. It all seemed like a game to Karen. Which had its attraction, but not something that would have too much staying power. We'd have to see.

Going down the private elevator to the lobby, I realized I had no idea where the Samurai Restaurant was or how I was going to find it. But when the doors opened, my escort of the previous evening, was again waiting for me.

"Would you like to go to your dinner appointment, Mr. Morris, or would you prefer to try your luck at our casino?"

I searched my brain for his name and thankfully noticed his name tag. "Henri, no I think we'll go straight to the restaurant and try our luck at the tables after dinner."

"As you wish, Mr. Morris. Follow me, please. And Ms. Clarkson, might I say you look stunning this evening."

I did a double take to make sure that Karen wasn't wearing a name tag too. She wasn't and I just chalked it up to one more reason why this whole hotel experience was beyond belief.

"Well, thank you, Henri. I'm glad someone noticed," Karen answered. It was a good jab, more than a glancing blow, and I probably deserved it, but I would survive.

We followed Henri down the same hallway as the night before, but turned off to a doorway on the right at the end of the carpeted pathway. I chuckled to myself, the person who designed all these secret pathways and private halls had to be certifiable. When Henri opened the door for Karen and me, we were in the private lounge area of the most spectacular Japanese restaurant I had ever seen. The floors were square glass panels with twelve to eighteen inch koi, still big goldfish to me, swimming by underneath us. Huge tanks and aquariums served as walls, with dozens of varieties of rare and spectacularly colorful fish. The tables were simple and square teak of various sizes to seat parties of four to twelve. Each table had its own three-walled private enclosure, with a six foot by three foot steel hibachi grill serving as a barrier in front. To top it off, there was a private bridge to each of these special tables that crossed over open water below, with the huge goldfish passing by. Bonsai trees of three to six feet dotted the dining area and created a feel of being a world away.

"This is cool" Karen said, genuinely impressed and once again happy to take my arm.

Our maître`d, Masaki, bowed and said, "Mr. Morris, so happy you have chosen to dine with us. May I show you to your table or do you prefer to wait in our lounge for Mr. Maydock?" His English was nearly flawless, though his accent was thick and once again I felt like everything I did was on a news ticker being broadcast everywhere in the hotel.

"No, I think we'll sit down at our table and have a drink there. Thank you."

"Hi," he said, the Japanese affirmation and added with a bow again, "very good, Mr. Morris. Would you and the lady follow me, please?"

Masaki led us across a bridge to the corner table. He angled the table out so that Karen could slide into the middle couch-type seat against the wall, while I chose to sit against the far wall, diagonally next to her. We could have both fit on her bench, but I thought it would be awkward when Roger came.

We ordered Kirin and Sapporo beers to keep with the mood and marveled at the fish surrounding us, trying to determine how big the tank must be and how much this extravagance must have cost to build. I wondered to myself how I'll handle drinking two nights in a row, when once every couple of months was more my style.

As we made small talk about the fish and the aquariums we had as kids, I could feel Karen's toes playing with my pant leg and socks and thought, oh no, I'm not ready for this. Thankfully, Masaki's delivery of Roger altered the concentration capabilities of her toes.

Roger was all smiles, though none directed at me as he said, "So you weren't kidding, after all. And who might this be and more importantly, what did J. Thomas tell you to get you to have dinner with him tonight?"

Karen was ready to play. "Actually, I was the one that seduced him and forced him to take me out to dinner. So, you must be Roger." She batted her eyes and offered her hand. Roger, the consummate flirt, kissed it and slid in next to her on the bench seat. So much for worries about awkward seating arrangements.

"And hi, how are you, Thomas, would be an appropriate greeting," I said scolding Roger. Unfazed, he kept his eyes on Karen, obviously drinking in her looks, her beauty and then staring unselfconsciously at her breasts.

"Nag, nag, nag," he said. "Can't you see I'm busy right now?" He grabbed Karen's hand and said, "So tell me how on earth did you get mixed up with J. Thomas and do you have any idea what a rare event this is?"

Karen was enjoying the attention. "Whatever do you mean?" she prodded. "And why do you call him J. Thomas?"

"Ole J. Thomas hasn't told you about our misspent youth? Well, I'll give you a hint. What do you roll and smoke and can get you in a heap of trouble... has a pungent odor..."

Karen giggled and smiled a sweet smile. "Shame on you for not telling me! You know I could've probably gotten a joint from one of the young flight attendants. They always seem to have friends that they hook up with and party with till all hours when we travel. Especially in LA and Vegas."

"Thanks but no thanks," I said quickly. That was the last thing I needed. Roger, on the other hand, was not so defiant.

"Hmm. That's an idea. For old time's sake, J. Thomas?"

"Thanks, but I think I'll pass." Sure it was an intriguing thought, but that's not why I was there, not to relive and re-enact some of parties of years ago. 'Why am I here?' I wondered. I should be home with Missy and the kids, and now I was trapped in a situation that was quickly losing its appeal.

"Party pooper," Roger said with a tone that made it clear he was willing to head out to the parking lot right then and there to have a toke. "Do you realize, Karen, that J. Thomas here has been a priest for the last thirty years and just left the monastery a week ago?"

"Okay, Roger," I interrupted, "that's enough. And thirty years? Let's not let this little fabrication of yours get too far from reality. Karen knows my history. We met on my plane flight out to L.A. a week ago and she just happened to be in Vegas this weekend on a layover. Let's just change the subject."

"Layover, huh?" Roger chuckled, "Now there's a great dual entendre."

Karen giggled and I rolled my eyes.

"I bet J. Thomas hasn't told you about our little game, has he?" Roger asked, still focusing on Karen, looking deeply into her eyes.

"No, not at all," Karen replied also seemingly transfixed by Roger's stare. "What game?"

"Well, whenever we get together, we play a little game. A challenge really. I try to stump Thomas on a word origin. You know he is incredibly well educated, all the best schools, etc. Thomas, in turn, tries to stump me with a useless piece of Yankee trivia. It's a lot of fun. You should join in." Finally, Roger took his eyes off Karen, looked brightly at me, long enough to say, "Go for it, you're up first," before turning his gaze back to Karen. "Stump us."

"Yeah, go ahead," Karen chimed in, finally looking over my way.

"All right," I said ready to play our age-old game. "Babe Ruth's called shot..."

"1932 World Series, Game 3" Roger answered interrupting the question.

"No, that's not the question. It's in three parts but yes, you are right so far. But since you jumped the gun, no credit yet. Number one: Who was the pitcher? Number two, who was on deck? And Number three, what did he do?"

"Ah, that's easy," Roger complained, but obviously pleased that I was going to make him look good in front of Karen. "Charlie Hoot, now that's a hoot of a name," he slapped Karen's arm with a big motion but no force, leaving his hand there. "Lou Gehrig on deck and he homered too! You must have watched 'Pride of the Yankees' again in the past week or two."

It amazed me how he could recall this baseball trivia in an instant, while I had to write notes to myself about questions to ask Roger before we went out for our ever-less-frequent dinners.

"OK, OK, we're impressed," I said, in mock disgust. Karen just smiled and wanted more. "Three points, swish, nothing but net," I said, doing my best impression of a well-known New York sportscaster and displayed a picture-perfect follow through of an imaginary basketball shot, with fingers finishing the wave. I held the pose for effect for a few seconds, much as a professional would as he watched the ball sail through the net.

Roger took over. "And now batting in the bottom of the ninth, my arch rival and nemesis, J. Thomas Morris." He hissed a crowd sound that didn't sound at all like a crowd, but hey, it was all in fun. I braced myself. Would he give me a fat one down the middle or start me off with a change of pace or curve ball?

"We'll start you off easy," Roger said and winked to Karen seeming very interested in how this game was going to progress.

"No, make it a hard one," she argued playfully.

"I'm going to leave that one alone" he said to Karen playfully. "You left yourself wide open on that one and you obviously don't know what you've gotten yourself into with me." She giggled and Roger's satisfied smile indicated just how comfortable he was playing the flirt.

"OK, enough foreplay. Where did the word fiasco come from and why did it come to represent a complete failure?"

"Oh, that is hard" Karen remarked.

Roger, however, knew that I knew this one. He had stumped me on it before and reveled in telling me its origin. He was now giving me an opportunity to look good in front of Karen.

I played along with the game and spent at least ten seconds acting as if it might be hidden in the vast depths of my brain somewhere, if only I could find it. I could sense Karen looking at me, even though I had closed my eyes for effect.

"Hmmm," I started softly, not sure how much to play it up and how to sound as if I were putting this together on the fly. "Let's see. Well, it does sound Italian and the Italians were world-renowned for the fine glass and stained-glass windows they made. Did you know that when glassblowers are attempting to make a glass bottle, they must blow it perfectly? It's an incredibly precise and skilled profession."

"Keep it clean," Roger joked.

Karen giggled.

"Anyway, when a bottle has the slightest little flaw, the glassblower will scrap the bottle and make a common flask. And you'll never guess what the Italian word for flask is." Karen kept her eyes on me and smiled, but appeared unsure how to respond.

I paused for effect and then answered my own question, "Fiasco!" Roger winked at me and our secret was intact. The bond was still tight, regardless of what had transpired over the past few weeks. I decided it was time to wrap up the game. "So fiasco came to represent the glassblower's failure. So endeth the lesson," I added, quoting Sean Connery in the movie "The Untouchables."

"Bravo," Roger said, clapping his hands in mock applause.

"That's neat," Karen chirped in. "How did you know that?"

Roger answered for me, "A deprived youth is the only explanation."

"Thanks," I said.

"What's an easy one like?" Karen asked. "I want to play."

"Okay," I said, trying to regain control of the situation somewhat, "Where does the word "jeep" come from? You know, like an army jeep."

"I have no idea," Karen answered quickly. "...weren't jeeps just cars for the military originally?"

"Very good start," I commended her. Yes, jeeps were used by the military, and they were considered General Purpose Vehicles or G. P.'s for short. Over the passage of time, G.P. became jeep. Lots of words start that way."

"That's neat," Karen said. "Fascinating," she added. "I want more. Give me another one."

"Okay, do you know where the word tip comes from? You know, what we are supposed to give waiters and waitresses?"

"No idea, whatsoever," Karen answered quickly. "Where did it come from?" She turned to Roger. "Do you know this?"

"Oh yeah, we were past these easy ones by the time we were in our mid twenties."

"Where does it come from?" she begged.

"Tip comes from the abbreviation TIP, which originated in English taverns and inns. Taverns would put a box on the wall for customers to put coins in for the benefit of the waiters or waitresses and there was a sign on or above the box that read 'To Insure Promptness' the initials TIP became standard and lo and behold, the word tip was born."

"Amazing" she gushed. "I want to try this out on my friends. Tell me more. Better yet, do you have one that will stump Tommy?"

I cringed at the name, which I hadn't been called since grade school, but didn't say anything. Roger smiled and said, "I just might."

"Okay," I said, "but this is the last one or we'll never get to dinner. We still haven't even ordered."

"Pooh," Karen responded with a frown. "Every party needs a pooper."

"All right, Roger. Bring on the heat."

"This is a tough one, Karen," Roger warned. Old J. Thomas could go down swinging on this one." I was happy to hear one of my preferred names being used again.

"Where does the word salary come from?"

Fast ball yes, but no movement and I could hit this one. 'How much should I milk it?' I thought. Enough of the games, I told myself. I needed some food to go with my empty bottle of Sapporo.

"Do you know Karen," I started in lecture form, "that in ancient Roman times soldiers were given an allowance to buy salt. Critical stuff, in those days for preparing food. So, their allowance was called salt money or a salarium, with sal being the word for salt. So that's where the word salary comes from. Pretty neat, huh?" Roger was impressed, Karen was wowed and I was happy.

"Now let's figure out dinner," I said, trying to move things along.

"Okay" Karen answered. "But right now I've got to go to the ladies room. Wonder where that comes from?" she giggled. "Just order me the shrimp and chicken if they have it." I stood up to let her out of my side, since Roger had pinned her between us, and I angled the table as Masaki had. "Back in a flash," she said, as she slid by me, putting her hand on my arm to steady her or to let me know we still had a connection. I couldn't tell which.

I sat back down and Roger and I watched her sashay across our little bridge to find the ladies room. She carried herself confidently and knew we were staring at her every move.

"Where on earth did you find her?" Roger whispered as she walked away. "Is she really a stewardess or did you hire her for my enjoyment. She is unbelievable."

"Calm down, boy. Keep it under control and in your pants. Yes, she's a stewardess, divorced and obviously lots of fun.. You two are very similar, really, in a way. You both love games. Which reminds me. How the hell did I ever let you talk me into this Ocular gig? Terry Burroughs is the devil incarnate, you know?"

"Yeah, I know," he confessed guiltily. "Sorry about that. And now today, I find out that I might not even need your help getting rid of him."

"Say what!?!" I couldn't believe my ears. "What the hell are you talking about? Do you know what I've already been through for you… and what personal danger I might be in for crossing his path?"

"I know, I know. But don't worry. It looks like this could turn into one of the easiest half mill you've ever made."

"I doubt it," I answered. "So what's going on? Have you found out that he cheated on his income tax, which I bet he did, or have you gotten wind of some shady dealings with some local mobsters? You know, I just might have found your smoking gun."

"That's great. We may want to keep that in our file. But our game plan is playing out even better than we thought it would. Spindletop was so sure they were going to hit in the Slaughterhouse Trend, they made some very, and let me emphasize very, aggressive lease deals in the area. As you know, when oil companies think they have a really good prospect, they usually try to lock up the surrounding acreage so that if and when the well hits, they can control development in the area and keep a big piece for themselves. Well, what we've learned is that the boys at Spindletop were so sure they'd know details on the well by the end of the month, meaning two weeks ago, that they leased three different acreage blocks surrounding their little exploratory well. These lease deals require them to either have a well drilling, or spud as the drillers say, within a certain period of time or lose the license. And get this, the lease deals are going to expire in the next two weeks. They got the leases cheap, because they were short-term, drill'em or lose'em, and now they are scrambling to get three rigs on location and wells spudded on the surrounding acreage or they are going to lose their leases."

Roger took a breath, but could not contain his excitement. He continued "So now they are on the ropes, scrambling for cash. They called us up today to see if we would waive their net worth and working capital covenants and, oh yeah, lend them another ten million dollars by next week." Roger leaned back, put his arms out and rested them on the top of his bench seat and smiled smugly, proud of him and reveling in the plight that had befallen Spindletop.

"And what about Terry's idea of lending them the money and doing a quickie private deal?"

"No can do. Now that Spindletop is in violation of our lending covenants, we control the cards. Game, set, match!" Roger was on top of the world and absolutely loving his view.

"So what happens now?" I asked.

"Well, it goes a little like this. Monday, they announce that they are going to have to halt trading in their stock for the proverbial 'News Pending'. At around three o'clock in the afternoon, we should have the finishing touches on a deal that converts our debt to equity, provides them with a fifty million dollar capital infusion and gives us a claim on the assets of the company. We own a majority of their lone debt deal so we can dictate to the other bondholders that they have to go along with our plan. We offer existing bondholders a choice of one hundred cents on the dollar for their bonds or a sliver of equity and sixty cents on the dollar. They'll all go for the cash except the smart vulture funds that play distressed companies."

My mind was spinning trying to keep up with him as he explained Monday's play by play, "And what happens to the existing stockholders," which I then realized and added, "including people like me?"

"And Terry Burroughs," he gleefully added.

"Yeah, what happens to us?"

"Do you know what the derivation of the word dilution is? Terry is about to find out. You, on the other hand, have just made more as a consultant than you ever would as a stockholder with your five thousand shares. But I still think you are going to make big money on that as well. Don't worry. Trust me."

What, I thought as Karen worked her way back to the table looking radiant and smiling broadly at Roger and me, is the derivation of the word trust? And then I remembered the old joke; "Trust me" was the Yiddish word for intercourse.

CHAPTER THIRTY THREE

I'm not sure exactly at what point Roger and Karen seemed to fall into their own world, connected like two teenagers on their first date, giggling, touching and locking each others arms. I think it happened once we made our way to the Craps table and Roger started having Karen blow on the dice for good luck. What began as a date for me, became a threesome and then a twosome again, with me feeling like an outsider. It was a scene played out dozens of times in our youth, but strangely this time I felt relief and no remorse or anger. I wasn't really sure where Karen and I were going. I knew Karen could satisfy my sexual needs and the animalistic lust I felt for beautiful women in general, but she didn't fulfill my emotional or intellectual needs. She wasn't an airhead and quite a few levels above the "Babes" that Roger usually trotted out for show, but for me the excitement had worn off. Roger gave me a wink as I excused myself to go to the men's room and Karen barely noticed my departure. I was glad that they were hitting it off and snuck off to my humble palace in the sky at about 10:45.

Once upstairs, I decided to check my e-mails and voice mails at the office and home, hoping that I would hear another message from Missy on my home phone. With no important messages on my e-mail or home phone, and nothing more from Missy, I sat back on the over-stuffed leather chair and put on SportsCenter to catch up on the world of sports. Yet, my mind kept wandering back to my brief one-on-one conversation with Roger.

What did he mean when he said he wasn't going to need me? Was my whole consulting gig a farce? Or was I the ace in the hole that would only be used if necessary? More disturbing was when I tried to tell Roger that I might have found what he needed or was looking for, he showed no interest whatsoever.

What was I going to say in my meeting with Stanford Sowers of the SEC on Monday morning? I knew that they were after Roger, but I didn't know any more about Roger's company's operations than I did a week ago. Come to think of it, let them fight their own battles. Roger might play tough, but as far as I could tell, he hadn't broken any securities laws or regulations.

Quite frankly, I was going to be happy when this whole affair, bad double entendre I thought, was over.

I needed a breath of fresh air and didn't want to sit alone in my glass palace on a Saturday night in the gambling mecca of the world. A good night of gambling would take my mind off the SEC, Roger, Karen, Terry Burroughs and the uncertainty at home. I staked myself to twenty-five hundred dollars for the night, twice what I would usually bring, put the five hundred emergency stash inside my wallet's secret compartment and said to me, myself and I, "Let's all have some fun."

The three me's went down in the elevator, without our usual companions, the Blackberry or cell phone. This was my free time and I was going to enjoy it.

My departure from my room was obviously not part of the hotel's planned script, for when I arrived downstairs, a concerned and out of breath assistant manager by the name of Ralph was there to greet me.

His tie was askew and I sensed that he was not expecting to be on call or needed at this hour.

"Is everything all right, Mr. Morris? Can I get you anything?"

"Everything is fine," I answered noticing his tense demeanor soften as if a weight had been lifted. "I just thought I might hit the town for a bit. Maybe check out some of the new casinos on the Strip. It's been a while since I've been in Vegas and just felt like getting out for a while."

"Absolutely, Mr. Morris. Your driver is pulling up as we speak and will take you anywhere you want to go." He seemed relieved to see the limo's headlights pull up to the cul de sac and Mr. Don't Fuck With Me opened the door without ever looking at me. I had no idea what Mr. Don't Fuck's abilities were, but I knew if I were ever picking up sides, I would want him on my team just for his presence and attitude.

My limo driver, a new one stood at the ready with my door open and asked, "Where to Mr. Morris?"

"Let's drive up the strip towards old downtown. I want to see what has gone on in the last ten years and if I don't ask you to stop, keep heading towards Binion's. I might want to play a little poker."

"Excellent," he said closing my door and in an instant we were off.

The strip had changed even more than I had imagined. When I looked outside from my room upstairs, the strip was just a jumble of bright neon and bold flashing colors. Now, down at street level, I noticed just how far all the casinos had gone to lure gamblers. We passed theme parks, not casinos. From New York, New York, Empire State Building included, to the swashbuckling facade of Treasure Island and the volcanoes of the Mirage. No expense had been spared to be different and appealing. Atlantic City, I thought, could take a few lessons on how to build a destination, rather than a casino.

Traffic was brutally slow, but I didn't mind crawling along the Strip. It gave me an opportunity to take in not only the changing ambience from block to block, but to observe the throngs of people walking down the sidewalks trying to find Lady Luck. Unfortunately,

I knew the vast majority of them would more likely find one of Murphy's cousins or relatives, for the law of averages were stacked against them.

I was happy not to be out there among the masses and told the driver, "OK, I've seen enough. We can head to Binion's now."

"Very good, sir," came the response and we quickly got off the Strip and onto the Expressway to Downtown.

As we got closer to Binion's, I could feel my heart beat stronger and faster as the anticipation of battle approached. I was dying to put my poker-playing skills up against the regulars and wanna-be gamblers who descended on Binion's every weekend. I had watched the movie "Rounders" and played some low stakes poker in Atlantic City at the Taj Mahal, and felt like I knew enough to hold my own. I reminded myself, "Stay focused, don't try to make things happen and when you have good cards, play strong." But I had to remind myself to bluff on occasion, act like a rookie and change how I responded to different situations. Otherwise, my face and mannerisms would tell more about the strength of my poker hands than the cards in front of me.

I walked into Binion's, where Karen had wowed the crowd the night before, and I noticed that no one gave me a second look as I passed on my way to the Poker area.

As I approached, a woman's voice came over the loudspeaker to let everyone know that a two thousand dollar buy-in No Limit Texas Hold 'Em game was about to start and there was still one seat available, with the winner having a chance at qualifying for a seat at the upcoming World Series of Poker Tournament. It must be fate, I thought and as I approached the woman announcer at the front desk at the entrance to the Poker area, I said with all the false confidence I could muster, "I'll take it."

CHAPTER THIRTY FOUR

F our o'clock in the morning is no time to be trying to decide whether to stay in a hand with an open ended straight, but that's where I found myself and the two other finalists from the evening's event.

The numbers on the cards were beginning to lose their clarity and I was having trouble maintaining my focus after more than four hours of calculating possibilities and odds, and seeking all forms of divine inspiration. It was little consolation that my two foes had to be feeling the same wear and tear as me, for they had probably rested up for this event and I'd probably see their names and faces on some of the pictures that dotted the walls of Binion's Poker pit.

In Texas Hold 'Em, everyone gets two cards, you bet, there's a "flop" of three community cards for all to see, another round of betting, then two more community cards, with betting on each one. We had all seen the flop, a nine of diamonds, a ten of diamonds, and a queen of clubs. My hole cards were a jack of clubs and the queen of hearts. So with five of my seven cards known, I had four cards toward a straight with the kicker being that I had a pair of Queens also. It was late, I was tired and I decided it was time to make my play before I crashed and couldn't focus anymore.

"I'm all in," I said, which meant that my entire pile of chips -- four hours of winnings -- was what I had bet. If one of my two competitors were to stay in and I lost, I was done, out, finished, and heading to bed.

Cowboy Jed, as I had nicknamed him, sat on my left. He sat quietly for about ten seconds, deep in thought behind his cigarette, sunglasses and dusty black cowboy hat, and stared at the cards on the table. Looking up, he said, "Hell, I'm in too. All in," sliding his chips into the middle to the table. Oh shit, I thought. This is where I find out what a fool I am.

Mensa, the nickname I had for the barely legal, teenage-looking kid sitting on my right, was the only other player left at the table. He spoke little, but could be seen calculating percentages and odds in his head all night long and corroborating his calculations with a twitching motion of his fingers. He seemed to only play hands that he won and caused groans from both Cowboy Jed and me when he said softly, "I'll call too."

So there we sat as the other poker tables around the room fell silent and most of the room's players rose to come watch the final hand. Someone was going to go home with a big pile of money and the entire room sensed the drama that was unfolding before us. I knew I had amassed over seven thousand dollars in winnings and had determined that my pile of wealth in chips was similar to Jed's and Mensa's, but figured that Mensa had a slight edge on both of us. Since all three of us were in, this was going to be the last hand. We were informed that Jed had slightly less money than me, and that since we were both "all-in, we were instructed to turn over our hole cards. Mensa decided that it did not really matter if we did or did not know what his hole cards were since there would not be any more betting and turned his cards over as well.

With all of our cards open to public view, we learned that Cowboy Jed had a pair of Jacks in the hole. But since I also had a Jack, he knew that the best hand he could hope for was a straight or a full house. Mensa had the seven and eight of diamonds as his hole cards, so he was working on a straight, a flush, and the unimaginable straight flush, the best poker hand possible.

In Texas Hold 'Em, the fourth community card is called the Turn or 4th Street, and when the Queen of diamonds was turned over, whistles and groans arose from the table and the crowd. I now had three of a kind, but Mensa now had a diamond flush and still had the possibility of a straight flush. Cowboy Jed realized that he was toast, as his best hand of a straight was not going to beat a flush and his possibility of three of a kind was not going to help either. The only Jack missing was the diamond Jack and if that were to show up, Mensa would have his straight flush. Sweat poured down the back of my neck and I stood up to watch my fate. Cowboy Jed walked away from the table not sure how to react, but after three or four steps, stopped and turned to watch the finish.

The dealer announced that the pot was $30,450.00, and explained that if I were to win, Mensa would still have $520, but that Binion's' house rules required that tournament games ended when the last opponent had less than $1,000. I couldn't focus, couldn't hear and couldn't understand. I had flashbacks of Steve McQueen in the Cincinnati Kid crashing and burning in a game of five card stud and Matt Damon getting crushed by John Malkovich in the beginning of the movie "Rounders." This was going to end badly for someone and I was ready to slink off into the darkness and hide in my plush bed for some much-needed rest.

The queen of spades on the River, or the fifth and last community card changed all that. Four of a kind. I sat down numbly trying to make sure I had the cards I thought I had.

Hooting, hollering and cries of "Oh my God," came from the surrounding crowd. "Holy shit" and "Fuck me" came from Cowboy Jed in the background and Mensa respectively. I sat there too stunned to move or speak. A light bulb flash temporarily blinded me and I was caught staring at the cards on the table and unable to turn away.

"Well say something, you idiot," came from behind me and I realized it was Roger's voice. I turned around to see Roger with Karen wrapped up in his arm on the other side of the railing.

"How long have you been here?" I asked, dumbfounded.

"Oh, I don't know, only about the last two hours, I guess. Isn't that right, Karen?" he said turning to Karen.

"At least," she said. "I was wondering if this was ever going to end."

"Uh," I stammered. "How'd you know I was here?"

"There are no secrets in Vegas, J. Thomas. You should know that. The only question is, who knows. You forget I have some friends in very high places in this town." He smiled. "And you did use the hotel's limo, ding dong. Now come on, collect your money. We have some celebrating to do."

"Yeah," Karen said coming to life. "Where to now?"

The tournament director, one of the pit bosses, was dressed in a black tuxedo. He approached us, pardoned the interruption and said, "Mr. Morris, if you would follow me, we have some forms for you to sign and we would like to have your picture taken for our Wall of Fame. It is something we do for all of our tournament winners."

"I guess so. Sure," I said, confused about all the goings on. I hadn't expected this. "What's the big deal?" I asked, still wondering why this was such a big deal.

"Well as you know, you have qualified for our World Series of Poker Championship, which happens on May 2nd through the 5th and we need some biographical information for our promotional materials. I promise it will just take a minute or two."

"Is it all right if my friends come along?" I asked pointing to Karen and Roger.

"Absolutely," he answered, "Francine, please let these people through" and the announcer from four hours earlier escorted them from their spot along the rail to the entrance and into the Poker area with me.

"You are one cool customer," Roger commented when he and Karen joined me in the pit area. "Do you realize your eyes never left the table while you were playing for the entire time we were here?"

"Yeah" Karen added, "We thought you'd at least look around and see us. We kept thinking that you would notice us, but you had that focus. You know, like last night, when you were playing blackjack."

The tournament director interrupted us, "Excuse me, Mr. Morris, but we really would like to get a picture of you in front of the table of chips and then ask you a few questions."

"Sure" I said. "Just a minute. And Rog, I'm not in the mood for too much celebrating. I'm feeling pretty whooped right now."

"Think how the other guys feel," Roger joked.

The photographer came over and started orchestrating the picture, with me standing at one end of the green felt table with all the game's chips in front of me. I remembered in the World Series of Poker, they had piles of cash on the table, but hey, who was I to complain?

Pictures taken, the tournament director wanted to find out where I lived, occupation and marital status. I paused uncomfortably for a second on that one, but answered, "Married with three children." He gave me a packet of information on the World Series, for which I qualified and which would occur during the first week in May. He really hoped that I would be able to come, as they were so happy to have a non-professional qualify for the tournament.

"Adds to the excitement, David versus Goliath stuff, and all that," he said.

I told him I would certainly try my best, but would have to check out scheduling, family commitments, etc. As I said it, I thought to myself, 'Yeah, like Missy is gonna want me to go off on a trip to Vegas to play cards for a few days! That could put an end to our getting back together and quick.'

Public relations duties accomplished, we went downstairs for a complimentary breakfast buffet, with most of the people there looking at me, not Karen or Roger, and whispering or saying things like "Nice playing." "Way to go." "Congratulations." One older, tall lanky man with gray white hair said, "I'll see you in the World Series." I had no idea who he was but replied, "Sure, sounds like fun."

Our waitress noticed my lack of recognition and said, "That's Mark Nelson. He's won the World Series twice in the past four years."

"Ah," was the only response I could manage. I ate unconsciously and didn't join in Roger and Karen's conversation too much, reliving hands that I had lost in the hours before and trying to figure out if I had misplayed them or misread the odds. It was a similar process my mind went through when I purchased a stock that didn't work out. My mind would churn for hours trying to figure out where I had gone wrong and where my analysis had been flawed.

"Earth to J. Thomas Morris," Roger said. "Earth to J. Thomas Morris. Anybody home?"

"Sorry," I said. "My mind is still wired over the game. I think it's time to head to bed."

"Do you want some company or do you want to go home alone?" Karen asked. I wasn't exactly sure what she meant about company for she and Roger seemed as if they had all the company they wanted.

"You know," I said, "I'm not going to be much fun, so why don't you kids stay and have some fun and don't worry about me. I hope you don't mind, but I really think I'd rather be alone tonight, or this morning, or whatever it is."

"Sure, no problem," Roger answered. "We'll be just fine. Tell you what. Want to get together for a late brunch? Maybe one or two this afternoon?"

"Sounds like a plan," but looking at my watch, I added, "You know, come to think of it, right now it seems really early. Why don't you call me at two and we'll figure it out from there?"

"Roger that" Roger said, and Karen chuckled, wrapping her arm in his and squeezing closer as I got up to leave.

CHAPTER THIRTY FIVE

S leep on the red-eye from Las Vegas to Newark was not a problem, as exhaustion never completely took over my body on Sunday. Karen and Roger woke me with their two o'clock call; I took a pass on brunch and told Roger I would catch up with him tomorrow by phone. I had a massive headache all afternoon from either the stress of my life or the card-playing from the previous night. Heck, who was I kidding, that morning's cards! It didn't much matter which was the culprit. I spent the day trying to relax and to put together my plan for the week ahead, making myself a list of priorities of what I had to do.

The list started with Missy and the kids. I had to get that straightened out first, followed by getting ready for my next meeting with Stanley Sowers of the SEC, and finally putting together a formal report for Roger on Ocular and its possible transgressions in trading and allocating purchases and sales among Terry's personal account, the firm's client's accounts. I made a note to call Susan at Ocular to make sure she was okay and that Terry had followed through on our agreement.

With my list in order, I closed my eyes and figured I could deal with Monday when it arrived at the end of my plane flight home. Thankfully, the rest of the passengers seemed to be in a similar state and after the last few drunks in the front of coach settled in and fell asleep, the plane full of passengers fell quiet and/or asleep within an hour.

I refused drink, food and flirting with the pretty stewardess, warning myself, "Been there, done that." It was time to get my life back and take control of it. No more running across country for Roger and no more shilling for the SEC.

I sleepwalked through Newark Airport, found my driver, grunted monosyllabic responses to his questions, followed him to our sedan and said a silent thank you. Sedans were far more comfortable than limos and I'd had enough of the stretch and super stretch routine of LaLa Land and Vegas.

Upon my arrival home, I saw Missy's car in the garage, grabbed my bags and walked quietly upstairs. The dogs, I remembered, were in the kennel and thus would not disturb my entrance. When I opened the door to our bedroom and saw Missy sleeping on her usual left-hand side of the bed, my heart leapt.

She stirred, but didn't awaken as the door creaked and I put down my bags. I stripped off my clothes, set the alarm for seven o'clock, an hour away, and slid under the covers.

I didn't need or want sex. I was just happy to feel her warmth near me. We could figure out the state of our marriage and relationship later. Right then all I wanted was to have her close. I put my head on the pillow, settled into the rhythm of her breathing, stroked her pantied bottom and rolled over to sleep.

In my dreams, I imagined we were alone on our honeymoon, drunk with champagne, but enjoying our bodies and our closeness. When I realized that my dream had fused with reality and Missy was fondling my manhood and coaxing it to life, I opened my eyes. I said, "I love you, Missy." She answered, "Shush, go back to sleep," and mounted me, a position she knew gave me great pleasure but that we seldom did anymore.

I closed my eyes as ordered, reached under her beige silk lingerie top and fondled her breasts while she rocked herself above me. It was a treat that she rarely allowed, but I figured if I were dreaming, I might as well enjoy it.

We didn't speak, but I could hear her telling me she needed me, needed us. It was all a mistake. She never should have left. She would never leave again. She was apologizing and I was accepting her apology. We would be stronger knowing how much we needed each other, how we completed each other.

Afterward, we hugged each other and drifted off to sleep silently, fitting perfectly into each other's arms.

The alarm clock startled us out of our reverie and I saw that it was time to get up. For the first time in weeks, I felt recharged and ready to get up and face the day head on. I knew what I had to do at work, home was falling back into place, and I was going to make sure that we never fell into that hole again.

"Will you be home for dinner?" Missy asked as I turned off the alarm and headed for my morning ritual of shower and shave.

"Yes, of course," I answered, though I realized there was nothing guaranteed about me ever getting home from work at a certain time. "I promise. I'll be home by six-thirty. Then, why don't we take the kids out to dinner?"

"Okay. I'll get them after school and make sure they get their homework done. Maybe we should just meet you at Monte Cristo's. I know you won't be late for that." She said it with a smile, and I lamented that there had been too few smiles lately.

"Capital idea," I remarked. "I will meet you all there at six-thirty. I promise." I added the promise part to make sure she knew that I would be there. I didn't break my promises. I just had a history of not promising too much, especially when it came to making dinner dates on time. Work always had the priority. Not anymore, I told myself.

CHAPTER THIRTY SIX

B ack into my routine, I was at the office by seven forty-five, consumed a diet Coke and the Wall Street Journal in the first half
hour and attacked my e-mails and Bloomberg messages in the next
thirty minutes.

Tina poked her head in a couple of times to see how I was doing
and realized I was in the zone and left me alone.

I called a quick meeting with my traders and analysts for eight forty-five and answered some phone calls to still-nervous clients. Some
were nervous about the terrorists attack, while others were concerned
about the *Wall Street Journal* article and rumors I was not going to be
spending my time on their assets.

"Rubbish and hogwash" was my response to the latter. "You know
how hard I worked to build this firm and I wouldn't do anything to
jeopardize our clients. Don't forget," I added, "I am still one of the
firm's largest clients and am not going to take my eye off the ball. I
have a vested interest in making sure we all do well."

It was a convincing argument and they knew it. It was no different from what I had told many of them a half-dozen times before, but

they needed to hear it again, "from the horse's mouth" as one client put it.

"And you're a horse's ass for questioning my integrity and motivation," I felt like adding, but didn't.

My meeting with the traders and analysts was short and uneventful. They weren't expecting any news on any of our holdings, and the markets appeared to be headed for a slightly higher opening. When I punched up the news headlines for my personal holdings, I saw that Spindletop Energy had been halted from trading with "News Pending" given as the rationale, the normal obtuse excuse given for any and all sorts of market moving developments. The follow-up story indicated that the company would be issuing a Press Release at ten o'clock.

Tina interrupted my catching up on the news stories and watching the markets open by knocking and entering my office with an "Excuse me."

"Yes, Tina," I answered, looking away from my terminals.

"Sorry," she apologized. "Two things, one, your friend Roger is on line three, saying it's very important, and two, Mr. Sowers from the SEC is here to see you. Shall I stall him?"

"No," I said. "Please tell Roger I saw that SPE was planning a ten o'clock press release and I'll call him later this morning. And go ahead and send in Mr. Sowers. I want to get this over with."

She did as I asked and I saw line three flashing on hold and almost picked Roger up anyway, but then I saw it go solid red, indicating he was no longer on hold and that Tina must be talking to him. A minute later Tina was escorting Mr. Sowers into my office. He was clad once again in an old and faded, but freshly pressed gray suit, carrying the same twenty-five year old leather briefcase.

I stood up to greet him, but Stanley said, "No, please stay seated, Mr. Morris. Thanks for agreeing to see me again on such short notice." He sat down in the same chair as last time and began to fish papers out of his briefcase.

"You know me," I said light heartedly, "always willing to do what I can for the SEC." And I've done my last good deed for you guys, too, I said to myself.

"We wanted to get an update on how your trip to Las Vegas went and what you might have learned about First American and Ocular Asset Management."

"Okay" I said; ready to give him my rehearsed little speech. "I've been thinking about your issues with First American and honestly have no new information on what they may or may not be doing. I work for them as a consultant, all very legal and above board and have spent my time analyzing how their subsidiary, Ocular, conducts business. After spending a lot of time going through their policies and procedures, I do believe that there are material violations of SEC and other Investment Company Act rules concerning how trades are allocated among client accounts and how the founder, Terry Burroughs has cleverly escaped detection from you guys. I have a folder here that outlines how Terry Burroughs would start off buying a small amount of stock. If it went up, he would put it in his own account and hold off buying it in client accounts for anywhere from a week to a month. However, if it went down, he would allocate it to client accounts and keep buying more. Really an ingenious way for him to limit his own risk and use the assets of other Ocular clients to protect him."

Stanley T. Sowers didn't say a word, but scribbled notes, nodded his head and even "humphed" at least twice during my discourse.

"Fascinating" was the word he came up with as he raised his be speckled eyes at me. "And you believe you have proof of this?"

"Absolutely," I answered. "It's all in this Fed Ex envelope with color coding and notes in the margins."

"And what, do you believe, is First American's role in all of this?" Stanley looked at me questioningly as if he didn't realize what I had just laid on his lap.

"First American?" I asked incredulously. "How the hell would I know? Like I told you, I don't know any more about First American than when I went to Vegas."

"Hmm," he grumbled, looking down at his pad. "We were really hoping that things would have moved faster and that you would have learned more, especially after the *Wall Street Journal* article. We thought that would have sped things up a bit."

All of a sudden the truth came pounding its way into my thick head. "So it was you that planted that story in the *Wall Street Journal* about how I was the leading candidate to take over Ocular. You sons of bitches."

"We did what we felt was needed to move the situation along," Stanley argued. "As I told you a week ago, we've been looking into First American and Ocular for a long time with no success. We felt that if we pushed things a little bit, we would flush out somebody or something that we could use."

"So you used me, created hell for me, my employees and my firm, all so you could nail someone you think may be doing something wrong." I was pissed and I wanted him to know it.

"I apologize if we have inconvenienced you or your employees, but it was a risk we felt we had to take, and if what you say is true, then it could shed some light on what is going on at Ocular."

"That's enough," I said getting fired up. "I really don't want to hear any more of your rationalizations. In fact, I think we have nothing more to discuss. You can have this file of papers and have some fun going after Ocular, but I'm through being your pawn. If you want to go after Roger Maydock and First American, go for it, but you are not going to get anymore out of me."

"And if we bring up your trading in certain securities that First American has dealings with?" Stanley threatened.

"Yeah, I've been thinking about that too. If you really think you have a case against me, go for it. But you know what, I don't think you do. So unless you want to start apologizing or want to hear how I'm thinking of suing you and your buddies at the SEC for all the shit you've pulled in the past two ,weeks, I think you better leave now!" I realized that as I had gotten into my tirade, my voice had gotten louder and that I was nearly shouting at Stanley, a mere five or six feet away from me.

"I uh, guess I will be going then," Stanley said as he rose from his seat. "I'm sorry you feel that way. But we did what we had to do."

"Bullshit," I answered. "Oh and by the way," I added, "could you tell me the name of your boss so my lawyer will know who to contact if we decide to sue you?"

He seemed shaken and stammered, "Um, that would be Randolph Brewer, the manager of our New York office." He slinked away without any further pleasantries and left without even saying goodbye.

CHAPTER THIRTY SEVEN

It was 9:59 AM and I couldn't wait for the news, so I had First American's news page on one Bloomberg screen and Spindletop's on the other. The headlines and news stories would pop up when released and as summarized by a cub reporter as fast as he could get the salient details out of the press release.

In a flash, it was a case of dueling headlines.

"First American Insurance announces it has successfully restructured $100 million of Spindletop Energy's debt in a debt for equity swap, establishes new $50 million senior secured debt facility."

"Spindletop Energy renegotiates bank lines, updates investors on exploratory drilling program in Slaughterhouse Trend."

"First American confident financing will satisfy Spindletop's capital needs for next twelve months."

"Spindletop announces wells in Slaughterhouse Trend nearing target depth, plans additional wells in area."

"First American indicates new financing deal will cause fourth quarter earnings to exceed analyst expectations."

"Spindletop to hold conference call with investors in two weeks to review drilling results."

"First American announces that Terence J. Burroughs, President and CEO of its subsidiary, Ocular Asset Management, passed away suddenly over the weekend. Company officials term the death tragic and unexpected."

I couldn't believe my eyes. I cancelled the Spindletop page and focused on First American.

"Roger Maydock, Chairman and CEO of First American stated, 'Terry Burroughs was an exceptional money manager and his talents will be sorely missed. At this sad time, our thoughts and prayers go out to Terry's family. Ocular Asset was built from scratch by Terry Burroughs and will remain his legacy for decades to come. While no one could replace Terry or his vision, we will conduct a search for a new Chief Investment Officer of Ocular in due course. In the meantime, we are confident that the investment team at Ocular is capable of safeguarding and managing Ocular's clients' accounts.

I think I went into a form of mild shock. The story seemed so out of place and knowing how Roger felt about Terry, his kind words seemed so fake, almost plastic in their feel. I thought back to the run-ins I had with Terry over the past weekend and how alive he was when I saw him a short day and a half ago. Staring at the screen, waiting for more news to come out, Tina interrupted me again.

"Not now," I said as she entered.

"I'm sorry," she apologized. "But it's your friend, Roger, again. He says he really needs to talk to you. He's on line 3."

I looked at the flashing light and said, "OK. I'll pick him up, but after this no more calls." Then I corrected myself, "Actually, if Missy or any of the kids call, I'll obviously speak to them."

"Of course," she added with a smile, before leaving me in peace.

"Roger, what's going on?" I said as I picked up the receiver. "I just read the news about Terry. What happened?"

"Thomas, you won't believe this. Sunday morning he goes into the office, sits down at his desk and puts a bullet through his mouth. Gruesome stuff. Your assistant, Susan, was the one that found him, first thing this morning. She is pretty shaken up about it, too. The police have had her in for questioning all morning."

"Why? What would she know about it?"

"Well, they are not convinced it is a suicide yet, even though he left a note. So they are questioning everybody. Susan told them about the fight you had with him Saturday afternoon, as well. They will probably be calling you too."

"Great" I said, just what I needed. "I can't wait."

"You might have to come out here to give them a statement. I have to fly out there for questioning this afternoon myself, though I don't see why."

"Well after all," I replied, "you and I were not his favorite people. Come to think of it, you probably had more to gain by his being dead than anyone other than his family. I bet he had a pile of insurance."

"Don't even joke about stuff like that," Roger said, obviously not pleased with my appraisal of the situation.

"Well, I am sorry that Terry is dead," I said, honestly hoping that I hadn't driven him to take his own life. Then again, maybe his suicide was the result of the mounting pressure that Roger and First American had put on him in recent months, as he felt his firm, his baby, slipping away from his control.

"Yeah, nobody wanted him dead," Roger agreed, but without much emotion or remorse.

"All right, well I guess I should get back to work," I said getting ready to hang up. "Keep me posted. Oh and by the way, I saw you got your deal done with Spindletop, just the way you planned."

"Yeah, some times things just happen to work out the way they are planned. Wait. Don't go yet."

"Why not? What else?" I asked.

"Well, with Terry gone, we're going to need someone to step in and run Ocular. There's nobody there that can do it and with your knowledge of the firm, my executive committee suggested that perhaps you would be the perfect person for the job."

"You have got to be kidding," I said with disdain welling up inside me. "Not on your life."

"J. Thomas, hear me out."

I could tell he was about to launch into a well-rehearsed script.

"No thanks Roger. I gotta go. I've done my time and now I've got to get back to my life. I've done more than I should have to help you out and now we are even. Not happening, no way, no how. But good luck." I hung up the phone and heard Roger trying to stop me.

"But," he started.

No buts for me. Click went the receiver as I hung up.

CHAPTER THIRTY EIGHT

Roger was right about one thing. The Las Vegas Police Department did want to talk to me and called about 11:30 on Monday morning. Tina came in looking upset and worried.

"Uh, Thomas, there's someone from the Las Vegas Police Department on the phone and it doesn't sound like one of your usual friends making a prank call."

"Don't worry, Tina. I was expecting them to call. Mr. Burroughs of Ocular committed suicide yesterday."

Her jaw dropped. "Oh my God," she said, making the sign of the cross, something I had only seen her do once before when we heard that one of our employees had been in a car crash. I knew she was Catholic, but religion didn't often seep into the halls of an investment house. Having been on trading desks at some of the major brokerage firms, I knew it never showed itself there.

"I'll pick him up immediately. Don't worry about a thing. It will be all right." Tina did need reassuring on a regular basis.

I turned away from Tina and picked up the flashing line. "Hello, Thomas Morris."

"Mr. Morris," came the serious reply. "This is Officer Lang of the Las Vegas Police Department." I wasn't exactly sure of his name, but I didn't want to interrupt and wrote it phonetically on the yellow pad on my desk. "I was hoping that you might be able to shed some light on your conversations with Mr. Terence Burroughs this past weekend. I understand you met with him."

"Yes sir. But it wasn't exactly a planned meeting. I was in the offices of Ocular on Friday and again Saturday, and I did speak with him both times. Both days, I mean." Stay cool I told myself.

"And what was the nature of those conversations?" Officer Lang requested. I could picture a tan, clean-cut policeman in navy blue with dark sunglasses taking notes on a little pad. I kidded myself that I had obviously seen too many police shows and movies.

"Well, they were certainly not what you would call social. We had discussions about the way Ocular Asset was structured, how things were done there. I'm sure you are aware that I have been hired by First American as a consultant to review how Ocular was being run: what policies and procedures they had and to evaluate if there were any ways to manage the firm more efficiently." I sounded clinical but solid.

"And how did Mr. Burroughs feel about your being hired to in your words, 'evaluate' how his firm was being run?"

Things were getting stickier as we spoke. Was I a suspect? Should I be thinking about getting a lawyer? I trudged on. "Honestly, he was less than thrilled and I believe he felt it was unnecessary. Terry founded Ocular and obviously was very proud of what he had created and didn't appreciate anyone having the authority to question the management of his firm, which was obviously his pride and joy."

"I see," said Officer Lang and I could picture him scribbling furiously away. I wasn't sure if I was supposed to continue and quite frankly didn't know what else to say.

"And at any point did you say anything that may have been threatening to Mr. Burroughs?"

I didn't like where this was heading and felt it was time to put a stop to it. "I'm not sure what you mean," I answered. "But before we go any further, am I a suspect and should I have a lawyer present while we do this?"

"If you like," came the curt response. "I was just trying to get some answers so that I could save you a trip out to Las Vegas. I understand you just flew back last night on the red-eye."

"Yes, I did," I answered, not wanting to piss this guy off.

"Why did you ask if you were a suspect?" Officer Lang asked curiously. "No one said that this was a homicide investigation."

"No, no," I assured him. "Just the way the questioning was going, I was starting to feel uncomfortable."

"Why were you feeling uncomfortable, Mr. Morris?" I could feel the beads of sweat forming on my forehead and could sense the dampness on the back of my shirt.

"No reason, really. Where were we?" I tried to get back to the Q&A.

"I asked you if you had threatened Mr. Burroughs."

My mind saw the images of Terry Burroughs yelling at Susan, but I couldn't remember a word that I said to him. And I couldn't remember exactly what I had said in his office.

"Well, I know that I told him rather forcefully to leave my assistant, Susan Emery, alone. When I arrived on Saturday, I walked in as he was yelling at her about the work she was doing for me."

"Yes, Ms. Emery mentioned that," he said. "Go on."

"That's about it really."

"And what work was Ms. Emery doing for you that Mr. Burroughs was so upset about?"

I wasn't sure how much to tell, but I really didn't want another trip to Vegas, especially for a visit with the police. "She was putting together an analysis of the trading procedures employed by Ocular and its employees."

"And what was the result of her investigation?"

"Actually, we could find no direct evidence of any violations of the firm's trading policies and procedures." He didn't need to know what I had sent the SEC and I knew that I hadn't told Terry about what we might have found. "I did, however, have some concerns about how the trades were allocated among client accounts and in fact did tell Terry, ah, Mr. Burroughs that I felt certain procedures needed to be tightened up. I have forwarded this information to the SEC and met with them this morning." I was not sure that Officer Lang had any idea what I was talking about, so I figured I should shut up now. After about a ten second delay, I wondered if Officer Lang was still there.

"Hello?" I asked.

"Yes, Mr. Morris. Just taking down some notes." He got his notes together and jumped right back in. "And when did you last see Mr. Burroughs?"

"That would have been Saturday afternoon around two o'clock I think. I was there working until about four thirty, but didn't see him after about two o'clock. I assumed that he was still there when I left at four thirty."

"And did you see or hear any noises or evidence that he was there after two o'clock?"

"No, I didn't!" I answered.

"And from there, what did you do?" That was a lay up.

"I went back to my hotel, had dinner, gambled a little, then went to Binion's downtown and played poker until four in the morning."

"Yes, I have that in my notes. Thank you. If I have any further questions, should I call you at this number?"

I was confused. "Yes, sure, but don't you want to know what I did on Sunday?"

"No, Mr. Morris. I don't think that will be necessary. By the way, how well do you know Ms. Emery?"

Curveball, I thought we were done. "Not very well, really," I answered truthfully. "She worked with me for the past few days and I found her to be very professional and capable. Why do you ask?"

"No reason. And what time did she leave Ocular on Saturday?"

I thought back to having sent her off with packages to send FedEx cross country and remembered wanting to get her away from Terry. "I think it was about two or three o'clock. I'm not sure. She certainly left well before I did. I didn't want her to be around Terry, I mean Mr. Burroughs after the way he had treated her earlier that day."

"I see," Officer Lang noted. "And that was the last you saw of her on Saturday?"

"Yes, actually, that was the last I saw of her all weekend."

"OK. Thank you very much for your time," Officer Lang said, implying that this time he really was finished.

"But I don't understand why you don't want to know about what I did on Sunday?" It seemed odd that there would be all these questions about details and no mention of Sunday.

"The coroner has fixed the time of Mr. Burroughs death at about six or seven o'clock on Saturday night." I was stunned.

"But I thought he committed suicide last night?" I said.

"No, actually his body was found this morning and it was incorrectly assumed that Mr. Burroughs died last night, but the coroner has placed the time of death or suicide, if it was a suicide, at between six and seven o'clock on Saturday evening."

My mind raced back to Saturday afternoon. Left Ocular, went to pick up Karen. Back to the hotel. Shower and shave. Headed down to dinner with Roger and Karen. If it wasn't a suicide, who could have done it? Certainly not Karen or I. Would Susan have been so upset that she went back and shot him dead? As I hung up the phone, a worse thought crossed my mind. Where was Roger before dinner and what was his alibi? What time did he show up for dinner and when did I talk to him? Was it 6:00 or 6:30? I couldn't remember. It was a blur and I didn't want to even contemplate the possibilities that were bouncing among the synapses of my imagination.

"Is there anything else officer?" I asked, wanting to end the line of questioning if I could. I certainly didn't like where it was sending my thoughts.

"No, that should do it for now," Officer Lang answered. "We may want to talk to you again though."

"I understand," I answered, hoping that I would not, in fact, get another call. "If there is anything I can do to help, just let me know."

We said goodbye and I tried to shake the thought of whether Roger could have been involved in Terry's death. I told myself that Roger would never go that far, reminded myself that with where things stood with Spindletop, he didn't have to get rid of Terry. I turned back to my Bloomberg trying to focus on how the markets were doing, but could only see the green and red colors, unable to focus on such irrelevant data as the prices at which stocks were trading.

CHAPTER THIRTY NINE

F or sanity I took a break from the Bloomberg and e-mail screens at about 11:30. I had told Tina to hold all my calls and it was a good thing I did, for no less than a half dozen newspapers had called to get my comment on speculation that I was going to be the next CEO or CIO of Ocular Asset Management.

Clients were starting to call as well, so I drafted a one paragraph comment that I told Tina to give to all newspapers and clients.

"There is no truth to the rumors and speculation that Thomas Morris will be serving in an interim or permanent capacity as an officer or employee of Ocular Asset Management or First American Insurance Company. Mr. Morris is committed on a full time basis to managing the investment firm he founded in 1994 and will have no further comment on the matter. Mr. Morris stated that, "We are all saddened to learn of Mr. Terence Burroughs' untimely passing. However, my priorities are my family and my clients and it would be imprudent for me to entertain offers to take on any added responsibilities at the current time."

I read it over and debated whether the message was clear enough, changed a few words and commas, but felt on the whole it was a good effort. Workable for now.

I called Missy to see if she was home and when she picked up, felt like I'd won the lottery. It was great to hear her voice and sense a positive tone.

"Hello?" she said.

"Its me," I answered. "How's your day going?"

"You know for some odd reason I feel like I've been up forever." She laughed as she spoke and was her old self. "You know I had this dream last night that you came home in the middle of the night and attacked me."

"Funny," I said jousting back, "I had the same dream."

She got serious for a second. "Now don't tell me you're calling to cancel dinner tonight. You'd better not be." The tone was threatening and even if I couldn't make dinner, I don't think I would be able to say so then.

"Absolutely not," I assured her. "Just calling to confirm. Do the kids know yet?"

"No," she said. "I'm going to surprise them when I pick them up from school. I've already told my mother to back off and give us some space. I thought about it a lot and she wasn't helping the situation. I told her as much and she wasn't very happy about it. I don't think she'll ever change, but I'm not going to let her get between us again."

I wasn't convinced, but certainly glad to hear it. "Sounds encouraging," I responded, trying to be upbeat about the prospect of no more mother-in-law interference. Great idea and concept, but I gauged the chance of success somewhere between slim and none, and slim was probably hiding.

"We need a vacation," Missy interjected. "I've started to look online at some resorts and spas. Just the two of us. Do you want it to be golf oriented, tennis, skiing? How about a spa? Where would you have the most fun?"

A wry grin crossed my face as I thought about the past weekend's card playing and how I now qualified for the World Series of Poker. It would be interesting just to see her reaction, maybe I should wait for dinner. But then I remembered the rest of the weekend's news.

"Before we get into that, I think you should know Burroughs, the founder of Ocular committed suicide this weekend."

"Oh that's terrible," she said quickly. "Why did he do that?"

"No one knows for sure right now, and the police are conducting an investigation as we speak. They've questioned everyone, myself included, as I appear to be the last person to have seen or spoken to Terry."

"You're not a suspect, are you?" I could hear the concern in her voice and it was reassuring to feel her warmth.

"No, I don't think so. At least they didn't tell me to not leave town, or in this case to come back to Vegas."

"Well that's reassuring," she offered, and it was true. "So what do you want to do about a vacation?"

I had almost forgotten where the conversation had started. "Oh yeah, my lttle news. I played some cards this weekend."

"I'll alert the media," she joked, stealing John Gielgud's line from the movie "Arthur." "No big surprise there."

"Right, but in so doing, I actually won some money in a little tournament and qualified for Binion's World Series of Poker."

"What's that?" she asked, oblivious to what the heck I was talking about. "I thought the World Series was for baseball."

"It is," I said a little exasperated. "But there is one for Poker also. There's big money at stake and the winners can make a pile of dough. Really fascinating stuff."

"So how much does it cost to get in this World Series?"

"That's the good part. Most people have to pay ten thousand dollars to enter, but since I won this weekend, I get to play for free!" I was proud of myself and couldn't help but brag a little.

"And how much can you win?" she asked, getting more interested.

"I think the winner can make like two or three million dollars."

"Wow!" she said, obviously impressed.

"What are the dates?" Missy asked.

"The tournament starts in a couple of months, just about when I think work will be winding down a bit. Maybe we could have a vacation together out in Vegas?" As they say, 'nothing ventured, nothing gained.'

Missy wasn't buying it. "Some romantic vacation, me getting to watch you sit at a table for endless hours, calculating odds and tuning out the rest of the world. Thanks, but no thanks. I said a romantic vacation." She was obviously disappointed about my choice of venue for a romantic getaway. I thought about mentioning some of the fun of Vegas, promise her a heart shaped tub, but thought better of it.

"Where would you like to go?" I asked earnestly. "This is supposed to be for both of us." I had regained control of my senses.

"You know where we had a great time, got pampered and really enjoyed ourselves with the golf and tennis? The Phoenician in Scottsdale! That was one of my favorite places we've been too."

I remembered it well. A favorite conference venue for many Wall Street firms, I had been out there five times, loved the golf courses, and had talked Missy into tagging along for a high yield conference a half dozen years earlier. It was one of the most relaxing getaways we had in recent memory, as the distance required us to get our children a full time nanny for a week. Recent vacations seemed to be an overnight getaway sandwiched around athletic events, dance recitals and parties. Our lives were no longer our own, and while we lamented our lack of freedom, it was Missy who always nixed the idea of the two of us really getting away from it all. Countless times when I tried to talk her in to coming to a conference or taking a vacation to the islands, she would say, 'Pretty soon they'll all be out of the house and we should be around while they still want us to be a part of their lives.' Her tune was definitely changing, and for the better, I thought.

"That sounds like a great idea!" I answered enthusiastically. Marriage was about compromise, and if I had to skip the World Series of Poker to work on my relationship with my wife, it was well worth it. At least that was what I would try to make myself realize in the coming months. "We had a great time there. Remember how we played backgammon for hours and got drunk that one night." I smiled as I remembered the evening, the weekend, the sex. The World Series thoughts were drifting lower in importance as the memories came back.

"Yes, I was thinking of that earlier today," she said with a hint of melancholy. "I miss those times."

"So go ahead and book the trip. How about in a month or so? The sooner the better. I don't need to do the World Series of Poker. Pick any weekend and we'll make it work. A Thursday to Monday trip sound good?"

"That's just what I was thinking. But don't worry about the World Series thing. You can still do that. This trip will be for us. That trip will be for you. Call it a peace offering."

God how I loved her. How great marriage was when you could take care of each other's needs with pleasure, selflessly.

"You're the best, you know," I said, meaning it.

"Enough already," she said, trying to stop my groveling, though obviously enjoying it. "When are you sure you can get away?"

I thought about the turmoil in the markets, the troubles at Ocular, the SEC investigation, Roger and First American. I wished I could get away from all my issues immediately, but knew that it would take some time to put out these fires and do what I knew had to be done. "Tell you what, any time a month from now. There are going to be some fireworks on the business front for the next few weeks, but in a month or so, things should be settling down. You pick the weekend and we'll make it happen, no matter what. I promise."

"I'll book the flights today," she said, contentedly.

Things were looking up and my problems suddenly seemed much more manageable. I was beginning to well up with emotion and was afraid I would start crying with happiness to have Missy back, the way it used to be. I blurted, "I've gotta go now. Love you."

"I love you too, Thomas."

CHAPTER FORTY

Susan called at about three o'clock, or about twelve noon her time and sounded beat.

"Mr. Morris?" she asked meekly.

"Yes Susan. Please call me Tom. How are you holding up?"

"Surviving I guess, but it was pretty brutal today. I was one of the first to arrive at the office this morning and I'm the one who found Mr. Burroughs. I walked past his office and something smelled foul, so I knocked and went in and found him. I started screaming and then blacked out, I guess."

"And the police think you had something to do with it?" I asked less gingerly than I intended.

"Initially they didn't because people assumed it happened yesterday. Then the coroner came and said it was Saturday and they had to check everyone's alibi for then. Thank God I went to the gym and then out with my friends. If I'd stayed home, I'd probably be in jail right now."

I could just see her on the Stairmaster, building up those beautiful calf muscles. 'You pig', I thought. But those calves just might have kept you out of jail.

"So I was wondering, what am I supposed to do now? No one knows what the hell is going on here. Clients are calling. We've already had ten clients call in or fax their termination letters today and the news is just starting to get out. I feel like this is entirely our fault. I mean did he kill himself because of what we found?"

"Don't give it a second thought. Absolutely not," I assured her. I had thought a lot about it and had come up with my own conclusions. "Terry never should have sold his company in the first place. When he began to realize that he no longer had control of his baby, the company he had built, it was just a matter of time before he walked away in some fashion. I think it was so difficult for him to let go that when he realized he had lost control of the thing which mattered most to him, there was no reason to go on."

Sure it was amateur psychology 101, but it was the best rationale I could come up with so far and the one I was trying to convince myself was true. With Susan's alibi seemingly sewed up for the time of death, that left Roger as the only other suspect that I could think of. After all, he had the motive, was alone in Vegas and had the most to gain. As much as I tried, I couldn't get it out of my head.

"But what should I do?" she asked. "I'm sitting here in your office and everyone's asking me what they should do and what's going to happen. I don't have a clue. It's scary, eerie. The smell of the body has filtered out to the whole office."

"OK, here's what you do." I knew she worked well with lists and was better at organizing information than most CEOs I had ever met. "First, you need a statement or press release from First American that tells the employees and the world what they are going to do. Until then, refer all calls to First American, they are your parent company and it's their headache. Give anyone who wants more information the name of the CFO, General Counsel and CEO of First American and the main phone number there. The names you will find on Bloomberg or they could be in my notes. The CFO's name is Hanes, like the panty hose and the General Counsel has a very British sounding name. The CEO is Roger Maydock, but you already knew that."

"Gotcha."

"Three. Tell all employees that right now you are a call center in crisis mode and that all client requests must be in the form of a fax or written to the attention of Roger Maydock, CEO of First American until such time as an acting head or CEO is named. Furthermore, tell all employees that they should keep a log of all calls they get or make with phone numbers and comments on what the call is about. Create a simple spread sheet for them to use to put the data in the respective boxes.. Date, time, client, phone number, comment section and collect everyone's at the end of each day. It will be invaluable to whoever gets thrown into the middle of this mess."

"Got it." I could tell she was back in her overdrive mode, taking fast notes. "Anything else?"

"Yes, I would like the traders to cancel all open buy and sell orders and to only act on client instructions that come in the form of a fax or in writing. No verbal directions whatsoever. It can only lead to bigger problems and confusion.. Finally, but do this now before you do anything else, call everyone into my office, which is now going to be your office, and tell them what you are going to do."

"Wow. Sounds like you have done this before. Are you going to come save us?"

"Thanks, but I really can't. And yes, I've had to do something like this before. It's not a lot of fun. But with proper planning and organization, which you bring to the table, it is manageable. You're going to love the rush. Just wait and see. It'll be the most fun you've ever had. You know what you have on your hands?" I asked.

"Yes, a disaster," she answered.

"No, a fiasco," I answered smiling to myself. "Do you know what that means?"

"A real mess."

"Yes, but a fiasco is what you get when you make the best out of a bad situation. I'll explain it to you sometime."

"I have no idea what you are talking about, but I know that I wish you were here to help," she said anxiously.

"I will be, but I'll be your silent and distant co-pilot."

"Thanks. I'll get right on this and honestly I can't tell you how much I enjoy working for you." I could almost sense tears of happiness.

"The pleasure is all mine. Now get cracking. The one thing that Ocular employees and clients need more than anything right now is a plan of action and you're going to give it to them."

"Got it. Thanks. Can I call you later?"

I looked at my watch, thought about dinner with Missy and the kids and said. "Actually, I'm just about done for the day here and will be leaving soon. Call me first thing in the morning and going forward just plan to call me at lunchtime every day. That will be nine o'clock in the morning your time and give me a quick update on how you're doing. You can always e-mail me, too. I check them pretty regularly."

"Thanks again," Susan said sincerely. "You're the best."

"Enough already," I protested, "flattery will get you everywhere."

She chuckled and hung up.

CHAPTER FORTY ONE

The rest of the afternoon was a blur of answering e-mails and phone calls. Even though I had the Press Release comment prepared, it seemed that clients and

Friends still wanted to know what I knew and what it all meant. How was Ocular going to survive? Why did Terry commit suicide? What about the rumors that there was a chance he was murdered?

Wall Street loves rumors and it was having a field day with this one. My friends loved gossip as much as anyone and they just couldn't restrain themselves from calling.

"No, I'm not going to run Ocular," I kept telling them; but a few just didn't seem to believe it. The more I thought about Ocular through, and the situation it was in, the more I saw the logic in taking over the management of their accounts. But if there was one thing I had learned in the past week or two, it was that I would never work for Roger again. Don't mix business with friendship. I told myself, for friendship are more important and can be ruined by business.

The stock market was muddling through in listless fashion, though the same could not be said for Spindletop, First American or the stocks that Ocular was thought to be involved in. Because of securities laws, firms like Ocular and First American were required to file a list of their holdings each quarter. With concerns mounting that Ocular's clients would be leaving in droves, quick-trigger portfolio managers and short sellers were trying to make money on the troubles at Ocular. Knowing that Ocular's funds would be facing redemptions from its mutual fund investors and client defections and terminations as well, the short sellers were swooping in on holdings that would be vulnerable to selling pressure. It was a bloodbath, as many of Ocular's publicly disclosed holdings were down between five and ten percent. Most of First American's largest equity holdings were down sharply as well.

Spindletop was a story unto itself. The stocks finally opened at about noon on the New York Stock Exchange at fourteen, down three points and had been sliding ever since. Investors were fuming that they had not been told how tight money was at the company and didn't appreciate that with the debt for equity swap that First American had engineered over the weekend, the company had magically diluted their existing stockholders interests by a cool twenty percent. Instead of one hundred million shares outstanding, there were now one hundred twenty-five million and First American now had a priority claim on Spindletop's assets. If I owned it in my clients' accounts, I would be pissed too. With a half hour left in the trading day, the stock was now at $11.75 per share, down a whopping forty percent on the day.

Then it happened. The quote machine froze as I was watching people bailing out of Spindletop. The news headline came across. "Trading halted -- Spindletop Energy -- Order imbalance."

That meant that the specialist on the floor of the Stock Exchange had had enough. He had tried to match up buyers and sellers all day and now there just weren't enough buyers to satisfy the portfolio managers and investors trying to get out of the stock at any price. Not only had Spindletop diluted its shareholders, but it was a major holding of Ocular and First American. Three strikes and you're out.

When trading was halted in Spindletop, it only added fuel to the fire for those other stocks owned by Ocular or First American which investors were trying to unload. It would not be a pretty day for either firm's clients or mutual fund investors and it looked to me like the "Ocular Effect" was starting to cascade through the market. Stocks across my screen were now turning red and sell programs were starting to kick in.

I could only imagine how Roger was dealing with the onslaught. I wondered if he was maintaining his cool demeanor through all this. He had won the battle with Spindletop, gotten control of Ocular in ways he never imagined and look what he had gotten in return.

I debated calling him and thought better of it. He might try and talk me into fixing Ocular for him again. We would need to talk again and soon, but not yet, the timing wasn't right. I had a plan forming and training would be critical.

One by one, more of Ocular's stocks were halted for order imbalances, even though the stock market was closing in less than fifteen minutes. It was one of those rare times when the specialists had to be getting killed. They were required by charter to maintain an orderly market and to keep bidding to buy stocks as they fell, and usually made a mint when stocks bounced back. It was one of those rare days when the bounce wasn't happening and they were crying "Uncle"

At 3:50, the press release from Roger hit the wires. I was glued to my Bloomberg watching the stories come across and wasn't totally surprised. I actually thought that Roger would have issued a statement sooner.

I read along as it hit what we used to call the broad tape, where news stories came out, as opposed to what was called the ticker tape, which only showed stock symbols and each individual trade.

"Roger Maydock, CEO of First American Insurance, the majority owner of Ocular Asset Management issued the following statement to the news wires this afternoon. Mr. Maydock stated that; "The significant decline in the stock of First American Insurance and the stocks held by Ocular Asset Management is unwarranted and the result of short selling by hedge funds." He added that "Even with the passing of Ocular founder, Terry Burroughs, Ocular is not in trouble and the situation is under control." He reminded investors that "noted value investor and turnaround expert, Thomas J. Morris was hired by First American recently and that Mr. Morris is intimately involved with and is overseeing the operations at Ocular Asset Management on a day-to-day basis."

Roger's use of my real name showed how seriously he viewed his plight. That still didn't give him the right to use me. I felt the proverbial body blow to the gut and suddenly I couldn't think or breathe. I wondered what a heart attack felt like, and decided if I was having one and survived, I just might kill Roger myself.

CHAPTER FORTY TWO

B y 5:50, I'd had enough. The stack of phone messages was growing exponentially and there was no way I was going to get to all of them. My whole body ached and as I stood up from my chair, I felt my knees creak, my thighs and calf muscles complain and my back scream. The tension and stress of the day had settled in body parts that were ill suited to deal with the onslaught and now I was paying the price. I wanted a hot shower, massage and bed, but I knew I had dinner with Missy and two of my children. I settled for three Advil and a swig of Diet Coke before I left the office.

My black Tumi briefcase was bulging with research that had piled up during the day, and when I put the heavy shoulder strap across my shoulder blade, another muscle group joined the chorus of complainers.

I felt like a baseball player that had played an extra inning night game only to be followed by an afternoon doubleheader. But baseball players had an off season to look forward to and in the investment business, your longest off season break to get rejuvenated was a whopping three days. The New York Stock Exchange Board of Governors had decided long ago that if humanly possible, there would never be a trading hiatus of more than three days. It was the first time I could ever remember thinking 'maybe I can't do this for another ten or fifteen years.' I had always assumed I would be managing money well past when all the kids were finished with college. Now all of a sudden, I wasn't so sure.

With negative thoughts coursing through my mind, I headed off to my dinner with Missy, Kathleen and Michael.

I stepped outside into the cold night air. It was already dusk and it amazed me how quickly fall had turned to winter. The leaves on the trees were heading for the places where they hide for the winter, being blown off their branches with authority as the wind picked up. Was I so cold because I had gotten used to the warmth out west, or had the stresses of the day and lack of sleep worn me down? I didn't know and didn't care, but wished I had an overcoat for my short walk to the car in the parking lot.

I dumped my briefcase in the back seat and climbed in quickly to escape the elements and pulled out of the parking lot to head to Monte Cristo's.

Just thinking about the restaurant made me realize how hungry I was and it suddenly dawned on me that I had been so busy and caught up in the day's events that I didn't order or eat lunch. I hoped that Missy and the kids were on time because I was starting to obsess about the hot bowl of French Onion Soup I was going to order and the cheeseburger that would follow, soft cheddar cheese spilling off the burger, impossible to contain with a bun.

The ring of my cell phone pulled me out of my soup-and-burger dream and without checking to see who it was, knew it had to be Missy.

"Hey babe, I'm on my way," I said cheerily. "I'll be there in less than five."

"Well then OK babe," Roger said, "but you're going to have to be beamed out here if you're going to be here in five."

"Oh, it's you Rog," I said dejectedly. "Sorry, I thought it was Missy."

"So things between you two are patched up?" he asked, though I knew he had no real interest in the status of Missy's and my relationship. He was calling because he needed me or to apologize. I guessed the former.

"Yes, things are patched up, as you call it. I'm heading to meet her and the kids for dinner right now. So I really don't have time to talk and I don't want to get into an accident. Besides, I didn't appreciate your press release at 3:50. You're making my life hell."

"Hey buddy, you signed up for this and are getting paid pretty damn well for it, I might add." He showed no remorse and, if anything, seemed peeved with my attitude.

""I didn't sign up for this." I tried to remind him. "Whatever happened to the 'Just help us figure out what Terry's doing and it will be the easiest half mill you ever made?'"

"Okay, so it didn't pan out exactly as planned. But hey, I spoke to your assistant at Ocular, Susan, and she told me how you were helping to orchestrate the crisis management plan. Really a stroke of genius. Just what was needed?"

"Gee thanks," I said.

"No, thank you," Roger said. "I would have done it myself, but I was a little tied up."

"I'm sure you were. Listen, I'm almost at the restaurant, Rog. I gotta go. I'll talk to you tomorrow, okay?"

"No, just give me a minute. I need a favor."

"Sorry, I'm all out. Gave at the office," I said managing a chuckle.

"Ha ha, very funny, but this is serious," Roger said with emotion.

"So is fucking up my life, dammit," I almost shouted.

"Calm down, Thomas, you've got nothing to worry about. I'm the one that the police have as their number one suspect in Terry's murder."

"Murder," I said, "I thought it was a suicide. You said it was a suicide."

"Yeah, that's what I was told, but now the Vegas PD is not so sure. They had me in a goddamned interview room with two way mirrors for two hours today trying to check out my alibi for Saturday afternoon and night."

I pulled into the parting lot of Monte Cristo's and eschewed the valet, parking in a far corner of the lot to finish the call. I saw Missy's car was already there.

"So what do you want me to do?" I asked, fearing the favor I was about to be asked.

"Vouch for me on Saturday late afternoon. I told them about how we had cocktails in my room at six before dinner."

"Roger," I said firmly, "I think I talked to you in your room around six-thirty from my hotel room phone, but I'm not going to lie."

"So that's the thanks I get. Remember our little incident in prep school. Made a mess out of my college application process."

"Roger, I can't. We're grown up now. Why don't you just tell the truth? You were in your room alone and then met us for dinner. I'm sure the hotel will vouch for you. Won't they?"

"See, that's the problem. I wasn't in my room. And I'm sure they won't believe the truth."

"What is the truth Roger?" I asked exasperatedly.

"I promise I'll tell you the truth when I see you later this week."

"What are you talking about? I'm not going to be in LA or Vegas later this week and by the way, nothing you say is going to change that."

"No, I wouldn't ask you to do that. I'm going to be in New York on Wednesday to meet with the sell side analysts, some of our big institutional investors and meet with the rating agencies, S&P, Moody's and Fitch. Figured I'd come down and buy you dinner."

"That's not necessary and I don't know what my plans are yet." I didn't want to lie, nor to be a pawn again in one of Roger's schemes. "I think I'll take a pass. Your latest stunt has made my life hell, thank you very much. I'm not sure I can handle any more of your great ideas for a while. Sorry, Rog, I really am."

"But I didn't do it, Thomas, honest," he pleaded.

"Then tell that to the police. Be honest dammit if you're really innocent."

"I can't," he objected.

"Yes you can. Rog, I gotta go." I got ready to disconnect.

"But I did go to Ocular Saturday afternoon. To see you, but you had already left. I must have just missed you."

Oh shit, there went my appetite and ability to digest. I gulped and wished I had working salivary glands.

Roger continued, "But he was alive when I saw him, Thomas, and alive when I left. Honest."

Roger was right. His hell was worse than mine. But I had absolutely no idea what to do with this little piece of news and whether or not I could believe him.

I headed into the restaurant and as I entered the maitre d's waiting area, Michael and Kathleen saw me and rushed up to give me "I love you and missed you" hugs. It felt great. Missy was more reserved, but gave me a big smile and might have been holding back a tear with the Norman Rockwell scene of family reuniting.

It was great to see Missy again in her 'I want to look good' mode, with her hair flowing freely the way I liked it, makeup done as if we were going out on the town and a classic black cocktail dress which she knew I liked. She looked terrific. She even squeezed her toes into the black high-heeled pumps that made her legs look great, but that I knew would make her feet ache for hours. She was pulling out all the stops and I appreciated it.

Unfortunately, I didn't show it.

"Hello, are you there?" she asked once during the onion soup and even Michael chimed in with "Earth to Dad" more than once while I sleepwalked through my Cheddarburger.

I blamed jet lag, the markets, a tough weekend in Las Vegas, the death of Terry, but made no mention of my latest call with Roger. When Missy tried to make casual conversation, I tried to form answers that I hoped would show I was interested and cared, but when she asked, "How's Roger?" I froze.

"Is everything all right?" she asked with concern. "You look like someone just hit you in the stomach."

"No. I'm fine. Roger is OK. I saw him in Vegas Saturday night. The news about Terry Burroughs's death has hit his company's stock pretty hard and right now he's scrambling pretty hard to keep a positive mood. He's running out of options and things are getting dicey. I'm worried about him."

"I'm sure he knows that," Missy said, consoling me or the absent Roger, I wasn't quite sure. "You'd do anything for him," she said.

'Would I?' I asked myself.

CHAPTER FORTY THREE

One thing that was constant in my life since Roger had gotten me involved in his little consulting project was that I never knew what surprises were going to be in the day's newspapers or what news stories would pop up on Bloomberg. I half dreaded and half relished reading what the journalists were going to say about Roger, Ocular, First American, and yesterday's plunge in those companies' equity holdings. I didn't expect the lead article in the first column of the Wall Street Journal to be about me.

The headline, "Ocular on the Ropes" in bold print stood out for all to see, with the secondary heading, "Can Morris Do It Again?" Shit, there goes another day, I said to myself.

I sat down at my desk and all of a sudden felt like I hadn't gotten any sleep the night before. I had, and after a round of God I missed you lovemaking, slept like a baby for almost seven hours. Right now, I felt like I'd gotten about twenty minutes of fitful sleep and I could hear the phones ringing outside my office. 'Thank God, they don't ring in here' I told myself, best move I ever made.

Tina come in looking more concerned than her usual self of late and I set about trying to manage the situation. "Don't worry, we'll get through it. No, I'm not going to Vegas. Nothing has changed from yesterday."

"But the papers," she argued.

I cut her off. "Are full of shit and are looking for ways to make things interesting. Now, let me have some time to read this crap and get ready for the day and I'll start putting out the fire in about a half hour. We've got over an hour and a half until the markets open and I'll have a game plan well before. Come to think of it, please run a set of labels for all of our clients and consultants and start a draft of a letter to tell them all there is nothing to worry about. My first priority is and always will be Morris Asset's clients and managing their money professionally and to the best of our ability. Use yesterday's notes that I put together as a guide."

"OK, I'll get right on it. Between phone calls, that is." She turned to head out of the office and then turned back as an afterthought. "And what should I do with yesterday's calls that we didn't get to or the ones that were left on the voicemail overnight?"

"Just try to organize them and tell the staff we are going to have a meeting at nine, traders, analysts, secretaries, everyone. If we all pitch in today we'll make the firm stronger than it's ever been." She smiled and I could tell got back some confidence about the day ahead. I wish I had convinced myself.

The story was mostly a rehash of previous speculation that I was slated to take over Ocular, with the only added fact being Roger's press release that in the author's mind cinched the deal. The author acknowledged that "a spokesman at Morris Asset denied speculation" but determined that our public response was to be expected. The only question in the author's mind was how would we merge the two companies and how much of an interest I would have in the new combined venture.

"Where do they get their ideas and who lets them print this shit?" I said aloud to myself.

"It's a little early to be talking to yourself," Tina said, having come back into my doorway without me noticing the open door.

I looked up and said, "I'm not ready yet."

"I know. I didn't think you were, but Roger is on Line #1 and really wants to talk to you. He wanted to know if you had gotten to Section 3 yet.

I didn't know what she meant or why Roger was asking, but I sensed it wasn't good. "No, but hold on."

I flipped to the third section of the Journal, which is the section that concentrates on the market, giving the previous day's closing data on all important stocks and bond indices, individual stocks, futures and mutual fund data. The articles usually focused on yesterday's newsworthy stories and as I expected, this was where they went after Roger.

FIRST AMERICAN FUNDS UNDER FIRE
WORRIED INVESTORS DUMP STOCKS

The story went on to detail the carnage in First American's and Ocular's mutual funds, which were "among the biggest percentage decliners in yesterday's market meltdown" The article noted that Roger Maydock had assured investors late yesterday that the firm was not in trouble and reminded investors that "First American hired noted turnaround expert, Thomas J. Morris, only weeks ago to oversee Ocular Asset." (See related story, page 1, column 1.) The article continued to try to flesh out the weakness in Ocular's and First American's stock holdings. "Investors remain concerned, however, that First American's meteoric rise of the past decade is dying out and question whether the company can effectively manage its diverse businesses, ranging from insurance and brokerage companies, to investment management services for wealthy individuals and institutions. Built largely through acquisitions, First American used its highly valued stock to scoop up a hodgepodge of assets, many of which are now struggling. Now the big question on investors' minds is if Ocular is in trouble, why is it in trouble and why did founder Terence Burroughs commit suicide over the weekend. (See related story, page A3, column 1.) Are there more skeletons in the closet?"

The rest of the story was background stuff on Roger and First American, but with a definite negative tone. I sensed that this was a story that had been in the works for a while and wouldn't die off soon. I could sense the climax and capitulation of investors was near at hand and it was about time for fireworks.

Tina was still standing there and Roger's light was still flashing. "I'll pick him up now and yes, we're still on for a nine o'clock staff meeting," I said to Tina, who dutifully exited and closed the door behind her.

"Yo Rog," I said in my cheeriest sarcastic voice. "And how is your day going so far? Thanks so much for the nice mention in the *Journal*. I really enjoy the little surprises I get every day."

"It's not my fault," Roger interjected, not wanting my false praise to go any further. "And yes, my day is hell so far, but at least the news that you are on board seems to have helped stabilize things a bit. Some of our stocks were actually up this morning in the pre-market."

The pre-market was a playground for the early risers and hedge funds; they could get a jump on the rest of Wall Street by trading stocks and futures with crossing networks and firms that were willing to make markets in the wee hours. They specialized in trying to develop markets and liquidity for those who needed more than the six and a half hours the rest of us confined our trading activity to. These guys were able to make big profits as the bid/asked spread between where they would buy and sell stocks was huge. It was a great opportunity for those firms willing to put their capital on the line.

"So, how were the redemptions?" I asked. No matter how the markets were reacting, if your mutual fund investors wanted out, they could call and exit your funds almost immediately and at times like these, the mutual funds never seemed to have enough cash on hand and had to sell into weak markets.

"It doesn't look too bad so far. We still have a cash cushion of 3% or more in all of our funds. We did sell some stocks early yesterday when we started to get hit. Precautionary stuff. It didn't help yesterday's action but a necessary evil. But hey, that's not why I called."

"I can only imagine," I deadpanned, feigning interest.

"We thought it would be helpful if you would put out a statement or press release indicating how involved you've been with Ocular and how you want to help them recover from this devastating loss. We put together a draft of a Press Release you could put out, if you want." He was pleading, but I couldn't do it. I'd already done too much and dammit, Roger had done too much. Our relationship would never be the same. It was a sad revelation.

"Thanks Rog, but I can put together my own press release and quite frankly it's going to emphasize how limited my role is at Ocular, limited to the analysis and oversight of trading and business practices -- whatever language is in my consulting agreement."

"But they'll kill us," he complained.

"No they won't. Not because of me at least. The papers will be having a field day with this for the rest of the week and you know it. It'll blow over in a week or two. Just hang in there." It wasn't like Roger to lose his cool. He always seemed to be five steps ahead of everyone else and for once he was being forced to react instead of acting and planning out what was going to happen.

"Come on, Thomas, throw me a bone, would you?" His plea had progressed to begging and I felt bad for him.

"Don't worry. I'll put something in there to keep them guessing about my role. That's the least I can do. No actually, that's the most I can do."

"I'll take it," he said with a sigh of relief in his voice. "Talk to you later?"

"I guess so, but let me get through the day, okay? By the way, have any of the papers picked up on the fact that you were being questioned by the police yesterday?"

"Just one of the locals, nothing too damaging. Just listed me as one of many being questioned about Terry's untimely death. Better than I had hoped for, really." I could tell he was at least feeling less pressure about potential fallout from the police inquisition.

"Sounds promising," I said. "Hang in there buddy. This, too, shall pass."

"That's right," he said upbeat again, like his old self. "What doesn't kill us....."

"Makes us stronger," I said, finishing his quote, happy that he was finding his old self again.

"Oh and by the way, now that Spindletop has announced that it's done its financing with us, you are no longer restricted from buying or selling its stock."

"Oh great, just what I was waiting to hear," I said with mock interest.

"Don't joke. I really think you might want to take a look at it again. At these levels, it seems pretty damn interesting."

"Thanks. Later, Rog. I've got to get back to work," I said getting ready to hang up.

"Thomas, I'm serious. This could be a great buying opportunity. With our redemptions, we're not going to be able to buy any here, but you should really think about it. You have high school and private school bills to pay. Not that many five or ten baggers out there you know."

"OK. Get a letter from your crackerjack lawyers saying I'm no longer in possession of material non-public information and I'll think about it."

"They're drafting it as we speak. The fax will be there before the markets open."

"Later, Rog."

"Thanks, J. Thomas, and I mean it, for all you've done."

"Yeah, after all, what are friends for?"

CHAPTER FORTY FOUR

My fifteen employees were waiting in the conference room at nine, as requested, and like Tina, they felt immensely better once I laid out the plan of attack for the day. If the markets fell another two percent, we'd get our buying hats on again. We did still have more than five percent discretionary cash in client accounts and yesterday's carnage had created some decent values. The rest of the day we would spend assuring clients that our primary focus was and would always be to manage their money. Yes, I was going to put together a Press Release and they would all have a copy of it before they made their calls. Tina would type it up as soon as the meeting was over.

When I asked if there were any questions, silence followed for about ten seconds so I got up to end the meeting when one of my traders spoke up.

"Mr. Morris, there's a rumor going around that you won one World Series of Poker tournament this weekend. Is it true?"

I couldn't believe how little privacy there was in the world, and how did trading desks always get the information first, no matter the subject! "Well not exactly. I did, however, win a little satellite tournament."

"I didn't know you played competitively," he answered.

"I don't, but thanks for bringing it up," I said smiling. "Now get to work and find some truly useful information that has something to do with stocks. Heck, maybe even a company we're invested in."

"Yes, Mr. Morris," he said smiling, but slightly embarrassed.

"OK, troops, that's it. Today won't be that rough. Tina will hand out the Press Release and calling lists in about ten minutes. Go get some coffee, have a smoke, go to the john and be ready to kick ass when you get back. Lunch is on me today, so get your orders in early and don't be bashful. Order whatever you want. You are going to earn it."

Tina followed me into my office, where I lit up a cigarette and quickly apologized. "I know, I know. I promised not in the office, but sometimes it just feels like the time for a smoke and this is it. And we really don't have time for me to go outside for a walk around the parking lot, do we?"

She nodded her head, but said nothing. I knew she hated the smell and after three drags, I stubbed it out.

"Thanks," she said. "Now what am I supposed to do?"

"Just hang here for a minute. I'll finish this Press Release. While you are waiting, please decide who should call whom."

I buried myself in the Press Release that I had been working on, which indicated that while I was concerned for the welfare of the Ocular clients and would help to the extent possible due to my consulting agreement, there was only so much I could do as my role was actually quite limited. I would continue to concentrate my efforts on managing my own firm and its clients' assets. Nevertheless, I would give whatever assistance and direction I could to help them through this trying time.

Tina read it and shrugged her shoulders, "This doesn't really say you are or are not involved in running Ocular."

"Then it's perfect. Keep 'em guessing, I always say. But for our clients, the message is clear. I am here and not in Vegas and am focused on managing Morris Asset Management. Does that seem clear enough?"

"Yes, I guess so," she said unconvinced. "I'll type it up and give it out to the troops. Do you want it to go to the wire services?"

"Absolutely and when they call, I am not available for comment. Also, we need to send a copy of this to all of our clients and consultants and naturally I want it to go out in this morning's mail."

"Naturally," she replied sarcastically. "Piece of cake – we'll stuff envelopes in our free time between phone calls."

I knew it would take all the secretaries a good two hours of envelope stuffing but that somehow they would get it done, while they answered the phones and dealt with the everyday crises of running a business. They were the best, not because they were the smartest, though some of them were, but because they cared about their work and had pride in their abilities. I enjoyed watching them respond to pressure and knew that they loved challenges. The best always do.

Settling in to review the morning's news stories and e-mails, it looked like the markets would be down a little at the start of trading, but not a panic-type opening. Most investors seemed to be sitting on the sidelines waiting to see how the markets were going to react before committing to buy or sell.

In the perverse world of investing, most portfolio managers and investors felt better buying stocks which were moving higher and selling stocks which were going down. It takes years of experience and some gray hair to realize how much performance you will give away following the crowd, but it is probably the hardest and most important habit to break. As a result, most of the market gurus at the major wire house firms were being cagey in their recommendations, suggesting if stocks went down they could fall further, but if the markets found support and started moving higher, it should be safe to buy. 'And people pay them big money for this crap' I reminded myself.

Tina came in with my copy of the Press Release and a fax from none other than Mr. Carl Huthwaite, General Counsel of First American, saying that I was no longer restricted as an "insider" with respect to Spindletop. I punched up the stock symbol and saw that it closed last night at $11.45 per share.

"Tina, put in an order for my personal account to buy 10,000 shares of Spindletop at the opening and another 5000 at 11 and 5000 at 10.50, GTC."

GTC stood for 'good till cancelled' and meant the order would be out there all day unless I cancelled it, but Tina knew what I meant, didn't ask any questions and scribbled the order instructions on her pad and went back to work. I hoped Roger was right about this one because not only did I have private schools and prep schools to pay for, but college was looming ahead for Tommie in a year. No amount of planning or saving seemed adequate in a world of ever-increasing educational expenses!

I moved on to attack the list of client calls that needed to be made and lost myself in work for the next few hours. Clients always need hand holding at the worst times and this was one of them. I kept my eyes glued to the Bloomberg terminal as I made my calls and when the market caught a bout of selling at around 11:30, I called my traders and gave them the simple instructions. "Buy 'em!"

"Yes sir, Mr. Morris. Any new limits?" the head trader asked.

"No, right here ought to be good. Buy half positions at the market and fill in the other half if we drop another two percent on the averages. Got it?"

"Roger," he said and I immediately thought about how much fun this had to be for Roger. Then I thought about Ocular and Susan and figured it was time to check in. I hadn't heard from her yet and wanted to see how she and the people at Ocular were holding up. I dialed the main number for Ocular and got a busy signal. Bad sign, I thought and tried again. This time it rang. Thank God, I said to myself.

"Susan Emery, please," I asked, recognizing the elder receptionist's voice. "It's Tom Morris."

"Yes sir, Mr. Morris. I'll put you right through," she said as if I were extremely important. Very professional. I hoped all callers were getting the same VIP treatment.

"Hello, Mr. Morris. I was just getting ready to call you," she said with a nervous but upbeat lilt. "But it's been so busy around here with all the phone calls from clients and reporters, and the police have been taking turns questioning the employees."

"No problem," I assured her. "I'm just calling to check in and see how things are going out there. Hadn't heard from you and wanted to make sure you were holding up." I pictured her as we spoke and I could only come up with two visions: the pained look on her pretty face as Terry screamed at her in my conference room office and the view of her walking away from me in the front of the building. God, those legs.

"We're holding up," she said, sounding a bit more self-assured. "Your little idea of having a company-wide meeting and prepping us on how to react to the onslaught of phone calls was a great help. Everyone here knows that it was you that got us moving forward and focused on what had to be done and we all hope that you'll be here to take charge soon."

"Not gonna happen. At least not the way things stand now. As you can imagine, I'm pretty swamped myself. Nevertheless, I will do what I can to help." It was rewarding to hear that the Ocular employees no longer viewed me as the bad guy, but I could only do so much.

"I told them that you would probably say that, but they were hoping I could change your mind. You know, talk you into it somehow. Tell you how much you're needed. Terry was so involved in how everything ran here that people are afraid to make decisions."

"I'm sorry about that, but the real leaders will find their way forward. Don't worry, it'll happen soon," I said, knowing it would be true. Most of the people at Ocular seemed very well qualified and very knowledgeable about their jobs yet had been so scared of screwing up and incurring Terry's wrath for so long, they had lost confidence in their own abilities. Let the reins out a bit and you would find out who could run. Just like a thoroughbred, you have to find out how much natural speed, stamina or ability a horse had before you could train it. Find out what tendencies he possessed before trying to fit him into a mold. The great horse trainers could train sprinters or distance runners and didn't have a preference which their horses were. They knew that the most important thing was to get the most out of the horse under their care. That's how they would be most successful.

"So that's what we decided," Susan said and I realized I hadn't heard a word she had said as I daydreamed about horse trainers and watching horses work out in the wee hours during my summers as a teenager, mucking out stalls for three dollars and hour. It was where I learned how to play cards too, as I tried to make a more reasonable wage by playing cards with the mostly Spanish speaking hot walkers and grooms between the morning workouts and the afternoon races.

"What did you decide?" I asked, afraid that they might have gone too far, too fast.

"That we would keep dress casual and still have Tuesday as hero day," she said confused, obviously repeating herself.

"I'm sorry. What's hero day?" I asked feeling like I didn't learn much from the second attempt either.

"Every Tuesday, Ocular pays for lunch and we usually order a six foot hero. We set it up on the park benches outside in the winter months and in the conference room, I mean your office, in the summer months. People eat in two shifts so we always have phone coverage and people on the trading desk."

"And Terry hung out with the employees at these lunches?" I inquired with surprise, not being able to picture him in casual conversation with employees that feared his every move.

"Oh no, of course not. He had lunch delivered every day from the same deli. Simple guy really, either a tuna fish or chicken salad sandwich with a bag of Lays potato chips and a Diet Coke. Same thing, every day, he either ate at his desk in his office or on occasion at his desk in the trading area."

"Exciting guy," I remarked, thinking how lonely his life must have been.

"Yeah, sad really. Everybody's always said that his firm was the only thing he really cared about, other than politics, that is. He did love being a muckety-muck in the Republican Party. Went to all their big fancy dinners, thousands of dollars a plate stuff."

"Enough history for me. Well, it seems like you have everything pretty well under control. Any emergencies?" I asked.

"Only about one every five minutes," Susan answered in an almost joking sarcastic tone. "But we've taken care of most of them and sent a bunch off to First American. The crew is kind of getting used to saying, 'Please put that in writing and fax it to us' or 'You'll really have to talk to First American about that."

I am sure Roger and his trusted brain trust must be having night-mares about Ocular by now. Just wait until they try to get to sleep tonight, I thought.

"Just remind everyone to keep a log of every phone call and orga-nize it on a spreadsheet," I said, reminding her.

"Already done, and everyone is following orders. They're even starting to brag about who has answered more calls. The mood is still somber with Terry's suicide and with everyone convinced the firm is going to implode, but there is a 'what the heck, we'll make the best of it while we're still here' attitude among the employees." She seemed relatively pleased with the current mood at Ocular and we both knew that we had played a large part in having a positive resolution to the crisis at hand.

"It truly is a fiasco, isn't it," I said smiling to myself.

"You said that before," Susan responded questioningly. "I didn't understand what you meant then and still don't. A fiasco is a mess, that much I know."

"Yes," I said. "But it comes from Italy, where a fiasco is the word for a flask."

"Huh?" she asked totally lost.

So I explained about the glassblowers of Italy and how they turned their failures into flasks, making the best of a bad situation.

"Ah," she said. "Now I get it. That's neat."

I only hoped the resolution of all these crises would turn out as well as the flasks turned out by those craftsmen. Could Roger, Susan, Tina, Missy and I craft a solution to our problems and defects without breaking. There were small signs that our mess was becoming more manageable, but with a lot of work left to be done. It was as if we were playing a game of no limit Texas Hold 'Em. Each player knew their hole cards, the flag was there for all to see, but there were a few cards yet to be dealt and they could dramatically alter the outcome of the game. Nevertheless, Susan was right; it would be 'neat' if it all worked out.

I looked over at my Bloomberg screen and saw that the market was down another 1.2% and fading. It wasn't going to be easy, but then again, it never was, was it? One thing I knew for sure, tonight I was heading home early, in time to watch Kathleen play a soccer game. It was important to her because if they won, they'd be in the playoffs. It was important to me because I needed a break from the markets, Roger, Ocular and the SEC. I wanted my life back and I was going to get it.

CHAPTER FORTY FIVE

I t's easy to like Wednesdays otherwise known as hump day, because Thursday and Friday are waiting in the wings. You can handle just about anything on a Thursday or Friday because the promise of two days of relief is just around the corner. Survive Wednesday and you've got it made.

From the moment I turned on my car at 7:20 in the morning and heard the first business update, I knew it wasn't going to be easy. The European markets had gotten the "Ocular retinitis" a clever radio journalist observed, and the US market pre-opening indication based on futures trading was downright ugly. S&P futures were "limit down" which in laymen's terms meant 2% or more of investors' wealth would likely vanish this morning, on paper at least. The only real losers would be those that sold into emotional downdrafts like this. I, on the other hand, still believed the economy was OK, the Federal Reserve was doing the right things and corporate earnings were improving. All in all, with the market down nearly 5% in a week, I liked the opportunities that were presenting themselves. There's no such thing as a sure thing, but most investors watched too much TV and bought and sold with emotion and not logic. When stock prices fell, you were supposed to buy more, not sell. It was one of the first and most important lessons I ever learned. "Buy Low. Sell high." The second most important rule was, when you felt like turning off your quote machine because you couldn't stand the pain of watching your wealth disappear, remember rule #1.

I got to the office and scanned the pages of the Wall Street Journal and was glad that I had been spared a follow-up on my potential employment situation. Roger wasn't as lucky as the Money and Markets Section had a series of easy to read charts and graphs showing just how poorly the Ocular and First American mutual funds were performing. The word ugly was on tap, with ouch as its chaser.

"How long can Roger Maydock keep the rating agencies at bay?" the story asked. I remembered Roger was due to be in New York to meet with the rating agencies to convince them not to worry. One thing I knew for sure, the rating agencies were gun shy and did not like companies being the subject of negative articles in the financial press. It was a self-fulfilling prophecy, where lost investor confidence spilled over to lost confidence by the rating agencies, which were afraid of reacting too late. So they would downgrade the "financial strength" of the company in question, which further reduced investor confidence and caused still lower stock prices for the company in question. Once the downward spiral started, it was nearly impossible to turn things around quickly. Troubled companies were often forced to sell whatever assets they could to stay afloat, and what they could usually sell the fastest were their best properties. The analyst community was already speculating which assets First American had on the block and how much Roger's company would need to raise to avoid a "liquidity crunch" otherwise known as a run on the bank.

I put my paper away, called in my traders, told them we were spending the last of our cash reserves this morning and gave them the stocks that we had to buy if we got the panicked opening the futures envisioned. My junior trader protested, "But did you hear that

First American could get downgraded to junk status today and there are rumors a hedge fund specializing in small caps might have blown up and be closing its doors today?"

"That's when you buy," I lectured him. "When there is blood in the streets. When you feel like you're going to puke if your portfolio goes down anymore and it does. Trust me," I said, "This is what we live for and why we get paid."

As I said it, the logic seemed compelling even to me, and reinforced what I knew I had to do.

"Tell me when we're done," I said. "It's important, and it should all be done in the first half hour. I'd like to get a least half done on the opening, but let them indicate them down big first, then come in with small orders to feel things out."

"Yes, Mr. Morris," the senior trader said. He knew he could and was supposed to call me Tom, but the salutation was in my mind a way of him reminding his assistant who the boss was and who was making the decisions.

After they left, Tina came in, more nervous than normal, which unfortunately was normal for her lately. "Is everything OK? I hear we are going to have a really big down day today."

"Tina," I said, "that's a good point. Everyone thinks it's going to be a big down day and yes, it probably will open down big, but after that, who knows. Do you ever go to the races?" I asked, thinking I should lighten up her mood.

"You know I do, Tom. My girlfriends and I go about one Saturday a month. What about it?" She didn't have a clue where I was taking her.

"Is there any payoff for picking the horse that's first out of the starting gate?"

"Well no," she said.

"And does the first out of the starting gate always win?"

"No," she answered sheepishly, starting to understand. "Especially in longer races, the winner usually comes from behind."

"Very true," I said smiling, "and this is a long race."

"Ha, ha" Tina said, chuckling to herself. "Very cute."

"Not a bad metaphor, if I do say so myself."

"Aren't we proud of ourselves today," she said in a half mocking tone, but smiling again and in the proper mood to attack the day.

"Before you go, do me a favor," I asked.

"Sure," she said.

"Call Roger's office to see if you can get Paula on the line. I need to know exactly what Roger's schedule is today. I have to talk to him sometime between 10 and 10:30. It is very important."

Tina looked at me quizzically. "Is something up? I heard the news on the radio and Joey showed me the article about their funds. Are they in big trouble?"

"Nothing that Roger can't handle with a little help," I said winking. "People could go broke battling against Roger. He doesn't lose very often. He really hates losing, and that goes for sports, women, business, life."

Yeah, Roger was one of a kind, and now that he was on the ropes, people would see what I knew. Roger was a winner, a survivor. He just had to find the ace in the hole that always seemed to be there when he needed it. In our Texas Hold 'Em game, he needed help on the turn or the river.

"Oh and one last thing," I said as she turned to head out of my office, "please call my broker, Teddy and have him buy me another ten thousand shares of Spindletop this morning. I'll pay anything below yesterday's close."

"Did Vegas get the gambling bug in you or something?" she asked with motherly concern.

"Nah, but thanks for worrying, ma," I countered. And with a smile, she was off.

I went back to the e-mails that were piling up, discarding most as trash. No, I still didn't need a bigger penis, bigger breasts or a new mortgage. I asked myself 'How does this spam get through all those expensive filters that we are paying for?'

When I saw Tommie's email, I felt a rush of joy. "Hey Dad, What's up? Talked to Mom. She sounds better. Hope you're OK. The WSJ article is making the rounds here at school and you've become something of a celebrity, but it doesn't sound all that great. Hope to see you this weekend. We've got our first game of the hockey season and we're going to put those Bulls through the meat grinder! Love ya. Tommie."

It was neat that the same slogans for the rivalry weekend were still the same as when I was there. I quickly typed a reply.

"Tommie, as they say Down Under, 'No worries mate.' All is well. Keep your eye out for tomorrow's WSJ. Might make an encore appearance. Yes, of course I'll be there Saturday. Study hard and make some hamburger. Love, Dad."

I loved e-mail more than I hated it because of the chance to have this relationship with my son. No one wrote letters any more especially children. I remembered the only letters I wrote in school were to girls I wanted to go out with and the letters I wrote to my father when I knew he was dying. I hated having to wait a week for a reply and at times like that a five-minute phone call on Sunday night just didn't cut it. With technology, I was able to converse with my son a couple of times a week, far more frequently than I know he would call.

Heading back into the mass of spam I noticed a message from Karen, and opening it, saw that it was her updated flight schedule for the next few weeks. No note, no nothing. I knew it was over anyway, but still vanity or pride or some failing wanted more. As I was about to close and delete the e-mail, I noticed Roger's e-mail address was on the distribution list. I looked back at her schedule again and saw that, lo and behold, guess who was flying to LA this weekend. "Roger," I said aloud, "you dog."

CHAPTER FORTY SIX

At precisely 10:25, I called Roger's cell phone as Tina and Paula had determined that Roger would be in a car being driven to a 10:45 meeting downtown and would be able to speak without interruption for fifteen minutes. He answered on the second ring.

"J. Thomas" he said without a hello, caller ID hiding nothing. "What's up? His voice seemed worn and without the usual energy. He was harried and it was showing, very uncharacteristic Roger.

"Just wanted to check in and see how you were doing. Sorry, I can't make dinner tonight, but hope you're having success with all your meetings."

"Thanks buddy. Yeah, I'm doing well. The analysts are beating me up pretty good, which I expected. But I just saw Moody's and you'd think we were carrying some sort of rare contagious disease. I think they're going to drop us a notch or two, even though we're still going to make this quarter's earnings projection. What a pain in the ass. They said we'd like to see more liquidity on the balance sheet! 'Who wouldn't,' I said. But, what am I going to sell? All of our acquisitions are so intricately merged into our operations and divisions;

it doesn't make sense to undue all the synergies we've created. Of course, Ocular is the last big one we did and is still a stand-alone entity, but who is gonna touch that with all that's going on? I'd love to get rid of it now that Spindletop has done their deal with us, but I'm not sure I'd get five cents on the dollar if I tried. To get the cash I'd be happy to get ten to fifteen cents on the dollar, but that's not going to happen this week.

"Yes, it is," I said. "I'm going to give you seventeen and a half cents on the dollar. I was thinking I'd go as high as twenty, but you showed your hand too early.

"Are you serious?" Roger asked incredulously.

"Dead serious. I've thought a lot about it over the past twenty-four hours. I've got a value shop. Ocular's a value shop. There's not that much difference in how we do business, just the size of the companies they invest in is different. I'll bring a few key people from Ocular to be part of my team and run it out of my offices, here in New Jersey. But for this to have any value, we have to do it immediately. Like announce an agreement in principle has been reached this morning."

"I'll have to call my Board of Directors. I'm not sure that I'll get a decision that quickly." He spoke in a rush and had his engines recharged. The juices were flowing again.

"And when do you see S&P?" I asked.

"Right after my luncheon with our bankers." He knew that this time I controlled the proverbial deck, and I could play the cards as I wished. I had a winning hand and it was not a question of whether or not I was going to prevail. That was already determined. The question was how much I was going to bleed him and First American.

"So this is the way it's going down. We're going to use last night's closing prices to determine the value of Ocular's assets under management."

"Last night's," he said. "OK, if that's what you want." He and I both knew that the market was down two percent this morning and Ocular's funds were probably down more. "Sounds very fair so far," he said, obviously writing it down furiously. "Last night's closing assets."

"And I'll pay 90% of the annualized revenue associated with the asset base as of last night's close, less any terminations that have already been received or are received by the end of the month, which is two and a half weeks away." I gave him a second to digest it.

"Ninety percent of annualized revenue, I paid five times revenue for this company two years ago." The shock was starting to set in.

"That's right," I said. "But the math works. Twenty cents on the dollar would have been one times revenue. But when you realize that if you don't do this deal, you're not going to get anything out of Ocular but losses and a big headache, it could actually be the shot in the arm that you need. It would be nice to show S&P and all those analysts that you have a cash cushion just a few weeks away, wouldn't it?"

I could sense him playing out the scenario in his head and could hear him furiously scribbling notes on a paper as I waited. "It's not nice to steal from friends," he admonished me without malice, as the realization hit that I was his savior, but no saint.

"Come on, Rog. All's fair..."

"...in love and war. Ha, ha. So now you're going to play rough for a while, huh? Turning the tables on me, are ya?"

"Hey, I'm just trying to help you out. Tell you what, I'll even throw in a kicker, just to show there's no hard feelings."

"I can't wait to hear this," he said, none too pleased. "Shoot."

"Seriously," I said, "I'm going to give First American a five percent equity interest in Ocular and a right of first refusal if I ever sell Ocular Asset.

"You'd do that?" he asked suspiciously. "Why?"

"Because you are my best friend, dammit, and we've been through everything together. But I do have one final condition, and yes it's a deal breaker if you say no."

"Go ahead. So far, I know I can sell this to my Board, the analysts and the rating agencies."

"I want indemnification from First American for any violations of SEC rules or regulations by Ocular or any of its employees up until our closing." Above all else, I reminded myself, do not let a great opportunity blind you to the risks of that opportunity.

"That's the condition. Shit. Thomas, I can't give a blanket indemnity. You know I can't do that." He wasn't happy, but he wasn't supposed to be.

"Hey Rog. I told you it was a deal breaker. I'm not going to jail or paying any fines for things that happened before I got control of this company. You wouldn't either and you know it."

He knew it. I knew it. We all knew it. But still it wasn't easy for him to swallow. But what were his options. He correctly concluded, none. "You're done," he said, Wall Street parlance for a deal being struck. It was an oath as binding as any handshake or ritualistic agreement, and in our world a lot stronger than anything a team of lawyers could put on a piece of paper.

"I'll get the term sheet off to your General Counsel and CFO by noon and will wait to hear from you before issuing a statement."

"No need," he said quickly. "My Board gave me permission to get rid of Ocular at any price. They said the headline risk alone could take down First American and to get rid of it. Period."

'So who had outplayed whom?' I thought. It didn't really matter, as we both got what we wanted and were still friends through it all. We both knew that our relationship had changed, but a certain part of the bond would never be broken.

I hung up the phone and called my bankers to let them know I'd made a deal to buy Ocular and I was going to tap into the credit line I had established years ago. I had never used it before, but renewed it every year for my business' security and potential emergencies or opportunities. This was not an emergency, per se, but Morris Asset was growing and they were going to need to get started on the paperwork.

CHAPTER FORTY SEVEN

No one really knows what makes a market bottom at a certain time, but usually exhaustion plays a role. The sellers have sold what they felt they needed to sell and nervous individual investors have capitulated. Then, suddenly, as the selling starts to dry up, the specialists take note and buy as much cheap stock as they can get their hands on. Other investors on the floor, tracking and following the activity of the specialists, jump on board. On TV at night, the announcers always attempt to pinpoint an event that caused the market to turn up or down, but they're making it up to portray the stock market as a simple cause and effect environment. On this day, the newscasters and pundits all pointed to the bold move by First American Insurance to sell its troubled subsidiary, Ocular Asset, to the "respected" investment firm, Morris Asset. They added that the deal was expected to close quickly, providing First American with needed cash and a reprieve from the rating agencies who, the newscasters added, seemed pleased with the development.

I'm sure it was more coincidence than fact, but was glad that my son, Tommie, would be able to hold his head high at prep school if the gossip traveled there. For my part, I was just happy for our clients, who benefited from our purchase of stock near the morning lows. The snap back and near panic buying in the afternoon enabled most market indices to close up nearly two percent on the day, almost a five percent swing off the lows. While the purchases of the previous week were still slightly under water, the combined purchases put our clients slightly ahead of the game. Now I just had to hope that the market had reached at least a near-term bottom. It had taken a while for the idea to buy Ocular to come together, complicated by the fact that for the gamble to really pay off, everyone, including Roger, needed to believe that there was no short-term viable fix for Ocular's and First American's troubles. The hard part for me was still ahead, as I was going to have to convince my clients that Morris Asset's takeover of Ocular was not going to negatively affect their portfolios. While I would become the Chief Investment Officer of Ocular, it was going to remain a distinctly separate subsidiary of Morris Asset.

Tina came in while I was reviewing the closing prices and checking performance and put two crumpled dollar bills on my desk.

"What's that for?" I asked, clueless as to the meaning of the cash.

"You were right. It was a distance race and that's what I always bet at the track," she said with a smile.

"But you don't have to do that," I argued. "We didn't have a bet between us."

"I know, but after I left your office this morning, I asked your broker to do what you would do if you thought the market was going to turn around and he said he bought me some Spyders and Q's and some index calls in my IRA, whatever that means. Anyway, he said I did well today, very well," she giggled an embarrassed smile. "So when do I sell?" she asked.

"I'll keep you posted," I said. "But please keep the two dollars."

"Not a chance," she said firmly. "The lesson was worth it, oh wise one" and bowed in mock praise with her arms outstretched, reminding me of Mike Myers and Dana Carvey in "Wayne's World" saying, "We're not worthy."

"Enough already. Who do I still have to call?" I asked. "But keep it down to an absolute minimum, as I'm leaving in a half hour. Soccer game to go to."

"Right, you told me. The papers really want a word with you, CNBC, too."

"No," I interrupted, "clients only."

She rattled off a few, gave me the pink phone message sheets with the client's names and phone numbers and said, "Oh yeah, I forgot to mention, you did buy your 10,000 shares of Spindletop. It opened down a half point, so your broker got you filled at the opening."

"Thanks," I said and realized I had been so busy I hadn't taken a look at it since lunchtime. When I punched it up, I shouldn't have been surprised that it was up $1.17 or nearly ten percent, as the Ocular and First American stocks had led the market higher in the afternoon. I noticed that there was a star next to the symbol on the quote machine and that there was no bid/asked spread shown. That usually meant a trading halt and punching up the news story, I saw that Spindletop Energy had, in fact, been halted from trading in the aftermarket and on the Pacific Stock Exchange due to "News Pending." Reading down the headlines, I saw that they were going to have a news conference and analyst meeting at 8:30 the following morning.

I suddenly wished I hadn't bought so much of the company's stock. Trading halts were usually bad news. Sure, once in a while they were due to a takeover, but when it was combined with a conference call to update investors on business conditions, it usually was bad news.

There was nothing I could do about it now, so I called a half dozen clients to reassure them that all was well and was surprised to find that most of them weren't at all concerned about the acquisition as the market had gone up big today, legitimizing the purchase in their eyes.

I grabbed my black Tumi, left my Blackberry in its charger and headed off to the soccer game. I had done enough work today and had enough research reports with me to keep me up well past my bedtime if I was so inclined. After all, who needed to read e-mails that came in after five o'clock? Not me. Not today at least.

As I turned out of the office parking lot, my cell phone rang and remembering the last time, checked caller ID. It was Roger. Instead of saying hello, I asked, "Do you have people stationed outside my office to let you know when I leave?"

"I'll never tell," he said cheerily, back to his old self, brimming with confidence with every word. "S&P's going to affirm our ratings tonight, the analysts are all going to come out with buy recommendations tomorrow morning saying the worst is over and it's all due to you. I just wanted to call and say thanks."

"You're welcome" I said, suspicious that there was more to the call. I paused, waiting for more, but when it didn't come, I filled the gap.

"Did you see they halted Spindletop after the close?"

"No, I've been in meetings all afternoon, but when I checked in with the office fifteen minutes ago, they told me about it."

"So, what's the story?" I asked.

"Probably news on the well or the drilling program," he said calmly. But I knew that First American had a lot more riding on Spindletop's fortunes than I did. Come to think of it, Ocular, my new company, had a lot riding on it too.

"Aren't you worried?" I asked. I was starting to feel a bit more uneasy as I realized the importance of tomorrow's news.

"Nah, you know what they say. Que` Sera, Sera."

"Whatever will be, will be," I finished. I'm glad he could be so blasé about it. I couldn't. But now I had to focus on the driving and getting to Kathleen's soccer game. "Talk to you tomorrow" I said.

"Later," Roger replied and disconnected.

CHAPTER FORTY EIGHT

While the papers on Thursday morning wanted to focus on the "stunning turnaround posted by stocks yesterday" and the "bold move" made by Morris Asset to take over the "beleaguered" Ocular Asset Management, all I could focus on was the upcoming news conference by Spindletop.

At 8:00AM, the Press Release hit the news wires.

8:00AM - Spindletop Corp. announces successful exploratory well in Slaughterhouse Trend. Terms well "commercial discovery."

8:00AM - Company says well reaches target depth of 25,300 feet.

8:00AM - Well encounters 412 feet of oil-bearing pay sands.

8:00AM - No oil-water contact found suggesting "significant reserve potential."

8:01AM - Company announces increased exploratory budget for remainder of year. Three appraisal wells spudded to help define field size.

8:01AM - Company estimates reserve potential is "substantially" in excess of 500 million barrels of oil and oil equivalent.

8:02AM - Slaughterhouse well encounters "extremely high formation pressure"

8:02AM - Well flows estimated 9100 barrels of oil per day in limited production test. Extensive flow testing to occur over next few weeks.

The entire press release wasn't out yet, but on the surface it sounded pretty damn good to me. I called Tina on the intercom and asked her to put in a call to my friend, Frank Howell at Bakersfield Petroleum. He understood drilling results better than anyone else I had ever met. If he was in the office, he could save me a lot of time and effort wading through the analysts' comments after the conference call at 8:30. My gut told me that this was a big find and was what those wildcatters had been searching for over the past two or three decades. Someone had finally gotten a well deep enough to find out what was there and it sounded big, really big. But what did I know?

Tina interrupted, "There's no answer and there doesn't seem to be an answering machine or voice mail. Are you sure that you have the right number?"

I smiled, "No, that's the right number. Frank's not big on modern technology." I thought of how simple and sparse his offices were and how the rotary phones probably couldn't keep up with the technological requirements of a voice mail system. Either that or he was just trying to save the five bucks a month. "Keep trying every five minutes or so" I hoped like most oil men he was an early riser, but figured he probably had no idea or interest in what time the markets opened on Wall Street.

I called my trading desk and asked my senior trader to see if there was a pre-market indication on the Spindletop stock, and he promised to check out Instinet and some of the major houses and get back to me in a couple to minutes. Instinet was an electronic trading platform that was similar to NASDAQ in that institutions would advertise where they would buy or sell a particular stock when the New York Stock Exchange was not open for business. The problem was, the spread or difference between where you could buy and sell a stock was usually huge compared to the market on the Big Board, as the NYSE had come to be known. While the Big Board's specialists would usually make a market for a liquid stock of no more than 8 to 10 cents, for instance showing a 21.10 bid for 10,000 shares and an offer of 5,000 shares of 21.15. The same stock, in after-hours or pre-opening trading, could be quoted on Instinet at 20.75 bid for 1000 shares and 21.35 offer for 500 shares. When there was news and excitement about a stock, the size of the bid or offer on Instinet could swell and the spread tighten up dramatically as brokerage firms and institutions wanted to get involved in the action.

When my trader called, it was clear that lots of people wanted in on the action.

"The market on Instinet is thirteen and three-quarters bid for 7000 and 500 offered at fourteen and a quarter. I checked with Goldman and they said there's a short squeeze going on but they'd make a market of fourteen to a half, 2500 up and Merrill said they were 14.10 bid for 50,000 with nothing for sale."

Who needed to hear a conference call when the market was telling you what you needed to know? The news was good. Those who had bet against Spindletop by selling stock they didn't own now had to try to buy the stock to cover their losses. I wondered how many of those short orders were made because of the troubles at First American and Ocular, and how many thought that Spindletop was going to run out of money or hit a dry hole. It didn't really matter now. They were getting hurt and it was going to cost them. It sure is expensive betting against Roger, I thought to myself.

I thanked my trader, thanked God, and decided I had time to get through some more research before the 8:30 call for Spindletop. I knew the news was good, but I still didn't know how good.

Tina buzzed me with the answer to my prayers. "I've got Frank Howell on the line," she said. "Line One."

"Thanks," I said. "I'll pick him right up." I grabbed the receiver, punched line one and said, "Hello Frank? Tom Morris here."

"Yes Tom, what can I do for you?" Our monthly production reports won't be ready for another day or two if that's what you're calling about. But it looks like we had a good month." He sounded apologetic and concerned.

"No Frank, nothing of the sort. You know I trust you guys completely. I was actually calling about another matter."

"Well then, go ahead, shoot. What can I do you for?" I could picture him in his office, leaning back and smoking his Lucky Strike, wearing his denim outfit and having a cup of black coffee.

"Thanks," I said genuinely. "I appreciate your taking the time and glad you're in the office early today."

"No bother. I'm usually here about 5 or 5:30, call anytime." I didn't doubt it.

"Anyway, do you remember that conversation we had when I was out there about the Slaughterhouse Trend?" I asked trying to jog his memory.

"Shit, yeah" he answered quickly. "I told you I knew a bunch of catters that poured a ton of money in that play and got nothing but problems and used drill bits."

"Exactly," I said. "But it now seems that someone has hit pay dirt and struck oil. Sounds like it could be big."

"No kidding. Yeah well, we all knew it was there. I guess it was a matter of time before somebody got to it. How big did you say it was?" He seemed interested or at least intrigued.

"That's what I was hoping you could help me with. I'm not really sure. The company says they think it could be 500 million barrels of oil or more, 400 something feet of pay."

"That does sound big," he commented taking it all in. "Did they give a flow rate?"

"Yes, they said 9000 barrels of oil per day in a limited flow test."

"No shit," he said with a whistle. "That is fuckin' huge. Did they say what choke size on the tubing was, ¼ inch or ½ inch, or anything about bottom hole pressure?"

I didn't know what he was talking about and realized how little I knew about drilling. "Not sure, I didn't see anything in the press release about it. Is it important?"

"For certain wells, yes, but if it's flowing 9000 barrels a day, it doesn't much matter. Sounds like you've got a gusher." I liked the sound of that.

"So what's it worth? Ballpark guess will do. Whaddya think?"

"Well hell, it's gonna take some proving up and appraisal wells, step outs to make sure you got what the company thinks they got. But if those wells work and they prove up real reserves, you can figure about three bucks a barrel at a minimum. What's the quality of the oil? Sweet? Sour?" He had quickly gotten out of my league. "Can they tie into a pipe nearby?"

"I have no idea, I hate to say. Don't forget, I'm not an oil man."

"Yeah, but you seem to do OK. See if the oil is sweet, that means low sulfur and it's worth more. Doesn't have to have as much done to it. Not as much refining needed to turn it into gasoline and all those ethanes and butanes and such, ya see. You also need to know the gravity, or how light it is. The lighter it is, the easier to transport it through a pipeline, if you have a pipe nearby. All these things could mean another dollar or two per barrel."

I appreciated his tutorial and tried to summarize. "So to be conservative, three bucks a barrel, but it could be higher if it's better quality oil and there's infrastructure nearby."

"Yeah, that about sums it up. I told ya you do OK for a Wall Street guy."

"Thanks," I said earnestly. "I really appreciate your time and if there's ever anything I can do for you, please just let me know. Okay?"

"Sure thing, Tom. My pleasure. You've always been a good partner and I don't mind a bit. And come visit any time you're in the area." He said it like he meant it and I thought how nice it was to have someone like Frank, who didn't bullshit, had no airs. He was a straight shooter and the kind of guy you could trust with your wallet.

I hung up and buzzed Tina and told her to send Frank a note and a really good hunting knife as a thank you for his help. It was time for the conference call and I now knew what to listen for as a result of Frank's tutorial. But I did the math in my head. At $3 a barrel, 500 million barrels meant $1.5 billion. If the oil was the good stuff, it could be even higher. Even with the dilution from Roger's debt/equity swap, $1.5 billion divided into 125 million shares very nicely to the tune of about $12 per share. And Roger had said that Spindletop's assets without the Slaughterhouse Trend were worth one and a half times the stock price, and that was before the recent collapse. So if the Spindletop assets were worth north of $15 per share and the Slaughterhouse Trend was worth $12 or more a share, Spindletop could be worth over $25 per share. Hell, the market's enthusiasm and over-zealous traders would run it to $30 if it was worth only $25. No wonder the shorts were getting squeezed and trying to cover before the market opened and the company's conference call was over. This could be fun. Not only that, but my new company Ocular owned a lot of Spindletop stock. "Better lucky than smart," I reminded myself out loud.

CHAPTER FORTY NINE

I was in a giddy mood all morning, as Spindletop headed higher and higher. I called Susan at Ocular at 11 AM to see how things were going at my new company. I hadn't had a chance to speak with her or the staff at Ocular the previous day and now that the deal was agreed to in principle, felt that it was time for me to address the troops. I also didn't know how much Roger or his brain trust had said to the Ocular employees. By now, they had read the papers, seen the Press Releases and had to be wondering what the next step was.

"Susan Emery, please," I asked when the receptionist answered at Ocular.

"And who may I say is calling, please?"

"Tom Morris," I said, wondering what response I would get today.

"Oh, Mr. Morris, I can't tell you how happy everyone here is that you are going to be taking over Ocular." She was obviously happy and seemed genuinely pleased by the turn of events. "I'll put you right through," she said.

Within seconds, Susan answered.

"Tom? Ah, Mr. Morris, I mean," she apologized.

"No Tom is right. So how are things at my favorite turnaround situation?"

"Honestly, everyone here is ecstatic. They didn't know what was going to happen. Was First American going to absorb the firm and move it to LA? Were they going to put a bean counter in here to count the money as the firm imploded? No one expected we'd be sold, let alone to you." She was bubbling with happiness.

"You realize it's still not going to be easy. People are still going to have to break their butts to save this. And it's going to be even harder with me here in New Jersey."

"You're not going to move out here for a while?" she asked suddenly realizing the downside of being bought by a firm headquartered 2500 miles away.

"No. I'll visit on occasion, but ultimately we will probably be merging the company into my base here. How do you feel about New Jersey?"

"Ugh" she answered without thinking. "I'm not sure right now. I hadn't really thought about it. Will you be moving everyone?" Her concern had shifted from herself to her co-workers. "Many of them have settled out here and have spouses that have jobs locally."

"I know, I realize that," I said apologetically. "And it's not going to happen immediately anyway. Don't worry. We'll make sure that the people that help us get through this are not only well compensated, but we'll find jobs for those that don't want to move east. But let's not focus on that, okay. We've got to get Ocular turned back in the right direction and fast. I want you to get everyone assembled in the conference room in fifteen minutes and I'll give them an update on where we're at and where we're going."

"Okay, I'll get right on it," she said without her usual energy.

"Susan," I said, before she could leave, "this is going to be a good thing for everyone involved. Trust me."

"Okay, I'm sorry. I'm sure it will. I was just thinking of my friends out here, my roommates."

"That's a long way from changing," I assured her.

"Sure, okay" she said feigning a more upbeat tone. "I'll get the troops assembled."

"Talk to you in fifteen," I said in my best upbeat tone. I wasn't expecting such a negative reaction from my "eyes and ears" and realized the initial enthusiasm for a takeover by Morris Asset was going to wear very thin very quickly if I didn't play my cards right.

We hung up and I called Tina in. She had a draft of the letter I was planning to send to all clients of Ocular Asset via overnight mail. I wanted to let them know that Morris Asset, like Ocular, was a value-oriented firm and the principles and discipline of investing for both firms were similar. While I did not promise an ability to beat the markets on a quarter-by-quarter basis, I was enclosing a copy of our track record over the past nine years which showed that we had outperformed the market seven out of nine years, basically tied once and lost once. A credible record, an honest record, and one which I felt could be duplicated in their small cap universe with the proper discipline and resources. I assured them that Ocular would continue to be run as a stand-alone subsidiary for the first year after the merger, but that Ocular would be merged into Morris Asset after the first year. I didn't beg, but suggested that since Ocular and Morris Asset were low turnover shops, there would not be a radical portfolio repositioning. As such, the prudent course of action would be to give us a year to determine if we were a manager with whom they could feel comfortable developing a long-term relationship.

"I'd stay on as a client after I read that," Tina commented as I read the draft and made minor changes to the wording. "It's a good no-frills, trust me, we're decent honest managers letter and your sincerity comes through. Do you want to put in something about how well the funds have performed since the announcement? Three of Ocular's funds were in the top ten listing this morning." I had seen the numbers, too, but knew that concentrating on a day's, week's, or even a quarter's performance was a risky strategy that could blow up on you.

"No, I don't think so," I said calmly. "Remember our little discussion about horse races?"

"How could I forget?" she asked with a smile. "It cost me two dollars."

"Well, the race we're about to start is a marathon. The start of the race is important, as you don't want to get stuck behind the pack or you'll never make up any ground. But, after the initial sprint to keep up with the lead pack, we're just going to settle in to a nice solid pace that we can keep up for a good long while. We'll pass plenty of runners along the way. Trust me," I said.

"Where do you get this stuff?" Tina asked with a wry smile. "Do you have a little book with these corny little metaphors tucked away somewhere? I mean, I like it and all that, but I never know what you're going to come up with next.. Yesterday it was horse races, today marathon running. What do you have for tomorrow?" She was making fun of me in a kind way and I enjoyed every minute of it.

"Hmm, have I told you about how the market is like a boxing match?" I was kidding her back.

"Oh stop it," she said with a laugh. "Enough, already."

"Now, what's this about a reduction in fees of ten percent," she said with worry.

"As I say in the letter, it's for the first year only. It's a way of tying them up for a year and giving us a chance to prove ourselves. I bought the company for cheap enough that even with the fee reduction, I can make the purchase price back in about a year. Not to worry. I'm an idiot sometimes, but I'm not stupid." It was time to move on. "Okay, now let's get Ocular back on the phone. We've got some work to do."

I got my notes together. Tina came back in to tell me the Ocular team was waiting for me on Line 2, assembled in my conference room office. I picked up the phone, welcomed them all to Morris Asset and reassured them, "First of all, we're going to make this work, we're going to have fun doing it, and everyone has job security for at least the next twelve months."

I could hear some muffled clapping in the background and audible sighs of relief. "Next, everyone is getting a raise of ten percent starting today. You are going to be asked to work hard and I want you to know up front that you will be rewarded for doing a good job. This is my way of letting you know that I trust all of you to do what's best for Ocular and Morris Asset and I consider it a good will down payment. If we do this right, there will be more where that came from and if we don't, I made a bad decision. But so all of you understand how this works, with the price I paid for Ocular, if we keep all the assets under management for one year, I've gotten all my investment back. If we keep half the assets for two years, I'm at break-even as well. So the way I look at it, I'm not going to do it alone and for all fees that we earn in excess of that 50% mark over the next twelve months, I'm going to take one quarter and put it in a bonus pool for employees. So to keep it simple, Ocular had about fifteen million dollars in revenue last year with about five million in expenses or about ten million dollars profit. I paid nine million for Ocular. For all profits over five million, I'm going to share it with all of you. So, now you know just what we are shooting for. There's some serious money at stake here for all of us. I know we can all benefit from turning Ocular around and make a great living for us and our families. Are there any questions so far?" I took a breath, not knowing if my new team understood the financial part of the deal and how they could benefit.

"Yes, Mr. Morris, I have a question. This is Jerry, the head trader at Ocular. What happens to the profit pool or bonus pool if we have a trading error or a fine by the SEC or something like that?" I knew the real question in his mind was the potential for SEC fines, for every investment firm carried errors and omissions policies with insurance companies that protected them against catastrophic trading errors, usually in excess of $100,000.

"First of all, everyone is to call me Tom, not Mr. Morris. Second, I know the SEC has looked into the trading practices at Ocular and I want you to know that First American has indemnified us for any fines that could be levied by the SEC for actions prior to my purchase of the company. So, we've all got a fresh start and we don't have to worry about that if we do our jobs honestly and to the best of our ability. And if the SEC should call or visit, be honest and open and let them know exactly what role Terry had in the goings on here. Let me make that very clear. The one thing I expect from each of you is to try your best and be honest. If you make a mistake, it's no big deal. We can fix or deal with honest mistakes. But if you try to hide a mistake or lie about it, try to cover it up, you're gone. Period. End of story. Anything else?" I hope I wasn't too rough, but if there was any doubt in anyone's mind, from clients, consultants or prospects that we were legit and honest, we'd never make it.

Hearing no more questions from the crowd, I launched into reporting responsibilities. Who was going to work with whom. Susan had walked me through who did what and it was pretty clear who should report to whom. I also gave them the names of the appropriate contacts and counterparts at Morris Asset who I was sure could answer any questions they might have. I told them that we would have a company-wide conference call every Monday at 10:00AM EST, 7:00AM for them and that everyone was required to attend in person or by phone unless they were on vacation, so that we could review strategy for the week. They were to coordinate their efforts with Susan, who I was going to talk to at least twice a day to answer questions and give direction. After about a half hour of the game plan, I felt it was time to go on the attack and told them to hit the phones and get our bonus pool growing.

A female voice I didn't quite recognize said, "Mr. Morris, one last thing before you go."

"Yes, I'm still here, and please, call me Tom."

"Thanks. Thanks from all of us." And the room started to clap and voices piled on. "Yeah, thanks." "Thanks so much." "We're going to do it." "Let's kick some ass."

I didn't know how long they would go on or quite what to say, so I just jumped in with a "No. I thank all of you and in the immortal words of John Belushi in "Animal House," 'Let's do it!!'" They cheered and I hung up. This was going to be fun. What a rush to be in a turnaround again and to be at the controls.

EPILOGUE

Within six months of the closing of the Ocular acquisition, it became obvious that the team Terry had put together was more than capable and in most instances, exceptional. After an initial drop of ten percent of the client base, we were adding clients within three months and at the mid-year mark had more assets than when the acquisition closed. Spindletop became the best performing stock on the New York Stock Exchange for two quarters in a row hitting $55 as further successes in the Slaughterhouse Trend were announced and reserve estimates soared to more than a billion barrels of oil.

Roger and I spoke less frequently as time wore on and had settled into our monthly update chit-chat with promises to get together again soon and more frequently. "Wasn't Vegas great?" he would ask me each time we spoke, seemingly forgetting that his "date" for the weekend had started out with me.

I kept my promise to Missy and remained the absentee owner/ manager of Ocular and Morris Asset did control the investment decision-making process from New Jersey. We did have our getaway to the Phoenician and played backgammon until the wee hours for old-times' sake. Played golf and tennis, were massaged and pampered for four days and had a wonderful time. It was a second honeymoon where we found not just the romance, but the intimacy that had been missing for too many years.

I fulfilled my dream of going to Las Vegas and played in the World Series of Poker. I slugged it out for four grueling days and made my way to the final table, only to be the first one to be eliminated. Nevertheless, I was rewarded with $56,000 for my efforts and an invitation to return again the following year with the compliments of Binion's.

The Las Vegas Police ultimately ruled that the death of Terrence Burroughs was indeed a suicide, and while the police threatened Roger with a charge of "Obstruction of Justice" for not telling them initially about his late afternoon visit to Ocular, either his lawyer or "friends in high places" got the heat to back off.

The SEC took a chill pill and recommended a number of modest changes to procedures at Ocular and First American and a small $10,000 fine for each firm. Mr. Sowers said that if Terry was still alive, they probably would have gone for the jugular, but why 'beat a dead horse.' And I thought he didn't have a sense of humor.

It was a clear, sunny day late in May, with the trees full of blossoms and the birds chirping outside, when Roger called.

"Did you get the Fed Ex yet?" he asked.

I said no, put him on hold, buzzed Tina, who said yes, I did have a Fed Ex from Roger and delivered it to me.

"Tina is bringing it in now," I said. "What's up?"

"You have to open it up," he said, playing coy and enjoying my suspense.

I pulled the tab on the Fed Ex box, found a square, beige, thick envelope inside and had a sudden realization what it meant.

"Who is it?" I said, adding, "And When?"

"Open it!" He demanded.

Inside I found the beautifully engraved invitation:

Roger Scott Maydock and Karen Clarkson
Request the honour of your presence
at their marriage on June 27

"You son of a gun," I said smiling. "So you're finally gonna set-tle down. I thought you had sworn off marriages after the last two disasters.

"Hey, be nice, go easy on that finally stuff. I'm not that old and you are, after all, only six months younger that I am. Besides, I have a favor to ask, old buddy."

Oh shit, I thought, what now? What troubled adventure was he going to try to send me on now? A little favor, hah! "And what would the little favor be?" I asked dreading the answer.

"Would you be my best man? I wouldn't think of asking anyone else."

He was sincere and at a high point of his life. The answer came easily and without a second thought. "I would be honored. After all, what are friends for?"

I called Missy at home and told her we had another trip to plan in late June to the west coast and that Roger was getting married again.

"He's getting to be an old hand at this," she joked. "Anyone we know?"

I wasn't ready for the question and suddenly not sure what to say. "Actually I did meet her on one of my trips out west and she seemed nice." I felt guilty and the remorse over my affair came rush-ing back.

"Well that would be a change," she said with a chuckle, "the last two were airheads."

"Yeah, I know what you mean," I answered flatly, glad for the change of focus.

"Tell you what," she interjected with an excited tone, "the kids will be out of school. Let's make it a special trip and take them all to the Grand Canyon or Disneyland and then go to the wedding."

It was a great idea, something we had always talked about doing. "Let's do both, Grand Canyon and Disney and then the wedding."

"Are you sure?" Missy asked. "That's a pretty big trip."

"Of course I'm sure," I said. Then it came to me, and I said with a chuckle, "That's what I do! I make vacations!"

ACKNOWLEDGEMENTS

Writing Fiasco has been a lifelong dream, one which would not have been possible without the support and assistance of some dear friends. Mary Jane Sauer typed and edited every page of chicken scratch I created, pushing me to continue chasing the dream and the story. Without her, Fiasco would still be on my bucket list of unfinished dreams. Paul Taylor provided encouragement and a level of technical expertise regarding oil and gas drilling which made the story plausible and factually defensible. Greg Greene gave me the book which gave me the permission to write the book before I knew where it would take me. If anyone is ever thinking of wring a book, either become friends with Greg or buy Steven King's "On Writing".

My prep school buddies Emery, Roger, Pat, Chris, Grover, Juice, Bear, Wee Dave, Tad. Trucker and the rest helped create the memories and fodder to bring Fiasco to life. To them I give my humble thanks for letting me be me in those horribly awkward years, accepting me the way I was. Finally, my greatest thanks go to my wife and children who put up with me and love me through all my misadventures.

Made in the USA
Lexington, KY
10 November 2014